A SECOND-HAND LIFE

Books by *Charles Jackson*

The Lost Weekend
The Fall of Valor
The Outer Edges
The Sunnier Side
Earthly Creatures
A Second-Hand Life

A Second-Hand Life

CHARLES JACKSON

Well, heaven forgive him! and forgive us all!
Some rise by sin, and some by virtue fall . . .

Act II, Scene i, *Measure for Measure*

THE MACMILLAN COMPANY: NEW YORK

First Printing

The Macmillan Company, New York
Collier-Macmillan Canada Ltd., Toronto, Ontario
Printed in the United States of America

To

My daughters:

Sarah Jackson Piper

and

Kate Winthrop Jackson

with almost all my love

CONTENTS

I

RUMORS OF THE PAST

IN the yellow sunshine that was just beginning to warm the morning, Miss Winifred Grainger sat in the last of the lawn chairs that had not yet been put away for the winter, holding in her hand, which lay in the lap of her corduroy skirt, a black-bordered announcement. It was a day of blue and gold, autumn at its peak. The early dew still lay on everything: it glistened on the palings of the white Palladian fence at the edge of the lawn, on the wide garden gate and the chaste square columns supporting it, on the black heavy flanks of the iron roller beside the dove cote—it shone in diamondlike slowly traveling drops even on the clothes-lines in back of the well-kept barn (a three-car garage now), drops that moved along the ropes to collect and finally fall where the lines sagged in the middle; and above, on the sloping roof, faint wisps of steam rose from the drying shingles in tiny expiring clouds. But Miss Grainger saw none of these things, nor was she looking at the printed card. She gazed nostalgically across the shining lawn at the abandoned summerhouse beyond the old tennis court, once immaculately sanded and taped but rank now with mustard, clover and nettles—all it lacked, she thought ribaldly, were long purples, or, more appropriately, dead men's fingers—the fabled summerhouse that had been the scene of so many hours of love, so long ago . . . But that had been nothing!—for so too had been the back seat of his old Marmon and her Cadillac; the well-groomed ninth green below the Club veranda during or after the dances on Saturday nights; her parents' cottage at the Point and the hypnotic beach there, loud with a beautiful rumble, prismatic with tumbling surf like palely colored glass; the balsam-lined road near town known in Arcadia as Lovers' Lane but called by themselves just The Pines (oh, she remembered, and could have named, a dozen such expedients and backgrounds, and was still able to smile as she recalled their satiric use of such a time-tried phrase as "*I* know a good place!"); his rented room often and sometimes, in bolder desperate moments, even her own large bed-room right in her own house, right under Belle and Dad's noses practically, where they had had to stifle their keyed-up irrational laughter, like the laughter of children in class or in church, all the more difficult to repress because, of course, they must not make a sound. . . . Now she looked again at the card in her lap, which announced the bare fact, and little more, of his death; then glanced at her wristwatch. It was time for Belle's morning constitutional.

Miss Grainger was aware that it was this morning walk with her almost-blind mother, and the turn around the block in the late afternoon, which, fully as much as the widely known facts of her life, gave her the reputation of an old maid. But for more than twenty years she had been past caring. Had she cared, she would have left Arcadia long ago—not stayed on to become an object of amusement or curiosity to the younger generation and the well-bred scorn of the older. She stuck the announcement in the pocket of her suede jacket and crossed the wet lawn to the glassed-in sun porch. She gave the short family whistle, saw Irma come from the kitchen and help her mother up from the wicker chaise longue, and a few minutes later they had started out.

When, arm in arm, they reached the corner and slowly turned down Maple, she knew that the housewives along the block could have set their clocks by it—just as, in her childhood, when Mr. Morse went by with his brindle Scotties on a leash, her father had always taken out his heavy worn Waltham, flipped open the gold lid with his thumbnail, and scanned the Roman numerals of the dial, less to check the accuracy of his neighbor than of his time-piece; and then he would announce: "Half an hour to dinner— there goes old Morse with Twist and Twig." She saw Mrs. Bald-ridge peering at them from behind a parlor curtain. Not to spare the woman embarrassment, but out of indifference and even com-passion, Miss Grainger did not look back and catch her at it: like everybody else the poor soul had little enough in her life, Heaven knew, and if it gave her any pleasure to spy on others . . . Belle whined: "The leaves seem to be falling earlier this year. Goodness knows I can't see them but I can certainly feel them underfoot." Indifferently she answered, as she had answered last year and the year before that, "I guess they are." Then, because her mother was almost totally blind now, she added: "But they're a lot prettier than they used to be, seems like. Wish you could see them, Belle." A moment later came the whimpered complaint: "I wonder why seasons change. Oh, I don't mean change, I know why they change. I mean why summers are hotter, winters colder—things like that." "I haven't the foggiest," Winifred Grainger said "—but isn't it supposed to be the other way around? At least that's what people are always saying." "And just tell me this," the old woman wailed querulously, "why in the world don't people sweep their sidewalks any more? All these scratchy horrid leaves! We do, don't we?" "Yes, we do. Or Irma does." "In my day, people kept their sidewalks clean. It's only right! Well—don't you agree?" "Oh yes. I certainly do. Absolutely." They were talking to themselves.

When her mother was tucked in on the sun porch again with a cup of bouillon on the small tiled table beside her, Miss Grainger went upstairs to her bedroom. She sat down at her writing table and looked out across the drying lawn at the summerhouse—its floor was rotted and sagging now, the weather-worn benches that lined three sides of it were warped, and through the open window she could hear how the flimsy trellis overhead rattled in the mild October breeze with the dried stiff leaves and stems of trumpet vine. Almost automatically she addressed an envelope to Harry Harrison at his office in the city; but, still bemused by thoughts of the past, she held off the letter a minute or two longer. For she could remember, if she put her mind to it, how that vine and those leaves had filled three months of summer midnights with a heady pungent smell, how the screening leaves had gleamed in the moonlight like steel or kept the rain off on showery nights, how her clever lover had quickly learned which boards in the creaking floor to avoid, and how—nonchalant, kidding, matter-of-fact at last, and all but a stranger—he had always, no matter what the hour, left too soon. When she finally began to write, she revealed nothing of these memories: to Harry it would only have been an old story.

". . . There was a printed card this morning from Betty Finletter saying that Jack Sanford had died. The funeral will be held at some home in Watkins Glen on Friday afternoon (Betty *Sanford* of course, and I must *keep it in mind*)," she wrote. "Nice of her to include me in; I didn't think she would. Just for the hell of it I think I'll drive down and attend. Anonymously, sort of; except that Betty, if anyone, will recognize me. Lord maybe she won't! Would you be free to go with me? I wish you would, Harry, but I have no idea why. For that matter there's no reason for my going either. But it does seem a pity if some one of us from the old days doesn't show up for old sake's sake, to pay our Last Respects to old Jack. 'Old Jack' is good—do you realize he'd be sixty no less? Imagine. It doesn't seem possible, not when I think of things. The guy who dove from the top of the lighthouse and went to work at eight A.M. after staying all night with you-know-who at you-know-where—could he ever be *sixty?* Fifteen years older than we are, which at this time of life, just as when we were kids, seems another generation. But when I was twenty there wasn't that difference, I guess because girls are just naturally older than men." She paused, and then added: "I said I didn't know why I wanted you, but on second thought that's not quite true. I want you with me at the funeral because you knew what a love affair that was and you're the only one who did know—everybody knew of course but you knew *what it was,* as I always told you everything at every stage of the game. Always; you could probably play it back to me better than I could tell you now. Anyway—would you be a gent and escort an old biddy to the last rites? My God it will be like attending my own long-delayed bridal!"

She looked the letter over, and then added a postscript: "Does that sound like self-pity? But you know better. I had my bridal. Anyhow let me know."

HARRY HARRISON pressed a button with his well-manicured finger to speak to his secretary in the outer office.

"Miss Ordway, don't let anyone disturb me, please. I have some private work and don't want interruptions." Then, constrained to add his famed light touch, nobody ever knew why and a few wondered, he said: "Now don't go getting ideas, doll. I just feel the need to commute with my soul."

He got up from the Queen Anne chair on the far side of the resplendent cleared desk and moved absently across the carpeted floor to the windows that gave on Seneca Street, six floors below. He gazed down unseeingly at the midday traffic and thought of Winifred Grainger's letter and request.

He was puzzled once more to discover in himself, as he had been doing dozens of times in recent months (he who couldn't afford such things), sudden unaccountable emotions, disturbing and deep. The letter had affected him more than he would have believed possible. Harry Harrison went about his daily routine, and his heavily social evenings (for he was much in demand), with an outgoing gay personality, bright remarks when occasion demanded, charm, graciousness, esprit, and quips for everybody. But alone—alone the picture was different; the mood, when he was alone, would have astonished and puzzled his many friends who welcomed him so cordially and envied his popularity: he had what many of his friends longed for and knew they would never have— popularity-plus, and the "plus" meant one thing to them: Personality. But there it was again: death and thoughts of death, matching his own growing secret obsessions, a burden or bafflement that he seemed to carry about with him everywhere lately, day and night, that constantly called for increasingly extra effort in the Personality Department, a strained but still effective stepping-up of that charm that was expected of him and without which, so he believed, he would be nothing. But this! What was it—our old friend *taedium vitae,* ennui, distaste of self and all his ways? He was shocked, too, he realized; not by the news in the letter but by Winnie's reaction to it. If she of all people could take the thing so calmly, so cavalierly it almost seemed, why couldn't he? But of course Jack Sanford's death had nothing to do with his depression; Harry Harrison had never cared for him really, or even known him very well. As if tired out, fatigued through and through by a more than physical strain, he dropped into one of the big leather chairs and put his smoothly shaved cheek, still smelling faintly from the morning cologne, on his palm. From his breast pocket he took out an immense linen handkerchief with an inch-wide border—it was monogrammed in dark blue with a severely modern, overlapping double H, resembling the segment of a diminutive picket fence—and dabbed at his dry lips. He gazed, abstracted, across the loved room, which, except for his apartment at the Sagamore and his small cottage at Parson's Point, was the nearest he came to having a home of his own.

In all ways, Harry Harrison believed in living his life in the civilized manner. The office of the successful man must not look like an office. Ledgers, typewriters, files and filing cabinets, the secretary herself—all evidence of the business one conducts is off stage, as it were; behind the scenes. Thus Miss Ordway occupied a small outer room of her own; and the drawing boards, the overhead fluorescent lights, the compasses and inks and T-squares and blueprints, and even the young draughtsmen with whom and through whom he made his money as architect of country houses, were confined to the large studiolike room on the floor above. His own office—that is, the elegant room where he received clients and friends—must represent his personality rather than his profession.

But a man's picture of himself is highly fallible; a wish to seem interesting, to himself as well as to others, may lead him, on a superficial level, to outright misrepresentation; though on another, buried, unconscious level to what might be called (though he would never know it) stark exposure. A photograph of his father in a silver frame stood at one end of the refectory table against the sage-green wall opposite, and at the other was a Mayan head interestingly defaced that he had picked up in Yucatán. On his desk was a gold-framed photograph of his mother. For a paperweight he had a sizable bronze replica of Romulus and Remus taking their storied nourishment from the Wolf, symbol of ancient Rome, that he took a special pleasure in, the more so when, as sometimes happened, the expression on a client's face reflected the thought that it was not "nice." On the wall between the casement windows were, one above the other, a pair of good reproductions mounted tastefully on beige linen under glass: Gauguin's *Spirit of the Dead Watching* and Manet's *Olympia,* reclining nudes both; and on either side of the door to the outer office hung a Renoir *Bathers* and *Mother and Child,* the latter a portrait of Mme Renoir suckling her infant son. At the right arm of each of the two leather chairs was a mahogany end table, with a cocoa-veined marble ashtray, a crystal box for cigarettes, and a silver lighter shaped like a small Aladdin's lamp. Glancing down, he saw, or thought he saw, that the table at his elbow was just perceptibly coated with dust. He reached out a middle finger and drew its tip along the surface; he must speak to Miss Ordway, and see that she stayed one evening and spoke to the cleaning woman. He turned the finger upward and examined the scarcely visible smudge. He was about to rub it away with his handkerchief, but rose instead from the chair and went into his private bathroom to wash his hands.

Finished, he straightened his sober blue four-in-hand in the glass above the washbowl, and then became absorbed in a study of his reflection. He placed both hands flat on the cold edges of the bowl and stared intently, intensely, at himself.

Harry Harrison saw a man whose face, for all its forty-five years, exactly, to the month, showed scarcely a line, and indeed could be thought of as strangely, even somehow unbecomingly, young; a rather attractive man with still sandy hair, and all of it; with gray, clear eyes; a good nose, the nostrils of which flared slightly as if scenting some distant, faintly unpleasant odor not detectable to others; a chin neither weak nor strong; a firmly closed mouth. But within half a minute he saw none of this; the face in the glass vanished as he lost himself in thought.

Should he talk it over with a psychiatrist, perhaps? (But talk what over?) That would be the correct, the modern and civilized thing to do. But psychiatry or analysis—what could they accomplish but the digging up of a lot of tiresome, unnecessary and ludicrous details of sexual stirrings during a lonely childhood long since over and done with? Aware that his bachelor way of life tended, in the very nature of things, to make him self-absorbed, self-involved, imprisoned within himself for all his cultivated and calculated outgoingness, he feared that analysis would only make him more so, turning him inward upon himself even more, further cutting him off from the stream of things which he would like to have entered into more freely and fully but, by temperament, could not, and knew that he could not, except superficially and for the most part meaninglessly—and doubtless what ailed him anyway, if anything ailed him, was nothing more than advancing years and the passage of time, an oppressive sense of the transiency of life which any man of sensibilities goes through as a matter of course when he approaches the milestone of fifty. He still had a few years to go, to reach that milestone, but those coming up would be a fast five years indeed.

Sure, sure, we all grow older—but could this fact alone account for his persistent, his increasing thoughts of death? Actually he knew better than to lay his obsession to the rapidly passing birthdays: forty-five was nothing in the modern world, was nothing anyway, and very likely he had many more years ahead. But— wasn't that just it, those many-more-years? For lately, more than once, the suspicion had entered his mind that this involuntary preoccupation with death had less to do with age than with a sense of failure, the sameness of his days and the bleakness of the future. Oh he was by no means a failure in the material sense; few if any of the men he had grown up with in Arcadia had done so well as he. Nor was it because he was unmarried, and had no one to share his "success" with, except possibly Miss Ordway, who was single-mindedly devoted to him at just the right distance and who was well paid for her devotion and service. Did the feeling of failure spring, he sometimes wondered, from a reluctant, an unconscious distaste of people, a desire to remain apart and aloof, untouching and untouched? This was a secret and buried fault, and he had long been on guard against it by cultivating, much of the time successfully, that popular social manner of his that was communicative and carefree, at least on the surface, and enough so (for who has time to hear our troubles, who is interested, who cares about us at all really?), and often gay. Except when he was with his lifelong dear friend Winifred Grainger, and also inwardly, in a place no one must ever know (for it was a weakness certainly, a fault, a lack, unmanly and ungrown-up), was he aware of a peculiar void amounting at times to desolation, a longing for something he had never had and didn't know of, as he puzzled the question—not, like so many men, Where along the way have I missed out? but *What* have I missed? He was not unhappy, certainly not miserable; if he had been, that would have been something positive at least. In a sense it was worse than unhappiness, it was apathy; and apathy could seem—did often seem—more dismal than frustration, disappointment, or actual grief. And it was so tiring to keep up a front, and put a bright face on things, when all one wanted to do, half the time, was . . . sigh: over what?

He glanced at his hands spread flat on the porcelain rims of the washbowl, and again, mysteriously, an imminence of death came over him, as if a door or window had swung open and a tangible breeze blown past—chilling or warm, it was all the same. A tiny mound of pink fat swelled up between the signet ring and the knuckle of his ring finger; the half-moons showed pink and clear on the well-kept nails; the fingers were squarish, and short rather than otherwise. These hands, he found himself thinking—how soon will they be less than pink, and cold then, and folded forever over the breast of his Oxford-gray suit? Morbid—even comic. But such previsions had come to him too often lately to be entirely a joke. At times, waking abruptly and unaccountably in the middle of the night, he had caught himself listening, actually apprehensive, for the beat of his own heart; and the reassurance that it ticked on as steady as ever was no reassurance at all. And only the other day, lunching alone at the Rochester Club, he had suddenly looked up at the silent, ancient, familiar waiter almost in alarm, and with difficulty restrained himself from reaching out and taking hold of the white starched sleeve, because he had been on the point of saying: "Do you realize I won't be coming here much longer, Albert—that one of these days . . ." But there was the thought, too, the undeniable certainty: Would Albert have cared? Nobody would care; nobody will care. For what oppressed him more and more as time went on was not really death itself but the fear, and the knowledge, that once he was gone no one would remember him, he would be forgotten, his passing would not leave a gap in anyone's life; it would be just as if he had never existed at all. What reason did he have that anyone *would* remember him, what had he ever done or given, whom had he ever meant anything to? Why did people remember people? To have "created" a few dozen country houses wasn't enough, surely; wasn't enough, counted for nothing. But what was enough, what did count, was *why is* a man remembered?

Sighing deeply, conscious that the sigh rose not at all from despair or anything like it, he returned to the beautiful room that was his office and sat down at the beautiful desk and took up Winifred Grainger's letter and read it again. It mattered not a damn to him that Jack Sanford was dead, but he wouldn't for a moment think of not going to the funeral with Winnie. He reached for the button to tell Miss Ordway to get Miss Grainger in Arcadia; then changed his mind. The occasion demanded a letter; she had written him, he would write her. He drew from the drawer a thick white sheet of his personal Tiffany stationery and wrote down the date and "Dear Winnie." After a moment of tapping the pen against his lower teeth, he began:

"Having just left orders with Griggs to have my shroud of basic black in good order for Friday . . ."

WITH HER CUSTOMARY BOSSY AIR, her self-assurance that she was the sole authority without whose vigilance and efficiency the whole household would go to pot, Irma strode into Miss Grainger's room at two o'clock without knocking and roused her out of a sound nap.

"Wake up, Miss Winnie," she commanded, prodding her shoulder. "Letter for you, dear."

Winifred Grainger turned over and looked up, first with foggy surprise, then anger. "You mean hound, couldn't you let a fellow sleep?"

"Special Delivery"—which excused everything.

"It could have waited till I came down, you silly bitch." She swung her legs over the side of the bed and took the letter from Irma's hand. "Now beat it!"

Pleased, Irma pointed her chin in the air and sailed from the room.

Winifred Grainger slit the envelope and lay back again to read the letter. Oh God, she said to herself as she caught the drift of the opening paragraph—Harry in a playful mood; so she skipped ahead to find out what she was looking for, and found it: the news that he would come to lunch and then go on to Watkins Glen with her for the funeral.

She took a cigarette and sat up again, fully awake now. Good old Harry. But she had expected nothing less. With whatever he had to give of himself that could be useful to her—and over the years this had amounted to a good deal, and many hours of sympathetic listening—he had never failed her yet. His was a deep-seated, an unshakable loyalty, which meant all the more to her because she well knew she was the one person in his life, with the possible exception of Carol Clyde, for whom he had such a feeling. More: he had always, from his earliest years, been her "stalwart champion," even though she had sometimes been embarrassed by his virtuous defense of all her erring ways. If she was a sinning Guinevere or worse, he was a Galahad whose heart was pure—a role not without charm in a youth, or even in a young man in his twenties, but a little unbecoming (though she could not have said why) after a man has reached thirty and forty and was now pushing fifty. Many people around town thought of him not only as virginal, of course, but also priggish; yet he had always, for some mysterious reason of his own, been the very opposite of priggish in his very liberal attitude toward her past. It had been a real support to her, many times, and she did not know what she would have done without him in her life.

Harry Harrison was one of those men, not rare in American life—Winifred Grainger knew several even in Arcadia, though the type usually gravitated to the cities (well, Harry had, too)—whom other men think they envy, and who, like priests and other celibates, pique the curiosity of women: secretly women can't stand it, they want to get in there and *do* something about it, muss him up, upset him, put him at a disadvantage, pull his zipper, even take him over out of nothing more than sheer mischief or curiosity. Neat and well kept, fastidious, conservative, attractive enough, clean, intelligent, faintly androgynous, often talented in his safe field and usually successful, he is the extra man at dinner, the fourth at bridge, the godfather of other people's children, the "Dutch uncle," the confidant of wives, the loyal friend and sometimes formidable enemy. Men admire his ease with women, deplore his single state and envy his freedom, and decide what he needs is to settle down with a good wife; women are inclined to mother him and sister him and take him in charge socially, with match-making in mind, and many of them think he has not married because, in his sensibly cautious way, he is merely waiting for the right girl to come along. If asked for her opinion, Winifred Grainger, meaning no disparagement of her friend at all, would have deliberately replied, typically (such a question deserved such an answer): "Balls, picnics and parties!" She knew these ideas were myths, for she knew him better than others did—knew all sides of him: a man like Harry Harrison doesn't want a wife and never did, and for him there's no such thing as the Right Girl; the type, if such he may be called, is *sui generis*, sufficient unto itself. In any case, she didn't trouble her head about "placing" Harry Harrison or indulging in the always fascinating game of match-making as far as he was concerned: she only knew him (only!) as certainly the best friend *she* had ever had, though how, or in what way, she herself would have been hard put to explain. She got off the bed and went to the telephone to thank him.

". . . The funeral's at two-thirty, the announcement says. It will take a little over an hour to Watkins Glen, so why not knock off early and come here for lunch at twelve noon? Sharp—you know Irma. If that's not taking too much of your day . . ."

Harry Harrison had planned to take the whole day, after going to the office to look over the mail first; and since it was Friday, he would not return till Monday. In fact, after they came back from the funeral, he rather thought he might drive out to the lake and spend the weekend at his cottage at Parson's Point. Would she go with him?

"We'll see, Harry. Must think. There's no one to leave Belle with except old Irma."

"That's easy. Why not take them along with us? It's all in the family."

She ignored this. "See you tomorrow. Come early enough for a drink. And thanks, Harry, you Old Faithful you."

She went to the closet for her suede windbreaker, then descended through the big house to the sun porch.

"Come, Belle. It's time."

"Time?" piped the querulous voice. "Why, it just doesn't seem possible, I hardly got comfortable . . ."

"Is, though. And here's Irma with your—Well look what *she's* got, for God's sake."

"Now that's not fair, Winifred, you know I can't see . . ."

"That old Norfolk jacket of Dad's. Harris tweed—it will outlive us all. Where did you dig that up, Irma?"

"Oh, I found it," she answered airily. "Thought it would be just the thing, these nippy afternoons."

"Right. And very smart, too. Really, Belle, you'll look terriff. I'd wear it myself if I weren't so broad in the beam."

The fallen leaves ran after the cars on East Avenue as Winifred Grainger and her mother moved along the sidewalk like figures in a dream. Little Barton Dunning played at the curb, filling a red cart with dead leaves. As the shadow of the women passed over the spot where he squatted in the grass, he rose up and stared at the women as if he had never seen them before. "Hi, Barton," Winifred Grainger said. He said nothing, just stared solemnly back. But she scarcely noticed; for she was thinking of the boy's grandmother, Isabel Barton, with whom she had gone through grade school and most of high school and who had married so young. Well, one didn't have to be all *that* young to be a grandmother at forty-six or so. It was Isabel who, "safely married," had been the first to warn Jack Sanford—had told him for his *own good* (as one always does these things) when he hadn't yet been in town long enough to have discovered it for himself—that going around with or even being seen with a girl of Winifred Grainger's reputation, even if her father was the banker and her family, locally the oldest and best, was something he just couldn't *do* in Arcadia, not if he wanted to get ahead in this town. You had to think of these things; know the facts. But she couldn't blame Isabel and never had. Isabel had acted from the best of motives, moral guidance, thinking only of Jack's future; and in any case Isabel had only been one of half a dozen or more who had steered Jack away with the same tune—members of that tightly knit group that centered around the so-solid (then) Betty and Herb Finletter and their perpetual open house.

There was a wonderful smell of burning leaves in the air, but the flames of it, wherever they were, and even the smoke, could not be seen anywhere: it permeated the chill afternoon like the pale yellow sunlight itself. The smell of burning leaves, a home-town smell, part of your growing up and your childhood, it went all the way back . . . This, Winifred Grainger thought, is the true smell of autumn; *is* autumn; far more than the smell of harvested apples or smoking jack-o'-lanterns or the cool fishy tang of Lake Ontario which, at this season only, for some reason, sometimes reached across the county as far south as Arcadia, twenty miles from the lake. The burning leaves meant October as surely as the sickly sweet smell of the Sugar Bush meant springtime; the burned gunpowder of the small brass cannon that started the races at the Yacht Club meant summer; and the pungency of the birch logs crackling and flaring brilliantly in the fireplace of her father's library meant winter. This is the season I love best here, she thought, as she sniffed the scent of the burning leaves; but it wasn't true: Winifred Grainger loved Arcadia and home at any season of the year.

The regulars at Morses' rooming house were out on the porch, or a fairly representative group of them—it was amazing, no matter what the hour, how there always seemed to be the same gallery to give them a thorough, but silent, once-over, across the low stone balustrade of the ugly Victorian house, as mother and daughter passed by. Old Morse himself was dead now, Twist and Twig were long since gone—but there had been a succession of Twists and Twigs, so that the two brindle Scotties now lying on the top step with their melancholy heads between their forepaws, gazing mournfully at the passers-by, seemed to be the original pair that Winifred Grainger remembered from her girlhood. Old lady Morse still carried on, a prodigiously informed dowager who was able to fill in, for the benefit of a newcomer to her coterie, the background and history of any soul who walked by; she mourned the fact that so few people walked these days: passengers in cars came and went so fast that she was unable to point them out to her roomers, who of course (so she thought) were palpitating for details of scandal, however remote. As usual, when the Graingers came along, an eloquent silence fell over the group on the porch, a silence that was but the prelude to history, as if, during that mute moment, Mrs. Morse was gathering breath before she launched into her tale, or tales.

Half a block farther on, a car drew up at the curb, its wire wheels making a crisp crackle among the dry leaves as it pulled in close and stopped. It was a small English sports car, in dark red, with two red leather bucket seats and a stick shift; the driver was a man in a blue flannel blazer and tattersall shirt, dark bow tie with white polka dots, and a soft pearl-gray felt hat with the brim turned up all around. At first glance one would have thought him barely middle-aged, but Winifred Grainger could remember that very hat, or a dozen others just like it, as far back as her early teens, and had damned good cause to remember them. Calvin Cunningham—or Cal, as he loved to be called by everyone, young and old alike—wore it the year round, winter and summer; it was the hallmark not only of his wealth but also of his calculatedly rakish good looks and perennial "youth," or at least of the young blood or blade that he tried still to be; and though real old age showed at last on the once handsome face, he continued to deny his years with every accessory that money could buy. Older than God, she thought; imagine him still driving a car, being *allowed* to drive a car, well it just goes to show what fortune and pull can do: he'll go to his grave a sport, in that soft gray hat and polka-dot tie.

Mr. Cunningham, nonchalant, collegiate, leaned sideways from the wheel and called out brightly: "Well well! And how are we today, ladies?"

Belle Grainger paused in her slow-motion shuffle along the sidewalk and pressed her daughter's arm inquiringly. She raised the other arm tentatively into the air and opened and closed finger and thumb as if trying to catch a pinch of something invisible to others. "Let me see-e-e, now just a minute," she quavered, looking up unseeingly at the almost leafless branches overhead, "I know that voice as well as I know my own name. No, don't tell me, Winifred! Isn't it—why, it's Cal *Cunn*ingham!"

"Himself! Good afternoon, Belle. And good afternoon to you, Winifred. Isn't this simply a ripping day?"

"Swell," Winifred Grainger answered noncommittally, thinking how often in the past, and with what intimate, whispered, and sometimes panting inflections, he had called her "Winnie."

"Can't I give you ladies a lift?" he asked, leaning over the low door in casual, boyish fashion. (But of course, because of the two-seater, it was all pointless, the invitation was compulsive and automatic, it sprang from old habit merely, one of those gestures the old bird still thought was expected of him.) "Or a joy-ride perhaps —a little spin out into the country on this delightful afternoon?"

Mrs. Grainger chuckled in appreciation of the flattering offer. "Now you mustn't sabotage our good intentions, Cal. This is our constitutional—it's most important."

Joy-ride. A little spin. The old boy's sure slipping, Winifred Grainger thought. Twenty-five and thirty years ago, when he had been a member of the board of her father's bank and one of the closest friends of their family, he had certainly been more in touch with the speech of the times—had spoken no more like her father, oh in more ways than one, than she had. The youthful touch had ever been, in all things, Cal Cunningham's speciality; and there were a few years there, several years—yes, she had to admit it— when he had been very good at it.

"Then I'll be on my way, ladies. I'm happy to have refreshed myself with this glimpse of you, however brief—it's really made my day! I might add that you're looking mighty fit, Belle."

"Remember me to dear Grace, won't you? Tell her to come and *see* me, for heaven's sake. She knows I can't get out."

"I'll do that little thing. 'Bye now"—and the car slid away.

"Old mealy-mouth."

"Winifred!" But the old lady bent her head and laughed softly to herself. "Between you and me and the gate post, I've always rather wondered about him and Mrs. Mott, haven't you?"

"Not at all. Everybody knows about him and Mrs. Mott. I only wondered what they saw in each other."

"Oh come now, Winifred, Cal Cunningham was a very good-looking man. A very *hand*some man."

"Yes, you've got to hand him that. He sure was."

After a long silence, and half a block farther on, "I'll tell you a secret," Mrs. Grainger said, with a little toss of her head. "Calvin Cunningham kissed me once. He really did, cross my heart. We happened to be alone for a moment in the music room during one of Nell Harper's evenings. Now don't you ever dare breathe that to anyone. Anyone. Do you hear?"

"He kissed me too."

"Now really, Winifred, that's not the same thing at all and you know it. So don't be silly."

You're darned right I know it. Not at all the same thing. Oh Mother! . . . Aloud she said: "Why isn't it?"

"Why, you were probably only a little *girl.*"

That's right. Only a little girl. Eleven. And twelve. And thirteen and fourteen and fifteen and right on through high school. And, Mother: Not only kissed . . .

As they came down Dalton Street, Winifred Grainger saw the curtains at Mrs. Van Benschoten's parlor window fall back into place. Judging by her invariable opening remark when calling on a neighbor, Mrs. Van was one of those women, like Emma Bovary, who spend their lives checking up on the street. Her tales always began: "I just happened to be passing the front window" or "I had just gotten up to close the window" or "I was just going over the window sill at that moment with a damp cloth . . ."

Irma met them at the door with the inevitable cup of hot bouillon and led her mistress off to the sun porch. Winifred Grainger went upstairs to her room and took off her suede jacket. She sat down at the dressing table and combed her hair, barely glancing at her reflection in the glass. There was still a long time to kill before Irma served dinner at six. She thought of writing a letter to her older sister Mercedes, who had a ranch at Palm Springs, or of driving around and dropping in on her oldest sister Alice, whose husband, tall lanky dull Bud Winship, had been mayor of Arcadia for years and years; but Mercedes never answered letters and Alice never gave her anything stronger at the cocktail hour than a cup of tea. Besides, poor washed-out strained Alice always put on a company smile for her and made conversation as though she were someone not related at all, a smile which bravely declared that she was determined to Ignore Everything and treat her as though her life had been as orderly as anyone else's; and Mercedes—well, Mercedes, in spite of the fact that they had a lot in common, men mostly, had never really had much time for her except during those periods when she had been lonely in Reno or home in Arcadia between husbands.

Now this is just plain idiotic of me, Winifred Grainger said to herself: balmy, screwy, but what the hell—don't all miserable females do things like this at one time or another? She opened the bottom drawer of her desk and rummaged through some papers till she found what she was looking for. She took the photograph and went to the window with it, to study it in a better light.

It was the picture of a man about thirty with bright alert eyes, rather small eyes and perhaps a bit too close together; a lean ruggedly masculine face with prominent cheekbones; a firm mouth and firm chin, with a deep cleft just below the lower lip (she remembered how, when sometimes she had watched him shave—to her a fascinating process, though she couldn't have said why—he always put his tongue in front of his lower teeth and pressed against the flesh there to "iron out" that deep cleft so that he could really get at it with the razor and shave it). His light-brown hair was parted in the middle and slicked down smooth after the style of the movie heroes, like Richard Barthelmess or William Haines; and he wore a small neat mustache carefully separated into two equal halves by the razor and pointed at the ends, like Lew Cody. The man gazing intently and even almost anxiously from the picture was clearly no world-beater when it came to looks (she had had at least forty who were better-looking), he didn't look like a particularly interesting person or even a very nice guy; but, there he was, and what she had loved, what had made her suffer, what she had never been able to forget, was this. Further—and this was unique in her considerable experience—he had loved her, for a while. People could say what they wanted to say about her, and they had said it; but he had loved her and even been in love with her for almost three full months. Perhaps three months of love wasn't too little in a lifetime; it might well be that many another woman, married, with children, and a husband over many years, had never known so much as three—not, at least, the kind of love she had known with Jack Sanford. As for the powerful, unique, and ineradicable image of him that, long after it was over, seemed to have stood in the way of her ever finding love again in another man, no matter how many times she had tried and how many she had slept with since—well, maybe it was true that he had spoiled her for others, but not for worlds would she have missed it. Look how potent it still is (she thought), look how it still holds, lasts, never ends, can still cause in her body involuntary shivers and tensions like a shock! For out of those less than three months so long ago she could still call up and feel again not ten or a dozen or twenty but surely as many as a hundred startling, stunning, wholly unexpected moments that had once left her all but faint as her whole body and heart suddenly quickened in total response: sitting beside him innocently one afternoon, to name just one, on the green-slatted bench beside the tennis court at the Club, the two of them watching another couple finish a set of singles and waiting their turn, Jack nonchalantly leaning back with his arms raised in their short-sleeved tennis shirt to clasp his fingers at the nape of his neck and tilt his face up to the sun, so that she, turning unaware to say something to him—how all at once, without any preparation at all (and really it almost seemed she should have been warned somehow, it was too breath-taking coming unexpectedly like that, too difficult to suppress the helpless gasp that gave her away), she found herself looking down into the short half-sleeve and straight into the hollow of his tawny, white-shadowed armpit, secret and beautiful and intimate and beyond all reason exciting, as if she had suddenly been given a too-privileged glimpse (almost, curiously, an unwelcome one) into one of the most private recesses of the person of that adored remote man every inch of whom she knew and loved so well, an isolated set-apart detail that, in little, pointed up and promised how entirely that night or later that afternoon she would give herself to and receive the whole of him, already so familiar to her yet always and continually so surprising. When, that fall, he had gone on to Betty Finletter and broken up the Finletters' marriage, she had hated her own loneliness for months, for many months, but she had never complained or even resented Betty Finletter's having him. If he was weak enough to be persuaded by others against her, if Jack Sanford couldn't love her as she was, she had not, however much she loved him, wanted him at all.

On the lower wide margin of the photograph he had written in green ink: *"To the trumpet vine, to the wisteria, to the summerhouse."* Cautious Pete, she thought with a smile; he had been so careful that other eyes should not read too intimate an inscription. And she smiled, too, over the memory of their quarrel as to the spelling of "wisteria." She had insisted that it was spelled "-aria," he that it was *"e,"* and he had settled the matter by doing it his way. Such things had mattered a lot in those days.

All I ever wanted in the world, she thought to herself as she put the picture away, was to make one man happy, keep house for him, and love him. So many women seem to have that, but it sure passed me by.

QUICKLY BUT EFFICIENTLY Harry Harrison ran through the morning mail, and made a few notes, and gave them to Miss Ordway. He had brought to the office a small flat case with a few overnight things in it—he could not sleep, for instance, without pajama tops and bottom, and buttoned right up to the chin, like a shirt—in the event that he should decide to go on to Parson's Point later. It was Friday, and a weekend at the lake might be very pleasant at this time of year; on the other hand, it could be depressing, too, for the place was deserted mostly, this late in the season, and everything closed up. The prospect of the afternoon was bad enough; at his stage of life, five years the good side of fifty but keenly aware that time seemed to have accelerated awfully fast lately, and he had to go it alone, funerals had come to take on a more personal meaning, a kind of identification, than he cared to acknowledge. Acknowledge it he did, though—his states of depression would not let him ignore the matter, and he was no fool—but acceptance was something else again.

"Goodbye, Miss Ordway dear . . ." he sang as he came through the outer office.

"Don't you want to give me a number where I can reach you, or anything?"

He put an actorish hand flat on his upper chest, the fingers spread. "Now who in God's world would ever want to reach me? Have a nice weekend, Miss Ordway. And *be good!*"

His last impression of her, as she watched him leave, was all too characteristic and familiar: she looked both older than her thirty-some years, and much younger—maternal, uxorial, and filial all at once.

As he drove out Rochester's well-bred and well-barbered East Avenue toward Pittsford and Wayne County beyond, and the city began to fall away behind him, he noticed for the first time that morning that the day would be a fine one. The bright late-October air was cool, and so clear that he could see for miles; in spite of what lay at the end of the journey, he could look forward to the drive, after lunch with Winifred, much of it along the shore of Seneca Lake—the prettiest of the Finger Lakes by a long shot. He supposed Winnie would want to take her own car and do the driving. He didn't mind, for she was one of the best drivers he had ever known. Whatever she did, she did well, whether it was horseback riding, sailing, designing her own clothes (there had been a few years there, in her early thirties, when she had even flown her own plane), gardening, running the house, or taking care of that terrible mother of hers, who, he had always believed, was to blame for so much. But in all the many years he had known Winnie— since childhood really—she had never shown the slightest resentment of the old lady, or indeed, it seemed, of anyone else—she who had so much cause. For if ever there were a girl or woman who had been taken advantage of . . .

Harry Harrison avoided the main highway as tiresome, and took an older, less direct route instead, the surface of which was often broken and crumbled, hard on the tires; but it was a route filled with fond associations of the past. Between Fairport and Macedon, entering Wayne County now, where he came from, the road swept gradually up and around a long low hill in a wide, very familiar arc. As his coupé began this slight ascent he recalled with a rueful, almost an abashed smile a childish daydream he had had so often, many years ago, about this very spot. Why the dream had centered on this particular curve in the road rather than another, he did not know, but here at any rate was the scene and background of that boyish fancy. Driving to the city with his parents in a car from Stevens' livery for a Saturday's shopping, and also when returning home, the same delightful vision of the future took hold of his imagination whenever this upward curve in the highway came into view. He saw himself as a grownup, as old as thirty or more, driving up and around this attractive curve on a beautiful day in an expensive light-colored convertible with the top down—or being driven in such a car, rather; for the very essence and charm of the daydream, so sure to be realized when he grew up, was that behind the wheel was a uniformed chauffeur, while he himself sat at his ease on the other half of the broad front seat, idly watching the passing landscape and now and then making pleasant but impersonal remarks to his driver in the most democratic fashion, not too comradely, but not aloof either: the emancipated rich employer secure enough in himself to be comfortable and considerate and even conversational with a servant. For years he had seen this picture in the certain future; and even much later, far from his home town, in distant parts of the country or in foreign cities, that picture and this place where he was now driving a quite different car, a closed car in fact, had stayed in his mind like a promise.

A promise to whom? To himself? He did not know and it did not matter, for the promise had long since come true; he had fulfilled it or it had been fulfilled in every particular. But when, six or seven years ago, the realization had finally been achieved, it had not, for some reason, come up to the dream. Almost it might be said that the realization did not remotely match the original design —yet in all literal ways, in every possible outward detail, they had been one and the same: the expensive pale-blue convertible, the clean-cut personable chauffeur, his own forearm and elbow in good cheviot or gabardine or summer white linen resting idly on the car door, and the friendly, democratic, but impersonal small talk. Thank the Lord he had had enough of a sense of humor to appreciate the irony of it when, that first time, on reaching this curving stretch of road in his new car with his new driver in the new uniform, his face had figuratively fallen. In spite of the mysterious failure of the dream to live up to the promise, he had kept on the convertible and the chauffeur for a year or two, out of a kind of stubborn or faithful loyalty to that boyhood vision—out of an inexplicable embarrassment, too—and then given both up. Older now, he appreciated the freedom of being without a personal servant, the pleasure and solitude of doing his own driving, and the comfort of a closed car the year round.

With the bright morning sun glittering on the tin peak of a farmer's silo, on the waving weaving surface of a field of grain, on the blades of a reaper mowing in a field, and flashing back from the windshield of each oncoming car, it was hard to realize that at the end of today's journey lay death. Where was Jack Sanford now? Lying in a funeral parlor at the foot of Seneca Lake deader than a doornail. It could hardly matter less to Harry Harrison. He hadn't seen Sanford for twenty-five years (he'd be damned if he'd think of him fondly as Jack, even to please Winifred). In spite of the man's abilities and good looks, his gaity and undeniable charm, there had been something suspect about him. He had been a guy on the make. This in itself was nothing too much against him; certainly it was the natural role or at least common role of many men in this world, including, to a somewhat different degree, Harry Harrison himself. But more than unusually unbecoming, somehow, had been Jack Sanford's opportunistic drive, his too obvious eagerness "to belong," and his cleverness in being able to get a great deal for the expenditure of very little. Oh, he had not spared himself; he had put himself into it heart and soul, he had given everything he had, to win everybody over—that coruscating personality had flared and flashed around town without stint or abatement—but only when his shrewd intuition had guaranteed the returns in advance. He had played the game: a perfectly respectable pastime or profession in Arcadia or anywhere else—indeed the most respectable. But unlike many others who were equally careful to make every moment count, whether in business or at play, Sanford had had an unattractive habit of walking out on a situation that had proved awkward and letting someone else pick up the pieces. It was all right to turn your back on old ways and old friends, it was even a common custom to do so if you had outgrown that way of life; but the custom also included the stipulation that the turning-away be done gracefully, unobtrusively, certainly not publicly. On these latter points, Jack Sanford had gone against the social grain; yet the force of that personality and charm had been such that his new friends Betty and Herb Finletter and all their closed circle had taken him up, taken him in, without demur.

But Harry Harrison had known full well, as had everybody else, that the Finletters' wholehearted acceptance of the climber (what else could he be called?) was due not so much to their willingness to overlook his breach of custom as to the fact that the girl he had walked out on was "only Winnie Grainger." And of course no one was really to blame but Winnie herself, whose reputation had been an open scandal since her mid-teens. It was a curious social fact but a true one that, though she came from one of the best families in Arcadia, none of the boys or young men had dated her publicly during high school or after. It was one thing to allow themselves to be picked up in her car and driven out to the pines after dark—anybody could understand that; after all it wasn't the guy's fault and they were just doing each other a favor, all understandably on the q.t.—but it was quite another to take her to a party at the Country Club or to the Yacht Club at Parson's Point, for it would be the equivalent of an open declaration that you were taking Winnie Grainger out for one thing only; and most young men, accountable to prying sweethearts or parents, couldn't afford to have their sex life thus publicly aired. The only young man in town willing to be seen out with Winifred Grainger in those days had been himself, Harry Harrison; and once he had even gone so far as to invite the notorious Winnie to the annual Assembly Ball in preference to his own girl, Carol Wilson—trusting the baffled and unaccountably hurt Carol to understand the altruism and charity of his motive, a wish to be generous to a girl who would not otherwise have been asked. Now, looking back over many years, he asked himself uneasily: Was that really his motive?

A curious thought occurred to him; and though it was not surprising in itself, it did surprise him that he had not thought it before. During all the years when he had dwelt on that daydream of the future—and it had lasted into his mid-twenties—the figure of Carol Wilson had never been a part of that picture. In fact there had never been anyone else in that car, ever, but himself and his driver; and now there was only himself. And yet he had "gone around" with Carol since they had been twelve years old, and she had been the only girl he had ever thought of marrying. "Thought" of? Why, he hadn't even *had* to think of it—it was just sort of automatic, it was just always there: the fact that they would some-day be married had been so inevitable that he had hardly ever spoken of it, much less planned it; it would just naturally come about of itself, like growing up. Their eventual marriage (so he once had thought) had been as certain of realization as the car and the curve and the uniformed chauffeur. And what had happened? How could one explain why some things turned out and some did not? Was it—could it be that the dreams that didn't come true were the ones you didn't put your heart into?

Carol was Mrs. Stewart Clyde now, and had been for nearly twenty years. They were still good friends and always would be, in spite of Stewie's irrational jealousy which—idiotically enough, he often thought—persisted even to this day.

AN HOUR BEFORE NOON Winifred Grainger stepped onto the sun porch where her mother lay half asleep as usual in the wicker chaise longue.

"You won't like this, Belle, but you're to have your lunch out here today, on a tray."

"Oh no!"

"Oh yes. Got a guest coming and I'm excluding you out."

"Who is it, if I might deign—"

"Go ahead and deign. It's Harry Harrison."

"He's not a guest! Why, Harry's always been just like one of the—"

"Never mind, Belle, you're lunching alone all the same. Irma will bring you a tray. You're lucky enough it isn't cold out here."

"What have you and Harry Harrison got to talk over that *I* can't hear, for heaven's sake?"

"Nothing. But that's the way it's going to be. Then while you nap, we're going for a drive. Irma can take you out this afternoon, I won't be back in time. Fact is, Belle, Harry and I might even wind up spending the weekend at the Point."

"Are you crazy? You'll freeze to death out there."

"We'll find a way to keep warm. If we go."

"You and Harry?" Her mother chuckled obscenely. "Never."

"No cracks, please. Eggs benedict coming up, okay? That's what I told Irma."

"Anything. You know I never eat."

"Only like a horse is all. You and your old heart trouble, your asthma, your aches and pains—I'm on to you, Belle, after all these years. You'll outlive us all."

"No pity, that's what I never get around here."

Winifred Grainger stepped back into the house and went to the dining room, with its shades half drawn against the bright sunlight.

It was important to see how the table looked—Harry always noticed these things.

Irma had remembered the right glassware and the Minton china. At the two ends of the small table were the place mats of finely cut bamboo that he had sent her once from San Francisco. And good for Irma—she had even remembered Grandpa Blake's napkin ring that Harry had used on those occasions in the past when he had spent the weekend with the Graingers. Satisfied with the look of things—satisfied that Harry would be satisfied—she walked through to the white drawing room and sat down on a hassock at the front window to wait for him.

It was, as Belle had said, always awfully cold at the lake this time of year but it might be fun to go out to the Point for the weekend, after all, either at his tiny cottage or at her larger one. Well, fun was not exactly the right word, but a change at least. She and Harry always had plenty to talk about; they never seemed to run out of conversation and probably never would. That easy companionability of his was the thing she liked about him most: he was so easy to be with; and though he would not have liked the idea, she always thought of him as some kind of comfortable old relation. He wasn't any good to ride with—he hated horses—or to sail with—he was downright apprehensive on the *Penelope*—but for somebody to sit around with and do nothing he was perfect. It was like talking to herself to talk with him; he knew her every thought, they made no social effort with each other, and after months or longer of being apart they had always been able to pick up the thread of things exactly where they had left off. Every woman ought to have some man in her life, she reflected, to whom she could tell everything and anything—and she was the only woman she knew who had such a man. Other women confided in men, too; but in the very nature of things they held back as much as they told. Not so with her and Harry. She even doubted whether she would have come to certain conclusions about herself and her life if she had not had Harry to talk them over with. Wasn't *alter ego* the word? Yet that couldn't be right, either; for no two people in this world could have been more *un*like than Harry Harrison and herself.

Parson's Point had seldom meant Harry to her. He had often

been a guest at the Grainger cottage as a boy and young man; but mostly it meant—always connoted, brought up ineradicable memories of—Jack Sanford. Their weekends together there, all concentrated in a little less than three months of one summer, had been among the happiest of her life, the happiest since early childhood. Many a time, with Belle and Dad right under the same roof, she had stolen out of her own room at midnight and crossed the hall to the guest room where Jack was, or he had come to her. She was certain her father and mother had both known of this (it was like her smoking cigarettes when she was fifteen: her mother didn't want to know of it or catch her at it, and thus have to "do something"), but in their anxiety to get her married—her father's anxiety particularly—they had closed their eyes and ears to it. Belle had been almost ostentatiously blithe about the whole thing, keeping up a festive attitude as if the most acceptable of bridegrooms had appeared on the scene at last; but her poor father, less artful, had been unable to conceal his secret distaste of the situation. It had been clear to her that he accepted Jack as a prospective son-in-law only because nothing better had turned up and probably never would, for he was fully aware of her reputation in the town. And when she had finally given Jack up—and she it was who had made the break, even though she possessed the one ultimate weapon with which to capture him for good and all, if she had cared to use it—her father's reaction had been one of mixed relief and disappointment. As for her mother—Belle of course went blandly on as before, pretending nothing had happened whatever, one way or the other.

Winifred Grainger was twenty when Jack Sanford came along, and she had had a wild hope then, almost a desperate one, that their love affair would obliterate all that had gone before. Without his knowing it, his love for her must certainly erase her obsessive memory of Cal Cunningham utterly (and it had); of Tony di Santo, so handsome and accomplished in bed that the "presence" of it had never let her alone; of Henry Wales; and the garage attendant on West Union Street, whose name for some reason she had never been able to remember; and Newton Griffin, George Stanton, and every other man in her life up to then (and it had, it had, at the time)—erase them so completely that she would never want another man but Jack. After he had left her, she plunged into sexual experiences again, hoping they, in their turn, would erase her fixation on Jack Sanford so that she could forget him as he had forgotten her (and they hadn't, they hadn't). Now she remembered, and could repeat to herself almost with a smile—rueful perhaps, but a smile all the same—a quotation she had read somewhere: *Strong is your hold O mortal flesh, Strong is your hold O love . . .*

And of course one other who had not been erased—for there had been nothing in their relationship to wipe out in the same way—was Harry Harrison, who was at this moment pulling into the drive in his black Buick coupé.

She went out to the side porch to greet him.

"Hi!" she called.

He blew her a mock-gallant kiss. Stepping to the graveled drive, he said: "We picked a fine day, Winnie."

"We didn't. If anybody did, it was Jack."

He gave her a glance. "Well that's a quaint thought. A little shudder-making, maybe. Am I on time?"

"On the nose, as always. Listen—there it goes now . . ."

For a silent moment they stood immobile looking at each other, she on the side porch, he in the driveway below, listening to that agonized wail of the siren downtown on top of City Hall, only a few blocks away, that did double duty as noon whistle and fire whistle. When the long groaning howl had died out in a hoarse rattle (sounding like some sea monster expiring under the waters of the deep, or a dinosaur yielding up some vast orgasm), they smiled at each other, and he came up the steps.

"I didn't bring you a present."

"You brought yourself. What were you thinking, Harry?"

"Oh I don't know. That sound takes me back a million years."

"Does me too. Do you remember the first time they tried it out? It was a big event in Arcadia! I was riding Beauty that afternoon; think of it, I was way out in the country, all the way down past the East Arcadia cemetery. And yet, even that far, Beauty reared up on her hind legs whinnying in panic, like Tom Mix's Diamond— remember *Diamond?*—and almost threw me. She never did get used to it, never. Dandelion doesn't like it either. None of them ever have."

"I hate it. It's so godawful small-town."

"You have no imagination, trouble with you. It can really give you quite a thrill in the middle of the night. I start up from my pillow picturing a fine spectacle like the old Opera House going up in flames—except *that* one was in the middle of the afternoon, wasn't it, in broad daylight—or the box factory or the paper mill, and it's always only the dump again."

"No wonder you like the movies." They went inside.

"Why, Mr. *Harri*son!" cried Irma histrionically as she came to the table with the cups of onion soup. "As I live and breathe!"

"You mean I'm the last person in the world, Irma, you expected to see? You didn't maybe have a sneaking suspicion that just possibly the man who was coming to lunch—"

"Now Mr. Harrison! You old fooler, you. Anyway it's just lovely to see you in our house and at our table again."

"Thank you, Irma. And thanks for remembering that beat-up old silver napkin ring of Grandpa Blake's—it makes me feel I'm still part of the family." When they were alone again, he said: "I should have gone out and said hello to your mother."

"It'll keep. She knows you're here. She's a little sore, though, that I wouldn't let her join us."

"Why wouldn't you?"

"Lissen! I see Belle practically twenty-four hours a day. It's a break for her, too, to get away from me."

"You didn't give me an answer on the phone about the weekend. I wish you would go with me, Winnie. I don't like going out there alone."

"That's not like you, Harry. You've always loved being alone."

"Sometimes. Sometimes not."

"I sort of played with the idea of asking Carol Clyde to have lunch with us, then decided against it."

"Stewie would not have liked that. Why did you think of inviting Carol?"

"Oh, I thought she might like to see you."

"I'd rather like to see her. But not today, especially."

"That's right, today is ours. Still we might drive over there before we leave town and say hello for a minute."

"Do you think it's strictly necessary?"

"I'm glad Carol isn't here to hear you say that. . . . Do you know, I've always thought Stewie Clyde was just about the handsomest man in town. And there are a *lot* of handsome men in this town. Well, everywhere, for that matter."

"What's so handsome about him?"

"Just that he doesn't know it. He has absolutely no idea, ever, of the impression his good looks make on people. There's a kind of innocence there. It has simply never occurred to him that he's good-looking. And for my money, that's what makes good looks in a man every time—provided he's personable enough in the first place. Though oddly, somehow even that docsn't matter much."

After Irma had brought them their eggs benedict and returned to the kitchen, Winifred Grainger said: "I keep thinking of Jack Sanford, of course."

"Of course."

"Now there's a man, incidentally, who did know he was good-looking, every minute. Actually he wasn't, really."

"*I* never thought so. Slick was the word for Jack Sanford."

"Don't you keep thinking of him too?"

"Well . . ."

"After all we are going to his funeral. The guy's *dead*."

"Yes . . ."

"Oh, I know you weren't exactly crazy about him."

"I never said, did I?"

"I could tell though."

"How?"

"I don't know really. Certainly you never showed it. You never showed anything."

"I'm afraid I'm not liking this much," he said.

"Cool, calm and collected—those are the words for you, Harry."

"I wish it were true. Don't you know what goes on inside? Oh, I don't mean me, I mean everybody. *Every*body's puzzled, disturbed, unhappy, lonely above all—no matter what they show on the surface. One learns to cultivate a technique."

"Impassive," she went on, as if she had not been listening. "Imperturbable."

"Oh, people—everybody, I don't care who they are!" he said with startling sudden emphasis. "Do you think people really are cool, calm and collected?"

"You are."

" 'So may the outward shows be least themselves'—haven't you heard that one?"

"In high school. But, Harry, if there was anyone who ever presented the serene untroubled countenance, it's you. Why, *look* at yourself."

"Worse and worse."

"If there've been any traps around, any pitfalls, upsets, even emotions, you've skirted them. That marvelous self-protective sense of yours . . . I know you awfully well, Harry."

"Nobody knows anybody."

"Oh come."

"You make me a zero, you reduce me to a nothing—don't you know that?"

"I don't mean to. Actually I'm paying you a compliment. You're not a slob who wears his heart on his sleeve, like me."

"I don't know where I wear my heart. An awful confession to make, isn't it?"

She didn't seem to have heard. "It's true, somehow, that your expression never changes, Harry. Good news or bad, it's always the same. That can be a gift, you know. A social asset."

"Now listen, Winifred. Will you please cut it out?"

"*I* could never make you uncomfortable—could I?"

"Everybody's vulnerable. Everybody. And you're making fun of me."

"Never, Harry dear. And, well, even if I were—"

"What then?"

"You wouldn't mind really. Not from me you wouldn't. Funny, but you've always been true to me in your fashion, and I'm grateful. You'd never turn against me."

"I wouldn't."

"We're stuck with it, Harry; stuck with each other. For good *or* bad. Habit; nothing more, but oh, nothing less."

"Yes, yes. Well, what's wrong with habit?"

"Nothing," she said. "It's not a bad one. *I've* had worse. I *have* worse."

"It's a habit I've lately thought," he said, "we ought to do something about, sort of. I've been half thinking about it a lot, lately."

"Oh no. *Oh* no."

"Why are you so sure? Hasn't the idea ever crossed your mind?"

"Not seriously enough, or yours either, or you wouldn't say things like 'sort of' and 'half thinking.' Come on, Harry, cut it out now, or we'll only embarrass each other. I don't think I could bear being embarrassed or self-conscious with you—you're all I have left. We're good friends and that's enough. Isn't that enough? Among the people we know, how many of them are even that? Now let's not spoil it by pretending it's something it isn't."

"You're a hard woman, Winifred."

"Yes I am. And I will not let you play games with me, and still less with yourself. That's the main thing: with yourself. We've known each other for too long for nonsense now. What are we trying to prove? Lord, you and *I* don't have to prove anything—not to each other we don't. So cut it out, or I'll begin laughing right out loud. You wouldn't like that. Not with your dignity and sense of face."

" 'Face,' " he repeated, looking down at his empty plate. "My God I haven't got any, that's the whole trouble. I have neither dignity *nor* face."

"Harry! Pull yourself together. You're not kidding me, are you?"

"I've never been more serious."

"A *very* trite line. I've used it often, said it myself—especially when I was trying to get some uncertain gent into the hay. It seldom works. Still," she added reminiscently, smiling faintly, "it has worked sometimes. Memorably, on one or two occasions. Which only made me feel like a fool afterward, when I was pulling on my stockings. Oh, those dreadful moments, dressing 'nonchalantly' while the guy watches you indifferently from the bed, like a stranger."

"You're not listening to me."

"All passion spent. Or was it passion at all, I've often wondered —or merely obsessive curiosity?"

"Come back!"

"You're right. Thank God Irma waiting in the kitchen wears a not-much-good hearing aid." She took a sip of coffee. "Sorry for that moment. Now what is it, dear Harry, you're trying to say? But for God's sake cut the comedy. Life's too short!"

"Life is too short, that's just what I mean. If you'll pretend that I'm not me, and you're not you—"

"That," she said, "I could never do."

"Well, make the effort. At least try to listen to what I'm trying to say, even if you don't go along with it."

"Shoot."

"There was a hint in that note of yours the other day, a definite overtone or undertone, about my never having really understood the story of you and Jack Sanford, even though I—and apparently I alone, because you always told me, you said—knew all the facts. But if I'm so stupid as all that, then what could you ever possibly have found in me to like?"

"I didn't say you were stupid. I've never thought that. I have thought, though, you were somewhat, well, uneducated. Not hep."

"Uneducated? Well, I'd be the first to admit that my experience of life can hardly compare with yours—and please understand that I say this quite without irony or malice."

"I know."

"But all the same, there is education and education. Yours has taken one form or route, mine another. And really—and it gives us a good deal in common, doesn't it?—they rather add up to the same thing."

"For instance."

"Again without malice—"

"Don't apologize."

"—what has it got either of us? Aren't we pretty much in the same boat? Haven't we arrived at more or less the same end? No matter what different routes we chose, or were chosen for us, we wind up alike. Unmarried at nearly fifty, with no prospect in sight, for either of us, but a lonely old age."

"You've got something there, Harry. I ought to feel a shudder. But I don't."

"Well, what are we going to do about it?"

"Simple. Drop it. Life's too short to kid ourselves."

"I'm very serious."

"You're not," she said. "You may think you are, but you're not.

What you're saying has nothing to do with me, or with us. You're speaking out of some peculiar isolation I don't understand."

"You do, or should. Because you're the same."

"Oh *no* I'm not. I've made my peace with the world, or with myself, I can't say how. Listen! I thought we were talking about Jack Sanford!"

"You don't want to talk about Jack," he said.

"He'll be very much on our minds today, nevertheless."

"Not on mine."

"You know, I keep finding myself thinking of Betty Finletter almost as much as of poor Jack. I can't help feeling badly for her. Damn, I must remember to say Betty Sanford."

"We don't need to think of Betty."

"You don't," she said. "I do. She probably hates me."

"If anybody, you should hate her."

"I don't though. I never have."

"I know. And I've always wondered why."

"You're hopeless, Harry. Really hopeless. You know why, or knew why. There's nothing I haven't told you, ever. Sometimes I even think it didn't register at all."

"That's not true. I remember everything."

"Maybe so. But how much of it you really got is another matter. Oh, you heard all the *words,* all right, but I'm afraid they often had little meaning for you. Like a foreign language."

"There's that stupid bit again. We're in a rut, Winifred. Stupid Harry Harrison. Well, I'm not going to get into that again." He got up and walked around the room. "It's true," he went on, "that you've always told me absolutely everything about yourself. It goes back as far as I can remember, to when we were kids."

"Always. The whole truth. I could even wonder why I did, why I kept having to."

"Some people need it."

"While you . . . Dear friends though we've always been, Harry, you've never told me the truth about yourself."

"I don't think I know what it is."

"Why, just . . . the facts, Harry. The facts."

"This is awful. Because . . . Because I don't think there are any facts. Something to tell about. I mean in the sense that anything ever happened. It's as though . . . It's almost as if my life had been lived in a vacuum."

After a pause, Winifred Grainger said: "Gosh. That's quite a fact in itself."

He stopped in his restless pacing across the carpet, turned, and looked at her. "I don't know why I let you say things like that to me." He moved back to the table, stood behind her chair, and put his hand on the back of her head. "I wouldn't take things like that from anybody else. I guess it's because we're such old friends, and I hope always will be. I need you in my life, Winifred, though I can't say why. Certainly I never do anything about it."

"You don't need to."

"Something's missing—I've only begun to realize it lately—and I don't like it much. Oh, it isn't really you I want, Winnie."

"I know that."

"But something, somehow . . . Somewhere along the line . . . I don't know," he said, moving away from her impatiently, "maybe it's just that I'm afraid to die."

"Isn't everybody?" Unexpectedly she gave way to a laugh.

"I fail to see the joke."

"There's no joke, Harry. Except—Belle wondered what we could possibly have to say to each other that we wouldn't want her to hear."

"And?"

She pushed back her chair and stood up. "Come, it's time to go."

Outside, as he had expected, they got into her car instead of his. The new Cadillac she had had every year had been replaced lately by smaller, more maneuverable cars: she was now driving one of the new cheaper, but smart, compacts.

A couple of blocks away Winifred Grainger turned the car into the driveway of a wide lawn in the middle of which was a large, square, very plain, clapboard house, typical of the older houses in Arcadia and nowadays something of an anomaly because of the newer preference, which Harry Harrison despised, for bungalows, split-levels, and ranch houses; this house was in fact very like the house in which he had been brought up. Winifred shut off the motor.

"You go in, I'll wait here."

"Why don't you come, too?"

"Listen, Carol and I run into each other several times a week, somewhere."

"I'll only be a minute. I'm afraid my heart's not in this, today."

"Go ahead, Harry. We've got the time."

He pressed the doorbell, then tried the knob and opened the door. As he stepped into the hall that separated the dining room from the living room, Carol came forward, from the kitchen. She was a tall attractive woman with bright but shy eyes, her hair a strikingly attractive mixture of black and gray, and surprisingly (he was always surprised by this, in recent years, when he saw her again) she still had the clear, high-colored, flawless complexion of her youth: it had been one of her greatest charms, in a girl who had always had beauty to begin with.

"Harry! Oh why didn't you come just a bit sooner; Stewart has only just gone back to work—you couldn't have missed him by more than two minutes."

"I wanted to see you, of course. You look wonderful, Carol. You always do. Almost breath-taking—it makes me realize what I have missed."

She ignored this, and took his sleeve in a comradely way, and led him into the living room. "Winifred tells me you're going to Jack Sanford's funeral, so I won't keep you."

"Yes, I can't stay. I only want to—well, see you, however briefly."

"I'm glad I'm not going. I don't like funerals."

"I can't say I do either. But frankly, I'm not exactly torn apart by this one."

"I know. It was so long ago that we knew him—if we ever knew him at all."

"I'm only going because of Winifred, of course. It means something to her."

"Of course. Still I don't know why even she would want to go, in a way. I never understood how she could have forgiven him. But—that's Winifred: all heart."

"Yes."

"He had personality, but is that ever enough? Still we had some

good times together, you and I, and them. A kind of foursome. I
remember one occasion . . ."

"One that wasn't so good, you mean. I was hoping you'd forgotten it."

"How could I, Harry? And in the long run, I could look back on
it as a *good* experience. Profitable, instructive. One of those experiences that taught me something, after I got used to it."

"Can't we drop it, Carol? It has nothing to do with what we
were talking about anyway—Jack Sanford."

"Maybe not, but he was there. He was very much there. And so
was Winifred, and the whole atmosphere they created, the aura
they cast over the whole evening. It wouldn't have happened, or
not happened, otherwise."

"Well, if we must be absolutely exact, they weren't there at all.
They spent the night in the boathouse. And I'm not ashamed to
admit it any more: *we* were alone in their cottage."

"Yes, that's true." Carol Clyde turned away. Her voice strove
for a lighter note, and succeeded. "Look, Harry, I want to show
you what Stewart has just finished. Look—our new fireplace!"

"I remember an old pine fireplace, with fluted columns and a
chimney piece severely simple—and quite lovely, I thought."

"Yes," she went on hurriedly, "but it was all coming to pieces
and Stewart tore it all apart and rebuilt it brand new, all by himself! He got all those stones from Bailey's Hill and lugged them in
and cemented them together, and—it's only been finished about a
week. We're very proud of it. I didn't know he could even *do*
things like that, but there seems to be no limit—" She broke off,
avoided looking at him, and allowed her eyes to linger caressingly
and admiringly on the ugly bulky fireplace, so out of place in that
simple, plain room. She lay a hand on one of the rough stones
(they glistened in spots as if tiny gold flakes or precious quartz had
been ingeniously embedded in the irregular surface) and touched
it as though it were something dearly prized. She spoke: "An
amazing man . . ."

He looked at her. He knew that she knew his thoughts, but he
said: "What's so amazing about him, especially?"

"Oh I don't know," she answered quietly, moving away. "He's
just an amazing man." The upbeat stress on the last word left no

doubt whatever of her loyalty and affection and her husband's "amazingness."

"You'd better watch the time, Harry. Winifred will begin sounding the horn."

"Really, Carol, this has all been rather pointless, my stopping in for only a minute or two. But I couldn't be in town and *not* come and say hello."

"I'm glad you did. You come back. Do please drive down from the city sometime and come to dinner with us and spend the evening."

"I don't know about that, but thank you, anyway. Tell Stewart I said hello."

"I will."

"Big success?" Winifred Grainger said as he got back into the car."

"Oh yes. Oh my yes."

"No ironies, please."

A block or two farther on he suddenly spoke out of a silence that had been puzzling them both. "Winnie, I'm afraid I don't understand people any more."

"What's the matter now?"

"Oh, nothing specially. They have this new fireplace . . ."

"I know. Carol told me about it the other day in the supermarket."

"A monstrosity. You wouldn't believe it. But I don't think that's the point."

"What is the point?"

"Carol loves it."

"I got that, too, when she told me."

"But she knows better! She has better taste than that."

"Does it matter? And is that why you say you don't understand people? 'Any more.' "

He didn't answer. He hadn't even heard her. Winifred drove the car along East Maple to where Route 22 began, the road to Geneva; they turned south here, and so drove off into the past.

"Is that you, Winifred?"

"Yes, Mother."

"Where are you going, dear?"

"Nowhere. Just out. Up the beach a ways."

"Pretty dark for that, isn't it? I mean a child alone on a deserted beach, in the dark and all. Are you dressed warm enough? It gets real cold these fall nights." The mother's voice comes faintly muffled, and listless, from where she lies wrapped up on a canvas-pillowed couch in the dark corner of the porch facing the lake.

"It's warm enough. And it's not all that dark."

"Why don't you ask Daddy to go with you?" the mother says aimlessly, as if she is thinking of something else, or not thinking at all.

"Daddy's taken the launch and gone over to the Point, as you very well know, to spend his usual evening with his cronies at the Yacht Club."

"Of course. I forgot."

"And if I really wanted someone to go with me—which I don't —I'd ask you."

"Now, Winifred, you don't need to be unreasonable. You know I don't walk much. 'Specially in the sand. It's too difficult." Which is true enough—at least about the walking. At their cottage on the bar, Mrs. Grainger almost invariably spends her evenings wrapped in a blanket, in what might be called a semiconscious state, on the wide porch that fronts Lake Ontario, which is an exact replica of the porch that faces the bay on the other side of

41

the cottage. Winifred sometimes wonders, though not very often, why her mother does this, what she gets out of it, and what she thinks as she lies there alone, in the dark, till bedtime. If asked, her mother would probably reply petulantly: "What? Why, I'm getting the lake air, of course."

"Well, don't be long, dear."

"Why not?" Winifred has, by this time, descended the four steps to the sandy beach.

"Why, just—don't be long. Do I have to give reasons?"

"No."

"And be careful."

"Careful of what?"

"Why, just—careful," the mother murmurs indifferently. "After all, you're only eleven. All sorts of dreadful things could happen to a young girl."

"It wouldn't matter if they did, would it?"

"No, I don't suppose it would," the mother says automatically. Then: "What?"

"What 'what'?"

"Winifred! What did you say?"

"Nothing. Skip it. Dry up. Pipe down."

"Win-ifred Grain-ger." There is a faint crackle and creak of wire springs, indicating a slight stir from the supine figure on the couch in the dark corner of the porch. "You know how I loathe and detest these—those vulgarisms. Heaven knows who you travel with."

"I don't travel with anybody. Who's there to travel with?"

"All the same, your father and I sim-ply de-plore such common-ness, and if you don't know it by now"—here her mother audibly suppresses a yawn— "then I think it's high time—"

"Save your breath. You and Father don't know I exist."

"Be reasonable, dear. Would I be saying all this if I—if your father and I didn't—"

"Love me to death, I suppose."

"Really, Winifred, I don't know what I ever did to deserve this.

42

I never knew such ingratitude. The younger generation today—"

"Blah blah blah. Go back to dreamland, Belle. If I get abducted or anything, or washed out to sea, you can read about it in the papers."

"Children today simply have no re-spect," her mother quavers as Winifred starts up the sand toward the lighthouse. "No feelings for their elders. They seem to think . . ." But the rest of what she says is wiped out by the marvelously musical wind, not loud, but not soft either, that blows in from the dark rolling lake.

Fifty or sixty feet farther on, Winifred kicks off her sneaks and leaves them where they fall. She loves walking in the sand barefoot: loves the feeling of the soft sand between her bare toes when she walks higher up the beach, or the hard, wet, cold feel of the sand when she saunters along the water's edge, which she does now. Sometimes she stands and lets the icy water swirl around her ankles; and when it runs off, the sand gives way under her feet, except at her heels, and then it is like standing on two hard sharp points as rigid as cement, or on golf tees. But as the water recedes, before it comes in with a rush again, these too give way, or are washed away, so that she stands a little lower now, in two deepening holes made by her own weight.

The breeze from the lake is cold, but she loves it. When she looks out, it is like looking out upon a dark ocean, fearful, beautiful, distant, restless, mysterious. Nothing moves out there, no light is to be seen, but all that mighty water is noisy and threatening and curiously promising in its turbulence, like the vague, distant, unknown and unknowable, vast future. Far far off, if she squints her eyes and doesn't look directly, she can see, along the far horizon of the lake—a thousand miles away or maybe only fifty—the faintest glimmer or glow of light, which may be Canada, may be the cities or towns along that far shore, Kingston or Coburg, or may only be something in the mind's eye, or the space around the planet, a pale phosphorescence that marks the far rim of the world.

There is a light though, a real and tangible light, ahead: the

43

revolving lamp of the lighthouse beyond the channel that separates Charles Point from the mainland of Parson's Point, which the bar does not reach across to. In the misty blowy night the lighthouse lamp, but only intermittently, for the briefest second, stands out like a torch suddenly brighter and larger than it should be, and then quickly vanishes as its beam sweeps the wide sealike lake before it turns inland, and then once again stares you in the face like a hurried, angry Cyclops who has no time for you, who is not really interested because he turns away so quickly, as you scuff on along the sand. When this happens, the dozen or so deserted cottages are dimly revealed in shadowy dark silhouette where they loom or sprawl in the turfy sandy ground fifty feet back from the lake shore, and, beyond, another fifty feet from the bay, with its placid boat slips and low boathouses, abandoned moored floats where the small waves slap, unheard in the tumult of breakers and breeze from the lake, and an occasional heavily jackknifed-scarred picnic table for outdoor suppers: nobody picnics on the lake side, because the wind always blows everything away.

Those cottages, those great, dark, shapeless, ugly barns . . . Winifred knows them all, knows everybody who summers in them, knows every room, almost, in every cottage: the sprawling raftered living rooms, the bedrooms with the unfinished partitions that go only halfway up, the mooseheads and elkheads and deerheads, the birchbark art and the burnt-wood art and the burned-leather art, the brightly beaded leather thongs that hang in doorways, the bare floors slightly warped, the sand under your feet like sugar on the kitchen floor wherever you walk, the leather Morris chairs with the brass rods that you can move into different notches to adjust the angle of the back for greater comfort, the sofas casually covered by Indian blankets with designs of swastikas and elongated stars, the indispensable pair or trio of folding bridge tables stacked in the corner behind the low bookshelf containing a few volumes of Zane Grey, James Oliver Curwood, Harold McGrath, Jack London and Frances Hodgson Burnett, the highly polished steer horns or the thick graduated Chinese gongs from the Nippon

Shoppe in Rochester that are used to call the wet kids shivering and blue-lipped in to dinner or supper—and the awful names, folksy or "Indian," carved into the shellacked surface of jagged wooden slabs hanging on short chains over the steps of the porches on the bay side: Idle-Awhile, Dew-Drop-Inn, Wahwautosa, Nokomis, Bide-a-Wee, or, more boldly, Chez O' Malley or Viva Villa.

Too silly for words of her mother to get into such a stew about speaking to strangers. There are never any strangers along the bar—that is one of its attractions, among the wealthier cottagers —for the bar is accessible only by boat from the mainland; and besides, it's out of season, mid-September, and the nearly twenty families who summer along here have long since gone back to town. Now she is approaching and nearly abreast of the showplace of the bar, the Calvin Cunningham place, where only a month ago she attended the lavish birthday party given by his parents to celebrate George Cunningham's twelfth birthday. Twelve years old, for Pete's sake, what was so wonderful about that? He acted like such a kid, while she herself, a whole year younger, was grown-up by comparison.

As she walks alone and barefoot along the hard wet sand at the last reach of the breakers sliding in from off Ontario, a voice calls out from the dark veranda of the Cunningham cottage, facetious gay, fatherly, sinister: "Whither bound, little girl?" A familiar voice; she knows at once who it is. She freezes almost in mid-step, but not from fear or even surprise; in an odd mysterious sense she has long expected this, without really knowing, and has even been waiting for it. There is something in that voice, as if a new note has been struck that she has never heard before though she recognizes it at once, that makes her stop in her tracks, listen with full alertness, answer politely, linger, and finally move up the sloping beach toward the dark veranda and the man sitting there on the hammock-glider waiting for her, George's father, Calvin Cunningham, waiting almost as if he has been certain all along, from far back, that she would pass by here tonight, that she would respond

45

to his call, and that she would come to him. She has this feeling even more when he takes her hand and pulls her gently down onto the canvas-covered seat beside him, when his embraces turn from short meaningless fatherly hugs into something quite different and more serious and strange, when he gets up for a moment and stretches her out flat along the surface of the sly settee, when he does not bother to cajole or talk with her any more, when all the world that she has known up till now is blotted out and a new world emerges, enticing, fearful, and promising, a world she feels has always been there and is really hers. And when, an hour later, she retraces her steps along the deserted dark beach to her parents' cottage, she whispers to herself, over and over: My father would kill him if he knew; my father would kill him. But she has no thought of exposing Mr. Cunningham, or of telling on him. She despises him, but she is fascinated, held, and wants to be with him again in that same way, and all the way; and as she finds and picks up her discarded sneaks in the sand, she knows that she will.

II

WHITHER BOUND, LITTLE GIRL?

. . . a few minutes past nine of a clear, mild, all but soundless evening in May.

Most of the store fronts along Main Street were dark, but anomalous lights still showed brightly in the windows of the Kandy Kitchen, Hanley's Drugstore, and Wilcox's Bon Ton Shoppe, whose forward-pressing young Wally Wilcox of the sensational penis for such a short fellow—wasn't it always the way?—had lately imported from the city a new lighting system that could be automatically set to turn off for the night after the second show at the Crescent. At this hour most of the people were home, many of them probably already in bed; some were about to reach home or were on their way there, having just left the first show, which was Gloria Swanson in *Manhandled;* and a handful of others were still inside at the Crescent, around the corner on Union Street, sitting out the second show.

Winifred Grainger sat behind the wheel of her father's Cadillac, which she had parked at the curb two hours earlier in front of Hoffmeyer's meat market, next door to Nick's Kandy Kitchen. She had just come from the movies, and was playing with the idea of going in and having a soda. It was not much of a struggle. She didn't mind going to the movies alone—lots of people did that— but the idea of sitting by herself at the soda fountain, conspicuous and undated, was different, somehow; and besides, Nick was just about as dumb a Greek as they come—he might have been attractive enough if he hadn't had those two big gold teeth, and judging by the heavy black intensity of him, she bet he really had something under that white apron of his; but she could certainly imagine a livelier conversationalist.

The backroom at Nick's had always been the place, up to only a year or so ago, where they had gathered after the movies or the basketball games on Friday nights—Harry and Carol and Isabel Barton and Chet and one or two others, now all away at college somewhere—because it was the only place in town you could go, if you had only a small allowance, as most of the boys did. It still was the only place to go, but there was no point in it now. What you did now was go home, tell Belle about the movie because she would be waiting up and wanting to hear who was there, or read her some asinine story in the *Journal* or the *Companion,* and then bed—Dad all the while silently manipulating his eternal game of solitaire with marvelous outward calm in the library, yet keenly alert to the chiming of every quarter hour from the hall clock and wondering serenely, as he placidly moved a red queen onto a black king, when the *hell* the two of them would go upstairs and get out of his way so that he would be free to sneak out and keep his regular date with that awful Mrs. Mott, who even now was probably already parked in their usual secret place on the canal bank behind the canning factory, with only the dimmers on to show him that she was there. Winifred knew this was the reason why her father, fully confident that she would be back at nine-thirty, had not only let her but even urged her to take his car instead of hers when she had left just before seven: it was supposed to tell them that he was in for the night and had not the slightest intention of going out again. My God, he had even put on his bedroom slippers.

The store fronts along Main Street after dark like this, lit by the pale glare from the few street lamps—yes, and sometimes even in the daytime too, in a certain light—looked unreal, looked two-dimensional like stage scenery, like the shabby canvas flats at the old Opera House that were meant to represent "Business Section: Small American City," so that it almost seemed that if you got out of your car and walked to the end of the row of flat façades and went behind, you would come upon, perhaps even stumble over, stagehands in shirt sleeves with tattooed arms shooting crap among the props and cables, the wires and slats and rickety framework that supported—back there in the dark, out of sight—the illusion of a street.

The old question, the question that puzzled her so often in idle moments, in her many many many idle moments, and that took up so *damned much time:* Which was illusion and which was reality? Or as they used to say last year in philosophy class at Miss Houghton's before she was kicked out, Which was relevant and which was real? *Only* relevant, she always added to herself, to make it clearer, and *really* real. Everything seemed to have a dual essence, a double possibility, an either/or that was somehow both; maybe everything was in seeming, and in fact, double anyway, with twin or opposite aspects of equal value, and all you had to do (all! oh, great!) was to find out, if you could only be wise enough, which was the thing for *you.* Would she ever be wise enough, have sense enough to be able to discriminate and know the difference (*was* there a difference?)? Drawn equally to love and to sensation regardless of the object, needing the one at the same time that she desired the other as much as or even more, scarcely able to distinguish between them or even care, the one getting in the way of and canceling out the other and making little difference to her at the time which was which—would she ever be able to resolve these divided drives in herself and discover at last—no, not *what* she was, for that would be too much to expect, but maybe what she was *more* than what she was less.

Winifred Grainger knew of course, everybody knew, that love and life as depicted in the movie tonight had nothing whatever to do with the facts of life as people lived them in the everyday world; it had been a confection merely, a dreaming-up; and most certainly she also knew (this was the baffling, the frustrating part of it) that reality had little to do not only with her speculation about what hung there inside the fly under Nick's apron but also with the thing itself. It had no relation to her at all, nor to her life, and had no relevance to the meaning or truth of life anyway. It was all extra, remote, a *spécialité.* Nevertheless the preoccupation with such things was real enough, ever-present, never letting her alone: *that* was real, if the object was not. It was an old friend and enemy by now, who had long lived with her like an unwelcome relative, interfering, upsetting. For whatever else was not real, the obsessive curiosity most certainly was; promiscuity and exploration even only in imagination were real all right, don't let anybody tell her different; real too was the constant secretive weighing of the possibilities and equipment of one male against another (the very word *male* encountered unexpectedly on a printed page was sometimes enough in itself to start up a swarm of erotic thoughts and fancies that distracted her for minutes, so that it was only by a deliberate effortful wrench *away* from the beckoning bypath that she was able to get back to the story again and go on): oh, all too real and a part of her, in short, the compulsive surmise—real indeed and enough, oh plenty, no matter how unwelcome or inconvenient such intrusive unrealities might be at the time.

The mild May night was so still that Winifred was suddenly aware, with a feeling almost of wonder, that she could actually hear Mr. LaPointe, the night cop, around the corner on Union Street, trying the doors one by one to see if they were locked as he made his rounds from store to darkened store. And then on top of that, cutting in on the quiet of the whole quiet countryside (but it was such a regular part of the evening, and Arcadia and she were so used to it by now that they seldom heard it), came the distant but penetrating iron-shriek of the wheels as the trolley from Rochester, due locally at nine-fourteen, took the long curve of Blue Cut at full speed three miles to the west. A few minutes now, and the slowed-down, monstrous, lumbering trolley, blazing with light and dropping big sparks from the overhead wire, would grind into upper Main Street from Maple Avenue, ponderously creaking as it brought home from the city a late shopper or two and a few traveling salesmen on their way through to cover Syracuse fifty miles to the east.

It was tough to have discovered before you were twenty-one (hell, long before) that sex had nothing to do with love. Not that this was so tough in itself; actually it was a damned good thing to know and many people never did learn the difference; but what was tough was the discovering of it, the having already had, so young, the kind of experience of life that dredged up such knowledge, that set you apart from your friends, that ever afterward you couldn't kid yourself about, that forced you to face up continually to the bald, harsh, not necessarily unattractive fact that desire for the purely physical was not love or romance and could be quite something in itself: tough because, on account of it, you didn't fit in. In a sense her approach to men was not feminine at all—at least not feminine in that she waited to be selected, for she had long since taken the initiative, now, and all but accepted the fact that this was the way it was going to be, for her, from now on, and any variation on this theme would be pure gravy. Girls who knew this about themselves, and knew it through and through—she knew nobody like that but herself: where were they and who were they? Certainly not in her crowd, not in Arcadia, not among the families her family knew. *She* had never known any of them, and from her considerable experience with boys her age or older it was damned clear that they didn't know any of them either, and would only have been thrown off and made ill at ease by them if they had, just as they were always thrown off by her if she forgot herself long enough to let them sense her acute physical interest in them. (Older men were different, thank God, especially for some reason married men.) A nice girl, that is if a nice girl ever had such interest or knowledge or desire, had to keep these things to herself when she was with boys—yes or with girls. Oh, girls far more. Judging herself by their attitude toward her (and it was nobody's fault but her own for being too frank with them), she was an alien in a foreign world, she was in fact a person living in *somebody else's* world and she must not forget it: beyond the pale, the sole black sheep in the flock, all but frightening because unique—while they, with their fastidiousness and solidarity and idealism and incuriosity, and their holy passion for the *status quo* of their physically inviolate persons: they were the norm; all white. How many times she had unwittingly shocked her friends (but actually been shocked herself far more by their reaction) when, in a bull session about boys and men, she had offered some intimate bit of information or observation intensely interesting to herself, fully expecting it to be of equal interest to them as girls, only to be reproached for being dirty. ("That's Winifred for you, just pay no attention, girls . . .") Confidences and exchanges of this kind had long since stopped; and while she had come to admire, in a way, their serene satisfaction with themselves as females, and even at times to envy their self-sufficiency, their needing nothing else—all the same she had often surprised in herself a sense of superiority, like the addict who in spite of his miserable isolation feels toward the unaddicted a secret contempt.

Inside the Kandy Kitchen she saw Nick move forward toward the display window and now he stood there in the bright white light, his glossy black hair shining even brighter, unaware that she was looking back at him from behind the probably reflecting (and thus opaque) windshield of the car. He leaned on the half-curtained rail so that he was visible only from the waist up, and stared morosely out into what must have seemed, from within, a deserted Main Street. Nick was idle too, poor guy, had nothing to do, there couldn't have been any business tonight, he too had time to get through, time to kill somehow. Killing time; what a life, and how well she knew it. Poor Nick, and while we're at it poor everybody-in-the-world. If she had been Nick she would have closed up and gone home; the dumb Greek, why keep open for nobody? Oh-oh, the common trap again that everybody fell into so easily and thus made so much trouble for everybody else, the trap of being presumptuous enough to think for other people who were not yourself. For she wasn't Nick, and how could she say what he should have done when she didn't know what it was like to be Nick—just as how much sense would it make if *he* said: "If I was Winifred I'd just keep my hands to myself, I wouldn't allow myself to think such things in the first place, it's as simple as that, just behave . . ." Ah, but you *aren't* me, Nick Scarmoutsos, so how can you really say what you would do if you were? . . . But apparently the joint did have some business after all: inside, someone now moved up to the counter from a table at the rear and stood beside the cash register at the far end of the fountain. Nick turned back from the window and took the person's money—some lone gent she couldn't recognize from here—and then, even through the plate glass of the window, such was the stillness of the night, she heard the *ding* of the cash register as Nick rang up the sale. A minute later the man appeared on the sidewalk, and it was no one she had ever seen before.

He stood there against the brightly lighted front of the Kandy Kitchen as if he had all the time in the world. (He too?) The brightness in which his figure was embedded, as it were, somewhat diminished his size. He turned his head to the left and looked idly up Main Street toward the spire of the Methodist Church and the Park, and the light behind him ate away his profile; then to the left toward her father's bank on the corner of Union and Main. He was medium tall and well built. Although his face was in shadow, he seemed to be good-looking; he could have been anywhere between twenty-five and thirty-five, maybe even forty. A couple came hurrying along from Union Street with lowered heads as if it were a cold winter night, not a balmy evening in the spring of the year—it was Mike and Ethel Connors, who lived on Dalton Street and who had been at the movies. The stranger nodded to them and said hello or good evening or something; either they didn't hear him or they paid no attention, for they hurried on without speaking. Now that wasn't nice, she said to herself; a lonely man like that . . . Then he moved forward toward the curb, and as he shed the bright light against which his outlines had been reduced a little, he emerged in his full size: broad-shouldered, rugged, an almost thickly masculine figure with a tendency to tilt forward as if aggressively, or perhaps just inquisitively. Now he stood a dozen feet away, looking over her car.

There weren't many Cadillacs around in those days—there never had been more than three or four in Arcadia anyway—and lately there was only this new one in town, her father's; but even so, she was surprised by the look of frank admiration, envy, and even avarice that showed on his face. It was so brazen, so exposed, so caught-off-guard that she wished she could disappear through the floor boards and let him examine the car to his heart's content all by himself. But she was trapped, and in a way it amused her. She knew he couldn't see her there at the wheel, because of the windshield throwing back the light—which also meant that she couldn't suddenly start the motor and drive away, not if she had any tact, not if she wished to spare him embarrassment as the car, empty as far as he knew, came alive. He moved a couple of steps nearer; his brow was furrowed, his lips were tight shut, and his eyes were fixed intensely as he took in every shining aspect of the beautiful car. Any minute now he would step around to the side and look in, and she would be caught—or would it be he?—for the side windows were down. And now he did just that: he stepped off the curb; and as he came abreast of her and leaned his arms on the window, she said, embarrassed herself, "Hi!"

"Well! I'll be darned . . ."

She grinned and hoped she did not look as foolish or as self-conscious as she felt. "Can't I give you a lift somewhere?"

He was already recovered, if indeed he had been thrown off at all. "Gee, I'd like that."

"Hop in."

"Except that—well, I mean it would be a kind of cheating, actually."

"How?"

"Well, I only live around the corner. At the Royale."

"Let's not split hairs. We could go the long way around," she said, and grinned again, knowing that she was giving herself away with every word she uttered (not a new sensation or experience, however), knowing exactly what he was thinking and who could blame him, and knowing too that he couldn't possibly know or have known how much she hated these moments even as she was helplessly drawn to them ("lowering herself," they called it, "cheapening herself"); hated having to go through them and get through them, that is, till she was safely over on the other side, where everything was out in the open and clear, and she could be honest with herself and with him.

"A really long way around?" he asked, getting in.

"Why not? I've got the time."

"And the inclination?"

Oh *no!* she thought. If he knew me better he wouldn't *say* things like that! Dullness of that kind, stultifying, depressing—my God, is this the way I'm going to have to pay, again, for an hour or two of . . .

"I take that back," he suddenly said. "Pretty crummy humor, if you ask me."

"Just what I was thinking," she said as she backed the car away from the curb. Then she swung the wheel to the left and slowly headed along the semi-dark deserted street toward the bridge and North Main, on the opposite side of town from home.

Keeping her eye fixed on the driving, she was yet very much aware of him, of his physical person. He had settled in, completely at ease, sitting part sideways with his back against the right door, relaxed and nonchalant, casual as all hell, yet his whole person was turned toward her in the most flattering and attentive way.

Keenly she felt the presence of him like an insistently animal aura ("It's only in your mind," people said), and was glad of the business of having to keep her attention on the driving so that she was unable to look at him, look him over, as she wanted to do. In the light from the dash she was acutely conscious of the left thigh and knee along the back of the seat toward her, the left foot hooked under the bent right knee—an attitude of masculine ease and well-being, somehow, that irritated her (he's assuming far too much) and that gave her an irrational, utterly unaccountable satisfaction just to know the anatomy was there, in her car on the front seat beside her.

"Do you know where we can get a drink, besides the bootlegger at the Royale—and that pap at the Kandy Kitchen?"

"I certainly do, and that's where we're going."

"I mean a place where we can sit down and everything, and get acquainted, with pink lampshades and fringe. I mean a *speak*easy —does this town have such a thing?"

"You're new here, aren't you?"

"How did you know?"

"If you'd been around I'd have seen you. And if I hadn't seen you I'd have heard of you. Everybody gets to know everybody else here very, very well in a very short time."

"Well, it's working now, I can say that for the system. Boy, am I glad. The only female I've talked to since Tuesday is the old beldame who waits on table in that so-called dining room."

"Mrs. Knappenberger."

"You know her?"

"That's the canal there. The Barge Canal . . ."

"Don't tell me. For three nights in a row I've sat and looked at it outside my bedroom window. My bedroom is in the back, where they promised it would be nice and quiet. They weren't kidding."

An attractive picture, almost dangerously attractive, and why was it always so? *Any* woman would respond to it, if she had a spark of imagination: an idle man, dingy hotel room, strange town, nothing to do, lonely, spoiling for trouble. She said: "Tell me something, but honestly."

"Anything."

In the dim light from the dashboard her smile was self-deprecating, almost a grimace of self-mockery. "What do you think of a girl who picks up strange men?"

"I don't think anything."

"I'll bet."

"I mean . . ."

"I know what you mean."

"Now just a minute!" he said. "You don't know what I mean at all, so stop right there. And let me tell you something else. Don't ever ask questions like that. Don't ever. You hear?"

"I'm sorry."

"I'm being tough with you because I'm a lot older than you are. You're such a kid, I feel I have the right."

"That's okay."

"And now, having got that off my chest, I'll answer you. And you specified 'honestly.' Well, it's very easy. I'll tell you exactly what I was thinking—in fact it will be a pleasure. I was thinking what a real break this is. I've been bored silly here, you can't imagine. And then all of a sudden, out of the blue—a pretty girl, nice car, no place to go, good company . . ."

"Thanks."

"That answer you?"

"Well, it's a lot better than I deserve."

"Christ Almighty, why do you say things like that? Maybe it isn't at all. If you're what I think you are, what I've seen of you, you deserve a great deal. Stop playing yourself down."

"Yeah," she admitted abjectly, "it's a habit of mine, from way back. How did you know?"

"I didn't know. But it's very self-defeating to be that way. It will get you nowhere. Nowhere."

She didn't answer; she didn't trust herself for a moment to speak. I must be getting soft in the head, she told herself, as she sensed tears beginning to well up somewhere back of her eyes, or in her throat, but thank God they didn't come; tears of something like gratitude (almost, where men were concerned, a new sensation entirely), gratitude mixed with a kind of amazement. This is some conversation to be having with a guy you've just met, she thought as they left the downtown section farther and farther behind; usually they hardly talk at all—they're not much, usually, for wasting time.

"Hey, where did you come from anyway?" she suddenly said. "How did you ever happen to hit a burg like this?"

"That's what I've been wondering about you."

"Me? Oh, I was born here. I grew up here. I've never been anywhere else, practically. Oh, a few trips abroad. But this is my home town."

"That's hard to believe."

"Not really. You just don't know small towns. We're not hicks, you know, or hayseeds. We don't even have to be Rotarians— some of us, anyway. That's old stuff: movies, comic strips, the junkier novels. I told you we even have a genu-wine speakeasy."

"I can't wait."

"You needn't be snooty. It's a very beautiful old place that I dearly love. Certainly the grandest old house, in the finest style, that you'll find in these parts. See, there it is now. See that place set way back, all lighted up?"

From its slight eminence above the road, and at least three hundred feet back, the Casa di Santo shone in the mild spring night with a garish glow from outside lights planted on the lawn that scarcely detracted from the beauty of its austere Victorian dignity. It was one of those increasingly rare, tall, handsome, red-brick, slate-roofed mansions still to be found occasionally, isolated in lonely grandeur, in Wayne County, Ontario County, Seneca, Yates, and so on, and oddly enough so often in rural areas, far from town; more often than not, too, nowadays, they had been converted to a roadhouse that played host to a handful of local night-owls and philanderers who had no place else to go. Arcadia numbered only about twenty-five of these restless individuals at best, and, unless the occasion were a special one, it was a rare night when more than eight or ten of them turned up at the place at one time; one might wonder how the Casa kept going. High up across its façade, just under the mansard roof, was an electric sign proclaiming its name in red and yellow letters that went out every now and then for the briefest pointless period, and then came on; and in this jumpy light a number of white iron benches could be seen placed here and there about the long, sloping, well-kept lawn.

As Winifred Giainger turned the car through the open wrought-iron gateway and went up the drive toward the high porte-cochère at the side, stables of red brick and slate came into view toward the rear, big enough to have housed a dozen horses and half a dozen carriages. The stables stood in darkened lonely splendor, ghosts of the past barely discernible in the dim pinkish-yellow light that came round from the front of the house.

"Boy!" her passenger exclaimed, sitting up. "The people who lived here must have been some punkins!"

"In their way, I guess."

They were met at the side door by a stocky, tuxedoed, handsome but expressionless man of forty or so with a dead-white pallor and blue-black hair. His manner was the very opposite of cordial, but he received you with a dead-pan unsurprise as if he had been expecting you all along. When he opened his mouth, you could see that his teeth were flawless, but he did not smile at all. "Hi, Winnie," he said, stepping aside to let them pass.

"Hello, Tony. Tony, this is my friend Mr. Smith. Mr. di Santo."

They shook hands and exchanged ritual please-to-meet-yous and Tony led them inside and through to a small table next to a white marble fireplace in the large, almost bare, front room, which clearly, because of its dimensions, yellow brocaded walls, and height, must once have been a drawing room of considerable elegance. Her companion turned in his chair and surveyed the magnificent room, his eyebrows raised, his lips tight shut. Tony di Santo took their order for highballs, and, after giving Winifred's new friend an experienced, silent once-over that expressed nothing at all, went away.

When she turned to face him again: "What else could I do?" she said with a grimace. "We didn't seem to get around to names."

"Well, it's not Smith."

"It never is. I'll explain to Tony the next time I see him."

"And then what'll he think?"

"Don't worry. We know each other very well. Tony and I are old friends."

"Then tell him it's Sanford."

"Thanks. Mine is Grainger. First name is Winnie."

"I got that. Mine is Jack."

" 'Jack.' Nice. I like that."

Now he looked her over, as, earlier, he had looked over her car. By current standards, her figure was not the best. The breasts were full, the hips a trifle too wide, but she was pretty—pretty with a kind of beauty (and it was a kind of beauty) that appealed more to the imagination and to the heart (and, frankly, somewhere below the belt, say) than to the eye. When she wasn't downright playing herself down, which seemed to be habitual with her, out of modesty or lack of ego, the eyes looked up at you with an unguarded expression that asked you to like her, to find her attractive, above all lovable. She seemed utterly without ordinary feminine guile; her femininity, outgoing and generous and giving though it was, asked somehow to be protected. The large candid eyes, the generous mouth, the peculiarly pensive way she had of resting her chin on her palm as if in melancholy thought—all these made you want to take her in your arms, enfold her, shut out whatever seemed to be or might be threatening. No matter what had been her background or experience (plainly a good deal; she was certainly a gal who had been around), he felt strongly—and he knew his hunch was right—that she was invincibly innocent. Yet her beauty was armed, too; you knew that when or if she gave she would give fully of herself, no questions asked, the equal of any lover. In fact she looked to be the kind of girl who, almost perversely, was more willing to give of herself than to take. And this giving quality—from her light-brown hair in casual disarray, her more than adequate arms that needed no one's help, her always (when they weren't turned down in self-mockery) half-opened lips, and the faint, scarcely detectable quality of breathlessness that was an undertone of her unsure, almost childlike voice—these qualities, while they subtly suggested plainer than words *Go ahead, take me, I'm yours,* also seemed to say—to men, that is, who liked to do the honors themselves—*That's right, I'm a push-over; if you don't like it, or if it scares you off, that's your tough luck—and mine.* So it was up to you: you were drawn and hesitant at the same time.

They were silent as Tony returned to the table with the drinks. In spite of his inscrutable tact, Tony glanced at Winifred inquiringly and she smiled artificially and found herself blushing; she looked down at her glass, hoping Jack Sanford wouldn't notice. Her wry self-deprecating smile, which was almost her most characteristic expression, so defenseless and so candid, all but said: *Okay, you found me out, I can't pretend, who do I think I'm kidding around here anyway?* The smile, so exposed, so vulnerable, indicated that what had been left out of her nature was the most ordinary sense of guileful femininity, even of self-preservation; and far from struggling to put on a semblance of something she knew she didn't have, she overaccepted, if anything, her lack of it. She knew what Tony di Santo was thinking as he lingered a second or two too long, pointlessly rearranging the ashtray and the bud vase: Here was Winnie Grainger with a new lover or at least a new prospect; would it amount to anything this time or would it be just another one-night stand? And though truly she didn't mind his thinking this, for it was nothing less than the truth and she'd be the first to admit it, what she did mind was the label, the being thought of automatically in locker-room terms. She minded it because these terms were basically untrue; things and people were never as simple or as simplified as all that. She believed she was aggressive with men because she did not think enough of herself to believe they could be interested in her; and when sometimes she did find they were genuinely interested, her gratitude and response almost drove them away. On other occasions of a new man's attentiveness to her, she often found herself thinking: Gosh, *he* can't be so much, if he's interested in me.

"This is some room," Jack Sanford said. "Some house, in fact. These ceilings must be twelve or thirteen feet high."

"They're sixteen," she said.

"I'd love to have seen this place in its better days. It must have been something!"

"Yes."

"You can't see from where you're sitting, but through that hall door over there I can see a circular staircase that I'll bet is solid mahogany or maybe walnut. We must go look before we leave."

"It's mahogany."

From the bar in another room came a loud peal of harsh, unrestrained female laughter.

"That's Ruby Pelletier."

"Who's Ruby Pelletier?"

"Oh, just a woman. She's at the bar with Charlie Collins."

"You know everybody, don't you?"

"You will too, if you stick around long enough. And they'll know all about you. It's a thing to remember in this town, if you mind such things. I don't. In a day or two, as a matter of fact, people will know that you and I were here tonight, and wonder how we met."

"*I* won't mind."

"Neither will I."

"Who is this Charlie character at the bar?" he asked. "Ruby's lover?"

"It's been going on for years, as far back as I can remember. He stays on and on with his wife, but he's never given up Ruby. It's very public, nothing sneaky about it, and I guess you've got to hand it to them for that. Everybody's always known it. A lot of people think it's awful but I don't, somehow. It's a true love affair. Really and truly. Like King Carol and that mistress of his, Magda somebody. Or like Hearst and Marion Davies. In the face of everything, they stick together. Nothing else seems to matter. I think it's quite wonderful."

"They sure pick the perfect background for an *amour,* a beautiful joint like this."

Winifred became aware that he was looking at her absently and she wanted to say, *You're not listening,* but she did not. His eyes, slightly narrowed, were fixed intently on hers, but blank; his head moved slowly up and down in mechanical assent, and to emphasize his inattentive attention his left eye, when she looked squarely at him, half winked, ever so slightly, as if they were in a kind of acknowledged secret cahoots, a semi-wink so slight she couldn't even be sure she saw it, yet at the same time it suggested a relationship intimate, conspiratorial, and curiously as attractive as an embrace. Perhaps it was only a mannerism, like a reflex action, but she couldn't help wondering whether it was really intimate and personal after all, or merely absent-minded. While the head continued to move up and down as if in agreement with what she had been saying, she sensed that his mind was on something else: he seemed to be speculating, looking her over in much the same way he had looked over her car. She was not offended; she was pleased, in fact. His concentration on her was intensely complimentary, if she considered it as a look of interest and appraisal—and she could see by his gaze that she was not found wanting. Self-conscious, she lowered her eyes and found herself helplessly looking at the wrists of the hands that lay spread on the white table-cloth on either side of the ashtray a hand's length from her own hands. The fingers and palms were appealing enough, but now it was the wrists which suddenly, unexpectedly, took her up as if into another element, not air, not fire, an element in which she found it all but hard to breathe but in which nowadays she seemed to spend half her time, if mostly only in imagination.

Thick and flat they were, male, like an ax helve, with beautiful firm skin like smooth hickory, and from under the leather watch strap a few spurts of hair insistently indicated more hair on the forearms, concealed in the shirt sleeves, and tufts and thatches of hair elsewhere on that broad body that sat opposite her, but so close, across the white tablecloth; and with this sudden heightened sensitivity to his strictly physical person she could almost feel herself falling, almost literally sliding in a kind of vertigo, into the inescapably alluring trap that seemed so often to lie in wait for her even when she wasn't expecting it or wanting it. Damn it all to hell! she thought, why did she have to be so goddam susceptible to male wrists—*and* fingers, and shoulders, and necks, and legs, and on and on—and always so damned oppressively aware that that attractive wrist (or shoulder or thigh or chest) was only attractive because back of it all, and over it all and under it all, lay the image of what she had come to find was the most beautiful thing in life, the human penis. Automatically her mind went back to the time, a time, one of many, all different and all the same, when a man clad only in an undershirt had leaned over her bed with an erection hard and clean as wood—what man it doesn't matter now, some man—and there it was again, the secret of what it's all about, the ultimate meaning of life, its very symbol, the firm clear utterance at the center, irresistible, overpowering, unanswerable, standing up there beneath that pulled-up undershirt and now here across the table from her and below the edge of the white tablecloth, out of sight but never out of mind. Why couldn't she simply admire the beautiful wrist for what it was and forget the rest? But without the rest the wrist wouldn't have been beautiful or even worth remarking at all. The same wrist on a woman, identical in shape and size and color and flat thick strength—if she knew it was attached to the figure of a woman it couldn't have held her interest for a second, aesthetically or any other way. But thinking of this kind, letting go to thoughts of this kind—the compulsive surmise, she called it—could spoil her evening, was spoiling her evening, could spoil everything, if she didn't pull herself out of it and quick.

"Jack," she said with some effort, "I told you that that banister and the spindles of the circular staircase in the hall were mahogany, as if I knew. Well, I did know. Jack, this is so unfair of me—I'm a real fraud, honest."

"What's the matter, honey? I don't get it."

"Ever since we came out here—well, I should have told you before, Jack, straight off. I used to live here. This was our old home where we lived with Grandpa."

"No kidding."

"I was born here and mostly brought up here, and so were my sisters," she went on hurriedly, as if eager to get through a bit of exposition that might prove embarrassing or even shameful. "We lived here until Grandpa died, when I was fifteen. Then we moved overtown, where we live now."

"What did your grandfather do to have a place like this?"

"I don't know. I don't think he really did anything."

"He certainly must have been rich!"

"Well, maybe. For these parts, anyway."

"Was he your father's father?"

"My mother's."

"What does your father do?'

"Dad? He's a banker."

"The banker I suppose, in a town like this."

"Well, yes . . ."

He leaned back from the table and looked at her with a warm smile. "Well I'll be darned."

"Why do you say that?"

"Oh, I don't know, the whole story. It just sort of fits."

"Fits?"

"I mean with what I've been thinking. I knew from the beginning, Winnie, that you were good goods. I could tell."

"Thanks." She looked down at her glass. "That's one of the nicest things anybody ever said to me."

"Good goods. It sticks out all over you."

"That's not true, but it's darn nice anyway. I guess people aren't much given to compliments, are they, and when they get one, they—"

"Meaning you. That right?"

"In a way."

"Listen here. You should go through life telling yourself that you deserve every single compliment you get. In spades! And a lot that you don't get, too!"

"That's what I meant. I don't get many."

"Then people are just thoughtless. They're too busy with their own lives. They don't think of each other. They take one another for granted—they don't really *care*. That's what makes people dull, not caring. They have only themselves to blame if they find life dull." He laughed, and added: "I didn't mean to sound off."

"Gosh," Winifred said, *"my* life is dull enough, God knows. Is that the way life is anyway, I keep wondering, for everybody? Or is it just here in Arcadia? Or is it just me?"

"It needn't be you."

"That's what I try to tell myself. And what's the good?"

"You sound awfully disillusioned for only . . . How old are you? Twenty? Twenty-two? Four?"

"About." She looked at him, and with the old keen sense of self-distaste she knew that her smile, in spite of her pleasure in the evening and in his company, was a give-away; the corners of the mouth turned down wryly, embarrassed. "I guess I shouldn't come out to this place, really. Oh, I'm not sorry I brought you here, Jack. I'm glad I did. But I notice lately that I sort of get all funny when I come here. The past, I suppose. I don't mind not living here any more, really I don't, or Tony's turning it into a drinking joint—it's not that at all. But I find myself thinking foolishly and sentimentally of the old days—and if you'll pardon my being sloppy for a moment, I can't help thinking of that little girl who lived here in this house and who was happier for a few years than anybody ever has a right to be and who loved everything in the world, all the whole marvelous world and my family and all the animals and the trees and fields and every living thing in it. Like the plants we used to have, even, on the side porch in the winter under a kind of crude glass greenhouse that Mr. Hinkle our gardener made for us, and the crops in the summertime, and the apple orchard, especially those marvelous few weeks when it was in full bloom, and the goats and their kids, and my collie Bruce, and Grandpa, who was such a wonderful-looking old man, and my beautiful sisters who were ten or twelve years older than I and their beautiful dresses and the exciting lives they seemed to lead, and dear Mr. Vandercook, who tended the stables and loved Dandelion and my pony Frisky as much as I did. And when I think of all this, out here, I can't help wondering whatever became of that happy little girl; because—because if that little girl was only meant to grow up and turn into the person sitting here at this table now, then there's no sense in anything—nothing makes any sense at all. I mean if that's all there is to life, and promise . . ."

"You mean there ought to be a law."

"Oh stop! It's nothing to kid about. I'm very serious. Because this was such a marvelous sensual happy world I grew up in here, and there was so much to do, the days weren't long enough, everything was so wonderful to touch and to smell and to watch grow and to learn about and come to know—and I was, I truly believe it, I was the happiest child that ever grew up anywhere. Anywhere! And what happened? What became of it? Where did it go—and why?"

Momentarily she was startled out of herself when he abruptly reached across the tablecloth and took her hand in his.

"This is getting," he said, "perilously like barroom talk. We'll be weeping in our drinks next."

She snatched her hand away. "No it isn't! Not the least bit! And I don't think I can *ever* forgive you for that!"

He reached for and grabbed her hand again. "Now we're making progress. We've had our first quarrel."

And then they were laughing, the nostalgic mood broken, and for the first time she began to believe that something might come of their evening after all besides the usual sexual tussle, that maybe he would let her get to know him, that maybe she wouldn't spoil things and cause him to write her off for an easy mark and thus lose interest after a few times, and maybe they would be friends as well as lovers. For she knew they were certainly going to be lovers sooner or later, if only for one time, maybe even tonight; she knew it because that was how badly she wanted him, and she was not one to hold back. The problem was to get through the evening without showing it too much, without giving herself away and thus losing him; but not to show it, not to make the opening move tonight: the hand on his thigh, the hand just partly in between his belt and his shirt—not to do these familiar routine things was asking a lot of herself, and she knew it.

"It seems a million years since I've had a talk with anyone," she said, looking down, twirling the ice in her glass, wanting to leave, because she had just seen him glancing at his watch, yet hanging onto the moment partly in fear of the test of leaving. "I haven't had a real talk with anyone in ages. Certainly not with a man."

"Don't your men friends talk?"

"Not much. Besides I haven't any. Not now."

"A girl like you? Don't kid me."

"Well, it's true. But I guess we have to go; you must have work in the morning."

"You don't want another drink?"

"No thanks. I'm never much interested in drinking."

"Neither am I," he said. "Let's go."

At the side door, Tony di Santo bowed them out. "Good night, Winnie. Good night, Mr. Smith. Thank you for coming."

"I made a mistake, Tony. It's Sanford, not Smith."

"Oh. That's good to know. I'll remember. Good night, Mr. Sanford. And thank you, sir. Come again."

During the slow drive back across town, Jack Sanford told her a few things about himself. He was thirty-five, unmarried, his home was Buffalo, he was a commercial artist, he had come to Arcadia to take a rather well-paying job with Baxter Brothers Box Company as a designer, designing ice-cream pails and charlotte-russe cups. ("And don't laugh." "I wouldn't dream of laughing. I respect anyone who can make a living at anything. Me, I have no excuse even for living." "There you go again, pulling yourself down.") He was supposed to sign a two-year contract and he had been here three days without doing so; he knew nobody except a very few people at the factory; he had thought he would hate Arcadia but now all of a sudden things were looking up. ("You know why, don't you?") In fact he could quite see that he might enjoy himself here.

Driving slowly, Winifred Grainger listened, attentive to this recital, yet keenly attentive, too, to another tale that was spinning itself out in her mind as he talked and as the car passed over the canal bridge into downtown again: the story of what it would be like if she kept the car headed up South Main, and then to East Maple, and then out into the country to the pines, to the sheltered, quiet, dark spot there where so many times she had played with love in the past. She thought of this with all her senses, all but actually experiencing it; and yet, almost without realizing what she was doing, she turned the wheel left at Union Street and drove slowly along the last remaining block of downtown to the Royale Hotel on the corner. The Crescent was dark, the movie over: old Burt Mason stood on a ladder changing the bill for tomorrow, taking down the bank of lights that had spelled out *Manhandled,* to be replaced with the next feature, Charlie Chaplin in *The Gold Rush,* its second repeat in a year.

Jack Sanford stood on the sidewalk beside the car in front of the Royale and leaned down, his arms on the window, just as when they had first met. The night was utterly soundless; she and he and Burt Mason seemed to be the only souls awake in the world.

"It's been swell," Jack Sanford said. "I want to see you again. I've got to."

"We're the only Graingers in the book, Jack, if you want to call me sometime."

"I certainly do. Your family won't mind?"

"I'm my own boss."

"Good night, Winnie. A million thanks." He turned and went into the hotel, where in the dim light of the single bulb that burned in the little lobby she saw him turn, wave in a kind of salute, and disappear up the dark stairs.

For several minutes after he had gone, Winifred Grainger still sat there behind the wheel, the motor running quietly. She looked up at the rickety upstairs veranda, for all the world like a setting in an old Western (two dark-shirted men should have grappled there in silent hand-to-hand combat, and crashed against the flimsy rail, and crashed through to the ground below, startling the horses tethered to the hitching posts), and remembered the one and only time she had ever been inside the Royale, and not only inside but upstairs in one of the bedrooms; and she wondered if anyone in Arcadia had ever known about it (except Harry Harrison, to whom she had told the story later), for she had been able to clude Arch Archer the night clerk both going in at ten-thirty and coming out an hour later—her body went hot for a moment in wild panic, as she thought of the risk she had run, for truly it had been the utmost in folly and danger. The man had been a cheap traveling magician, in town for a one-night stand at the Opera House—a seedy, tired, sickly handsome man with a horrible fascination for her just because he was so awful and different and strangely handsome, because she knew she would never see him again, and because he had stared at her with fierce weak eyes over a copy of *Shadowland* he pretended to be looking at when they met at the magazine counter in Roger's Store, stared at her through and through as if telling her *I must have you, come with me*—and she did, or at least followed him. She remembered vividly what went on in that dingy crummy room, on that creaky crummy bed (Why did these things, once past, even only a few minutes past, never seem to relate to her, never seem even to have happened?), and how, though she herself had inwardly rebelled and wished to get out within minutes after entering that awful room, she had remained, out of a kind of perverse loyalty, her kind of loyalty and even honor, a peculiar kind of good-sportsmanship against her better judgment which made her stay on and on even when she wanted to go; because after all it wasn't his fault that she suddenly no longer wanted it, nobody had got her into this dreadful situation but herself, and the only decent thing to do under the circumstances of her reaction was to stay and pretend and go through with it, no matter how much it went against her sensibilities and pride, such as they were. Now she pictured that same room or some room just like it with Jack Sanford in it, sitting on the edge of the bed alone and taking off a shoe and pulling off a sock, then thinking for a moment or two, thinking over the evening perhaps, then pulling off the other shoe and the other sock; and the picture was somehow so overpoweringly attractive, in spite of the fact that her realistic sense told her it was just another guy getting ready for bed as hundreds of thousands were doing all over the country at this very moment, that she found herself shaking her head in a kind of disbelief of self, as she soundlessly asked the question, Why did I let him go, why didn't I hang onto him for tonight at least, *how* could I have let him get out of the car so casually without starting something whether it would have been welcome to him or not?

As she drove up deserted Main Street toward home, even the Kandy Kitchen was dark now, and the street lamps made the dark store fronts look more like painted scenery than ever: so unreal in fact that she didn't even need to turn her head to see that the flimsy canvas flats surely rippled in the night breeze as she drove up the street.

"That you, Winifred?" her father said, coming from the library in his maroon dressing gown and slippers, with a deck of cards in his hand.

"Sorry I'm late, Dad. Couldn't be helped."

"That's all right, dear. Keys in the car?"

"Yes."

"I don't know if that's a good idea. I'd better get them. Arcadia has grown so, lately. Well, good night, dear."

In bed at last, listening to the car she had so lately left being backed as quietly as possible out of the garage and then down the crackling graveled drive to the street (Heaven knows what apology or explanation her father would make to Mrs. Mott now, or if she had still waited for him, or what hell the old bag would give him if she had), she thought of Jack Sanford lying in his bed at the Royale, while she lay here. She wondered if he was asleep yet. She knew just what he looked like, lying there on the pillow. And if he was not asleep yet, she wondered what he was doing; and if doing nothing, what he was thinking. And she wondered, with a bafflement almost beyond belief, why they had done nothing together. Fantastic though it was to think of now, they had not even kissed

—not even kissed. It was the first time such a thing had happened, or not happened; it was an entirely new experience with her, unique, and she wondered what it meant.

THE PHONE CALL CAME three days later, in the afternoon. When she heard the ring, Winifred Grainger knew at once who it was. She had not been unhappy, had not even been impatient. She felt sure the call would come sooner or later, for there were important issues pending that she could only think of as "unfinished business." Lighting a cigarette, she picked up the receiver.

"Yes?"

"Winnie?"

"Speaking."

"Hey, I thought you were going to call me!"

"Jack. Come on!"

"Oh, I was supposed to call you?"

"If you must have your little jokes . . ."

"Are you free this evening?"

"Well, if you twist my arm."

"Let's do something."

"What do you have in mind? As a matter of fact I'm free as the wind. As a bird."

"Great. Will you have dinner with me?"

"I'd absolutely love to."

"Suppose I pick you up at six. I know where you live—I've driven by your house several times, visualizing you in it. It wasn't hard. Winifred, it's grand. Good goods like you, through and through."

"I didn't know you had a car."

"Bought it a couple of days ago. A used Marmon about a thousand years old. Looks like a long old-fashioned tub, very high and round in the rear, but great style. Wire wheels and stuff. I love it. If you don't, we can take yours. Except my car's not very well known around town. Yours is."

"What's that got to do with anything?"

"I get it. Playing dumb."

"Jack, I do what I do. In any case, I'll love seeing you, no matter which car we use."

"Six o'clock then. I'll just drive into the driveway and sound the horn. You can hear it all over the county."

"No, don't *do* that. I'll know when you arrive, and I'll come out. But I do want to bring you in for a second, to meet my parents. It's only proper in a *jeune fille*."

"Oh, we must be proper at all costs. I've already discovered it's very important in Arcadia," he said.

"You're learning. But there are ways to get around it."

"Do you know them?"

"Where shall we go for dinner?"

"You think of a place."

"Okay, Jack. It will be enough for me, though, just to see you. I believe I've thought of you one thousand and sixty-two times since the other night."

"I've been doing some thinking myself. And feeling. But we do have to eat. Store up energy, and all that."

"Oh absolutely."

"Six o'clock then. It'll be fun seeing what you look like by daylight."

"I'm not so good by daylight."

"I'll take my chances. 'Bye for the moment."

"So long, Jack. Many thanks."

Dressed for her date in matching tan sleeveless sweater and unbuttoned cardigan of cashmere, with a brown pleated wool skirt without pants underneath, Winifred sat on a hassock near one of the tall front windows of the white drawing room, waiting for Jack Sanford. When he turned into the driveway a few minutes past six, she went out directly, through the side door.

"I love your car," she called.

"Don't you?" he said, getting out with a broad smile and coming forward.

"I don't think I've ever seen a Marmon before. I guess I'm too young."

"Well, you have now."

"Really there's nothing more elegant than an old car that was once elegant. I bet it cost all of five hundred dollars."

"Four. And it's got a klaxon. Do you know what a klaxon is?"

"I've heard of them."

"You'll hear *this* one all right."

"Just a boy."

"Who, me? Listen! I'm more than ten years older than you are at *least.*"

"The argument still stands."

"Do you know who once owned this car?"

"I have no idea," she said.

"Neither have I. But he must have been a big shot or a tycoon or *some*thing like that."

"He must have had a big family, too."

"Why do you say that? All that room in the back?"

"Yes."

"That room—all that space—can be put to pretty good use, and it doesn't necessarily need a family to do it."

"Never mind, Jack. Now come on in, Belle and Dad are palpitating to meet you."

"I'll bet. Who's Belle?"

"My mother. Now be *nice* to them, they need it."

"I know how to behave. Just don't tell me."

He followed her through the side door and into the small sitting room where her parents sat waiting. Mr. Grainger was pointedly absorbed in the Rochester *Times-Union,* and Belle sat on a small velvet-upholstered settee doing nothing with an anticipatory smile. Her father rose to his feet, the paper clutched to his middle.

"Mother and Dad, this is my friend, Jack Sanford. He's taking me out to dinner tonight."

"Ah . . ."

"How very nice to meet you," Mrs. Grainger said.

"It's a real pleasure for me, meeting Winifred's parents."

"Thank you."

"Thank you, Mr. Sanford. It's a pleasure for *us.*"

"I love this house. It's beautiful. The very finest type of Georgian."

"Oh? You know our house?"

"Well, I only mean I've driven by a couple of times, and couldn't help admiring—"

"You must get Winifred to show you over the place some day when you have the time."

"I'd like that."

"Where are you going for dinner, dear?"

"Haven't decided yet, Belle."

"*I* tell you. Why don't you drive over to Skaneateles and take Mr. Sanford to Krebs's?"

"Oh, Mother. All that *food*. And to waste so much time driving all the way there and all the way back."

"Waste time? What else is there to do?"

"We'll think of something."

"Krebs's is famous in these parts, Mr. Sanford. People come from miles around. And on *Sun*days you can hardly get in."

"We'll manage nearer home. I'm not fussy. A good hot dog or two would suit me."

"Winifred has never been much interested in food either. Isn't that so, Father?"

Mr. Grainger sat down and opened his paper again. "I'm afraid I don't remember."

"Anyway, wherever you go," Mrs. Grainger said, "have fun."

"We will."

"And *bon appétit*."

"Thank you."

"Do come again. Now promise. *Make* Winifred bring you."

"I'd like to, thanks. Hear that, Winnie?"

"I heard."

They had barely left when Mrs. Grainger said: "Now where do you suppose Winifred ever met *him?*"

"Can't imagine," her husband said, his eyes and attention already attuned to the financial page.

"I must say he seems a *nice* enough young man. Nicer than most of them."

"Nice enough, I guess."

"At least he was well *dressed* and everything. After a decent interval we must invite him for dinner one night."

"I suppose so."

In the car, the roomy old Marmon, now backing out with Jack Sanford at the wheel, Winifred said: "Well, that's that."

"Why do you put it that way?"

"You don't want to go through that again, do you?"

"It wasn't so bad. And since you ask—yes, I'd like to."

"Jack. Are parents people?"

"I'd like to get to know them—and them to know me."

"You may think so now."

"I'm steadfast, Winnie. I don't change."

"Most admirable. But Belle and her inanities . . . And Dad and his silences . . ."

"Have you decided where we're going?"

"Well, I think Tony di Santo's is rather out, don't you?"

"Why?"

"After the other night and all. I mean it's too soon to go back there again."

"You mean he'll think things?"

"I don't give a damn about that, ever. When you know me better you'll know that. I just think it would be rather pointless and even tasteless."

"You're the boss."

"There's a good place out on the Palmyra road. Turn left at the intersection, by Dad's bank."

"Fine."

"Oh, Jack. I *am* glad to be seeing you again."

"You knew you would, didn't you? Tell me the truth. You didn't think I could stay away, did you?"

"I love your car," she said. "I just love it."

For answer, he blew the klaxon: it made a roaring, rattling scream in the night.

"Oh, no!" she said.

"The hallmark. Got to test it once in a while."

"You must burn an awful lot of oil—and simply eat up the gas, an old tub like this. How many miles do you get?"

"Haven't had it long enough to find out. They tell me eighteen, but I'll bet it's nearer ten."

"Can you afford it?"

"I'll manage. I signed that contract today, committing me to two years; and the pay's not half bad."

"Oh, you did sign—"

"Of course I signed. My God, Winnie, after the other night, what else could I do?"

"The other night wasn't much."

"Was for me."

"Jack, you make me very happy."

"I'm happy too. So that makes two of us."

"But oh, let's not bank on it. Don't bank on it. Don't ever bank on anything."

"You're a cynical creature, aren't you, for a young girl?"

"Just realistic."

"Now cut it out. I told you to give yourself *credit* once in a while. Be*lieve* in yourself."

"Okay."

"You expect nothing from the future?" he asked.

"I don't trust the future."

"Thanks."

"Oh, it has nothing to do with you. I mean——"

"You mean you're not capable of love? You don't believe in love?"

"Too much is my trouble. And it has a way of letting you down. I've never found it."

"We'll have to fix that."

"It's a good line you're handing me, but even so, Jack, you *are* good for me. You can't possibly realize——"

"Good. I'm glad."

The Perroquet (*Perroquet,* my God; the only real Perroquet she'd ever been in had been situated a hundred yards back from the beach at Juan-les-Pins, near the Casino; and though that one, too, had been little better than a dive, it was a night club of sheer glamour compared to this one) lay halfway between Arcadia and Palmyra, a squat red brick house just off the road, illuminated by an excess of garish outdoor lights: no waves sliding in from the dark Mediterranean, of course; no yachts riding at anchor off shore; no multilingual clientele, no black tie in evidence anywhere or menu two feet tall. But the food was good, the drinks okay, the few diners or drinkers well behaved, at least at this early hour of the evening. When they sat down opposite each other at a table in a corner of the dining room, Winifred Grainger noticed, or thought she noticed, that a subtle change had occurred in his manner since the evening of their first date.

He looked at her with a pleased, even a possessive, smile; yet there was something about his expression that seemed also to indicate that he looked up to her, had indeed elevated her in his mind, as he had not done before when he had been so casual. Clearly she was "something" now, and the effect of his admiration was not lost on her. She thought: If only he knew; but God am I grateful! I must do everything not to let him down, not to disappoint him. She wanted and needed to be loved, and here it was, maybe. She could not believe in her good fortune; she felt like a fraud, and almost did not dare meet his eye, but after a couple of drinks they were having a marvelous time together, as if they had known each other for ages. Almost, because inwardly she couldn't help feeling that he did not really know her and never would know her. Or, if and when he did, the bottom would fall out of everything. Please don't let that happen, she prayed inwardly; I could really love this guy, and I think he's on the way to loving me.

They had beef Stroganoff and a salad; another highball instead of wine. Without curiosity they glanced around at the six or eight other diners and found nothing in them to talk about, though she recognized a man in his mid-thirties from Macedon whom she had once picked up for a quick evening (he had forgotten her, thank God) and a youngish couple from Arcadia who nodded when she intercepted their speculative gaze—"bowed," her mother would have said.

"Tell me about the factory and your work."

"The factory's lovely. Everything's lovely. I'm going to like it here very much. I'm liking it now."

"When you told me you'd bought a car," she said, "it sounded as if you had really settled in."

"Oh, I have. I have."

"Good."

"I've got a million questions to ask, but not now necessarily."

"What kind of questions?"

"You for one. Arcadia for another. And about lots of different people I've noticed and a few I've met."

"Why 'not now necessarily'?"

"Plenty of time. I told you I'm going to be here for a long, long *while.*"

"I'll tell you anything you want to know," she said.

"Not now. I don't feel much like it at the moment, and I don't think you do either. We could talk ourselves right out of everything, you know."

She looked down at the small dessert plate and pried into the frozen tortoni.

"Do you know what I mean?" he asked.

"I'm not sure. Maybe. Yes, I guess I do."

"You know—certainly you must know by now, Winifred, that I think you're a very attractive girl. A very nice girl."

"I hope so. I wish it were true."

"Well, I think it's true and that's all that matters."

After they had finished their dessert: "What shall we do now?" he asked. "Would you like to take in a movie?"

"Not especially."

"Neither would I. Come on." He stood up, pulled her chair back from the table, and they left.

The car was parked in a dark area of the parking lot. He opened the right door for her, and went around to the other side, and the moment he sat on the front seat beside her he reached over and pulled her roughly to him. There was not a word. There was not a word for ten minutes or more. Finally: "This is kid stuff."

"Don't I know."

"Winifred. Winnie. We've got to do something about this."

She did not answer.

"Don't you agree?"

She was so conscious of his shifting embraces, or his gifted exploring hands and lips, the quickening of his breathing, the pressure of his knee and thigh against her body, that she was confused. She desired him with everything she had and was; but strangely she felt at a loss, somehow almost at a disadvantage. Brother! Was the shoe on the other foot, the roles reversed! The novelty of being made passionate love to, of being on the receiving end for a change—of being wanted by someone who in one sense was way ahead of her and in another far behind, an innocent, because he didn't know at all, yet, that she wanted him fully as much as if not more than he wanted her—this duality somewhat held her back; though it was what she desired most in all the world, she had to take time, get used to it, remember that she was not the predator after all. Why didn't she, wanting him so much—why couldn't she take it as her due, as other girls did; dally with him, stall, play hard to get, if only to make herself more desirable to him? But games of that sort, though of course she knew they were standard practice and even expected by both sides, seemed to her the sheerest hypocrisy, deceitful, even hateful, and, if she had been capable of them, would only have made her ashamed of herself if not of her sex. Let me get my breath, she said to herself; let me try to start all over, on another level, be one with him in the way that will be best for us both. She could almost feel foolish—*did* feel foolish—that a girl as experienced as she was suddenly didn't know how to act. If he had been indifferent, or even passive . . . Clearly she had to find a new awakening in herself, a new dimension and depth, a new kind of health.

"Why don't you answer?" he whispered, breathless, close against her cheek.

"I can't. I can't speak."

He sat up, sat back; released, she almost slumped to the floor, as if exhausted.

"Darling Winnie. You don't think I'm rushing things too much? Or am I?"

She wiped her damp forehead with the back of her hand. "Don't worry. I know the facts of life, Jack."

"But I mean . . ." He left the sentence unfinished.

"I know what you mean."

"Do you want to, too?"

After she had caught her breath: "A while back you said we could talk ourselves right out of these things," she said, "if we talked enough."

"Let's stop right now."

"Yes."

"Talking, I mean."

"So do I."

As if she were a stranger, an anonymous passenger he had picked up and given a ride to, he gave his attention at once in the most businesslike manner to the car. He turned the ignition key to start the motor and drove out of the parking lot onto the highway.

Minutes passed in silence. Then: "What would you like to do?" he said.

"Like the fella says, I'm putty in your hands."

"Fella! Who wants that?"

"It's just an expression. I'm sort of whistling in the dark, I guess."

"Afraid?"

"Not of you. Oh, never of you, Jack. Of something else maybe. I can't explain."

"Of love?"

"In a way, no. Never. In another way."

"You don't have to say. Anyway, no talking now. Except I must ask the all-important question."

"What?"

"Where shall we go? Where can we be together."

"At the moment I can't think . . ."

"Shall we drive in to Rochester and go to a hotel?"

"Why go all the way to Rochester? There's a hotel in Arcadia. You've even got a room there—what more do we need?"

"Winifred Grainger. I wouldn't dream of taking you to that—that fleabag."

"Why not?"

"You can't imagine what it's like."

"If it's good enough for you—"

"Remember that Charlie character and his Ruby out at Tony di Santo's the other night? How I said they sure picked a good background for an *amour?*"

"The background isn't what counts."

"Gosh," he said, "you really mean it, don't you?"

"Of course I mean it. After all it's your home for the time being. I want to sleep where you sleep. In your own bed, not in somebody else's."

A few minutes later, as they left the Perroquet farther behind them and the lights of Arcadia, such as they were, glimmered ahead, he said: "Winnie . . . You really are a wonder. I don't deserve this, you know. But I promise you'll have no regrets. I'll be good to you."

"You're good to me now. Good *for* me, too. Now, no talking?"

As outwardly casual as if they were an old married couple, they passed through the shabby lobby of the Royale while Arch Archer gazed at them in openmouthed surprise from behind the desk, passed the three or four cigar-smokers and tobacco-chewers whose antiphonal mumble about nothing momentarily came to an eloquent halt, and went up the torn carpeted stairs, Jack Sanford leading the way. Winifred had forgotten how bleak, barren, almost dark, that upper hall was, lighted by a single weak bulb. They found Jack's room, and when they were inside he turned the key in the lock.

There was the single bed, unmade but clean enough, the straight chair and the "easy" chair, the department-store dresser and mirror, the small table that could be used as a desk, the tin wastebasket. The room had not been painted for years; its color was a nondescript gray-green slate, flaking off in patches. Over the bed— Winifred recognized it at once; either this was the same room, or the management had bought dozens of copies—hung the chromo, askew in its cheap coming-apart frame, of the boy Christ embedded brightly among a heterogeneous collection of oversized wild beasts, with the title in absurd Gothic letters below: "A Little Child Shall Lead Them." There was the door to the closet, the half-open door to the bathroom. At the rear, to the right of the hall door, was the plain wide window without curtains, with a cracked shade (like a Western map with a multititude of quirky rivers, forked, crisscrossing insanely, arriving nowhere) that could be pulled down, looking out onto the canal below and the bank opposite.

"There's a dressing gown on the back of the bathroom door," Jack Sanford said, "if you want to use it."

"I do, thanks. I'll only be a minute."

She draped her clothes over the towel rack and the toilet seat and got into the tartan plaid gown; its skirt fell almost to the floor; the cuffs hung at least ten inches below her wrists. Nobody could say I'm not well covered, she thought as she gave a final look at herself in the glass.

He was sitting naked on the edge of the bed, near the foot. She climbed into the bed and lay flat on her back, her arms crossed over her chest like a Christian martyr or one of the Saints, and looked up at him, aware that she was grinning foolishly.

"Shall we douse the light?" he asked.

"Doesn't matter."

"My God, on you that gown looks like a Mother Hubbard. Here, let me."

He leaned forward, pulled it back from her shoulders, and after much embarrassed wriggling on her part he had extricated the offending garment. He sat down again, nearer this time; and exercising almost superhuman control, she lay the palm of her hand as casually as possible along the expanse of his bare thigh, unbearably aware of the silky tantalizing hairs under her finger tips. Shivers of anticipation went through her.

He put his two hands on her shoulders, and caressed her neck. "I don't think I've ever known a girl," he said, "who would do so much for me."

"Like what?"

"Come up with me to such a cheesy, sordid, dingy, *dimsal* room like this, just to be nice to me."

"Oh well," she said, almost in a whisper. "You can never tell about love."

"Is it love, Winifred?"

"I think so. Or it's going to be. I hope."

"I think you're right." His hand, with the most sensitive, scarcely palpable, caress—light as if he were almost not touching her at all—drew its fingers down her body between her breasts, and came to rest lightly still, still caressing, on her abdomen. "You're an amazing girl, you know. And *I* love you *now*. I admit my head is spinning; and my body—well, you can see for yourself. But that much I do know!"

"Don't say it, Jack. Don't commit yourself. No need to."

"Very well."

He lowered himself over her, shifted his position, got into bed with her, reached under her with his left arm while her two arms spread wide to enfold him close against her, and they were together.

Twenty minutes later he pulled on his shorts and stepped over to the table-desk to get cigarettes for them both, then came back and sat on the edge of the bed where he had sat before. He lighted two cigarettes and gave one to her. As he puffed he leaned back, his free hand lightly restless between her thighs. After looking at her a long time, appraising but infinitely tender, he said: "You really know all about it, don't you?"

"I'm not a virgin, if that's what you mean."

"Am I glad! Deliver me from virgins every time. They're too damned hard work."

"Why the shorts?"

"Oh, I don't know, it's sort of distracting otherwise."

"I like distractions."

"Maybe I'm just modest, then. Too modest. One of my peculiarities. I can't sit around naked anywhere, not even in a locker room with other men. I can't even look at them, much less have them look at me."

"I could."

"In a locker room? You?"

"Just give me the chance."

"Now, Winifred . . ."

"Forget it."

He took a deep drag of his cigarette. "When I said you really know all about it, I'm saying—I guess I'm saying, in fact I *know* I'm saying, with admiration, how marvelously accomplished you are. How talented in bed. A man appreciates that. Some women just . . . Well, I can't think of any other way to say it."

"Must we say it at all?"

"I'm trying to pay you a compliment, of the greatest kind."

"Don't try. The greatest compliment you can pay me, Jack, is to . . ." She stretched out her arms as before. "Lie with me again. Hold me. I love you, Jack."

Some while later, once more roaming the room in his shorts, he said: "It's ten-thirty."

"Are you throwing me out?"

"I certainly am not. Quite the reverse. Do you want to stay all night?"

"You wouldn't get any sleep," she said.

"I hope I wouldn't."

"I can't, anyway."

"You could."

"No. Not this time."

"Your parents?"

"They never know when I come in."

"Why don't you then?"

"Some other time. I wouldn't want to be going out of this place in the morning, or make you get up just before dawn and take me home. Besides . . ."

"Yes?"

"I want to think things over. It may seem to you that I take this lightly, but I don't."

"Neither do I."

"Now if you'll just hand me that dressing gown."

He did so and kissed her two shoulders separately, lingeringly, before wrapping it around her.

She was dressed in no time. When she emerged from the bathroom, she found him still in his shorts, sitting at the table, writing.

"Well! Of all things to be doing. We're so do*mes*tic."

"I just want to get this off and drop it into the post office tonight. Won't take a minute. Do you mind?"

"Take your time."

She went to the rear window and stood looking out. Though one of its worst, the view was typical of Arcadia. She looked out on the broad flat waters of the Barge Canal, as still and unmoving in the eerie night light as a river of solid cement; and across, on the opposite bank, she saw dim lights in a few of the five or six shacks that were the homes of the very poor, lined up along what used to be called—what had been, when the canal was an active thorough-fare of barge traffic—the towpath, where teams of somnambulistic, bony, furry-eared mules had hauled, by long hawserlike ropes that sometimes slapped the water and sometimes remained taut in the air, strings of barges along the once-famous water route, all the way from Buffalo to Albany, or the other way around. And one of those dingy shacks across the way—the only one, in fact, that looked even remotely like a well-kept cottage, with a weather-stained picket fence and pathetic flower beds in the two patches of "front lawn" and rambler roses strung on wire trellises—one of them, that one, she knew very well; knew from the inside, as nobody else she knew in all of Arcadia knew it. Most people were hardly aware that these squalid dwellings existed, but she had been inside one of them, had spent nearly half an hour there, one unforgettable, grim, sordid night of all but unbearable tension:

A man on the street one day—a middle-aged man, tall, erect, too erect because strangely rigid, with mad eyes, whom she was later to hear spoken of as a "character," a "queer one"—had bought her a small bag of candy and walked along with her for half a block, his arms held rigidly at his sides as if he could not bend them; had led her to the canal bridge right beside her father's bank (all this in broad daylight; she couldn't have been more than ten at the time, though she didn't remember); had pointed out with a quivering finger and staring eyes the shanty with the picket fence on the towpath below, where he lived; had said in a constrained, rasping, barely audible voice, turning to her, but turning his whole rigid body toward her in order to do so: "That's where I live. Will you come see me tonight, after dark? I'll be sitting on the porch behind the vines, waiting for you." His head tilted farther back as he said these words; she thought he was going to have some kind of attack. His cheeks seemed frozen, his eyes stared transfixed into space. She did not answer. She moved away from him, frightened; she went back to the safety of the "right side of the canal." Nobody ever bought and gave *her* candy; didn't he know that she was the banker's child, that nobody needed to buy candy for her? And that night, just after dark, she went to the bridge again, found the steps down to the towpath that she had never noticed before, descended, went along the cindery path to the cottage with the picket fence, opened the gate, went up to the low porch, found him there. She did not know who he was, what he did, how he got along, what was the matter with him. Utterly silent, they went inside. (He was like a scarecrow, with a colorless surprised face and staring eyes that saw nothing.) He shut the front door and drew the blinds. He lighted a kerosene lamp, motioned her to sit beside him on a musty shabby sofa with broken springs, took a packet of photographs from the drawer of a small table, spread them out on the uneven surface of the broken sofa, pointed to this one, that one, his finger shaking as if he were having a spell. The suspense—but why? of what?—was unendurable, but she could not leave; not yet. He fumbled at his clothes, fumbled with hers, pawed her, pawed and stroked himself even more, quivering all over as if some invisible motor operated inside him, his eyes of staring glass all but starting from their sockets. Then something seemed to happen, though she did not know what; his sudden groans and moans were like breathless sobs: she understood and yet did not understand. A second later he scooped up the photographs, thrusting them with spastically trembling fingers back into the drawer, and she knew instinctively it was time to go, get out. Not a word was said between them; no good-nights even. She let herself out the front door, passed through the fence gate, went along the towpath, and climbed the cement steps to the bridge again. The next time she saw him, maybe a month later, two months, six months, he did not recognize her as he passed her on the street; and she went by as if she had never seen him before.

Now she stood in Jack Sanford's room looking across at the scene of that mysterious, incomplete, hazardous, compelling tryst. It had not happened. Oh, it *had happened;* she didn't for a second pretend it hadn't, didn't deny it privately or inwardly even to herself. But as for being touched by it, or reached, or involved or affected in any way, it was just as though it had never occurred at all. When things of this sort had taken place in her life—and they had many times, and worse—it was almost as if they had happened to somebody else. No one would believe it if she told them; she scarcely believed it herself, once it was over, though the memory was vivid enough. She only wondered why such things had happened to her and not to others (or had they?): what was there in her that, like a prescience of evil, even as a child, even before she was conscious of them, had attracted such things, and always had—and attracted those odd people to her unerringly, and she to them, as if she wore some stigma or "sign" on her forehead invisible to the general world but all too plain to the others? And as she stood now looking across the broad canal below, its watery expanse hard and flat as an abandoned roller rink, and barely made out from this distance the outlines of the small neat cottage with its curiously dainty picket fence and its climbing rosebushes, she couldn't put herself into that picture at all. She had been that child, that girl, but it wasn't she, either. Love is possible, in spite of everything, she told herself insistently, while Jack Sanford sat at the writing table behind her in his shorts. Love is possible. Love is possible . . .

"What are you doing?" he asked.

"Nothing."

"What are you thinking then?"

"Nothing."

"Do you still love me?"

"Oh yes." As she turned back from the room she saw him folding the written sheet, stuffing it into an envelope, and licking the flap to seal it.

"Okay," he said. "I'm about ready."

"I'd dress first, if I were you."

"Good idea."

She sat down in the one good chair and with the greatest pleasure, but remote, objective, watched him begin the somehow complicated process, which seemed to take forever, of getting into his clothes: balancing on one leg sometimes and going into a kind of one-legged dance for a step or two, thrusting out his raised chin as he buttoned his shirt, hunching up his shoulders as he thrust the shirt tails deep between his legs while the pants remained still only half on, held there by half-bent knees and spread thighs.

"I think one of the most fascinating sights in all the world," she said, "is watching a man get dressed, or undressed."

After the barest fraction of a second he asked: "Why?"

"I couldn't possibly tell you. It just is. There's a kind of innocence about it. The odd thing is that it's a luxury that women take as a matter of course all over the land, and most of them, I'll bet, don't even bother to look—just take it for granted."

"Want me to start over again?"

"I'd like nothing better, even though the innocence is gone now. But I can wait—I *will* wait—till the next time."

Before he unlocked the door he took her in his arms. "My darling Winnie . . ." He kissed her lingeringly and deeply, but tenderly, as if he had been fond of her for years.

"Dear Jack," she said as he released her at last. "Dear Jack . . ."

"Ready?"

"As much as I'll ever be. But oh, this is always such a terrible moment, the breaking off. I hate to stop."

"Just let me open the window and let the place air out a little while I'm out."

She stood beside him as he threw up the sash of the single window at the rear. Among the small row of dark shanties across the canal she saw that a single light still burned dimly in the one with the absurd picket fence and the pathetic flower beds.

"A real fleabag," he said as they went down the torn carpeted stairs. "Dimsal!"

As they got into the old Marmon parked at the curb in front of the Royale, he said: "Now is the time to sound the old klaxon, don't you think?"

"I do not."

They passed the post office on the corner of Main and Maple Court.

"Wait!" she said. "You forgot your letter."

"So I did." He did not slow down. "I'll drop it in the box on my way back. I guess my mind is on other things. Can't imagine why."

When he turned in at her driveway she said: "I'm not going to ask you in."

"No. It's late. We can sit a minute though, can't we?"

"All night, if you like. Except that we may have to move. I see Dad's car is out."

"Club or something?"

"Something . . ."

"Winnie . . . Come here."

She moved over. They embraced; they kissed. Their long silences were broken intermittently by scattered irrelevant sentences, conversational exchange of no importance or point, the idle talk of lovers unwilling to call it a night.

"That room of yours."

"What about it?"

"You called it 'dimsal' or something."

"That's right."

"Where did you ever pick up a word like that?"

"I'll tell you," he said, fondling her hand, holding it to his cheek, kissing it. "A long time ago I heard a little girl who had a funny speech thing, not exactly a spoonerism but something of the sort—I heard her say 'dimsal' for 'dismal,' just as she said 'temecery' for 'cemetery.' 'Dimsal'—I thought it one of the finest words I'd ever heard. It beats 'dismal' all to hell."

"It's marvelous."

"Isn't it? From then on I called her 'the dimsal girl,' and appropriated the word for my own use ever since. It's gotten so I don't hear myself saying it *wrong* any more. I have to watch out."

He parted her open cardigan, fumbled with the cashmere slip-on underneath, pushed it up, moved exploring fingers across her bare midriff and up to her breasts, holding his hand tight there, tighter as she felt his growing agitation. Her head was on his shoulder, her mouth half open, his mouth open and covering hers. It was like being in a suddenly descending elevator with the floor giving way beneath you. She thought she had never experienced such an intoxicating sensation in her life. This could last forever; but it couldn't. Sooner or later that halt has to be called to everything. She sat up straight and pulled away, rearranging her clothing; she opened the door of the car.

"Good night, Jack. You must go."

"Yes."

"Don't forget to mail your letter," she said, trying to recover her breath.

"Oh yes. That letter." He reached into the inside pocket of his jacket and drew it forth. "Here. Take care of it for me, will you?"

"What on earth . . ."

"It's to you. From me."

"Dear Jack." She slipped the letter into her purse. "Dear Jack. As if things weren't bad enough already . . ."

"I don't understand."

"You know I won't sleep as it is. Now this . . ."

"You'll sleep. We'll both sleep, damned well. Good night, darling."

"Good night."

As she closed the side door and entered the house, she heard him sound the klaxon once, good and loud. Idiot.

She went directly up to her room, undressed, got into her nightgown, lighted a cigarette, took the letter from her purse, and sat down on the edge of the turned-down bed. She read:

Darling Winnie:

You must know that it is more difficult to write a short letter than a long one, if it's meaningful at all, and God knows I haven't much time. I'm trying to do this while you're dressing in the bathroom, and I have no idea of what I want to say, just because there is so much to say. There, you've already come out. Talk about lightning-change artists. Now you're standing at the bleak window looking out onto that dimsal scene. And all I want to say, I guess, is thank you. I will never forget tonight. It's all wrong to be polite and say thanks after the act of love-making, it's one of those things one just doesn't do, it's a time for no words at all, period. But I do say thanks because I think, darling Winnie, you are the most generous girl I've ever known. I love you completely with my heart and body, and I also think I am in love with you.

Your

JACK

Abruptly, out of a deep, fulfilled sleep, Winifred Grainger woke to one of those baffling blanks of amnesia—we've all had them—when for many seconds, which seemed like minutes, she could not place her surroundings, did not know where she was; and worse: with whom.

Her instant automatic reaction, while she waited for things to right themselves, was to lie low and tell herself: Go easy now, it's got to be all right, don't worry until you *know* how bad it is, it may be okay after all—a wakeful nightmare not of terror but of caution. The low-ceilinged, unfamiliar room—narrow, sparsely furnished, its unfinished walls merely boards through the cracks of which you could see occasional slits of daylight—and that man standing with his back to her at the far end, the heels of his palms on the low window sill as he leaned and looked out into the misty gray morning: those broad but sloping naked shoulders, the beautiful twin-grooved back narrowing to the tight firm ass with deep concave hollows on either cheek, the legs like columns . . . Then she smiled with inexpressible gratitude; and the whole previous evening, which might have been so awful (it had been so often), came back and flooded her body and mind with sudden pure happiness.

"Hank!" she called out, in an excess of relief and impulsive high spirits. "Come back to bed or you'll freeze!"

He turned away from the window to look at her.

"And *I'm* frozen," she said, stretching out her bare arms. "This quilt! Come warm me up? Please?"

Jack Sanford sauntered across the bare floor, his hands on his hips, toward the narrow cot.

"So, I'm 'Hank,' am I?"

"Oh!" she cried. "Oh! How could I! *Jack* dear . . ."

"Must be that Smith friend of yours," he said, sitting on the edge of the cot. "Mr. Smith."

"Oh! Can you ever forgive me?"

"I'll try real hard." He took her hand in his.

"I just . . . I was still asleep, sort of, and drawing blanks all over the place."

"I'll say."

" 'Hank'—I don't know any Hank. Cross my heart!"

"I believe you."

"You've got to!"

"More important is," he said, "you asked me to warm you up."

"Will you?"

"I'm cold too. Certainly I will. It was mighty chilly, standing there at the open window, watching the mist curl up from the bay and the sun trying to burn through—a magical spectacle always— in nothing but my birthday suit."

"And such a beautiful birthday suit."

"Even though you thought it was 'Hank's'?"

"I didn't. I swear I didn't." And she meant it. "I was just looking at you, admiring again that breath-taking body, those stunning legs, and names just . . . They just . . . Names didn't seem to mean anything. One would have been as good as another. Isn't that awful?"

"Forget it. Move over."

"No. I want you right on top of me."

When he was in position—and that's the way she thought of

it—with one hand she pulled his head down and buried his face against her throat and whispered into his ear, almost soundlessly: "I love you, Jack. I love you, dear Jack . . ." He thought they were the most thrilling, blood-warming words he had ever heard in his life, but his instinct told him, exactly attuned to hers, that it was because of the tone in which she spoke, or murmured, the hushed intimacy, rather than the words themselves or even their meaning. *Any*body could have said the *words:* conventional, standard, expected.

They had driven out to Parson's Point for the first time last evening; Winifred had wanted to show him the place she loved so much, which she always thought of as her real home. After an argument at the Point, they had persuaded Jonesey, the Graingers' handyman during the summer who, out of season, lived in a rooming house at the Point, to let them take out one of the motorboats. The cottage had not yet been opened for the season, the bar was deserted, but there was no reason why they couldn't spend the night in Jonesey's narrow room over the boathouse, on the bay side of the bar, at the foot of the short path leading down from the cottage. The late-May night, though almost June now, had been cool; cold. It was exhilarating crossing the choppy bay in the dark (a good three miles), there were no hazards of anchored sailboats or rafts in the path, and with Winifred at the wheel the narrow high-powered *Isabel III* leaped and plunged onward like a champ porpoise out to set records for speed. At moments they were almost airborne, as if they had taken off into the misty, moist, chill night, the speedboat leaving in its trail—for the wind and the speed carried the sounds quickly away, left them far behind—a series of spanks and thumps and whacks as it momentarily hit the choppy waves before it seemed to take off into airy space again, as if into the elements of love and excitement. Thrilled, they could only glance eloquently at each other from time to time; they could not speak, for they could hardly catch their breath in that bracing speed and wind. When the *Isabel III* at last approached the Grainger boathouse on the bar, after a wide curving arc, it slowed down and settled deeper into the water, till, as it finally slid noiselessly with the motor off into the slip, it seemed certain the narrow motorboat would ship water and go down, and they would be swamped, forced to climb out and emerge standing knee-deep in the black still water between the two landings. Nothing of the kind occurred, of course; they tied the painter on one of the cleats, went out the door to the back, and while Winifred fumbled with a bunch of keys till she found the one that led up to Jonesey's humble quarters above, Jack Sanford stood at the entrance looking up at the bar, admiring what he could see, in this dim light, of the Graingers' splendid cottage. The same gratifying thought came into his mind that had occurred to him several times before: good goods. It was not, he thought, merely mercenary or material appraisal: everything he saw nowadays, everything associated with her, enhanced Winifred's value in his eyes, made him appreciate her the more, surrounded her with an aura of privilege and glamour that had been lacking in his life—that was certainly rare in *this* town—and that he aspired to and wanted. His love and gratitude were the greater for it.

As he lay with her now, that love—physical love—almost seemed secondary. After a while, after their morning love-making, he rolled to the side of her, held her still in his arms, and the two of them lay on their backs looking up at the cobwebby ceiling, enjoying that special luxury of being able for the moment to ignore each other as lovers; and they talked, spasmodically, indifferently almost, like two old friends thinking aloud.

"I want you to get to know Parson's Point and the bar as I do. This is my paradise, if that doesn't sound too pretentious."

"I want to, too."

"In another week the cottage will be open and the season will be on. There'll be all kinds of things to do, we'll be completely on our own even when Belle and Dad are here, and the days won't be long enough."

"That's what you said about your childhood, when you lived in that great house."

"My days of innocence. Well, it will be the same here, only more so—except for the innocence. Because there are two of us now, to enjoy it together."

"Except for the practical fact that I have a job. I work for a living, after all."

"I'm speaking of the weekends. Darling Jack, I don't want to run your life, or appropriate you—I'm not the possessive type, really I'm not—but I want you to feel this place with me, and enjoy it with me. When you can."

"I do now."

"Yes, I really think you do. Who else would come up with me to this bare barn of a room without heat or *any* comfort except this narrow cot like a trough—like a dugout, my God."

"You came up to my fleabag."

"You couldn't have kept me away; that was *your* place, and I wanted to be there. But oh dear, you've no idea of the wonderful things coming up—what the place is like when the full summer is on and there's so much to do."

"Dances, you mean? Parties?"

"Yes, there are those, too. But I don't go to them much."

"Why not?"

"Oh, I don't know. I could say I've outgrown all that, but it would be a little bit dishonest of me."

"In what way?"

"Truth is, I don't get invited."

"You? That I can't believe. You're not high-hat?"

"It's not that. Arcadia and Parson's Point—much as I love them, they're funny places, Jack. Funny things happen here. Funny discriminations."

"Funny?"

"You know what I mean. Or will know all too soon."

"*That's* easily fixed."

"How?"

"Do you belong to the Yacht Club, for instance? And the Country Club in Arcadia?"

"The family and I have memberships. But I don't go."

"Then *I'll* take you."

"But Jack, it would be just us—no foursomes and so on, like everybody else. Just the two of us. No dinners or anything beforehand; no gatherings after. Not even any mixing at the parties, really."

"Could it matter less? It's you I want, not them—whoever they are."

"Poor Jack. That's what you think now."

"That's *cert*ainly what I think now. And feel. Winifred! Don't you know I'm in love? Don't you?"

"Do you know, I really begin to believe you are."

"Well, that's the most dubious statement I ever heard in my life. You certainly didn't put your heart in that one."

"Oh yes I did, Jack. You'll never know how much."

"Tell me, then."

"What's the sense? Words are no good. I don't believe in them."

"Or in anything else, apparently."

"That's not true. I believe in you, in this, in what we've got here right now." She spread her hand and fingers over his bare abdomen.

"I believe in much more, as far as we're concerned," he said.

"You go ahead and do that. I'll just take it as it comes, and be thankful."

"You have no faith in the future? In our future? Winnie! If we don't believe in ourselves! . . ."

"Jack dear, isn't *now* enough? Isn't it all we have—all anyone has?"

"Okay. I see that I'll have to take over."

"I'm willing. If disbelieving . . ."

"And run the show."

"I'm willing."

When they got up, shivering in the damp morning chill, they stood naked at the open window where he had stood before, with their arms around each other, and looked out. Tiny twists of cloud rose from the calm, no-longer-choppy bay, individual tiny geysers that spiraled into nothingness no more than a foot above the water. Overhead, in the yellowing haze, the presence of a sun could be felt, waiting to emerge from the clouds and mist and warm the morning. The islands across from the bar, which even in bright sunlight looked like floating phantasms of moss and low trees and a few scattered, barely perceptible cottages, could not be seen at all. With all that hushed silence, pale light neither daytime nor night, and blurred outlines everywhere, the world and the morning seemed to be only theirs. It was going to be a marvelous day. But they had to get going; she had to get him back to town to his job, to work.

THE MEMBER of the household who was the most keyed up over the prospect of the evening, and in fact wholeheartedly disapproving of the guest beforehand, was Irma. Belle Grainger looked forward to the occasion with an irrational schoolgirlish curiosity; Lyman Grainger was depressed, characteristically, over the intrusion of a "stranger"—depressed, in any case, because of a well-founded skepticism that any date of Winifred's would amount to anything, in the sense that something good would come of it; and Winifred was a little edgy over the whole thing, not because of her parents' possible disapproval of Jack Sanford or that he might not pass muster, but because poor Jack was bound to be bored by the whole nonsensical but somehow necessary evening. Irma's agitation was caused by her preconceived and unshakable conviction (Irma was one of those untroubled lucky persons who always made up her mind good and firm in advance) that nothing, and no man, was good enough for her Miss Winifred, though she knew in her heart of hearts that Winifred was, in the most practical or pragmatic sense, lucky to be having a male guest at dinner at all.

Jack Sanford arrived at six-thirty; he boldly sounded the klaxon as he entered the drive. Bravado? Winifred wondered as she heard the horrendous sound from her bedroom and started down.

When she opened the door to him, he put his arms around her and kissed her as if he had a right to. He was wearing a proper dark suit, black shoes, white Oxford shirt, and a smart club-striped tie. That mustache of his (which in secret moments she smiled to herself about), meticulously separated in the middle by—it must have been—a straight razor, was freshly waxed at the ends.

"Hi," she said as he released her.

"Winnie! You look wonderful."

"Come on in."

"Your mother said you would show me over the house sometime, remember?"

"Sometime."

"Not tonight?"

"You're not here as a tourist, sweetie. Belle and Dad want to look you over, but thoroughly. Certainly you must know that."

"I know that. I want to look them over."

"Why?"

"I'm not saying."

"Scared?" she asked.

"Not a bit."

"No, I don't believe you are."

"Why the hell should I be? I'm somebody too."

"You're right. No reason at all."

Her father and mother were sitting in the white drawing room when Winifred ushered him in. Almost at the same instant, as if on cue, Irma arrived with four cocktails on a small silver tray.

"What a pleasure to see you again," Mrs. Grainger said, extending a hand. "A great pleasure. Isn't it, Lyman?"

"Oh yes." Mr. Grainger half struggled to his feet for a half-hearted handshake, and sank back into his chair again.

"Good evening, sir," Jack Sanford said.

Irma came close up to him, her face expressionless—which seemed more deadly somehow than if she had been openly hostile—and held the tray of cocktails almost under his chin; they were spiked with antimony, he surmised, at the very least.

"You might have offered a cocktail to Mother and me first, Irma," Winifred said quietly. "You must be nervous."

"Me nervous? Never!" A moment later she sailed from the room, the empty tray held for some reason against the flat of her back.

"Irma's got it in for you," Winifred said, "I can see that."

"Doesn't matter. *I* don't expect everybody to like me in this world. Why should they? There's lots of people I don't like."

"You'll like Irma in time. She just takes getting used to."

"Do you like Arcadia by now, Mr. Sanford?"

"I love Arcadia, Mrs. Grainger." What else would he say?

"I'm afraid the cocktail is a little—well, not what you're used to, perhaps. I don't know one from another. We entertain so seldom, you see, and—well, cocktails are just cocktails."

"It's not important," Lyman Grainger cut in curtly.

"I couldn't agree with you more," Jack Sanford said, all amiability. "It's a very good drink, whatever it is."

"Don't try so hard, Jack. Irma isn't at her best in the beverage department."

"Well, we drink so little, you see," Belle Grainger explained. "We're not accustomed to having people in, much—though I do enjoy it *thor*oughly, I must add. But times have changed so, don't you find? It's all quite different since Mercedes was home—she's Winifred's older sister, and *so* attractive. She's living now in Southern California with her new husband. Palm Springs, isn't it, Lyman? In the desert. When Mercedes was here, the house was just overrun *con*stantly with her many young men, and Alice was almost as popular. Oh, it was so gay then!"

"They weren't all so young," Winifred said. "I remember some of them had been married two or three times."

"In any case they were suing for her hand by the dozen—if I may use such an antiquated expression."

"See, Jack? That makes me the wallflower of the family. I told you I wasn't popular."

"Winifred *dear!* I didn't mean for a moment . . ."

"Skip it. I am what I am and I like it—I think."

"*I* like it," Jack Sanford said.

When they sat down at the neat oval table with a pure white damask cloth and the right appointments—the small silver urns for cigarettes, the silver candlesticks, the centerpiece of small white iris that could only have come from a hothouse or one of the better florists in Rochester—Jack Sanford was surprised to see that his heavy damask napkin was rolled inside an old-fashioned sterling napkin ring. He picked it up and looked at it, after withdrawing and unfolding the napkin; but the fancy monogram was so worn with age or interlaced with scrolls that it was indecipherable. A napkin ring; the thought passed through his mind: Did they expect him to be a more or less frequent guest from now on? Not bad, he thought; not bad . . .

"I love this town, I really love it," he said as he spread the napkin in his lap. "And this house. Are you aware of what a really beautiful house it is?"

"I think we are. Aren't we, Lyman?"

"I suppose that did sound impertinent. I only meant, most people who own houses like this—though there aren't many—just take them for granted, without even thinking."

"Jack, you can be quite sure that much careful planning and decoration and not least of all money have gone into this house—regardless of what might have been left out of it."

"Our Winifred," Mrs. Grainger suddenly said, with conversational brightness, "tells me you took in the opening dance at the Country Club, Memorial Day weekend. We didn't know about it beforehand—I don't know why she never tells me these things. Did you enjoy it, Mr. Sanford? Don't you think it's terribly nice for a town this size?"

"I had a very good time."

"It was a bust," Winifred said simply.

"A—a 'bust'? What *do* you mean?"

"A washout. A flop. A nothing."

"Well if you're too soph*is*ticated for our simple country ways, then I'm afraid you're, well, there's no pleasing you."

"Oh, it was all right, so far as it goes."

"Didn't you dance, and have supper, and everything?"

"We did everything."

"*You* liked it, didn't you, Mr. Sanford?"

"I thought it was very nice. A little on the cliquey side, maybe."

" 'Cliquey'?"

"I mean people didn't seem to mix much. I guess you've got to live here a thousand years before that happens. There's nothing more snobbish than a small town, where everybody knows everybody else, and who they are and where they came from—their backgrounds, I mean. Still I—I really thought it was very nice. An attractive club, attractive people for the most part, good music, good food. Very nice."

"Well there you are, Winifred!"

Aware that they had somehow strayed onto touchy ground, Jack Sanford changed the subject. "Tell me," he said, "do you folks know that large eighteen-ninetyish house up at the end of the street—the one with the funny stained glass in the front door and upper hallway and the cupola and that enormous circular veranda?"

"Of course, Mr. Sanford. We all know the house. We know all the houses."

"Why do you ask?" Winifred said.

"No special reason. Except that I've noticed, every night it seems, at least half a dozen cars parked in front or in the wide driveway, and the lights are on all over the house, no matter what the hour. Gosh, it's almost like a club. I almost thought it was a speakeasy, all those cars."

"You're quite right," Mrs. Grainger said. "*Some* people in the neighborhood don't approve at all."

Irma came in from the kitchen, went around the table with a Chinese lacquered tray and set down before each place a cup of *petite marmite*. When she had gone he asked: "Who are they?"

"A married couple by the name of Finletter," Belle Grainger said, sighing as if in pain. "I'm afraid Betty Finletter is the one who attracts the crowd. She's not from Arcadia, of course. She's an outsider."

"Who is Betty Finletter?"

"Oh, just a woman," Winifred said.

Jack Sanford smiled as he glanced at her. "Funny, that's the same phrase you used about Ruby somebody at Tony di Santo's a couple of weeks ago."

"Did I? I didn't mean anything specially by it."

"Winifred! You don't mean to say you were telling Mr. Sanford about Ruby Pelle*tier*, do you, dear?"

"I guess I was."

"Whatever for?"

"Well, she happened to be there, at the bar, and one thing led to another, as Jordan Baker prompted—and as Daisy echoed her."

"What *are* you talking about? Now you've got me *all* confused."

"What's the particular attraction at the Finletters'?"

"They're not people you're likely to know," Mr. Grainger said. And since it was almost the first utterance he had made since they entered the dining room, the other three involuntarily looked up at him as if he were a stranger who had wandered in from outside somewhere and sat down at the table with them unasked.

"For the record," Winifred finally said, "don't let Mother give you a bum steer, or Father either. Betty Finletter isn't 'just a woman,' as I so carelessly said—any more than Ruby Pelletier is 'just a woman' either. The point is, don't get the idea they're anything alike."

"I won't. I can't help wondering, though: Why all those cars every night?"

"The Finletters, I'm sorry to say," Mrs. Grainger said, sounding genuinely sorry, "seem to have a gift, a real gift, for attracting the ragtag and bobtail. The riffraff, you might say."

"*I* wouldn't say it," Winifred said.

"Well, I would, and I do. You're far too generous and broad-minded, a real failing, I think." Turning to Jack Sanford, she went on: "They keep a kind of open house, perpetually. People who do that, you know, are, well, restless to say the least. All the single men turn up there and a few married men too. Hardly ever any women. Oh, maybe one or two now and then. It's really most odd. Though I must say in all fairness, Herbert Finletter is a very nice, quiet person. I know his mother very well. We belong to the Shakespeare Club together and occasionally play bridge."

"Come on, Belle, as long as you're being so damned 'fair,' let's *be* fair. Betty Finletter happens to be a very attractive, lively, friendly woman, with personality to burn. She wasn't blessed enough to be born here, but what of it? She's from Boston," she added, turning toward Jack Sanford, "and has lived here only a few years. She must find it damned dull. Well, obviously she does. God knows why she ever married Herb. He's quiet all right, but it must be murder living with him."

"Winifred!"

"And she's a very outgoing person," she went on. "Likes people. And they like her."

"Do you?" Jack Sanford asked.

"I don't know her very well. I'm not one of those people who are always dropping in on them."

"Say, it just occurred to me. Was she the woman at the Country Club dance with black hair parted in the middle and worn behind her ears, wearing that brilliant green dress?"

"Yes, that's Betty."

"And that Palmolive complexion?"

"I see you did notice her."

"How could I help it?"

"How could you indeed," Mrs. Grainger said. "She dresses like one of those, well, one of those women who, well . . ."

"*I* think she dresses very well indeed. She doesn't happen to get her clothes at the Bon Ton Shoppe, if that's what you mean, Belle, or at Sibley's in Rochester."

"Well, every woman to her own taste, I always say."

Winifred ignored this. Mr. Grainger looked pained. Jack Sanford wondered what lay underneath all this.

"About this dropping in on the Finletters," Winifred said, "since you've already noticed it yourself. *I* don't, because I'm a girl, and it's men friends who go there mostly. Herb Finletter has a lot of friends. Damn! In my indirect way even *I* sound catty now. So please overlook it. The only point anyway is that Herb knows everybody, they run a good house, they stay up all hours, and Betty Finletter is an interesting woman who deserves all those friends she has, or they wouldn't go there, would they? But I should shut up: the situation needs no explanation whatever. This is the damnedest town, Jack. You'll find that out. You can't say the right thing without seeming to say the wrong thing. People read things into everything, if they're the judging type. Why the hell isn't there an *in-between* level where people can meet or discuss things with some kind of honest understanding and fairness?"

"Winifred Grainger. I must say it isn't very pleasant to sit here, or pleasant for your guest either—or for Father," Belle added as an afterthought—"and have to listen to all those—well, if I must say it, those damns and hells and Gods. And I know that your father most certainly agrees with me. Don't you, Father?"

"I haven't said 'God' once. But I will now, if it'll make you feel better. God, when is Irma going to bring in the roast?"

Whereupon Irma appeared from the kitchen as if positively summoned, as if on cue again. She passed around the lamb, which had been carved in the kitchen to spare Mr. Grainger, and the mint sauce, then went back in successive trips for the broccoli, the pan-browned potatoes, the tossed salad. Though her expression seemed frigid and unyielding as ever, they all noticed that she studied the guest surreptitiously but thoroughly; and Winifred, though she didn't care a damn, wondered what she thought of him. Jack Sanford was equally aware of her intense scrutiny, like a kind of flirtation in reverse; and purposely he avoided her eyes, smiled and was his most charming, to give her every opportunity to accept him. Almost reluctantly, then, she finally retired to her domain of the kitchen.

"Dad, I've got an idea. You won't like it, but . . ." She smiled wryly, aware that he would see through it. "Are you and Mother going to spend the Fourth of July at the cottage?"

"We usually do."

"Or is it maybe a little too early for you?" she suggested.

"Why, no, as a matter of fact, I don't think we are this year," Mrs. Grainger said vaguely, improvising. "Your father and I have other plans for the holiday this year. At least I think we do, if I'm not mistaken. Don't we, Father?"

"What's that?" he said, making no effort to conceal his surprise.

"It seems to me that you and I promised . . . Well, I forget who it is for the moment. I'll have to consult my date book. But didn't we accept some sort of engagement with the, well, with the Conrads, or somebody?"

"First I've heard of it."

"Now there's a man for you every time. Tell me, why do you ask, Winifred?"

"I'd like to spend the holiday weekend at the cottage, with Jack and a couple of others, say."

"Whom do you have in mind, dear?"

"I thought of asking Harry Harrison and Carol Wilson. We could all sort of chaperon each other," she added, frankly satiric.

"Why, I don't see why not. In fact I think it's a lovely idea, don't you, Lyman?"

"Thanks, Belle. I'll call Harry tonight. The only fly in the ointment is getting the permission of Carol's parents. She's only twenty."

"Well, so are you, dear."

"There's a difference."

"Perhaps I could ask them for you," Mrs. Grainger suggested.

"Mrs. Wilson seems a reasonable woman, though I must admit I don't know her very well."

"We'll manage. I can always tell Carol's mother that Jack is forty-five instead of thirty-something. You could look forty-five, couldn't you, Jack? Or at least act it?"

"I do it all the time."

"But that would be lying, dear."

"Wouldn't be the first time."

"*Win*ifred," Belle Grainger said with her company laugh. "If I ever took you seriously I'd be old before my time. Fortunately I know you through and through."

"It's all set then. How about it, Jack?"

"I don't know this Harry, or Carol either, but it sounds grand."

"And since you said you enjoyed the Country Club dance so much," she said, with that wry smile that turned down the corners of her mouth, "we might even take in the dance at the Yacht Club, the season's first. A real blow-out. It'll give you a taste of local high life that'll knock you cold. Boy!"

"Who goes to this shebang?"

"Everybody, of course. Or as we say in Arcadia, everybody who is anybody. Which means about one-tenth of the people, if that. Do you know, I once went to a grand affair in Palmyra, the annual Assembly Ball, and I happened to enter the ballroom at the same moment that one of my friends did, a girl from Arcadia, of course. The place was simply packed; there was hardly room to dance even. And my friend stood in the doorway looking over the crowd and practically wailed, 'Why, there's nobody here!' "

"I was just thinking, dear. Now mind, it's only something to be forewarned about. But there's, there is a slight, well, hitch. Mr. Jones!"

"Jonesey? What about him?"

"Well, on account of some other work, Mr. Jones isn't free to take over the care of our boats and move into the boathouse till the tenth, I believe."

"So?"

"Then there's Agnes. She isn't going to move into the cottage and begin her duties till after that, even."

"We don't need Jonesey. You know I can handle the launch and the speedboat as well as he does—I've done it for years. As for the cooking, I'm not helpless. I know how to wield a skillet and turn on the burners, and if worse comes to worse we can always go over to the Point for our meals. More fun anyway; takes me back to childhood. Come on, Belle, don't throw a monkey wrench in the works."

"Why, I wouldn't dream of spoiling your fun, dear. I'm only trying to *help,* of course."

"You'll help by staying out of the picture."

"Well, that's certainly putting it bluntly," and Mrs. Grainger managed a laugh. "Aren't they terrible, Father? I tell you: Kids today . . ."

"Jack's no kid. We're insisting on forty-five. Now remember that."

"What does a guy wear to this sort of shindig?" Jack Sanford asked.

"Up to you. I'll wear a plain sleeveless myself, probably white. I never doll up unless it's the Rose Ball just after Easter—to which I'm never asked. You can wear anything: slacks and jacket, or whatever you're comfortable in."

"In our day, I always wore a semi-formal to the Yacht Club dances, and your father wore white flannels and a blue blazer. Looked very handsome, too, 'specially in his yachting cap. Nowadays you can buy yachting caps *any*where: I think it's awful. In our day you had to be-long!"

After dinner, Mr. and Mrs. Grainger somehow made themselves scarce, not too ostentatiously, and Winifred and Jack were left to themselves, with the drawing room, the library, the sitting room, the "den" for their use. Even so they wandered outside, to the back lawn. They started to go out through the kitchen, but because Winifred was unwilling to interrupt Irma's dream world where she sat at the enameled table poring over *The Sheik*—she had been reading it for nearly a week now, and often spoke of it admiringly because it was so colorful (all those desert scenes and sand storms)—they went out through the glass-enclosed sun porch at the rear and down the couple of steps toward the tennis court. The grass was heavily wet with dew, drenched in fact, and Winifred took off not only her shoes but her stockings.

"That's the sun dial," she said laconically. "That's the dovecote. That's the garage, which used to be a marvelous barn. That's the fancy fence, Palladian, so-called, and in style I guess it is, that Dad had built when we moved overtown and that cost a fortune. That's the tennis court, unused most of the time. That's the peacock chair that's uncomfortable as all hell but Mother thinks it gives the place class: she saw something in a magazine. That's the roller, for both the court *and* the grass. That's the birdbath, a copy of Somebody-or-other. Beyond the court, way over there, is my summerhouse: I dearly love it. If you don't too, then everything's off. There, I told you I'd show you over the place someday."

"Funny thing is, I can hardly see a thing. I'm moon-dazzled or moon-struck."

"Flatterer."

"Oh, it's you too. But this moonlight is too much. It makes everything unreal, in the loveliest way. Even you."

"Hey, I'm real all right. Just try me."

"I can't wait."

"On to the summerhouse, then."

Nothing is more banal or theatrical than moonlight, she thought as she led the way. Moonshine it ought to be called. In novels you never quite believe in it; it's a device of the novelist too clever by half. All the love scenes outdoors at night take place by moonlight, and God knows the moon doesn't shine *that* much, that often; there are nights and nights when it doesn't shine at all. But it did tonight, almost embarrassingly so, as if it had been "arranged."

The night was a blurred green misty white, with a meretricious magic; the moon itself was absolutely full, an absolutely round and perfect moon riding high overhead, small, but illuminating everything below with a rare, unbelievably bright light: you could have read a newspaper by it, as they say. Because the full moon was at its very peak, it was almost as if, a few hours from now (just as a few hours ago), that geometrically exact orb, drawn with a precise compass, would be ever so slightly less round, as it was certain to be tomorrow night, the lower left rim imperceptibly (but perceptible all the same) blunted a little, like a round but soft balloon that had momentarily come to rest against an immovable object. But tonight—tonight it was full, and pure; perfect; solid-seeming, as if never to wane again. If you looked hard at it, you saw strange things on its surface, though the brilliance of its light made this difficult: faces that were not faces; the provocative profile of a woman with her hair worn in a kind of bun at the nape of her neck; valleys; declivities; deserts; mysterious areas of glowing white and off-white, almost shadowy, that might be anything—anything you saw in them. It was the color of chalk illuminated as if by a swelling and diminishing light from within, with the faintest, the most enchanting, overcast or tinge of yellow that vanished even as you looked at it directly. And far above and around and on all sides in the tremulous pale sky there was that so-called ring-around-the-moon that you both saw and did not see. For some inexplicable reason, the brilliance of the moonlight seemed all the more dazzling and even hallucinating because of the utter stillness of the night: it bathed the whole world in a magic radiance, but it seemed to glow and palpitate and shine for you alone—if you looked at it, were aware of it, and in love.

Walking hand in hand through the soaking wet grass, they reached the summerhouse and stepped up onto the low flooring of the ancient vine-draped structure. There was the pungent smell of the trumpet vine and Dutchman's-breeches that descended from the open trellis above, and in the radiancy of the moonlight, almost a ghastly light in a way, the surface of the large flat leaves dangling haphazardly from above gleamed like steel, white, silver, without a trace of their native green. The warped floorboards, exposed to so many weathers, creaked under their feet as they mounted the low platform; the warped rough benches at the three sides were damp, really wet, with dew.

"Shall I wipe this bench off with my handkerchief, so we can sit down?"

"No! It would be sopped in no time. *Towels* wouldn't be enough."

They sat side by side on the soaking-wet bench and looked across the lawn, across the tennis court, toward the brightly lighted house nearly three hundred feet away. The light shining from the many windows was anemic, pinkish and dull, like the pale but lurid light of a glowing cigarette in a night club.

"Darling. Let's sit on the floor."

"Let's . . ."

Then they lay down side by side, on their backs, he holding her body in one arm and her head on his chest.

"Tell me something."

"Anything. Anything."

"Who was that child," she asked, "that you called 'the dimsal girl'?"

"You remembered her?"

"How could I forget?"

"She was my older brother's child. Mary, her name is. Gosh, she's going on fourteen by now, maybe even more. Think of it."

After a silence she said: "I'd love to have a little girl."

"So would I."

"Or even a boy."

"So would I."

"Either, as long as it was yours."

"So would I."

"I guess there's small chance of it though," she finally said, turning her head away.

"Why do you say such a thing?"

"Well, we'd have to get married."

"Not necessarily. It happens without."

"God knows that's true."

"But the crux of the matter," he said, "the secret and meaning of the whole thing . . . I mean, of course, if it means anything at all . . ." He hesitated.

"I hope I know what you were going to say."

"What?"

"Forgive me for saying it, for putting words in your mouth. True and honest I don't want to put a burden on you," she said, "but boy or no boy, girl or no girl, the real thing is that I think I want to get married. Oh, not just get married! Marry you."

He tightened his arm around her, raised himself partly up on his side, gazed into her face momentarily shadowed by the trumpet vine, and whispered: "Do you really?"

"Yes."

He did not speak. She held her breath, in a tension of blissful suspense. At length he said: "I do too."

"Darling. Darling. I'm glad."

"God," he said, sitting up. "The least move and this damned floor creaks like a haunted house."

She laughed. "What difference does it make?"

"Got to come out here some Saturday with a hammer and some long nails and *secure* the damned thing."

"Who can hear us? And anyway I don't mind. Anyway."

"Neither do I really. Winifred. Darling Winnie. We're going to have that little girl yet. Or that little boy. Do you know that? *Don't* you know that?"

"I believe you mean it, dear Jack. I believe you really do. But gosh. Me, I never expect things like that to happen. It's too much."

"You're a big help, you are."

"Dear Jack. I do want to believe . . ."

"Then believe in me, for Christ's sake."

"All right."

"All right what?"

"I believe in you."

"Then seal it. With 'darling' or something, can't you?"

For answer, she turned her whole body toward him as they lay on the wet floor, put her arms around him, and embraced him passionately and held him that way, as if unwilling ever to let him go.

The moon, a little higher now, a little smaller, but bright as ever (brighter if anything), cast its radiant, unreal, almost too beautiful light on everything below: on the dew-shiny black roller beside the tennis court; on the old-fashioned outdated dovecote empty of doves long since; on the stopped sun dial; on the gleaming leaves of the trumpet vine that were not silver or steel at all, though they looked it now, but were actually green and would be green again tomorrow when the world righted itself; and on the two lovers wrapped in each other's embrace on the warped creaky floor under the flimsy trellis that was banal as a stagesetting which tomorrow would appear in its real guise: a falling-apart, all but tumble-down structure badly in need of repair by a few honest-to-God carpenters in jumpers and aprons, with hammers and nails and fresh boards to put it to rights, if it was worth it.

IN THE SEMI-DARK, marvelously blowy night Winifred Grainger held the wheel on the forward seat next to Jack Sanford, who operated the powerful adjustable spotlight; Harry Harrison and Carol Wilson were huddled against the chill and the spray among a pile of leather pillows in the slightly lower back seat, behind the second windshield; and even as Winifred cut the motor of the broad comfortable launch, not the narrow speedboat this time, that threw out at either side twin sprays of white phosphorescence as a snow plow spreads prodigal wings of bright new-fallen snow, she heard the band playing inside the Yacht Club for the opening dance of the summer season, which always took place on the Fourth of July. As the hissing waters died down, she recognized the tune—slow, low, a heavily accented, throbbing version of "My Man," and it started up in her, not without delightful thrills of a kind of homesickness almost, a swarm of nostalgic memories that went all the way back, oh years, to the children's dances that used to be held on Friday afternoon, with pop-eyed Mrs. Miles clapping her hands and calling out the beat, keeping an anxious eye meanwhile on each child present as if he were retarded. She thought too, with keen pleasure, of the more formal grown-up dances that took place every other Saturday night when she was in her early and mid-teens—but teen-ager or not, she had attended these occasions along with other young boys and girls because her father and mother and their fathers and mothers had been there and that made it All Right. Was this the reason, she wondered idly, why the Yacht Club band always played the same old song hits year after year in preference to the newer later songs—to please the older folk who didn't care for the new numbers and to hold them all together as families? It was expected at the Yacht Club, taken for granted, never questioned. And as she wondered idly about this while bringing the launch skillfully alongside the pier, the answer, or a variation of the same answer, occurred to her of itself: it was a subtle form of flattery on the part of the head steward to the tastes of the old-timers, the fathers and mothers who were the real mainstay and support of the Yacht Club and who always chipped in without a qualm to pay off the heavy annual deficit at the end of the season—what else was old money good for, for heaven's sake?

So perhaps in deference to them the Yacht Club band, however much they might want to try out something new, was impervious to change that would displease. Winifred certainly didn't mind; she loved it in fact: it was part of her growing up and her background. Old and tired though they may be, this evening she was certain to hear again, and again love, "Smiles," "Margie," "When My Baby Smiles at Me," "The Shiek of Araby," the beautiful "Beautiful Faces" with the beautiful lyrics, "Chinatown, My Chinatown," "Mammy," "Stumbling," "The World Is Waiting for the Sunrise," "Japanese Sandman," "Song of India," "Hindustan," "Avalon," "Whispering," and the lot. She had such a fondness for these old tunes, first heard outside in the alley where she fooled around with other kids and ate hot dogs, or while waiting, a little younger, for her parents in the launch itself tied up at the pier till nearly midnight, that she was almost ready to believe that if the Yacht Club band didn't get around tonight to "Dardanella," "I Never Knew" and "They Didn't Believe Me," the evening would be all but ruined. But of course the success of the occasion didn't depend on the music, though the music certainly helped if you responded to the songs of that era as much as she did; for her, it depended on Jack—Handsome Jack, as she felt like calling him tonight, in his white flannels and dark-blue flannel blazer with brass buttons (embellished unfortunately, however, with a hideous embroidered "shield" of gold, red and blue with so-British lions rampant that looked like a phony coat of arms or something, just above the patch pocket on the left breast). It depended too, somewhat, on how much they mixed with the crowd and were "accepted" by them: this, she knew, would mean much to Jack, and to a lesser extent it depended on Harry and Carol. God knows they'd known one another long enough (like brother and sister, she sometimes felt) and they could take care of themselves even if they did nothing but sit around, for Harry and Carol always had plenty to talk about and would enjoy the evening in their own way. Jack she could handle; still, if the Yacht Club dance proved a failure for Harry and Carol, she would feel bad, because they were, after all, her guests for the weekend.

Smooth as a lazy porpoise—or a broad indolent sea lion, rather —the braked launch half slid, half rolled into the slip reserved for it at the side of the Yacht Club, and somebody standing on the pier above caught the white rope she tossed up to him. It turned out to be Chester Hastings, who was waiting there for his date to arrive from Auburn Island in her Kris-Kraft.

"Hi, Winnie," he said—he with whom she had at one time or another shared at least twenty sundaes at the Kandy Kitchen and as many pleasures if not more of another kind in the back seat of his Studebaker or beside it, on a blanket on the ground, under The Pines on dark amorous summer or fall nights—"nice to see you here."

"Hi, Chet."

"I see you've got a date."

"Yes."

"I'm waiting for mine. Marian Williams—father's a big trial lawyer in Rochester."

"Bully for you."

" 'Bully'—I haven't heard that word since kid days."

"Neither have I."

"Don't see you around this place much any more," he said.

"Well, after all, it's only the first dance of the season."

"Yeah, thass right, thass right—and am I rarin' to go!"

"Chet," she said in a loud clear voice, as the wobbling launch steadied itself, enabling her to stand up, "this is my guest, Jack Sanford. Jack, Chet Hastings." She couldn't resist it: "My boat-man."

"Boatman hell. She's a great kidder, you know. But nice to meet you, sir. Hi, Harry. Hi, Carol. Say, how's old Yale these days, Harry? Understand you're taking up architecture or something."

As Carol first, helped by Chet's outstretched hand, climbed up the short straight ladder to the floor of the pier above, followed by Harry Harrison, Winifred turned to Jack Sanford with a grin and said under her breath: "Did you hear him call you 'sir'? So you *are* forty-five, after all."

"Too old for you, then."

"I've had older," she said casually.

"Hey! What goes here!"

"I'm kidding," she said.

"Anyway I got the 'sir.' But I feel fifty-five when I look at that

sophomoric adolescent masquerading as a man. Not even dry behind the ears."

"Listen! You're thirty-five to me, the very prime of a man's life.
I wouldn't have you a single day younger or a day older."

"You liked me all right yesterday, didn't you? And gee, what am
I going to do about tomorrow?"

"Oh shut up. I'm just trying to tell you I love you. It's always a
great mistake . . ."

Almost the first person Winifred Grainger recognized as she
passed by the orchestra stand with Jack Sanford in tow and entered the large room where the dance had been in progress for
almost an hour (the tune, wouldn't you know, was her old favorite, "I Never Knew," which she accepted at once as the perfect
omen) was Betty Finletter, dancing at the moment with Stan
Hewitt. She was wearing a severely simple sleeveless dress of pale
pink shantung with a green belt, and her blue-black hair was
bound with two narrow grosgrain ribbons of pale green and pink,
tied in a small bow on top of her head. She was not tall, and as she
danced she had an attractive way of arching her slim body far back
and looking up at her partner's face with the keenest attention, half
smiling with a kind of alert pleasure, as though he was the most
fascinating man in the world and she the luckiest dame to have
been asked to dance with him. The figure was perfect, supple, trim,
very slender—the figure of a young girl, half her age in fact, for
Betty Finletter must have been thirty at least. Winifred, who was
realistically aware that her own hips were an inch or more too
broad, her waist too thick fore and aft, envied and admired the
impression Betty Finletter gave of being able to wear clothes without having to think whether they were right or wrong. Anything
became her; and she could no more imagine Betty Finletter trying
on one dress after another before the mirror than she could picture
herself reaching into the closet and picking out a dress, any dress,
without thought.

She felt a hand on her shoulder, another around her waist.

"What are we waiting for?" Jack Sanford asked.

She turned and raised her arms to him and they moved forward
onto the dance floor. The trap-man was subtly whisking the snare
drum with a loose wire flyswatter; the clarinetist, standing,

apostrophized the ceiling as if in an ecstasy; the pianist with his beautiful teeth like pearls richer than all his tribe gave a little flirtatious smile to anyone who passed by. " '*I* never *knew* . . . I could . . . love anybody . . . honey like I'm . . . lovin' you,' " Jack Sanford half whispered, half sang in her ear; and to her surprise she wished he wouldn't: it sounded so old-fashioned, somehow, so much like a date who wasn't used to all this. She didn't doubt his pleasure in the music; she felt that it equaled or matched her own; but in an inexplicable way his exhibitionism of that very pleasure somewhat killed it for her. But such a reaction only made her dislike herself, not him. Why shouldn't he sing the damned song if he wanted to? she argued with wordless loyalty.

Harry Harrison and Carol were nearby, moving slowly, holding each other at arms length and looking directly into each other's faces, and the impression they gave was that they were not so much dancing as having one of their interminable conversations.

In a corner, Herb Finletter and a couple of his bachelor cronies were matching pennies on the surface of a small table—or maybe dimes or quarters. Spontaneous bursts of hilarity came from the trio now and then, and a hand slapped down hard on the table, while two other hands dug into pants pockets for more change.

Most of her mother's and father's friends were present, Winifred noticed: one of the "very nice things" about the Yacht Club dance at the Point (which was also true of the twice-a-month Saturday-night dances at the Country Club in Arcadia) was that the parents attended these parties in force, fully as much as the younger generation, and often seemed not only to outnumber but even to be having a better time than their offspring.

Every few minutes some girl or young woman pointedly leaned away from her partner and exclaimed with patronizing brightness: "Winifred *Grain*ger, where on earth have you been!" or "Don't tell me it's our old Winnie come up for air. Grand to see you!"

She glanced upward at Jack Sanford with a sheepish grin. "Anybody would think I'd come back from the dead."

"Yeah, what *is* this?" he said. "What's it all about?"

"Nothing new. Anyway you noticed it yourself at the Country Club dance."

"I did, and I don't get it. All this welcome!"

"It's not important. Only you can be damned sure they're not all that glad to see me."

"Why shouldn't they be? I'd be, if I were them—or they or whatever it is."

"I said it's not important, now forget it."

And it wasn't important. But secretly she couldn't help being pleased—oh, not because they spoke to her and seemed so glad to "have her back," but because of Jack's reaction of irritation at their solicitude, and still more, because here she was, at the Yacht Club dance now, and last week at the Country Club dance, with a date of her own. It had been a long time since she had been invited to affairs of this sort, and of course she knew, and accepted, the reason why: local young men couldn't "afford" to be seen in public with Winifred Grainger, especially a social occasion of this kind. Everybody in town knew her, of course, and liked her enough in their way; but public dances, where respectable people gathered, were out. Now she was back, and she felt a real curiosity in the air around her as to what was going on—maybe she wasn't so bad after all, maybe she had changed her ways—and who was this attractive man anyway? The waxed mustaches might have provoked a suppressed smile or two, here and there, but at least Winifred Grainger was circulating socially again and had acquired a man who cared about her enough to be seen with her publicly—twice now—at functions that were bound to be widely hashed over the next day: a ritual in Arcadia, so much so that it almost seemed their sole value was the topic they afforded for gossip and discussion at tomorrow's breakfast, tomorrow's luncheon, tomorrow's cocktail party, or wherever two or three people were gathered together—in offices, on the golf course, in the magazine store; when they pulled up alongside one another's cars and to hell with the people behind them; and most certainly tomorrow night at Tony di Santo's. But Winifred Grainger was happy, even at the prospect of being talked about: it would be, for her, a *new* way of being talked about. And she was aware—but characteristically wondered if she only imagined it—of a new status or position in the social group, of being an interesting curiosity, and sensed a kind of "approval." When at one point in the early evening Betty Finletter passed by with a dancing partner, for instance,

Betty gave her a genuinely beaming smile, a warm and cordial smile; and though Betty had never known her that well, she called out in the friendliest fashion, as though she meant it—as though it gave her pleasure to say it: "Hi, Winifred, old dear. Come and *see* us!"

Pleased, she clung closer but not ostentatiously—it was not in her to make herself conspicuous in public—to Jack Sanford. She put her cheek against his as they danced and sang quietly, barely audible: " 'I . . . can't sleep . . . I . . . can't eat . . . I nev-er knew a single soul could be so . . . swee-eet . . .' "

Jack Sanford said: "I love that tune too, but I've got to tell you: I don't like people who sing when they dance."

"Neither do I, isn't that funny? Because you were singing it a minute ago, and I found myself inwardly cringing for you."

"Did I really? And did you?"

"You did, and I did."

"Awful! Let's make a pact: no singing from now on while we're dancing."

"Like the talking, remember? How you said one night we could talk ourselves right out of anything?"

"Oh, that was before anything had . . . I mean it's not the same thing, but okay anyway. No singing! Shake?"

"I'm shaking as it is, like a leaf."

"Why?"

"Oh, happiness, love, you, stage fright, the Fourth of July—a million things."

"That's my girl. I like people who are keyed up, who don't go around blasé as all hell taking everything for granted."

"That I never do."

"Good. Do you know something else? I even admire a girl who can blush."

"Me, I blush all the time—not that I'm proud of it. It's awful for a minute or two. And the more you try to stop . . ."

"Blush over what?"

"Not the kind of things you're thinking."

"How do you know what I'm thinking?"

"I blush over the most ordinary attentiveness, or attention, and sometimes if somebody unexpectedly says 'Thank you' or is kind

. . . And God, if anyone goes so far as to give me a present or even *compl*iment me, I about die."

"Now we're getting gushy."

"Aren't we though? No talking, and no singing."

A moment later they were both singing together: " 'I never re-alized what a pair of . . . eyes . . . and a baby smile could do . . .' " When they heard themselves, heard each other, they laughed together in delight and quit the dance floor for the bar inside.

But in a moment he was up, as Harry Harrison and Carol Wilson came in. "Carol, *puis j'avoir cette danse, s'il vous plaît?*"

"I guess I know what you mean, and I'd love to." They left to go back to the dance floor, and Harry took a chair at a small table with Winifred.

"Tell me," he said.

"Tell you what?"

"Why, everything."

"Jack Sanford?"

"What else? Is he the guy?"

"I think so."

"Or just *a* guy."

"It's more than that."

"Happy about it?"

"I'll tell you later."

"When?"

"When I know."

"You don't know now?"

"Jack is new. He's only been here a short time. Month and a half at most."

"But you love him already."

"Oh yes. It doesn't take that long to fall in love. I love him, no doubt about that."

"I know. I can see it in your face."

"Do I show it that much? Just a green girl, simpering and preening and chewing her braids."

"But he's got to love you too."

"Oh no he doesn't. I never weigh these matters: how much do I love someone and how much do they love me back. Me, I don't think about it. I never think of who's going to get it in the end."

"It might be you," he said.

"It very often has been. But this will be very nice while it lasts. It's nice now."

"Winnie, you really sound in love."

"I am. And though I may be fooling myself, I believe Jack's fallen for me a little, too. Quite a novel experience," she said, lighting a cigarette as casually as possible.

"Look who's watching us," he said, lowering his voice, "from that banquette over there. Stern disapproval written all over her face. Typical."

"Who?" she said, turning. "Oh, Isabel Barton that-was. Our once dear friend Isabel. We were all such pals, growing up together. Well, nothing surprises me any more. Nothing."

"Who's she so disapproving of? Me?"

"You know better, Harry. And it isn't even me. It's Jack *and* me."

"Does Isabel know him?"

"No. That's why. What right have I to get a nice man like that—doesn't he know about me, hasn't he *heard?* Silly bitch. But actually I pity her, feel sorry for her."

"Winifred, are you sleeping with this guy?"

"What do you think? Come off it, Harry."

"I hope he's going to be good for you."

"He is now is all that counts. I don't believe in tempting fate by asking for more than that."

"But if he loves you?"

"I'm not really sure; I only hope he does. Oh, why do women have to go around weeping and wailing 'Does he love me?' What about *them?* Isn't it enough that *they* love—if they do? *I* never thought of it as a fifty-fifty-proposition-or-I-won't-play."

"Well, I can only say I'm glad for you," he said.

"I'm glad too. But keep your fingers crossed."

"It's so much better . . . I mean, it sounds really good."

"I know what you were going to say. 'Better than sleeping around with every Tom, Dick or Harry.' Pardon the expression."

"I couldn't be more flattered."

Carol came in from the dance floor and joined them.

"What happened to your partner?"

"We were cut in on by Chet Hastings. That child, that absolute child! It seems his girl never did show up from Auburn Island. And after a few minutes I had had enough, so I said I was tired. Funny, everybody used to seem so nice in the old days. I've enjoyed Chet Hastings' company many a time, and so have we all. But something seems to happen to people. Is this what comes from going away to college?"

"Not necessarily. Some of us grow up, some of us don't."

"What happened to himself," Winifred asked, "when Chet cut in on you?"

"Himself? Oh, Jack. Why, he just roamed around, looking the place over. He's attractive, Winnie. Personality all over the place."

"Yeah, he's got personality, all right. Plus a waxed mustache straight out of the movies. Like Lew Cody."

"I think it's cute," Carol said. "It takes a man with a lot of individuality and self-confidence to wear a thing like that. I admire him for it."

"Even though you don't like it."

"I didn't say that."

A blur of pale pink moving backward past the door of the dance hall caught Winifred Grainger's eye, and she saw that that personality, that individual with so much self-confidence, was dancing with Betty Finletter. Betty was leaning back and looking up at him as if entranced, but genuinely so; he was smiling as he talked, with raised eyebrows, and Winifred knew he was being his most charming self which, when it was good, was damned good just as Betty Finletter was. There was nothing phony about either one of them; they were two attractive people, bringing out the best in each other. She watched this without comment, admiringly even; and Carol and Harry rose from their small table to go back to the dance.

She felt a hand on her shoulder, friendly, paternal, but with the subtle pressure of a caress, so practiced that no one else, watching, would have noticed it.

"Where have you been, Winnie dear?"

She looked up without surprise into Cal Cunningham's handsome face, beaming down at her over his dark-blue polka-dot bow tie; he was wearing an immaculate white linen suit.

"Oh, nowhere. Just around."

"May I sit down for a sec?"

"It's a free country."

He took the wicker armchair with the cretonne padding next to hers.

"Why don't you come and see me any more, like old times? Or give me a ring? I'm at the office every night. Business as usual. Alone."

"Waiting for me?"

"I wouldn't say that, exactly. But it would be mighty nice. It always has been. Hasn't it?"

She didn't answer.

"I always thought you enjoyed it as much as I did. In fact I know you did, when I think of certain things." For the benefit of any possible onlooker, the expression on his face was calculatedly indifferent, as though he were talking about nothing more important or interesting than the weather.

"I did."

"Can't we go on with it? It's been five or six months now, Winnie. I've missed you."

"Cal, I'm not going to say I didn't enjoy what we did together. I still think of it occasionally, even. But Cal, it was just that and nothing more."

"And what's wrong with that?"

"Nothing. But I've been busy."

"Too busy for me? You never have been before, Winnie."

"I am now."

Two couples went by. "Hi, Winifred. Hi, Cal." They were gaily dressed, in a happy mood, they knew everybody, were having a good time, were popular. They were on their way to the dance floor, where the band was now playing "Avalon." Across the way, Isabel Barton kept up a running fire of gossip with an attractive man of thirty-five or forty, who had once picked up Winifred in his car and brought her home two hours later, but every few minutes she remembered to throw a watchful glance in their direction. If people only knew, Winifred Grainger thought ironically, what's being said at this table, this minute, while all around us . . .

"I see," Calvin Cunningham said with an air of brightness. "It's this new person you came with tonight."

"Cal, don't confuse him with you, or vice versa. It isn't the same."

"I understand."

"I hope you do."

"But when this wears off," he added with a friendly, neighborly smile, "I'll be waiting for you. Will you remember?"

She glanced down at the surface of the table, fingered a scalloped paper napkin, thinking: Funny thing is, I may even take him up on it, one of these days. She said: "You ought not to be sitting here, Cal."

"Why not?"

"Oh, I don't know. I guess it doesn't make any difference. At this late date."

"I have the right. We do know each other, Winnie. After all!"

"I'll say . . ."

"I see you're in a very bad mood. Or was."

"Far from it. I'm in a very good mood. Or was."

"In that case—"

"Yes, just move on, Cal. Don't interfere. Good night."

He stood up, gave her head a fatherly pat—inwardly it made her cringe far more than if he had frankly leaned down and kissed her—and went in to the dance.

She watched him go—watched Isabel Barton watching her watching him go—and in the outlines of the well-tailored white linen suit he wore, over the hefty but remarkably good figure, in the blue-black hair, the confident walk, the hands slightly spread at his side and the fingers open as if he received everything in the world (and everybody) with a tactile sensual touch, she was aware, with feelings of mingled titillation and self-disgust, of all that she had experienced through him, all that he had so often made her feel and might yet again. A father figure, the modern psychologist would call it; but he was anything but a father when they lay together, nights, on the wide couch in his inner office.

Momentarily the music stopped, and Jack Sanford returned with Harry and Carol.

"I hear there's going to be fireworks!" he said.

"Always, at the opening dance."

"They've got a big raft or barge, towed out into the bay maybe half a mile offshore, and they're going to go off any minute now. Ten o'clock, someone said."

"Who?"

"I think it was the band leader. I was talking with him between numbers."

"I'll need my coat. It's chilly out on the pier."

"I'll get them," Harry said. "Come on, Carol."

When they were alone together: "I didn't know you knew Betty Finletter," Winifred said, and immediately wished she hadn't mentioned it.

"I don't, really. What makes you think I do?"

"I saw you dancing together."

"Yes. It seems to be that kind of party. That Hastings sap cut in on Carol and me, and I walked around and saw others doing the same, so I cut in on Betty Finletter."

"Did you enjoy it?"

"Very much."

"I've never seen her look more attractive than she does tonight. I don't know her well, but I think she's nice."

"*I* thought so. Wonder what her husband's like?"

"Oh, he has his cronies, and they play cards and horse around and shoot crap and stuff. Too much money is his trouble. Nothing to do."

Harry and Carol returned with the coats, and they followed the crowd, already gathering, to move out onto the pier. They pressed toward the front. Jack Sanford lifted Carol up to stand on one of the thick square beams (they always smelled of oil, somehow) that marked the front end of the pier, and stood there holding her, with his arm around her waist, at the very edge. Harry and Winifred stood beside them, with linked arms; all four had a clear view of the bay in front of them, still dark except for a few dim low lights, promising activities to come, on the large flat barge that had been towed out into the water, fronting the Yacht Club.

In the crowd around them, waiting for the fireworks, many facetious derisive comments could be heard, belittling the spectacle in advance; but when the display began, starting off as always with a single high rocket that ended, as pink and green sparks fell slowly toward the water, with an unexpectedly loud *booom* like a thunderclap, the same thing happened that always happens on such occasions, despite the compulsive sophistication of the crowd: unanimous cries of "Ah-h!" involuntarily soaring up in sudden spontaneous chorus, then sinking in a slow descending scale, to be followed again and again by "Oh, look at that one!" and "Look at *that* one!" as a piddling series of Roman candles shot slowly up into the dark sky: preamble, after the initial rocket, to the pyrotechnics that were to follow.

The silhouettes of three or four men could be vaguely distinguished moving about among the few low lights on the barge, and as they went about their dangerous work Jack Sanford, holding Carol on the broad plank, turned and gave Winifred a grin of frank delight, then reached back and took her hand. He squeezed it affectionately, and somehow the pressure of the crowd around them and their own solidarity among all these "strangers" made his nearness dearer to her. She experienced feelings of their belonging together that could not have been as real if they had been alone: it was almost as if they had been married for years and had been through much together that gave them secret mutual understandings of each other that could never change now and break apart and be meaningless. It was as if they did not even have to speak to each other to know what each was thinking and feeling; and they did not.

A sudden small flare on the barge, a sudden movement of a bent-over figure hastily stepping out of the danger zone, and a long, slow, wobbly half-seen streak soared slowly aloft. "Ah-h-h" and "Ooh-h" cried the crowd, involuntarily, as the dark sky overhead was split open by a down-thrust spray of vermilion sparks, accompanied a moment later by a volley of pop-pop-popping; then a spray of white-green lights a little higher, with the same faint tattoo of small explosions while the beautiful colored lights floated down and went out one by one; and then a third burst of gas-blue lights, higher up, topping everything ("Ooh-h . . ." and "Ah-h-h . . ."), climaxed, as the last fading spark drifted indolently toward the bay, by a single blinding white flash with a shuddering detonation that actually made the boards of the pier floor tremble or seem to. "Oh, look at that one," "Oh, look at that one!" the cries went up again and again, as if the crowd had never seen fireworks before, and Jack Sanford pulled Winifred closer to him with his free hand and held her as though they were watching together, with breathless admiration, the first revelations of a brilliant doomsday approaching.

When it all ended, with a wild barrage of exploding color and deafening reports as half a dozen pieces went off together, a series of reverberating explosions in the night sky indicating that now all was over, they turned to one another with expressions of disbelief on their faces, each one speechless to express what he felt or had felt. A woman somewhere behind them was heard to utter clearly, for clearly she wanted to be heard: "Well, I've seen better"; and no one troubled to comment on her remark.

Not long after, for there seemed little reason for staying longer now, the four of them were in the launch again, homeward-bound across the dark bay toward the bar, and curiously silent. Winifred kept the motor to a minimum—barely enough to keep afloat, it seemed—as if they had all the time in the world. Now and again they passed red or green lanterns hung on the bobbing mast of an anchored sloop or lark, and in the distance under the starlit sky could be seen the shadowy floating masses of Auburn Island and Sodus Island—and miles away the faint lights of Lake Bluff which seemed to hang in the sky, because of the few cottages on the cliff's edge where people were still up. Finally the feathery cottonwoods strung at sparse intervals along the bar appeared ahead; Winifred brought the launch into the wide slip at the boathouse all but silently, and they were home.

The Grainger cottage was not a great shapeless barn like most of the others. Neat and compact, in better taste, it was painted white inside; there were nautical touches such as a ship's clock, a "wheel" from a long since submerged lake steamer, and a white looped rope that went up the stairway in place of a banister to the four bedrooms above. A white rope carpet covered the whole of the living-room floor, and Agnes the cook, who slept downstairs in a room off the kitchen, had spread out on the flat table, under the hanging ship's brass lantern of thick ribbed glass, an array of bottles and an ice bucket in case they wanted nightcaps, and two plates of sandwiches wrapped in wax paper.

"Good old Aggie. Anybody want to eat, or drink?"

"No thanks."

"Well, you two know where your rooms are. Or room is."

"We know," Carol said noncommittally.

"Well, you'll excuse us? I might as well come out with it. I made a deal with Jonesey to stay over at the Point tonight so Jack and I could use his room at the boathouse. That's why I drove the launch instead of Jonesey. Hope you don't mind our not staying in the cottage. We're leaving it all for you."

"I haven't heard a thing," Carol said as she started up the stairs, her hand on the loose white rope.

"I suppose it does look pretty bad," Winifred said as she pulled off her clothes in the dingy long room upstairs in the boathouse.

"On the contrary. I'd say you were giving them every break."

"It may be a break they don't want."

"That I can't imagine."

"Harry Harrison isn't like you. Or Carol like me. Life is very complex, sometimes," she said, "for some people."

"God what a joint this is. There isn't even a proper bathroom. And that exposed overhead light bulb . . ."

"We'll soon have it turned off, and then it will be just as good as anywhere. Heaven exists in the dark."

"I'm afraid I'm one of those guys who likes his creature comforts."

"Did you really want to sleep in the cottage? Why didn't you *say* so?"

"Why do you want to sleep out here?"

"Associations, call it. And it doesn't matter where I sleep, as long as we're together."

"We'll be together in that single cot, all right. It's like fitting yourself, along with somebody else, into a beached canoe."

"Listen, you," she said, not at all displeased, "I'm not just 'somebody else.' "

She slept marvelously in that narrow groove of a bed, and when she woke it was to find herself wrapped comfortably, as if from long habit, in Jack's arms.

"My darling," she said, low. "Are you awake?"

"Awake! Good God, how could I sleep?"

"That's fine. You're not supposed to sleep when you sleep with me. Oh, Jack, I do love you so. I love lying so close to you, being so much a part of you."

"So do I."

"We *are* one, aren't we?"

"As much as two people can be. Now remember our old maxim. No talk."

"Okay. I won't even murmur or moan, or cry out."

"But I like it when you do," he said.

"I don't do it on purpose. In fact sometimes I'm not even aware of it. It's something I can't help."

"Wait a second. I've got to pee."

"Use the window. It's all right, there's nobody around this early."

He went to the single window at the end of the narrow room and stood there a few seconds. Then she heard his water falling into the bay just below, loud, like a horse wheeing.

When he came back and crawled into bed, she said, "My, I'm proud of you."

"Why?"

"I loved hearing it. I even wanted to get up and stand beside you and watch you doing it."

"Why didn't you, if it meant all that much?"

"I thought, somehow, you wouldn't like it. Men don't, you know."

"Don't they? I wouldn't know." He smiled. "You're not only a child, you're a very re*tard*ed child."

"Now you've found me out. You'll know just exactly what to expect from me from now on."

"Oh no I won't. You're never the same. The things you are, and do!"

When they came into the cottage at nine-thirty, Carol Wilson and Harry Harrison were just finishing breakfast. Harry looked up brightly, and brightly called out: "Good morning!"

Winifred didn't need to look from one to the other to get it:

something was wrong. Something had gone amiss, or there had been a misunderstanding, or even a quarrel.

Harry's bright expression and cordiality belied this—belied it and at the same time gave him away. "We've already been out," he said. "Think of it, we took a walk along the beach before having coffee, even."

"You must be crazy."

"Oh, we're crazy all right," he said gaily.

Carol said nothing.

"I've wanted to walk to the Bluff ever since I first saw the place," Jack Sanford said. "Will you take me, Carol?"

She looked up at him with a shy, womanly smile and said, "I'd be glad to."

"Nothing doing," Winifred said. "At least not now. Breakfast first."

After they had gone, Winifred said to Harry: "Tell me."

"Tell you what?"

"Whatever happened? Something happened."

"You're imagining things. It's that overactive imagination of yours, that insatiable curiosity, that sees things that aren't there."

"I forgot. You were never one to talk, were you, Harry? So I apologize."

"There's nothing to apologize for."

"Whereas," she went on, "if anything happened to me, or happened between Jack and me as obviously has happened to you and poor Carol, I'd be the first to tell you."

"Why do you say 'poor Carol'?"

"Because she's unhappy."

"She'll be okay."

"Then I *was* right. Something did happen."

"Winifred, will you lay off, please? It's of no importance. Carol's all right. And so am I. We've had a *very* good *time*. We slept like logs, thanks to those very good beds, among other things."

"So did we, even though the bed wasn't that good by a long shot. But it couldn't have mattered less. It never does."

THE TALL ROW of very thick dark pines that lined one side of the bypassed road just beyond Asylum Hill—a side road, never used for traffic nowadays, beautiful and quiet, like something out of the past—they sat wrapped together here in the back seat of the old Marmon and listened to the haunting soughing and deep sighing of the wind in the branches. On the quietest, most windless night, the trees were never still; it was like the sound that emerges from the pink curling recesses of a conch shell when you put it to your ear: the sound of the sea, it is said. Same here: the breeze, even the slightest zephyr, moving among the dark massed pines, gave to those parked in the few cars below—four cars tonight, widely separated, and each with its lights off—a continuous music as of distant surf. It was lovely to hear, to give oneself up to: no other sound anywhere but the melancholy sighing and soughing somewhere above them in the dark, an accompaniment to love, and solitude, that was magical, mysterious, promising, all those foolish and, under the circumstances, empty words.

"Tell me," Winifred whispered, "what's wrong?"

"Wrong? Nothing's wrong. I'm happy."

"Something's on your mind."

"Only you."

"Lord, what an answer—when you're not with me at all."

"How could I be closer to you? I could hardly hold you more lovingly."

"Sorry. I only wondered."

He was silent for a time. Then: "If it's anything, it's only the whisper of the pines. It fascinates me. But it's deeper than a whisper; it's like the restless unquiet waves on a lonely beach. Our beach. We do have a beach, you know. Ours."

"We do."

"And isn't it ours? Yours and mine?"

"Who else's?"

They were silent again, listening to the pines. He stroked her hair, her cheek, her neck, reached into her blouse. She kept her hand flat on his chest, under his jacket, pressing against him.

"You know this isn't such a bad town," he said. "People *are* nice. And friendly."

"The right people can be, with the right people."

"Maybe you malign them a little. People here are really rather nice."

"Go on."

"Go on?"

"You're trying to tell me something."

"Not really. Only, well, somebody called me at the office this afternoon and asked me to drop in for tea. I thought it was very nice and friendly, because it was so unexpected."

"Who was she?"

"Does it have to be a 'she'? You women!"

"Don't be an ass, Jack. Do men do those things?"

"Yeah, you're right. Well, it was Isabel Barton, if you must know."

"Look here, I don't have to know at all. It's your business."

"What concerns me concerns you, doesn't it? Doesn't it? Isn't that the way it's got to be? And vice versa."

"Did you go?"

"Of course I went. Shouldn't I?"

"Why shouldn't you? Dear Jack, *I* don't care what you do."

"Well, you ought to care."

"Really," she said, "there's no pleasing you. Whatever I say is the wrong thing. Why are you so obtuse? I'm only too glad you're getting *around*. That's what you wanted, isn't it?"

"Naturally I want to meet people and have a sense of belonging in this dump."

"Well, Isabel Barton has helped you get a good start."

"Catty as all hell, aren't you? Women!"

"You're repeating yourself now, my friend. And I'm not catty. Isabel is someone I've known and grown up with."

"That's what she said. She likes you."

"Don't believe that for a second. I'm frank to admit I don't like her *at all*. Oh, for Christ's sake, Jack, what's it all about?"

"Nothing. If it had been anything 'out of the way,' I wouldn't have told you, would I?"

"Oh, I don't know. There are ways to disarm, and 'frankness' is one of them."

"Now look. She just wanted to meet Winifred Grainger's new friend. The new man in town. New men are a scarcity apparently."

"Who else was there? I really wouldn't ask, but it was you who brought it up."

"Nobody."

"*No*body. A tea?"

"Why should there be? Maybe the others couldn't come."

"Like me, for instance."

"Okay, I'll shut up in the future."

"So there's going to be more."

"I have no idea."

After a silence Winifred said, "Jack, the reason I'm surprised is because nobody else was there. Isabel Barton is married, Jack."

"I know that. Her name is Dunning. I didn't know you were such a puritan."

"Damn it, that's one thing you certainly know I'm not! Don't you?"

"Her husband has already left her and her kid."

"Poor Isabel . . ."

"Go ahead, be catty as you like, but she has no designs on me. I can certainly reassure you of that."

"I believe you. She has designs on me."

"Now what's that supposed to mean?"

"Oh, let's forget it," Winifred said. "It isn't important one way or the other." She held back the tears, tears of anger with herself mostly. She loved Jack Sanford; damn it, she was in love with him. And she could so well understand how a personable young man coming to Arcadia, and through her meeting scarcely anyone else . . . She sensed his dilemma, she pitied him for it, and even though she felt certain of what lay behind Isabel Barton's invitation to tea, she loved him because he (it was only human after all) hadn't been able to resist; and it was also only too human of him now to feel guilty of that innocent tea date and bridle at everything she said. Isabel had no designs on him, as such; as far as men were concerned Isabel was a cold fish and managed, whether she meant to or not, to drive them away. But Isabel was an operator, a rigid maintainer of the *status quo*, and Winifred knew she must have felt it her *duty* to wise up Jack Sanford and put him on the right track socially, even if it involved the sad duty of revealing, oh so reluctantly, a few details of Winifred's past. Poor Jack; if he loved her, how did he take these tidbits? Was he shocked, thrown off, hurt?

And was it his fault if an interfering female dropped a word or two of sound advice in his ear, the implications of which were most certainly that Jack's career would be circumscribed in Arcadia to say the least if he continued to go around with a girl of Winifred Grainger's reputation? It was a test of love that many men would find hard to weather. She only wondered, with pity and love for his helplessness (certainly *he* hadn't expected or wanted such a thing), how much Isabel had said in her practiced oblique way that had registered with him. Probably very little; Jack was so outgoing himself, so eager to enjoy life and enjoy people and belong in Arcadia, that Isabel's subtle invidious hints might well have gone right over his head. Hadn't he even told her about it himself, quite needlessly? But there had been a faint trace of sheepishness underlying the story; and the fact that he felt even this much guilt (if guilt it was) made him pitiable in her eyes, and even more lovable, or at least needing love. There was nothing wrong, nothing wrong at all, so long as she loved him and he loved her. Of her love for him she hadn't the slightest doubt. But besides that love, her faith in Jack, her trust and belief in him, had grown the deeper, the more secure as the weeks passed.

"Jack, come here. I want you. I always want you."

"Yeah, I've been wondering why all the talk. In a place like this, with that lovely sound in the pines? There probably isn't a word being said in any other of these cars along here. And I'm talking too much right now."

Together they slid into the corner of the wide back seat; after a while they took the car robe and moved out onto the grass. Overhead the sighing pines accompanied their love-making with the most haunting, the most melancholy music. It was the perfect music for love, unobtrusive but very much there, like a perfume, like the night, like the very breath and breathing of their mounting passion.

NIGHT; very late. The curling surf was by turns a dull silver-gray, like pewter, then a striking many-colored iridescence like colored glass tumbling over and over as the beacon from the lighthouse just beyond Charles Point momentarily swept the beach, its rapidly passing beam mingling with the lifeless but clear white light that shone down on the beach from the bedrooms above, where Belle Grainger lay in one room alternately reading and dozing off, wondering, when she thought of it, when those two were ever going to come to bed, and where Lyman Grainger, solely out of duty as a parent and father after all, still kept his light on, though he had long since forgotten the world and all its creatures, not least of them Winifred, who, he often thought during wakeful troubled moments, should be very much on his mind, though she hardly ever was.

Jack Sanford and Winifred Grainger lay side by side in the sand; they had scooped up and packed around them on the windward side a small wall of sand to protect them from the breeze and spray that blew in from off Ontario; but on a late July night it was never all that cold; and far less than the chill or spray they minded—yet enjoyed it, too, and laughed softly to themselves about it—the sudden gusts of sand that blew from off the top of their low battlement and stung their faces and sprinkled their bare abdomens, got into their hair and sometimes their eyes, and reminded them generally that they were intruders on the natural element of the beach and the sea and that their proper places were upstairs, in the house and in bed, where everybody else was supposed to be at this God-forsaken (and beach-forsaken) hour.

"Winnie," he murmured in her ear, and though she heard him clearly enough she didn't really take in the gist of what he was saying for a moment or two, "going to be awfully busy these next few weeks. Can't have any real dates. Unless we make it very late at night. And I mean late."

"How late?"

"Oh, twelve. One. Something like that."

"But you don't work such hours!"

"I will be working those hours for a few weeks to come."

She knew what he was trying to tell her, but she helped him out loyally. "That's not fair. After working all day, why should you . . . How could they expect you to stay so late at night?"

"It's this new line we're putting in. I designed the whole thing.

Very radical change. And most of the fellows I can't get to see, to look it over, till way after hours."

"I understand."

"Can I come and see you very late?"

"Of course."

"No matter what the hour?"

"I love you, Jack."

"And I love you. I wish you knew how much."

She laughed, to save the situation. "I wish I did."

He raised up on an elbow, and sand slid off his belly. "What are you doing, making fun of me?"

"Of me, if anyone."

"Well, I'll be coming round as usual, even if it is late, and we'll get what we can."

"Good God."

"Sorry. I don't think I'm the crude type, really. But you know what I mean."

"I do. And why do we bother?"

"Bother? Why shouldn't we bother?"

"I mean when it's late and you have to work in the morning."

"Because I need this too. And," he added, "I love you."

She was silent.

"Don't you?"

" 'Need it'?" she echoed. "Yes, I guess I do."

"That's not what I mean and you know it."

"We'll be quarreling in a minute if we don't watch out," she said, "without even meaning to." She laughed. "And it's no fun quarreling or anything when you're half naked with sand all over you, and bits of clothes to scrounge around for in the dark."

"I'm not quarreling. I love you too much for that."

"I love you, Jack."

"You'll never know how much I need and want you and love you. With all my heart, with everything I am."

She knew he was lying in his teeth now, and she placed her palms flat on his shieldlike breast. She loved him, she wanted him, she never wanted to see him go; but that day, she felt sure, was not far off now . . . Unless he just wanted to come around and have her when he had the time and felt like it. Even that, because she had no pride in the matter, she wouldn't mind; it was better than nothing.

The lighthouse beacon swept the beach, always too rapidly, and was gone again, so that, leaning over and toward him, she was unable to look into his eyes. A few feet away the breakers slammed and slid up the sloping black smooth sand, smooth as a dance floor, toward the piled-up small hillocks of sand above. As always, no matter whom she was with, no matter even if she was alone, the beach at night and the tumbling glassy surf and the hurried sweeping beacon created a magic that, though she had seen and felt it hundreds of times before, would be always new, hundreds of times again.

A WEEK or two later, on a Saturday noon in early August, Harry Harrison and Winifred Grainger, both of them momentarily self-conscious from the lifted looks that arose from the surrounding tables, followed the white-jacketed steward to the table that Harry had reserved for luncheon on the wide verandah of the Country Club, overlooking the beautifully kept golf course, the paper mill below, and, beyond, the gleaming eight rails of the New York Central Railroad, curving in a wide arc a little more than a mile away, intercepting the much traveled road to Lyons, eight miles to the east, so that many times during the day, and just as often at night (when you were more aware of it in the stillness of your bed), the scream of whistles of through-trains to Chicago and beyond could be heard throughout Arcadia—a lovely sound at night: all her life, it seemed, Winifred had lain in bed at home and listened to the fast express trains as they went through town, the passengers and the engineers alike probably unaware that there was even a town called Arcadia on the map at all, it came and went so quickly, and of course the through-trains never stopped there; the shriek of the whistles always made Winifred think of the great world beyond, had done so since early childhood, and did so still. To one with imagination, a thrilling and stimulating sound in the night.

They sat down at the small table that had been reserved for

them and picked up their menus in silence. Harry Harrison and Winifred Grainger, friends from childhood who it seemed had spent most of their lives talking to each other about everything under the sun, also had moments together when they scarcely spoke at all: it was that kind of intimate comfortable friendship and they were so used to it they scarcely noticed or even appreciated it. This was one of those moments of silence, for a while at least. She passed up the offer of a cocktail and ordered Vichyssoise, tomato stuffed with chicken salad, and iced coffee: a typical lady's lunch or a lady's typical lunch, though Winifred Grainger was hardly "typical."

"Not very imaginative, I'm afraid," she said as she put the *carte* aside. "But that's our Club for you, and it's enough for me."

"As long as you ordered what you want," he said. He greeted the waiter. "Hi, Johnnie," he said; they had all three known one another in high school. "I'll have madrilene and plain chicken salad, lots of mayonnaise."

"Okay, Harry, thanks. Nice to see you both. Anything to drink?"

"No thanks. Well, iced tea, maybe."

"Okay, coming up," and he went off to the kitchen.

Left to themselves, Winifred looked across at Harry, so correct and immaculate as always, and her smile was self-deprecating, the corners of her mouth turned down, as if she were embarrassed. Luncheon at the Club was a very rare occurrence for either of them.

"What's so funny?"

"Nothing's funny. I'm happy as a lark. It's just that you shouldn't be taking me to lunch, Harry. Do you know that nobody else does? But nobody! So of course I appreciate it all the more."

"Why shouldn't I, for Pete's sake. You mean I should have asked Carol instead?"

"Well, there's that, of course. But I mean . . . Look, you can't afford it. I know you can't."

"Oh no? I happen to be rolling. I've even saved money at that lousy summer job."

"How come? And if it's true, then you should spend it on somebody else."

"It's you I want to see, Winnie. Nobody else. At least not today."

"An occasion! How nice. Dear Harry, you make me feel good. I sure need it. Well, come on! Out with it."

"Out with it? I don't know what you mean."

"Oh don't you, you old sly-boots. Look, Harry, I know you awfully well, old dear. And I can tell by the reserved, I might even say the *guarded* look on your face . . ."

They were stopped, for the moment, as Johnnie brought their soups to the table, set down soup spoons, gave them napkins. Winifred Grainger glanced down the line of tables and across at the row opposite. As she did so, she noticed how old Mrs. Hazelton, facing in her direction and lunching alone, suddenly dropped her eyes to her single lamb chop, and for the next minute she was awfully busy poking around at it, examining it, turning it over, almost as if she expected it had been poisoned. Johnnie gone, Winifred stirred her thick Vichyssoise, submerging the chives, and addressed Harry again.

"Harry, let's not kid around. It's about Betty Finletter, isn't it?"

"What makes you think so?"

"I live in this town too, you know. And late the other night I drove downtown to get some cigarettes; I found I was clean out. I can almost wonder now whether I was unconsciously or deliberately out, so that I could . . . Well, anyway, coming home, I naturally passed the Finletters' big house at the top of our street, lighted up from top to bottom, with about a thousand cars parked in front and around the driveway. *And* quite naturally—I admit it willingly—I slowed down and naturally cased that conglomeration of cars. Female curiosity; I'm neither proud of it nor ashamed of it. And one of them happened to be Jack's *very* familiar old Marmon. He really should get a new car, something nondescript and ordinary."

"If there were a thousand cars," Harry said with a satirical grin, "you must have done some damned keen scouting."

"Oh I did. And as I say, there it was, parked in the street, large as life and twice as sick-making."

"I'm sorry, Winifred."

"So am I. It's been hard to take."

"Maybe it doesn't mean anything."

"It needn't, till Jack comes around very late the same night—and I like a damned fool am still up—and gives me the old malarky about being detained at the office. God, it makes me feel like a wife—the kind of lied-to wife I promised myself I'd never be, to anyone."

"What does he come around for? I mean why not explain the next day?"

"To put it crudely, for a quickie, in the summerhouse. And I fall for it. Fall for it without believing it at all, but because—oh Christ, I want him."

"You love him so much?"

"I have loved him so much."

"Well, now you know," he said.

"That's what you were going to tell me, wasn't it?"

"Only just this, because that's all I really know, and you seem to know it too. That Jack has been taken up by the Finletters; been tapped. He seems to have become a member in good standing of their perennial open house or house party or whatever it is. Wouldn't he though? Isn't he just the type?"

"It was bound to happen. I'm not surprised really. I even half expected it, in time. I'm only . . . Oh, nothing."

"Hurt?"

"Of course I'm hurt. Disappointed. Even angry. And the worst of it is, I can't show it. I have to pretend I don't know."

"Winifred, he was never good enough for you, not ever. I saw it from the beginning."

"Some of them have been a lot worse."

"But I'm not talking about that. I'm talking about love, and what's good for you, what's best for you."

"Look, and you've got to believe me. Jack did love me. He did. That's one thing I can't be fooled about. One thing that can't be faked. It was lovely till other people began to interfere."

"Don't mind my saying this, but I don't think it's true. Maybe, Winifred . . . Maybe you'll never find love in Arcadia. There are too many strikes against you here."

"Maybe there's no such thing anyway, Harry. For me, anyway.

Wait, drop it for a minute," she said with a dead-pan expression in a dead-pan voice. "Look who's coming."

Betty Finletter, in a simple white piqué suit, followed by Jack Sanford, alert, smiling all around, with eyebrows characteristically raised as if he didn't want to miss a thing, wearing an old tweed jacket and tan cotton slacks, were threading their way through the room and out onto the veranda. It was now an open declaration that they were friends at last. Johnnie seated them a few tables away, and pocketed the folded reservation card and stuck it in his pocket.

" 'Fate keeps on happening,' " Winifred said with a laugh, and then added: "God, what am I going to do now?"

"Nothing at all, do you hear?" Harry Harrison reassured her. "Point is, what are *they* going to do? It's their problem, not yours."

The question was settled almost at once, after a fashion. Betty Finletter, facing them, called out a friendly "Hi!" Jack Sanford, in the act of sitting down, turned in the direction in which she was looking, and saw them. At once he rose again and came over to their table in the most reassuring fashion. That alert, eager face, with the hair parted immaculately in the middle, the waxed mustache, and the raised inquisitive eyebrows—how could one think he was not genuinely glad to see them?

"Winifred! What a nice surprise."

"Isn't it?"

"Hi, Harry. Good to see you."

"Thanks."

"Well! What are you two up to?"

"Just having lunch."

"Winnie, you look great. I love that necklace. Pink jade, isn't it? I don't think I've ever seen it before."

"I wear it often. It doesn't show much in the dark."

"Touché!" he said good-naturedly. "I certainly led with my chin that time!"

There was the piercing wail of a through-train at the railroad crossing a mile across the golf course. *Wahhh! Wahhh!* Wah-w*ahhh!*

"Say hello to Betty Finletter for me. Lovely suit she's wearing."

"I will."

"Wish I could wear things like that, but my figure won't take those simple, good lines."

"Ah-ah, there you go again, playing yourself down. Remember what I always told you about that?"

"Forget it, Jack. Look, I've got to eat my soup before it gets hot."

"Right! Have a good lunch. Be seeing you." He bent over her, charming as all hell. "Tell me," he said in a low, intimate voice, the voice she knew so well, "would it be too bad of me if I kissed you? I wouldn't want to do the wrong things with all these dowagers looking on."

"Not here, Jack, and you should know better. Save it for when there's nobody else around."

With no further word he turned and went back to his table, where he sat leaning eagerly forward talking to Betty Finletter with the keenest animation and gestures.

"If ever I saw a man puzzled, ill at ease, or downright guilty," Winifred said. "It's so transparent you can't help feeling sorry for him. I do, at least, and it will be my downfall."

"You're too soft-hearted. I should only say: Well, that's that."

"No, it isn't Harry. I wish it were that simple. Listen, you had something you were burning to tell me, though you couldn't bring it out directly. Well, I have something to tell you. And you're the only one I'm telling or ever going to tell, except possibly my sister Mercedes."

He looked at her across the table apprehensively, not speaking.

Very matter-of-fact, she said quietly: "I'm pregnant, Harry."

"Pregnant," he repeated, in an awed but breathless whisper. "My God, how would you ever get pregnant?"

"How does anybody get pregnant?"

"But I thought . . . I mean . . ."

"Yeah, I thought so too. Fat lot of good it did me. I've got only one thought now, though. It's *the* one, and I hope I never forget it. Oh, but I will."

"What's that?"

"It's a man's world, and there are no two ways about that."

"But don't people . . . I mean girls get . . . Well, I mean there are abortionists, aren't there?" He hurried the word as if it were an acute embarrassment to him.

"It's too late for that."

"How too late? I'm afraid I don't know very much about these things."

"It's a little better than three months. Or a little worse."

"Winifred, you've got to find somebody."

"Oh, I've had abortions before, two of them—I remember I told you about them at the time. But they were much earlier, therefore easier, and not so risky. Besides, I've got to admit it: all along I secretly wanted this baby. I know better now. Things were different then, or they're very different now."

After a worried pause, Harry's face almost brightened, and he said: "There's another solution. The absolutely perfect one."

"Don't think I haven't thought of that too. But it's no good. Not any more."

"Just listen to me. Tell Jack Sanford about it. He's got to marry you now."

"Oh, all you people. You think the custom of the country is . . . the custom of the country. Maybe for some it is, but not me."

"What's wrong with it? If ever a case called for—"

" 'Case.' Harry, cut it out. I know you mean well but forgive me if I bow out of that one. No shotgun wedding for me, thank you."

"But you love him. You've told me so. You're in love with him, Winifred!"

"All the more reason . . ."

"For what?"

"For my being unwilling to trap him. I've got the winning cards, I know that—at least by local standards—but I'd be damned before I'd ever bring myself to use them."

"But this way you'd get what you want."

"No, I wouldn't. If Jack Sanford doesn't want me for myself, and it seems he doesn't, then I certainly don't want him just because he happened to get me pregnant. *That's* not too difficult to understand, is it?"

"But any other girl . . . Winifred, I never thought I'd see the day when I'd call you a fool. There's such a thing as being *too* honorable."

"Listen. Honor has nothing to do with it, so let's drop these high-flown whatever-they-are that can only sidetrack us. Please?"

"Does Jack Sanford have any inkling of this at all?"

"I've never mentioned it."

"But he'd *want* to know, and do the right thing. Wouldn't he? Wouldn't any man?"

"Not necessarily. But that's not the point. I'm trying to think what is the right thing for *me*."

"Got any ideas?"

"Very vague."

"Is there any way I can help, Winifred? Short of going to Jack Sanford myself?"

"Now listen. That, I absolutely forbid, do you hear, Harry? Absolutely! You'll be doing me a kindness by just forgetting it."

"I can't do that, of course. But okay," he said meekly, "I promise."

"Anyway I'm not entirely destitute. Nobody ever is, don't you know that? It's one of the great things about life."

"But I want to know what you're going to do. Good God, Winifred, I can't just sit around doing nothing while you're miserable."

"I'm not miserable. I've got a scheme or two up my sleeve. I'll tell you about it in due time, as I always do."

"Due time. I should think there wasn't much time left."

"There's enough. I'll call you tomorrow or the day after at the latest. I'll know something by then."

When they got up to leave, Betty Finletter waggled her fingers as a gesture of goodbye, and Jack Sanford, seeing this, half rose from his chair, half turned, and blew Winifred a kiss.

IT WAS a day of telephoning.

Beginning half an hour past midnight, after her mother had long since been asleep and her father returned from his tryst with Mrs. Mott behind the canning factory on the canal bank, Winifred Grainger softly closed the doors to the downstairs study and called her sister Mercedes in Palm Springs, California.

"Merce?"

"Yes? Yes? Who is it?" The voice was shrill and irritated.

"It's Winifred, Mercedes."

"Winnie! Where *are* you calling *from*? You can't be out here anywhere, are you?"

"I'm home."

"Good heavens. It must be way after midnight there. What on earth is the matter? What's happened?"

"Nothing. I just want to come out and see you for a while."

"*See* me? You mean stay with us? Now be reasonable, Winnie. This is terribly sudden, terribly short notice. It's just not possible, not just at this time. Greg has some people coming down for a week or two from Burlingame that I don't know at *all*, and it just isn't feasible, it's too, too awkward. How about early fall, dear? The desert is lovely then."

"I only want to stay a couple of weeks."

"But I tell you, darling, it couldn't be more . . ." There was a pause; Mercedes seemed to reconsider, even to change her mind. "Have you consulted Mother and Dad about this?"

"No. I thought I'd see if you could have me first."

"I see. Yes. Well." There was another pause. Then: "But of course you can come, darling! Any time you want, and I suggest the sooner the better. Those friends of Greg's seem to be increasing daily. I mean more and more of them are coming down, to ride and shoot and stuff; but we'll find a way to stick you away somewhere. One of the smaller guest houses isn't going to be used at all, and you can have that. When would you like to come, dear?"

"Right away. But I'll have to clear it with Belle and Dad first."

"Wire me. Call me. But do come! You're welcome as the flowers in May. Take the Sante Fé Chief to Pasadena—be sure you get a bedroom on the Santa Fé through-car on the New York Central, the Twentieth Century, so you don't have all that bother of changing trains, plus the stop-over, in Chicago. Got all that? I'll meet you at Pasadena; save us going into that hell-hole of Los Angeles. Just let me know *when*, darling. And please be very *precise* about your arrival—I mean because of daylight saving and the different time zones and all that. Oh, why does everything have to be so complicated these days! Anyway the station agent can tell you. And remember this, old dear, I can't wait. I'm simply be*side* myself to see you."

Some hours later, after breakfast, after her father had gone off to the bank, Winifred said: "Belle, I phoned Mercedes last night."

"*Mer*cedes? You did? Whatever for? And why didn't you let *me* in on it? You know how much I miss her, and how she never calls *us*."

"You were asleep, it was too late. I sat up and waited for the late night rates. And anyway, I only got the whim during the evening, after you'd gone to bed."

"What whim?"

"It's hard to explain, but all of a sudden for no reason at all I felt like going out and spending a few weeks with Mercedes and Greg at the ranch."

"But we hardly know him!"

"Time one of us did, then. Anyhow I just felt like it. I never thought I'd be homesick to see old Merce but I guess I am. Do you mind?"

"Why no, I don't mind at all, if your father's agreeable. But I thought you were having such a good time lately."

"I was. Still, I'd like a change for a week or two."

"It's a lovely idea really. I *like* the idea of you two girls wanting to see each other. That's the way it ought to be between sisters, I always think. And Mercedes *is* rather more like you than Alice."

"Thanks. I'll stop in at the bank before noon and ask Dad."

But before she did this, Winifred drove across town to the New York Central office to inquire about trains. The man called New York, to get her a roomette on the through-car of the Twentieth Century that was picked up by the Santa Fé Chief in Chicago, as

Mercedes had suggested. There was a slight fee for this. There was also a slight fee—less slight, really—for the train to make a special stop to pick her up in Rochester tomorrow night, half an hour before midnight: to stop in Arcadia was impossible. She paid for her reservation, the ticket to California, and the extra charges; then she stopped in at the bank to tell her father.

He had scarcely any comment to make whatever. "I don't have time now, dear. We'll discuss it tonight at dinner."

"But, Dad, I've already made the arrangements, have the reservation and everything. I only need to wire Mercedes when to meet me at Pasadena."

"I said we'll discuss it tonight. I'm very busy now. I hope you have a good time. And I hope you like Mercedes' new husband. Gregory, isn't it? I've never met him, you know."

Just before noon she dialed Jack Sanford at the office, a thing she had never done yet.

"Hi," she said when he came on.

"Winnie . . . Of all things!"

"Listen. I'm doing something to you I've never done before."

"Thrills, thrills. Tell me."

"I'm asking you for a date."

"Doing something *to* me? *For* me, you mean. What's it all about?"

"I'm going to California tomorrow night for a week or two. My sister Mercedes called me from Palm Springs and asked me to come out. It's been ages since I've seen her. So I thought I'd go. She's having some people and wants me too."

"Tomorrow night you're going?"

"Yes. Got my reservation today."

"Isn't this rather sudden?"

"Not too. We're a mad family. Unpredictable."

"Well, it is unexpected."

"I'm leaving tomorrow evening. Could I see you tonight and say goodbye?"

"Of course you can. Why, of course! I'm afraid it will be a little on the late side, but . . . how about ten or eleven? Let's say eleven at the latest."

"That's okay."

"Shall I come to your house?"

"Yes. Only don't blow that damned klaxon."

"Don't worry. I've gotten over that."

"We all grow up eventually."

"What?"

"I'll hear you turning into the drive and will come out and let you in. We don't need to go anywhere."

"Good. I'm a little tired."

"So am I."

"Thanks for asking me, Winnie. I'll be there."

"Thanks for coming."

At six she telephoned Harry Harrison, to ask if he would drive her to Rochester tomorrow evening, to make her connection with the Century at eleven-thirty, when it paused briefly in the Rochester station to pick her up. He said he would, gladly. Then she went up to her room before dinner to lay out a few things for Irma to pack for her in the morning; the most important item of all, for a very good reason, seemed to be her riding breeches.

A COUPLE of minutes before twelve Winifred went out to the driveway to meet Jack Sanford. Belle was of course in bed, Dad was luckily back from his date, and they had the place to themselves. He took her in his arms when he stepped from the car, then held her at arms length and said: "Tell me what's up. Kind of abrupt, isn't it?"

After she broke from his kiss, she said: "Not really. Mercedes has some house guests at the ranch that she wants me to meet, so I thought I'd go. I love it out there."

"She's not trying to marry you off, is she?"

"Of all the ridiculous . . . Look, my friend, nobody marries *me* off."

"That's my girl. Still, it seems awfully sudden," he said as he walked toward the semi-darkened house with his arm around her waist.

"Not too. I do it all the time."

"Must be great to be rich. All the way to California for a house party."

"Isn't it? I love money. Nothing like it."

"Say, there's something funny about you tonight."

"Quite the contrary. I'm very serious."

"How long will you be gone?"

"I don't know yet. Not too long. Come on, let's go round to the summerhouse. I'll swipe the blanket and pillow from Belle's siesta couch on the sun porch. Irma can put them back in the morning if we get carried away and forget."

"There *is* something funny . . ."

As almost always, the lawn was sopping wet with dew. There was no moon tonight, but they needed none: they could have found their way blindfolded. And when they did arrive at the familiar place and settled down and got used to the dark, the night, with only the faintest sprinkling of dim stars, was not half so dark as they had first supposed. It never is; and she thought she had never seen or known a really pitch-black night. Apparently there is no such thing: however dark the night, one can always see a little.

They made love, as so many times before, with complete concentration, passion, and quite the same physical joy. She clung to him after. She knew she had never really loved a man's body, because she hadn't loved the man, as she loved Jack Sanford's, and she didn't care how inwardly remote or indifferent he might have been tonight. Actually she felt an intensity of ardor in him that she had missed lately, yet she knew the ardor as effort, a special try. Still, he was the man for her, and she felt there would be no other, no matter how many more might take his place in the years to come. She was not saddened by it, though she was intensely aware that it was a farewell and would never be repeated. All the more did she savor every bit of him now, appreciate his every move and his kisses. Strangely, sex as such seemed to have little to do with her pleasure tonight, as it had with others. It almost didn't seem to matter; *he* mattered, who was fast slipping away from her in spite of his skills in the art of love-making, his techniques, his too conscientious, transparent attentions. She was saddened, she who knew the difference so well, only because he wasn't himself as she had known him, but a skilful lover making every effort to please.

"When will I see you again?" he said at last. "I've got to see you!"

"Heaven knows."

"Hey, come on! Give me *some* idea. I've got to have something to go on."

"I really don't know. Honest and true."

"Winifred. My darling Winifred. I'm going to miss you most awfully."

"I'll miss you."

"Do you realize that every single night since we met, except the first night, this has happened? We've had this?"

"Maybe that's what's wrong with it."

"Nothing's wrong with it!"

"Maybe it will do us both good to have a change."

"*I* don't want any change! Do you?"

"It's not good," she said, "to take each other for granted."

"I never took you for granted!"

"Nor I you. Ever. Ever, ever."

"Do you have any idea what you've done for me, Winnie? What you've given me all these months?"

"There've only been three of them."

"All the same, do you?"

"You tell me, Jack."

"You've given me, well, love. Do you think that's an easy thing to forget?"

"It isn't for me."

"And I've got to have you again."

"We can't make promises. We even talked once of having a child."

"What's wrong with that? Every man wants that."

"So does every woman, maybe even more. Oh, I'm not reproaching you, Jack dear. Believe me I'm not. We are what we are. But we mustn't make efforts that are just . . . efforts."

"We haven't. And you're being what you are is what has made me love you."

"Well . . ."

"Well what?" he said.

"It's time for you to go. I have a lot to do tomorrow, getting ready."

"Cold as ice."

"No, I'm not. I'll think of you a good deal. I'll miss you. I know

I'll never forget you."

"Good God, you talk as if you're not coming back for months."

"A lot can happen in even less time."

"For instance?"

"People change. They change even when things are going well. Distance has nothing to do with it. But, darling Jack, my dearly beloved Jack, please remember: I have loved you. I still do. Oh damn, none of this is even remotely like what I wanted to say."

"What did you want to say?"

"Just . . . so long, I guess."

"You could have done that on the telephone."

"Maybe I should have."

"How about one more time, to clinch the so-long for good?"

The large leaves of the trumpet vine overhead, the Dutchman's-breeches and other plants dangling from the open trellis above could barely be seen against the pale scattered stars, but their familiar pungency was everywhere.

"Say," he suddenly said as he shifted his position on the floor, "how come the floor doesn't creak any more?"

"I had a carpenter fix it the other day."

"Good girl."

In his renewed attentions, then, she couldn't help feeling a new not unexciting emotion on his part, an emotion stepped up because it may have sprung partly from relief, partly from guilty conscience. And she abetted him in this, to free him as she knew he wanted to be free. She was freed too now, in a way, but a prisoner of that freedom. How long would it last, she wondered, this aching involvement with him? If she believed that it would last forever, never let up, never lessen, she wouldn't have let him go for a second: rather than the prospect of a barren or promiscuous life ahead, she would have taken him under any conditions. Or so she told herself at the moment. In reality, being the person she was, she no longer wanted him. Reality in love was all or nothing—all, or nothing.

Half an hour later, in bed, she heard the night train go through, streaking around the curve down by the Country Club. *Whaaa-whaaa-wha-whaaaa*—a sound that carried her back to childhood and forward into some kind of future.

ANYBODY WOULD THINK I'd never been anywhere, Winifred Grainger thought as, for the third or fourth time during the sleepless night in the berth of her roomette, she raised up on an elbow, pushed up the stiff window shade, and looked out at the passing farmlands, dark mostly except for the flicker and flash of the speeding, dimly lit train. She had plenty to think about in the night—plenty to think about anyway. It almost seemed that her home town that she was rapidly leaving behind (for good?), that homely but so cozy village where she had started life as a happy untroubled little girl, had been lived in darkness: her whole life, she thought, using a phrase totally unlike her and one that she wouldn't have uttered to another living soul, had been seen (as they said in church) as through a glass darkly. Except for that single occasion at the Club when they had encountered each other by chance, she with Harry Harrison, he with Betty Finletter, it had been one of the few times she had ever seen Jack Sanford (he who meant so much to her) by daylight. Small wonder that he had remarked at the time, with admiration and even surprise, on the pale pink jade beads that she wore every day: they didn't show for what they were in the summerhouse, at night, or in the dark of The Pines, or on the marvelously shadowed ninth green below the Club veranda during or after the Saturday-night dances, and they paled to a sickly nothing in the fluorescent overhead lighting or in the glow of the too-pink shaded lamps at Tony di Santo's or the Perroquet. She could almost doubt whether he ever knew the color of the dress she wore—any more, really, than she remembered his necktie, for they discarded both as soon as it was convenient. His shorts were white in the dark, but they might equally have been blue, or tan, or yellow: it couldn't matter less. Once they had been thrown aside on the beach or under the whispering pines or on the floor of the summerhouse, they might have been—and were, for all that they were needed—a piece of colorless rag. As for her own underwear, her black pants and bra, they too blended into the dark landscape of love and were forgotten, till that awkward moment when she had to squirm into them again, colorless still in the dark night.

As she peered under the half-raised shade, a single flaring light

flashed by with a *ding-ding-ding-ding* sound; farther off a speckle
of lights indicated a small village somewhere, or a group of farm-
houses; and still farther, at a great distance, a single glimmering
pinpoint was all but stationary, so slowly did it move on out of
range and eventually, almost reluctantly it seemed, pass from view.
The farmlands of Ohio? Or had they reached Indiana? The landscape, the dark earth, was one tremendous revolving disk, it didn't
matter where, the few lighted objects in the foreground racing by
and vanishing at a startling speed out of all proportion to the
dimmer lights pricked out remotely here and there on the very rim
of the spinning wheel of earth. Railroad stations were sudden
flashes like startlingly illuminated store fronts, gone before you
knew it, to be left behind and remain forever somewhere in that
dark hinterland, while the train streaked on toward morning and
Chicago, gently rocking, faintly creaking, surprisingly silent but for
the muted clacking of the wheels which played an elusive tantalizing musical accompaniment to the night that you couldn't identify
("The Halls of Montezuma"? "Anchors Aweigh"?) over and over
again, all night, while you sang the nameless tune to yourself,
almost getting it but never quite. Now and again came that thrilling
Whaaa-whaaa-wha-whaaa far ahead in the onrushing dark, farther, it seemed, for it was blown away at once in the vast night,
than it had ever been at home, more than half the town away, a
good mile beyond the Country Club and the paper mill.

What am I looking at in this immense turntable of dark landscape? Or looking for? She found no answer, of course. She told
herself that she was just restless or sleepless—unaccustomed surroundings, change of scenery and all that—but she had reached a
crisis in her life and she knew it, had known it for weeks, for all
that she had been able to maintain, back home, the semblance of
indifference and even a tough nonchalance: with her parents, with
Harry Harrison, even with Jack Sanford. Not for nothing those
embarrassed deprecatory smiles, the self-mockery, the blushing
over things that people didn't blush over (she who had so much to
blush about). She needed love, needed it now; and she thought
almost sadly, yet with a satirical smile ("Now really!"), of the
handsome blue-black Pullman porter dozing on the small seat
under the blue night light at the end of the car. All she had to do

was press the button. Ah, if only life were as simple as that. He would answer her ring, but so objectively, so aloofly, really "getting" nothing, and with so much paternal kindness that he couldn't even be embarrassed—not a tenth as much as she would be when, after he had tended to her trumped-up wants (aspirin tablet, light quilt, another pillow), he had returned to his post again. Meanwhile it was a time to think: not of her erring ways, for this she had never done, but of what she had missed.

She had missed love, missed out on it, missed her one chance for love. Bitterly she knew it, and she wondered how much the fault was hers. In losing Jack Sanford who had loved her (she didn't doubt for a moment that he had, for several weeks), she had missed the one opportunity that had ever come her way to pull herself up out of the morass of compulsive meaningless sexuality in which she had been sinking so long, and rejoin the human race. Only twenty!—yet she was like a blasé divorcée more than twice her age who passed herself from man to man indiscriminately and could scarcely remember or distinguish one lover from another. If Jack Sanford had not been informed of the sordid details of her past—rather (for she blamed nobody) if there had been no messy background for him to hear about in the first place—all would have been different. But she had done those things they talked about, and worse; it was all true, it was her history; and in a town like Arcadia, with its tightly knit social groups that he himself had called "clicquey," he was bound to hear sooner or later. What of it if she was the banker's daughter—which was certainly one of the things that had attracted him to her in the first place? Belonging to the first family so-called, the oldest and best, had only made her sins (in all conscience, though, how could she think of them as such, when she had enjoyed them so much?), had only emphasized her errors, made them more prominent, more talked about. She couldn't undo them or deny them. And she blamed no one now, as the rocking train sped on through the dark countryside of Ohio, Indiana, the small strip of Michigan, and on into Illinois at last.

Chicago, LaSalle Street Station, bright morning, meant a drawing of the curtain and staying in bed, while, after the passengers had disembarked from the other cars with their attaché cases and smart luggage and hat boxes, the single through-car was backed out of the station again, shunted around a wilderness of yards, eventually to join the Santa Fé Chief at Union Station, after easing slowly into position with a caution that did not prevent a series of unsettling jolts that should have shattered every window and could have waked the dead in all those cemeteries on the West Side.

When her Pullman had finally been coupled between two cars of the new train and the new passengers had embarked, Winifred Grainger dressed and found her way along the corridors to the diner. There were two of them, besides two club cars, and she took the first seat suggested to her. She was seated at a table for four, but there was no one next to her; opposite, across the snowy stiff cloth, sat a man in his forties—a male—not handsome, but interesting enough in his rugged way. He cast a glance or two in her direction now and then, his expression almost devoid of curiosity, possibly merely trying to "place her" socially; but he talked animatedly to his wife beside him, gesturing with a fork or a finger as if what he had to say was very important; in short, he was attentive. The wife gazed abstractedly at her plate or dreamily out the window, and occasionally remembered to nod or shake her head as if to show that she was all ears. There was the piercing long toot of a whistle far ahead, very slowly the buildings on either side seemed to slide away on their own, and they were off.

When she could do so without attracting his attention, or his wife's, Winifred glanced at him and wondered what he was like under the table, where his knees almost touched her own. More than most women she knew what he looked like there, but she wondered all the same. Every man was different, or new, not like the others—until you had seen it or had it and then it blended in or blurred with all the rest, so that it became unimportant and unrememberable. But oh not at the beginning, not before it became yours. Then it had possibilities that none of the others ever had.

After breakfast-lunch she went to the club car. The atmosphere here was quite different from that of the club car on the Century. At either end there were blown-up photo-murals of scenery of the Southwest, the Grand Canyon at one end, the Garden of the Gods at the other; and below the latter, two moldy-looking creatures, looking more like prop Indians than the Real Article from the Pueblos, sat on the floor tailor-fashion wrapped in filthy blankets (doubtless concealing sharkskin suits), not unwilling to sell, provided you made the first move, beadwork, brick-colored pottery, war bonnets whose too feathery feathers would surely come apart at a touch. The tables, the two or three banquettes, the four settees were filled with jovial passengers getting together with a zest that would have done credit to a Grange meeting at home, or a mixed assembly of the Eastern Star. At the far end, in dramatic solitude, gazing mystically into space (though you couldn't tell where she gazed, really, because of her dark glasses), a young woman with beautiful legs, "perfect poise" (her publicity man would have said), platinum hair under a beige Garbo hat just shapeless and big enough, and a splendid *hauteur,* movie-queened it over the less glamorous company along the car who raised questioning eyebrows throughout, as each one wondered who she would turn out to be.

Winifred Grainger politely refused to join a gin-rummy game and went back to her roomette. She pulled the bed down and lay on top of it, disinterestedly watching the passing landscape of Kansas or maybe still Illinois, stretching to the farthest horizon in colors of the purest canary and sage green. She was tired through and through from her wakeful restless night, and soon fell asleep with her clothes on.

The reverberating *bonggg* of some kind of cymbal that she had heard before on shipboard (though this noisemaker was merely passing through the gently rocking corridor) woke her at last. It was time to go in to dinner. Without changing her dress (she merely pulled her wrinkled skirt straighter around her rather broad hips and ran a comb through her loose hair), she went to the dining car.

Somehow the movie queen in the dark glasses had wangled a table all to herself (preferential treatment, arranged by the studio) and there she sat, sipping a soda, moodily smoking a cigarette, the observed of all observers. Many glances were continually directed her way, some passengers even half rose in their chairs to get a better look, but because of the opaque lenses one could not tell if she was even aware of the attention, those dark glasses that were certainly as essential a part of her costume as if, fatigued, having just come off the sound stage, waiting to be powdered and touched up again by half a dozen attendants, she blankly regarded the bright set before her while she tried to recover in the canvas-backed chair stenciled Miss Whoever.

Again Winifred Grainger tried the club car—both of them—and never felt so lonely in her life: lonely and *passé* as the two moth-eaten Indians whom it would be a dead give-away as a tourist, a passenger unused to the sophisticated splendors of the Santa Fé Chief, to glance at at all, much less to buy from. Well before dark she returned to her roomette, undressed in the tight quarters, and went off almost immediately into the soundest, the blankest kind of sleep.

She awoke with a bright sun streaming in on her bare arm, neck and forehead, hot, and almost blinding. She had forgotten to pull down the shade at the window next to her bed. She leaned up on her elbow to look out, then sat up. Winifred Grainger seemed to be in a different world from any she had been in before, almost another planet. The train was moving slowly, upgrade. The countryside was bleak, rocky, mountainous; they seemed to be barely moving. And then she saw, not far ahead, the two locomotives that pulled the train up and over the pass, coming back her way. It was an odd, unreal sight. They disappeared from view, seemed to straighten out, and then they appeared again, as if coming back: winding horseshoe curves must have been the answer. The earth was rocky, chalky, barren, and the only color came from an occasional short or scrawny-looking cactus plant of a kind of greenless green, the shade or hue of a filing cabinet in her father's office. The sun was white; she felt the strain and pull, and heard the effort, of the locomotives in tandem. Because of the unexpected grotesqueness of that craggy colorless landscape, plus the full night's sleep she had behind her, she got up, dressed, and went down to the dining car. It was not yet eight o'clock, and she was one of only four passengers present. The desolate Indians had not been in the club car as she came through, squatting below the photo-mural; they were probably sleeping it off somewhere, and not fire-water either: 4-star brandy, more likely, vodka, stingers of white mint, Grand Marnier, even champagne. But where did they sleep it off—in a kind of barrow or gypsy's wain attached at the train's end?

"Where are we?" she asked the waiter as she opened her napkin.

They had just left Trinidad, Colorado, were now climbing over the Raton Pass, and soon would descend into the desert, traveling almost equally south and west. "I hope you slept well, Miss?" "Thank you. I slept great. In some ways I never felt better in my life." "Ah, the mountain air . . ." He poised his pencil, ready to write down what she wanted to order. "That's what we always hope for out guests on the Santa Fé, Miss," he added. "A good night's sleep. Coffee first?"

On her return through the train, Winifred Grainger found a considerable sprinkling of passengers lounging about in the club cars, waiting for their seat placements to be called by the steward before they could enter the now-filled dining car: a few over-dressed women, a few others in frankly tatty clothes, two or three smartly dressed as if they were Going to the City, in worsted flannel skirts with crêpe-de-chine or print blouses, one in gabar-dine of palest green, another in black serge; several men wearing the wrong ties, wrong shoes, suits of just the wrong gray. What's the matter with me, she asked herself: am I such a snob? I could never possibly like a man who wore a white necktie or a tie with an armorial shield painted on it, shoes of interwoven thongs, or suits the color of clay; I couldn't possibly! I wouldn't even want to speak to them; we'd have nothing in common! And yet . . . and yet . . . take off that offending tie, let him step out of those God-awful shoes, strip him of that all-wrong suit, and some-times wonders were revealed: wonders. She had many times dis-covered (to her chagrin, astonishment, and delight—even awe) that the man in the nondescript clothes proved a breath-taking monu-ment of beauty without them, a beauty he himself was totally, innocently unaware of, or he would have taken pains (like the dazzling bird or the male beast in the animal kingdom) to show himself off better, reveal a hint or two of his manifold physical charms in the strut or carriage of his figure, in the cut of the clothes, the tailoring or fitting. It was one of the mysteries of life that men for the most part hardly regarded themselves as objects of sexual or physical beauty: the display of the figure was the prerogative, the special mysterious domain of women exclusively, and men were all for it, content to be allowed in occasionally—figuratively crawling on their hands and knees, and even then scarcely believing their good fortune. Let them go to an art class someday, she thought, and stand up there as a model on the small dais before an appraising, objective group of students of both sexes interested in the purity of the body as such, not who or what it was: then they might get some vague idea, as she had so many times (through hardly vague, and under quite different circumstances), of the hard, compact charm of their physiques and the clean lines running throughout from head to foot, far outstripping in aesthetic attraction the sloppy, over-soft, rubbery bodies of the pendulous-bottomed, droop-breasted, flabby-bellied women. How had this idea ever come about? Propaganda, advertising, the fraudulence of art? When would they ever wake up to the fact that *they* were something too! she exclaimed silently but with vehemence; and then immediately remembered with dismay those braggart men, by no means a few—those saps! those conceited roosters, yes, cocks!—those insufferably flattering, oily, self infatuated gents who, when they spoke, spoke only for the benefit of themselves, with a total lack of imagination of their effect on women, to whom, of course, they were clearly God's gift. She blushed for him now, but she could say it honestly and without rancor: in spite of the fact that he had been in love with her for a brief spell or acted like it, Jack Sanford has missed this category, if at all, only by inches.

But how different they all were. That unself-conscious man sitting opposite her now, for example, one knee thrown over the other, with two-toned gray shoes, sleezy silk socks of mixed gray and white, with clocks—clocks!—and a couple of inches of bare shin and calf showing above the top. That inch or two of bare skin, that sprinkling of fuzz more downy than hairy so that you only saw it at the sides, that male leg . . . It wasn't bad (bad? hell, it was perfect). She couldn't take her eyes away, in spite of the offending accessories of shoe, sock, pant leg of a kind of clayey gray. If somebody should step over to him now, take him in charge and with a giant pair of scissors cut away the cloth, the cheesey paperlike leather, and the bad silk, that leg (such were its innocent, perfect proportions) would be revealed in all its glory: columnar, tawny, downy with strength, admiration of the artist for its purity, substance, lines, flesh—my God, what is more admirable or attractive in this world than good clean naked flesh? But: if somebody should commit an act so outrageous and beneficial, the poor guy would doubtless die on the spot, and his till now vapid and inattentive wife (for they were indeed the pair who had sat opposite her in the dining car) might well flee the train in shame and take off into the wild landscape, to disappear forever. Whereas if it had been Jack, he would have been conscious of his whole mien as he sat there, conscious even of the effect his leg, with its show of bare flesh, was having on any watching female; he might even have pulled up the pant leg an inch or so farther, to "feature" that appeal—and she would have seen through the gesture, now, and despised him for it. She smiled to herself at the thought. What was the matter with them, anyway? Whatever they did was wrong; they couldn't win. Maybe she was regaining her balance at last, or her sense of humor.

No, no. It wasn't balance, or even her old sense of humor, come back again. Who was she kidding? It was the same old obsession that rode her night and day (why?), as regular and compulsive as breathing. Would it ride her to the end of her life, would she ever get over it? No. She was fooling herself if she thought so, and she didn't. For all the good he had done her, or the benefit of their love, Jack Sanford might just as well never have existed. Certainly what she had to go through now, she had to go through alone. Who did she think she was kidding? Sometimes she thought her whole life, such as it had been up to now, could be expressed or compressed in that single phrase: Who am I kidding? At the same time she took a small pride in the thought and the fact that she was not kidding anyone, never had, never would, least of all herself. Life—and this was the deepest conviction of her whole nature—life is too short for such masquerades.

When she returned to her roomette she found it had been made up. She took down from her book bag, stored above, one of the dozen or so books she had brought along, and settled herself to read. It was *The Great Gatsby,* a novel she had already read twice that summer, with increasing admiration each time as she fell more and more under its spell. She thought it was not only the saddest book she had ever read, but also the most purely glamourous, in the exact sense of that overused word: it was glamour as she had never seen it on the printed page. But even during the familiar opening pages, she found that her eyes had strayed several times at least to the landscape flowing by, and by the time she came to the beautiful sentence, "No—Gatsby turned out all right in the end; it is what preyed on Gatsby, what foul dust floated in the wake of his dreams . . ." it was no good, not today, she had to give it up. She put the book aside and gazed with an admiration that was in actuality sheer awe at the countryside fleeting by, oh, all too fast.

The train had reached the real Southwest now, or the beginning of it, and the passing panorama beyond her wide window was a haze of pastel colors of every description, blending into each other along the desert floor. She was entranced and surprised. There was nothing to look at; and there was everything to look at. The distances, in spite of the yellow-white haze, were beyond belief, as if the contours of the earth could actually be seen for the globe that it was, and the land dropped away somewhere far off without horizon at all. It was unlike anything she had ever dreamed of, and she kept saying to herself: "Why didn't anybody ever tell me, why hasn't anyone ever told me it was like this?" She had seen travel folders and posters of Arizona and New Mexico dozens of times, but they had left her totally unprepared for the actuality. On her two trips to Europe, everything looked exactly as she expected it to look: Mont St.-Michel, Chartres, Paris itself, the Alps, Rome, Florence, Venice—in effect she nodded each time and merely checked them off, so to speak. But this . . . this . . . And though she didn't know it, she hadn't seen anything yet: seen what the mid- and late-afternoon sun would do with this wonderland.

All but hypnotized, hallucinated, she spent the morning in her cubicle of a room, mesmerized by the desert. She felt she was being taken out of herself (for her it *must* be something different, for none of the dozens she knew who had passed through this landscape before her had so much as mentioned it) and she felt inside herself, almost reluctantly, odd, quirky, unaccustomed stirrings of some kind . . . some kind of religion? No; by no means! She experienced an almost equally embarrassing attack of patriotism, no less, a kind of chauvinism that reminded her, with shy pride, that this was her country, this was America, there was no place else like it on the whole face of the earth—which made her wonder all the more why nobody had ever told her even that much. Or were people generally embarrassed by emotional stirrings of this kind and covered them up with whines of "The food, my dear. Now my advice to you when you leave civilization [Chicago] is to go on a *ridge*-id *die*-et. Eat nothing!" Meanwhile this, all this, was almost too much; the endless and ever-changing beauty of it would have left her speechless, if she had had anyone to talk to.

An hour past noon she went along the corridors toward the dining cars. Now it was her turn to wait to be called by the steward. She settled herself in a stiff leather chair in the adjoining club car and picked up a magazine from the glass-topped table. It was called *Sunset*. The two Indians cross-legged under the photo-mural must have been stuffed by a taxidermist: they looked exactly as before and sat in the same trancelike positions. One wore a battered plush hat with a rumpled feather in it; the other was hatless, with thick braids of horsehair to his shoulders, bound just below the ears with bits of yellow ribbon. Both were wrapped in heavy blankets as if they were freezing to death.

Across the way a broad-chested, theatrically rugged man slouched at his ease, though carefully holding on his sprawled tweedy legs an open book a little too upright: she wondered how he could see to read it. His hair was thick, bushy but meticulously combed in ironlike waves; his wide thick mustache went straight across, obviously shaved below as well as above by a straight razor. A gnarled straight pipe stuck straight out from grim lips. His look was gruff to the point of ferocity, accented by glasses with black, very thick rims. He was very conscious of being Somebody, and she became conscious of it too, so much so that the blond movie queen hiding behind her dark glasses took a back seat, figuratively speaking, regardless of her brilliant hair and stunningly plain chambray dress. And then Winifred Grainger noticed, with a kind of horror that should have been tempered with hilarity at the very least, that on the back of the dust jacket that covered the book he held on his thick thighs so upright she could not miss it, was a full-page photograph of a tweedy rugged man, pipe in mouth, wide straight carefully groomed mustache, staring at her fiercely as its model now stared at the open book held so uncomfortably, or at least unnaturally, upright. After a moment or two (oh, he needed it so, and no one else was paying attention) she leaned slightly forward and said quietly: "Excuse me for asking, but are you by any chance an author?" He glowered interestingly and replied in a baritone a full octave lower than normal. "Yes, Miss, I am. Why do you ask?" "I couldn't help noticing," she said, "that you look like . . . that you seem to resemble the man in the photograph on the book jacket." He turned the book around and looked at the picture with a frown, as if he had been unaware till then of the nature of the book he just happened to have picked up for a cursory glance. "Oh that," he said. "Yes, it's my mug, all right. Ain't pretty, is it?" She was aware that the "ain't" was deliberately chosen: the butch touch. "May I present it to you, Miss? It's called *One Road to Hell*." "Sounds interesting," she said. "Wait, let me autograph it for you." "You're too kind." He did so at once, with a wide stub pen and green ink, without asking her name. At that moment her number was called for the dining car. "Am on my way to Hollywood," he volunteered as, unsmiling, he handed the book over. "Goddamned nuisance, if you ask me. Going out to supervise the screenplay for M-G-M and Spence." "Spence?" she had to ask, knowing how badly he wanted her to. "Spencer Tracy. Not that they'll do it justice, but what the hell? As far as my works are concerned, the studios and the agents exist for the sole purpose of being taken advantage of—and, brother, I take them for plenty. The book is one thing and the movie is another, I always say." "Is that what you always say?"—but just then the steward put his head in the car again, next to the Garden of the Gods, and reminded her that she had been called. She clutched *One Road to Hell* against her chest with both hands, smiled good-bye, and went in.

Thank God for a laugh or at least a smile, she thought as she sat down opposite her usual partners and unfolded the stiff white napkin. So he's going to California to do a movie and I'm going out (which was more unreal?) to have a baby, an abortion, a miscarriage, whatever the experienced Mercedes could manage. It was all one to her, and her own indifference, both to the imminent experience and to the recent past, disturbed her. Jack Sanford mattered to her at the moment as little as the pipe-smoking straight-mus-

tached Author in the club car. But maybe, when she got back to
Arcadia again and Jack was still around . . . Maybe when she kept
running into him, as she was bound to do . . . Maybe, if he had
not seriously taken up with Betty Finletter . . . God, God: if
I have any pride left at all, protect me from that. Anything else
would be better, even Cal Cunningham—or the stolid, darkly
handsome, no-good, built-for-action-only Tony di Santo. Why
hadn't she seen him more often lately, as she was so used to doing?
The answer of course was that Jack Sanford, who had loved her
briefly and whom she had loved, had got in the way. She gave her
order to the waiter, then turned her head away and gazed out the
wide windows, first on one side of the train, then on the other. What
a country. It was like looking on a still sea of hot brilliant color, unlike anything in life, yet far realer, ever-lasting, something that
would always be there. The colors, the gently undulating landscape
as the train rocked along, the distant carved pillars of vermilion
sandstone reaching to fabulous heights against the champagne-
colored sky, irregular and ribbed and jagged, yet astoundingly
beautiful in their very irregularity—they seemed to belong to some
haunted and haunting landscape of the imagination, some compelling hallucinatory world of the spirit which, if you looked at long
enough and gazed deeply into—gave yourself up to—would reveal
things you had never known before.

When she returned to the club car she discovered to her utter
dismay that the window shades had been pulled down to the very
bottom on either side of the car. The men and some of the women
were absorbed in card playing, Monopoly, Mah-Jongg, sipping now
and then from highballs made of tequila. The bright sunlight distracted them, and in shutting out the sun they had also erased the
thrilling landscape apparently without a thought, as if it was something they were used to and bored with every day of the week, like
their own back yards, like State Street or Clark Street, or the
packed parking lot they looked out and down on from their antiseptic office windows. Winifred Grainger was not easily shocked;
in fact she thought she never had been shocked, in the ordinary use
of that word, in her whole life. But when she saw the shades drawn
to the sills throughout both club cars, saw how the card playing,
drinking, or merely gossiping passengers had shut out (shut off,

really) the golden sunlight and the continuously interesting glory (changing every minute, so that no one mile was like another) of the desert sights and colors through which they passed, providing a panoramic spectacle one could not have grasped from the most accurate photograph, she was shocked in her very being, and ashamed—ashamed for the callousness of her fellowmen. She quitted the club car at once as if she didn't belong there, as indeed she didn't, and returned to the peace of her small bedroom, which had only one drawback—that she could see the desert out one window only, and heaven only knew what she might be missing on the other side. But it was enough. Thinking of the drawn shades on both sides of the club cars, she told herself that one could be surfeited with too much of the desert beauty: this was enough. "Enough": it recalled an expression her father had used so often, years and years ago when she was a child, that she and her sisters had smiled about to one another, secretly, across the dinner or luncheon table as, pleased with himself, he got off his sententious phrase: "Enough is enough and more is superfluous."

In early afternoon the train pulled slowly into Albuquerque and stopped, for the first time since Kansas City. The porter rapped on her door to tell her there would be a twenty-minute stop-over, and if she wanted to get out and buy some souvenirs . . . She did; she welcomed the opportunity of a change; and as she stepped down to the concrete platform and sniffed the hot but dry and bracing air, walked through sunlight the color of sauterne, saw the palm trees hovering over the station with glimmers of white-peaked mountains far beyond, she felt excited and happy. She was in no hurry; they would be given plenty of notice before the train took off again. A row of handsome Indians, male and female, sat cross-legged on the sidewalk selling their wares of rust-colored ceramics, blankets that looked too new, beads, and woven baskets; few passengers bought from them, but made for the station shop instead, where cleaner and properer souvenirs, doubtless made in Japan, went like hot cakes. A silver and turquoise necklace took her eye; she tried it on, then decided against it because it looked all too plainly for what it was: a "souvenir." She bought some note paper, the Los Angeles *Daily Times,* a diaphanous scarf for Mercedes and a plain pipe for Greg. She headed back for the train, reluctant, somehow, to get on and resume the journey. The air was so fresh and dry, the sunlight so yellow and palely brilliant, that she could have stayed and stayed.

Slowly the long train of streamlined silver cars pulled away from Albuquerque, and the real wonderland of the desert began. For miles nothing was to be seen except brilliantly colored buttes, jagged but majestic, rising from the wilderness of red sand in lonely isolated grandeur; distant purple mesas so symmetrically formed they might have been erected by skilled if ancient architects; rugged yellow bluffs; cathedral spires of red sandstone towering against a colorless sky in solitary mysterious grandeur—but all spaced so far apart, with only vast stretches of green and yellow desert between, that each spectacular pinnacle (almost no two of them framed by the window at the same time) was displayed to perfect advantage, however remote, with a majesty of its own quite unrelated to another and even to the flat desert from which it soared up, aspiring, noble, eternal. The tears came. Why? What was she crying about? Again she experienced feelings of spirituality she was wholly unequipped to understand, because they had never been known before. She felt so little, so inconsequential— and when she thought of the unreal artificial cities through which the train had passed (and the shocking irony that, just beyond the mountains of Arizona they would descend to, and become a part of, Hollywood, of all places, the unrealest city of all, so unlike the unreality just beyond the train windows which, oddly, didn't seem unreal in the least, however strange), she sensed with awe that the breathtaking beauty of all this would remain (imagine it existing there in the dark, in the night, with no one to see); would always remain, unremarked, as it had remained just so for millions upon millions of years, as if it were the only thing that counted in this transient, empty, artificial world. It suddenly seemed of no importance whatever happened after this had passed from view: for it would not pass, it would stay as it was forever, whether anyone was there to admire or not. And the spell it cast got worse, or better, as the afternoon sun waned and sank. A new unearthly brilliance of color washed the entire scene. A sandstone butte of deep rose umber changed, even as she watched in a kind of breathless awe, to dark heliotrope, then blazing violet; a greenish mesa, so far away that she could barely discern its mathematically perfect outlines, became lavender, then rich purple, then blue-black, pulsing with darkest emerald all in the space of minutes, or a minute. I have never believed in God, she murmured to herself, blinking the unaccustomed tears from her eyes so that she might still see while there was still time; never believed in anything, really. But something . . . something . . . There must be Something behind all this. Embarrassed by her own emotion even in the privacy of her bedroom (why? there was no one around to see), she got up and went down to the club car. And when she walked in and heard the chatter (the dark shades still drawn against the intruding sun, against the fabulously rich desert rotating on either side) she wanted to call out something rude. My God, she was positively evangelistic! And who would have understood or even heard her? She waited then, alone as she had never been before, till the lowering sun darkened the glittering air outside, put out the splendor of the shimmering buttes and bluffs and distant mesas, and made it possible to raise the shades again so that everyone could get back to normal.

After dinner, returning from the diner through the club car, she saw the movie queen, her dark glasses put aside at last so that she looked like any pretty girl in a pretty dress, playing poker with three nondescript men, and laughing raucously as she drew a wanted card. Why, the girl was nobody at all! And neither was the scowling Author with his tweeds and Book, who might have been supplied by Central Casting. And neither was she. No one at all; none of them. She went early to bed and tried to read; but she was too aware of that passing panorama of awesome structures in the darkness of night beyond her window, and remotely far away too, stretching miles and miles out of sight, utterly indifferent to the speeding train which intruded, yet did not intrude at all really, on their mysterious mystic domain. The train was slow, and climbing as if with effort. They had reached and were passing through Flagstaff—which meant, not long after, a long slow descent to the viny hills and green fields of a more normal landscape: Southern California. For the first time since Sunday-school days she said her prayers, or at least the only one she knew. For no reason that she could name—for Mercedes was wise, understanding, capable, and resourceful as all hell—she dreaded the meeting with her sister. Yet Mercedes was the only one who could help her; wasn't she? Her dilemma was: did she really want that help? Well, she had to turn to somebody. The only thing was, she wasn't sure that Mercedes and her sophisticated magic were the answer. Mercedes was nobody, either; but not even faintly did she mean to belittle her sister by saying this or even thinking it. She meant something else—something vague that she couldn't put her finger on; but she wouldn't dream of trying to explain it to Mercedes, who wouldn't understand any more than she did.

When she stepped down in the morning sunlight at Pasadena and stood among her few pieces of luggage waiting to be recognized, it was she who did the recognizing. Some fifty or sixty feet away stood a handsome woman in her early thirties looking up at the cars. She had the slim figure of a girl; she was feminine in the completest sense of that word; she was one of the few natural blondes Winifred had ever known, with a real yellow in her hair (like the Prince of Wales); the expression on her pretty but somewhat haughty face seemed by nature discontented and even disapproving; and she wore a large floppy straw hat, glasses with green lenses to protect her eyes from the brilliance of the morning sun, and a snug blouse and skirt of Mexican cotton, very smart, no stockings on her bare legs (good legs), and black rope-soled shoes with white tapes tied around her attractive ankles. They found each other almost at once. Without preliminaries, Mercedes directed a porter to carry Winifred's luggage to her open convertible parked in the shade below, tipped him a dollar, and started the motor and drove expertly out to the highway without a word of greeting. Winifred understood; in a way, her sister's silence was a compliment.

At last she said, "Pasadena's a dreadful town. They're all dreadful towns out here. Cheap. We're lucky. The desert is the only place to live. At least we have isolation there and we're lucky enough to have a lovely place of our own."

"If Greg has that crowd coming down from Burlingame, it doesn't sound like isolation exactly."

"There's only a handful, and you'll have a place of your own. You may even like some of them," Mercedes added pointedly.

"Greg," Winifred said to change the subject. "We've never met him, you know. Number Three, isn't he?"

"If you must put it that way, yes."

Mercedes drove ably with one hand, the other held to the top of her head to keep her floppy hat in place.

"What's he like?"

"Dumb as an ox. Charming. Beautiful. And a pain in the ass."

"I know so well what you mean," Winifred said.

"Oh no you don't. He has to be seen to be believed. But aren't they all, anyway?"

"Not all."

"Right. We live in hopes, dear."

"I'm just saying . . ."

"Well, don't say. Feel. It's the only thing that counts."

"Oh, it counts, all right. It's been *my* downfall."

"You talk like a fallen woman. You're far too young for that. Besides, they've gone out, dear. Long since."

"I wish it were true. You know what I'm here for."

"I'll tell you, Win, what you're here for. And please remember for everybody's sake, and I don't mean just Belle and Dad, it is not to be discussed. Except between us. You're here to have a baby or an abortion, depending. Happens all the time. Could happen to anybody. So don't be tragic about it. When you phoned I got it at once. And I'll tell you something else."

"Shoot."

"It's probably Cal Cunningham. The wonder is it hasn't happened before."

"You couldn't be wronger, Merce. It's nobody you know at *all*. Anyway does it matter who? Does it matter!"

"Don't go getting hysterical."

"Me hysterical? I thought you knew me better."

"Women in your condition do get that way."

" 'My condition.' "

"I've got to stop for some gas."

She drove into an Esso station and a strapping young giant came out, attired in a white jumper. He seemed shy, probably because of the two pretty women, one of them as young as he was and (his expressionless face registered the fact eloquently) some baby.

" 'Morning, Bart. Lovely day, isn't it? This is my kid sister from New York. Ten gallons, please."

Bart disappeared behind the car and a moment later they could hear the regular splash of gasoline pouring in.

"Cute, isn't he? The husky phlegmatic type. Rather like Greg. Very much like Greg, in fact, if you add a few years."

"Seems pleasant enough."

"Would you be interested?"

"Oh, for God's sake, Mercedes . . ."

"Darling, I'm not pro*pos*ing anything. I'm only asking. Purely academic."

"No, I don't think I would. He's just a big—'scuse it please—a big hunk of meat who doesn't know that women exist."

Mercedes smiled. "Sometimes that type can be rather fun, you know."

"I suppose, sometimes."

"Meaning what, exactly?" her sister said sharply. "Are you speaking of me, or for yourself?"

"I suppose that you, well, play around occasionally."

"*Darling.* I wasn't born yesterday."

"Neither was I."

"Then it's time you learned *the ropes*. Get wise to youself."

"I know the ropes. But I don't play around, as *you* mean it. I'm deadly serious about sex."

"My, you *are* hooked, aren't you?"

"Sometimes I think it's the only thing I *am* serious about. Certainly it's been very important in my life, and that's no news to you."

From under the brim of her floppy hat Mercedes studied Winifred in silence. "Well, all I can say is, you're a damned fool. Charge it please," she said to Bart, who quietly appeared at her elbow, his chore done.

"Can't I wipe off the windshield for you, Mrs. Bickerton?"

"No thanks, sweetie," Mercedes said, turning the ignition key. "It'll give me all the more reason to stop again tomorrow."

"Thank you, ma'am. Nice to meet you, Miss." He touched his

brilliantined hair, as if he wore a cap there, and they drove off.

They were soon in the desert, driving fast along one of those broad highways of several lanes that even then were the pride of Southern California. Finally they both began to speak at once.

"Tell me about . . ."

"Tell me . . ."

Each broke off. Then: "You first."

"No, you."

"Well," Winifred said, "I was only going to ask, what about these people coming. Burlingame is San Francisco, isn't it?"

"In the way that Southampton is New York. Well, there's three or four guys coming down tomorrow who love Greg more than they love me. You know how men are. They'll shoot and ride and have all sorts of boy-fun. I'll feed them. Now I don't mean anything invidious by that, you understand."

"I know the type. Squash clubs. Stag dinners. Golf every weekend as if it were their one true love, which it is. What were you going to ask me?"

"The facts."

"Oh yes, the facts. Well, I'm pregnant."

"I told you I got that. How many months?"

"Too many, too risky anyhow, for an abortion. A little over three."

"How *could* you have been so stupid?"

"Maybe I'm just stupid."

"What do you plan to do about it?"

"Well, I did want to go ahead and have the baby, rather."

"You must be crazy."

"But I changed my mind."

"Well, I should just think! And I don't propose to allow you to have it out here."

"As I said, I have other ideas now."

"Such as?"

"Well, I thought I'd ride a lot, good and hard. And maybe jump off things. Overdo. All that. And see if I couldn't bring on a self-induced . . . well . . ." For some reason she couldn't bring herself to say it.

"Miscarriage."

"Yes."

"It *might* work," Mercedes said.

"You can do anything you want to, you know, if you try real hard."

"Except get the man to marry you, it seems."

"But I didn't want the man to marry me. Not at the end, that is."

"You said a while ago you had wanted this baby."

"Not at the end."

"Okay, if you don't want to talk."

"Mercedes, do you want me to go home? I appealed to you because, frankly, I couldn't think of anybody else. I'm going to try real hard to have this miscarriage. My heart's in this thing, just as it was before in another way. But if I'm going to be twitted, or quizzed, or prove an embarrassment to you . . ."

"Forget it. I'll help you all I can."

"Thanks."

"For all our sakes, though, there's no point in letting Greg know there's anything going on. Men get awfully moral about these things. But I do wish . . ."

"What?"

"That you'd tell me the name of the guy."

"Look, why don't you drive me back to the station? I told you you didn't know him. You've never met him."

"You've never met Gregory."

"That's different."

"Why should you protect him like this?"

"I'm not protecting him. I was in love with him for a while, and now I'm not. I should think you'd understand that."

"Very well," Mercedes said with a deep frustrated sigh. "Have it your own way."

"It isn't just that it's my way. Under the circumstances there's no other way. The man and his name don't count. Not any longer."

"Okay, Win. I won't speak of it again."

And she didn't.

THE BICKERTON PLACE turned out to be an old-fashioned hacienda of considerable style, elegance, and spaciousness, surrounded
by a long wall of pale pink adobe about eight feet high, which all
but concealed the many small-gabled roofs of red tiles above. They
drove through an archway into a wide yellow-sanded court, with a
round adobe well and a single palm tree in the center, the latter
casting a black shadow in the blazing sunlight; beyond was a low
garage that could have housed half a dozen cars, and, farther back,
a row of stables adjoining an attractive, large, white-fenced corral.
The inner courtyard had an upper gallery running around three
sides of the structure. To Winifred Grainger the whole place (such
was its beauty and style) looked like something out of the books,
but belonging more to a Mexican landscape than to Southern California.

"God, it must be wonderful to be so rich"—and the words
echoed in her own mind as having been recently uttered by, or
picked up from, somebody else, she couldn't remember, at the
moment, who.

"Yes, the Bickertons are rich," Mercedes said, "which means
that Greg's quite rich too, though that doesn't necessarily follow. But it's one of the things I love about him most, bless him."

A squat but husky young Indian came running (imagine running
in this heat, Winifred thought; but the heat was dry, she did not
even faintly perspire) and taking her luggage from the back seat,
disappeared at a trot.

"He's settling you in. His name is Concepçion. Isn't that a riot?
I mean . . ."

"Shouldn't I go and change or something, before I meet your
husband and your friends?"

"Not now. Let's lie about first, have a cool drink, get caught up
on each other, and then lunch. You can rest after. Besides, the boys
are out; I see half the cars are gone. Gambling in Indio, probably;
yes, at this time of day. Anything to pass the time. Indio's about
ten miles off; it's our nearest habitation. Don't be afraid; we've a
staff of exactly twelve stalwart Indians here, and they're loyal.
Palm Springs is a few miles in the other direction. We're part of
the Mojave Desert. Down that way is the south entrance to Death

Valley. Cheering to know, isn't it? Come on, we'll stretch out on the patio, though it may be cooler inside. Want to go inside?"

"Whatever you want to do."

"Anyway, for heaven's sake take off that jacket. Got something sleeveless to wear later, I hope? Let's have a drink. The patio is shaded. And it's got a fountain that *sounds* purley and cool even though the water is probably scalding. Me, I've never tried it."

They stretched out, supine, in long cushioned chairs and gave themselves up to the pleasant heat and the stunning, vast, almost throbbing silence. Far off a massive thunderhead, rearing up like a mountain of pink-and-lavender rock candy, towered against the black summer sky, trailing across the desert floor slanting skeins of rain that you could not be sure you saw. Another Indian, barefoot like the other but a woman this time, silently brought them tall ice-cool drinks of gin with a delicate flavor something like mint mixed with cinnamon or saffron. "After lunch," Mercedes finally said, through a resounding unsuppressed yawn, "I'll show you your own place—you've got the cutest place all to yourself. I decided it that way so you wouldn't have to put up with the boorish banging around of Greg and his chums when they get drunk at night."

"I wouldn't mind."

"You don't mind being alone either, do you?"

"No. I like it. I'm a great deal alone."

"How about avocado and a salad for lunch, and iced tea?"

"Anything."

"Well, anything you want or need, speak up. Liberty Hall, you know. I want you to be comfortable. I want to be good to you."

The tears came—for no reason. Quiet, hardly showing, almost private. To Winifred's inexpressible relief, Mercedes made no comment for some time. Then, matter-of-factly, she said: "Of course the thing to do is be indifferent."

"The thing to do is be invulnerable. And how does anyone manage that?"

"*I* manage."

"I guess I'm just a slob."

"I wouldn't go so far as to say that. But you do have a distressing habit of not thinking of your*self*. Me, I think of myself first. Always. It pays."

"I'm sure it does."

After a long drink Mercedes said: "Well, what do you want to do about this thing? I told you I'd help."

"Mostly I just want to ride like mad. Ride my fool head off. I think it might work. It's got to work."

"Do you want to see a doctor?"

"No. At least not yet. Wait till I need him."

"I know a good guy. Very understanding."

"Good."

After lunch, with her arm linked through her sister's, Mercedes walked her out to the small charming guest house she was to occupy near the corral: a neat two-room dwelling, with bath, simply and tastefully decorated, surprisingly cool inside, doubtless because of the thick adobe walls. After Mercedes had returned to the main house, the Indian who had toted her luggage from the car appeared in the doorway. He managed to make it understood that if there was anything she wanted or needed, she had only to bang on the small painted drum that hung just outside the door: he would hear her.

She looked him over, in gratitude. Concepçion was squat, rugged, thick, and about thirty-five (she guessed); his face was a dusky sunburned red, the color of a new-peeled horse chestnut, and as shiny. His hair was a thick dead black, hanging in a long bob on both sides, with bangs on his forehead to the eyebrows. Around his head he wore what she could only think of as a red rag, much folded over, and overlapping, like a long handkerchief that has been pulled straight, tied behind, and then pushed up here and there, and down, to make it somewhat even. He was dressed in a thin black cotton shirt hanging over his pants, with a red sash, and cheap white cotton pants below, very loose; he was barefoot. But the thing that took her eye was a stunningly beautiful necklace he wore that reached almost to his middle: pale silver, with bright Indian designs every inch or so, separated by smaller perfectly matched silver beads. At the botton was suspended a large inverted silver "C," like a moon not even at the quarter; and the whole was studded with bright blue or green (it was hard to tell which) turquoise.

Winifred looked at it admiringly and said: "Can I buy that? It's lovely!"

After a few seconds he understood, and at once became withdrawn as if offended.

"I'll pay you whatever it cost. Or more. Anything! I'm crazy about it." And she reached for her purse.

Backing out of the doorway, with strange small movements like gestures of horror, he said (in effect): "No, no, this is mine. No can buy it." And somehow she got the impression that to him it was beyond price, that it belonged to him in the way one's tribal insignia or escutcheon belonged to one: it was part of his family, the sign of the tribe from which he sprang; it would be a sacrilege if it passed into other hands, and most certainly it was not for sale for any amount of money.

Respectfully she accepted the rebuff; she even admired the fact that he was completely adamant, almost unthinkingly so, and could not be swayed by dollars. Still she coveted the necklace and made up her mind to own it, or one like it, before her stay here was over. It was not greed; it was pure admiration for a thing of beauty unlike any piece of jewelry she had ever seen before. Why didn't other men wear such things? Why did only Indians so decorate themselves—men of all human creatures? And the fact that Concepçion prized it so highly only made it the more valuable in her eyes.

To her surprise, she slept almost till sunset. And when, bathed, wearing a green cotton sleeveless dress and white sandals, she made her way through the courtyard toward the main house again, she could tell from the loud deep talk within, so loud in all that desert silence, that the "boys" had come back.

Although they had been lying all but on their backs on several couches, as if exhausted, as if flung down there from some great height, they rose as one when she came in and Mercedes introduced them: Greg (or Bick), Tony, Wally, Ted, Gareth, Huntley, and Pete. Three were from Burlingame, two from Oakland, two from Sausalito, but they all belonged to the same clubs in San Francisco: the P-U Club, the Bohemian Club, and the Mace Club. Almost at once they flopped down again and went on with their incomprehensible monotonous talk as if she were not present; but one or two of them, especially Pete and Gareth, kept looking her over from time to time out of the corner of their eyes, and Tony even got up again to make her a drink. Greg embarrassed her by calling her "Sis," but all these were token attentions at best. The men belonged in a world of men: women existed for the sole purpose of being dressed well, running an establishment like this one, agreeable to be taken places occasionally, danced with, and possibly slept with on occasion. Mercedes sat at one side hunched over a solid square table a little larger than a card table, working out a jigsaw puzzle that must have comprised a thousand pieces at least. She had got as far as the foliage at the top (heaven knew how many days it had taken her), and when Winifred, drink in hand, paused to look over her shoulder and see how she was doing, she said: "The man told me it was supposed to be Robin Hood and his gang in Sherwood Forest, but I don't know. Did they all wear green? If so, then I *am* in the soup."

Winifred went to one of the open doors to look out at the fading desert fast disappearing in the dusk. Everything was so strange. She missed home and her own things there, missed that comfortable, plain but beautiful house in which she had not been happy but where she had not been unhappy either. She missed her own car, and her freedom. She missed Jack Sanford. She felt homesick; she even longed for him. Maybe this minute he was at the Finletters'; maybe (almost certainly) she was, also at this minute, furthest from his thoughts, while he was glad to be free again; but she missed him all the same and tried not to think of him, tried not to remember certain places, moments, details. It didn't work. Far more than she wanted that handsome silver necklace, more even than she wanted and needed to get rid of their child, she wished he were here to take her in his arms. That would have meant everything, everything; but she knew, too, how little it would mean to him. She said to herself: Well, kid, it's just something you have to accept, you have no right to inflict your griefs on others, it does no good even to dwell on them yourself, because it's *something you really don't want any more, can't have, mustn't hang onto.* For you, it's *out!* She turned back to the room and idly watched Mercedes struggling with multiple pieces of green that all looked alike, even to shape.

That night, around ten-thirty or eleven, still wakeful, she stepped to the door of her little house and looked out. There was no moon; but dark as it was, the desert was strangely alive with light and with murmurous sounds. A rustling in the scrub or bush could be heard everywhere; coyotes barked and yipped or howled far off, or maybe just dogs; a greenish-blue luminescence hovered over the vast barren expanse that was almost phosphorescent. This was no wasteland; for all that it was desert, it vibrated with a peculiar mysterious life. Miles away a glimmer of lights could be seen— Palm Springs, or Indio—but the desert had its own light that created a kind of submarine effect as if the whole world were just under water, partly submerged but by no means drowning. Overhead, the stars sparkled and throbbed and beat in the sky with a fantastic brilliance—oh, too much. They seemed so near, so low, that you could have knocked them out of the sky with a stick one by one. She felt a longing to be taken up, somehow, into that half-dark, that opalescent dark, toward those outlandish unreal stars, and disappear into the throbbing night that was a haunting glamour as she had never known or thought of glamour before. The idea was so attractive, and seemed so easy, that surely it would require only a small effort of will to bring it about. Yet, leaning against the glowing white wall in the blue night, she was earth-bound and always would be. There was only one philosophy, if you could call it even that: everybody wants to get outside of himself. But we're stuck with what we are, forever and forever, and we have to take it. Not only take it but accept, make something of it—put it to some *use,* for God's sake. We haven't happened for nothing; there must be something behind it all. Meanwhile, all this beauty of the night and the desert, this unknowing immense unregardful beauty, this impervious imperturbable majestic haunting mystical beauty . . . One could only shake one's head in the presence of such grandeur and immensity, and ask: Who the hell are we, for Christ's sake? What is man that Thou art mindful of him, et cetera.

Before eight in the morning she had breakfast alone, in the main house; then, dressed in riding breeches and shirt, she went out to the corral to choose a mount. To her surprise, Concepçion, the Indian with the handsome necklace, was there too, as if he had been waiting for her. All prearranged by Mercedes? She chose what looked like a spirited mare—Concepçion said she was one of their worst, meaning best—and he saddled the horse for her. As she rode out through the gate the Indian, with the simplest and most natural movement, as if he were aimlessly straddling a fallen tree trunk, threw his leg over the bare back of a pinto pony, without saddle or anything but a bridle, and rode out with her. She brought her horse to a halt. "No, no! Stay home," she said. "I want to go alone!" He ignored this as if he had not heard, and maybe indeed he had not understood. She gave up, put spurs to the flanks of her horse, and shot forward. The Indian was at her side.

Not always. Sometimes her speed was such that Concepçion was left behind; sometimes he was right next to her, and sometimes he outstripped her and raced far ahead. When he did so, she gloried in the way he rode (in the way they both rode). His bare feet, without moccasins, were steadied by no stirrups: they stuck almost straight out, the toes spread. His cute ass in the thin white cotton pants bounced on the pony's back midway between rump and mane; he was sure of himself, far surer than she was, good rider though she had always been, with stirrups, reins, saddle. He held his back rigidly upright, the black cloth of his shirt fluttering in the speed, the silver necklace now hanging down his back, and his longish bobbed hair slapping at his neck and ears. He did have reins to hold onto but he used only one hand, and now and again a short sharp cry (of joy?) escaped involuntarily from this most silent, most taciturn of men. As they rode on, for miles, as hard and fast as they could, she wondered why he had come along. Orders? Were there dangers in the desert that he would protect her from? As the hours passed and the sun grew higher and hotter and the morning haze lifted, she felt that they were one or had become one or would become so, without the need for words or anything else. When they stopped to water their horses at an irrigation ditch, she saw why he wore the shapeless bright red rag around his hair and across his forehead. It held back the sweat from his eyes, for they were both streaming with perspiration by now.

Unlike the brilliant desert of New Mexico and Arizona that had so fascinated her from the train, with its richly colored barren sand in which nothing grew but an occasional cactus plant, this desert was covered thickly with short matted scrub that, when you looked down, was a riot of flowers, as the seed catalogue would have said. She recognized some of the almost buried or hidden blooms. Early, before the sun rose high to drive them out of sight till evening, myriads of white flowers like morning glories covered the desert floor, thrusting upward through the low tangled scrub. She saw lavender and verbena and marigold everywhere in a contrasting patchwork of smaller purple and yellow flowers that she didn't know the name of. There were white sand daisies, blue lupine and small scarlet blossoms with yellow throats, and always the bright-green, sage-green, and sometimes milky-green spiny cactus that grew no higher than ten or a dozen inches. White forget-me-nots caught her eye, and she wanted to move about and gather a real bouquet of them—but for whom? Jack was three thousand miles away. Concepçion, if he noticed them at all, took them for granted, naturally, as part of his everyday world. Mercedes would have said, "Look, dear, if you want *flowers*, we'll drive into Palm Springs. There's an excellent florist who gets fresh flowers every day from Beverly Hills." They belonged where they were, these delicate plants; they would not have been missed, if you should pick them; there were so many, and the desert was so vast . . .

Breathless (she at least was breathless), they pulled into the corral shortly before noon, both of them hot and sweaty. Concepçion tethered their mounts to the white bleached posts. She indicated that she wanted to be alone. He left, and then she did something which, if anyone had seen her, would have looked very odd indeed, possibly even mad. Assured that she was alone (but was Concepçion lurking in the black doorway of that shed nearby, watching her?), she climbed up the three or four horizontal fence rails till she was at least seven feet above the ground, felt her way carefully to one of the upright posts that supported them every ten feet or so, stood up, took a deep breath, and jumped off into space, to land on the ground stiff-legged with a jar that shook her whole frame with shock. Somewhat dizzy from the impact, she nevertheless managed to do it again, then again and again till she could no longer climb up, and could hardly see. Dazed, she found her way to her own small house, took a shower, lay on the bed a few minutes, and then, blessedly tired out as she wanted to be, crossed the great courtyard to the comparative cool darkness of the comfortable spacious hacienda. The others were just getting up, coming downstairs.

After lunch on the awninged patio, she said she wanted to retire to her own place for a nap, and partly she did so. Then she changed into her riding clothes and went to the corral again. Concepçion was there as before, their horses ready, though they had exchanged not a word of her plan for an afternoon ride, at a time when everybody else took a siesta, no matter how late they had risen in the morning. Without conversation or words of any kind, they rode out through the gate and off into the desert as one, riding almost as hard as they had ridden before. Now and again, as they reached a peak of speed, they gave each other a small look of mutual satisfaction, a smile on her part, a dead-pan acknowledgment on his that he admired her horsemanship. And again on returning, having dismissed Concepçion, the routine of climbing up and jumping off the corral posts, over and over again, as many times as she could take it. And when she turned up at the shaded patio a little before six, seemingly crowded with men except for herself and Mercedes, she might have been coming from the movies. "How was your day?" someone asked (Huntley? Tony?). "Swell, I had a real workout. I love riding." "We had a real workout too," Huntley (or Tony) said. "The slot machines in a joint at Indio. They were red hot when we got through with them. But did it do us any good? I tell you they're fixed, Greg. You can't win. They're fixed, I tell you. Why, I spent . . ."

In the evening the two sisters watched, with identical expressions (corners of the mouth turned down, foreheads furrowed in "surprise" should occasion demand), while the boys sprawled or knelt or crawled on the vast bare floor playing with Greg's elaborate trains: working the signals, halting miniature locomotives at diminutive water towers, arranging head-on collisions with an excitement, volubility and hilarity that put the two girls' apathy to shame. Greg, who wouldn't bend over to pick up a dime or a burning cigarette, seemed completely at home on the floor; he all but nestled beside the busy tracks, and sometimes he stretched out full-length on his stomach, his cheek resting on his palm, watching a speeding train with flashing headlight and listening delightedly to the warning signals (*ding, ding*) of the grade crossing with lowering gate as if he had never been more comfortable or content in his life. Mercedes might have been a million miles away, but did she care? her sister wondered. Huddled over an impossible jigsaw puzzle or working a needle-point pattern with the acutest concentration, she seemed perfectly content, too. She had her husband, whether he was aware of her or not; she was well provided for; she hadn't a care in the world; life was simple and even good if you expected nothing from it. Winifred went to bed.

She had barely stretched out in her batiste nightgown, looking through the window near her bedside at the tremulous never-silent blue night of the desert, when she heard a scratch and a tap at her open door, barred only by a screen, unlatched.

"Who is it?" she said.

"Me. Gareth. Did I wake you?"

"No."

"I just wondered, well, are you all right? It's a wonderful night, you've no idea."

"I'm all right," she said.

"Well, I'm not. Not by a long shot."

"What's the matter, too much to drink?"

"No, not that. I'm perfectly sober. I want to come in for a minute."

"What for?"

"Oh, I don't know. Just come in. Okay?"

Lying there in the blue dark, she considered. She knew what he wanted. She said: "Come in, then."

He did so, but so timidly, so awkwardly and shyly that she almost felt sorry for him. But not sorry enough.

"Sit down," she said.

"Where? On the edge of your bed?"

"Why not?"

"You're a brick, Winifred. I knew you wouldn't throw me out or turn me down. It's hell out here in the desert."

"Well, that's where you're wrong. I am turning you down."

"But . . . you said come in. I distinctly heard . . ."

"I did, Gareth, and I meant it. But listen for a minute. Think of me instead of yourself. I like you and all that. You're a very attractive fella. Clean-cut, I believe is the word." He did, indeed, look like an Arrow-collar ad by Leyendecker, and as lacking in humanity or personality and even glands; she couldn't imagine him sweating, for instance. "But look, I'm trying to get over something. Some other man. That's why I'm out here, to break it. I don't mind a harmless visit in the night, but, Gareth dear, maybe some other time. And I don't mean tomorrow night. I mean, the way I feel now, I don't care if I see another man again in, oh, months. Will you forgive me?"

"Well, that's laying it on the line at least."

"It doesn't mean I don't like you."

He was already standing again. "Well, if that's the way you feel about it."

"I'm afraid I do."

"Anyway," he said, backing off, "thank you for being such a good sport about it."

"Don't thank me. I wish I felt differently but I don't."

"Good night, Winifred. I didn't think there was any harm in taking a chance."

"No harm. Good night, Gareth. See you at lunch tomorrow."

He was gone.

God, if they were all as easy to get rid of as that; if they took it like polite little boys as he did. But she didn't want them to take it like that, ever. But she didn't want Gareth, either. If on the other hand it had been Concepçion . . . He at least sweated. But no, not even Concepçion. At least not tonight.

Several evenings later she suddenly couldn't finish dinner and asked to be excused on the grounds that she wasn't feeling well, for some reason. Too much sun maybe, she said. When she had reached her cottage, undressed, and was sitting in a hot tub, Mercedes phoned from the hacienda.

"What's the matter?" her sister said. "Anything wrong?"

"I hope so. I've got severe cramps, and I'm bleeding some."

"I'll be right over."

"No, I'm all right."

"I'll be over, I said."

When she came in, Winifred said, "Maybe this is it, Merce. God, I hope so."

"You're not to think about it, dear. Relax. Here, take these sleeping pills. Just a couple for a starter."

"I'm relaxed, except for the cramps."

"Take them anyway. I'm going to call Dr. Alonzo from Palm Springs. He's a good guy. I trust him completely."

"I don't need him. I'm okay."

"Oh no you're not, not if you're bleeding and everything. Listen. You're in no position to call the shots now, do you hear? You're a sick girl."

"I'm beginning to feel like it."

"Take these pills. They'll calm you down. And I've got more where these came from."

"Anybody would think . . ."

"Never mind. Do as I say." From the bathroom she brought a glass of water; Winifred dutifully, even meekly, took the pills.

"Now I'm going to call Dr. Alonzo. He's no Valentino but he knows his business. Promise not to go out if I leave you?"

"Out! Where would I go? I'm bleeding, I tell you. I feel awful."

"Good. Now lie down and let the pills do their work."

Winifred did as she was told. She was glad to be alone, even if the cramps did hurt. The bleeding seemed to be nothing—nothing you could feel, anyway, except a wet mess in the bed. She got up to get some Kotex, but felt too weak to rummage through her luggage. She even doubted whether she had brought any; under the circumstances, she probably hadn't. God, if she needed Kotex, she wouldn't be out here in the first place. She lay back again in the bed, pulled the blanket up to her chin against the night chill of the desert, and in a few minutes felt herself dozing blessedly off.

The yapping of a coyote nearby, followed by a mournful but shrill wail, woke her. She reached for the little bottle Mercedes had left on the bed table, next to a glass of water already beaded inside with motionless air bubbles like dead champagne, and took two more tablets. She fell asleep again.

Some while later, maybe an hour, maybe two hours or even more, Mercedes was shaking her awake. She sat up abruptly, confused, not knowing at first where she was.

"This is Dr. Alonzo. He's here to help you. You must do everything he says, do you hear?"

"How do you do, Miss . . .?"

"Grainger," Mercedes said. "My younger sister."

He put his palm on her forehead. Then he was shaking down a thermometer when she said thickly, "Sorry. I've got to go to the bathroom, if you'll help me. I feel all woozy. And the bed is soaked through. Can anybody change it? I can't lie in all that . . . It must be blood. It's got to be blood."

"I'll help you," Mercedes said. "Lean on me. Give up to me. You won't fall."

As they staggered slowly from the room like a pair of befuddled Siamese twins, Dr. Alonzo turned back the blanket and examined the sheets.

Some minutes later, when they returned from the bathroom, the bed had been freshly made, the sheets changed.

"Who on earth . . .?"

"I wasn't an interne years ago for nothing, Mrs. Bickerton. I can make beds. Now just get back in again, young lady. You'll be a lot more comfortable this time."

Without a word, Winifred, conscious but dazed, lowered herself to the bed and lay flat, looking unseeingly at the ceiling. She didn't even trouble to pull up the blanket but let somebody else do it.

Dr. Alonzo stepped into the bathroom, and after a moment he called out quietly, "Mrs. Bickerton, may I see you a moment?"

Maybe five minutes later the two emerged from the bathroom and stood on either side of the bed, looking down at Winifred. She lay quite still, eyes open, but breathing deep, distressed sighs.

"Winifred."

"Yes . . .?"

"Dr. Alonzo has something to tell you. Can you take it in?"

For answer, she turned her head toward the doctor; she gazed at him clearly enough, but remotely.

"The worst is over," he said. "In fact it's all over. You've had your miscarriage. You passed it without knowing it. I found it in the sheets when Mrs. Bickerton took you to the bathroom."

"Passed what?"

"While you were in there with your sister, I picked it up and wrapped it in a few Kleenex tissues to get it out of the way. It had been lying there in the blood. Then I changed the bed. When you came back, I took it into the bathroom and told your sister about it. We disposed of it in the toilet. So it's all over."

Tears trembling on her eyelids, Winifred said nothing.

"There's only one thing more," he said, "but that's up to you whether you want to hear it or not. The foetus was fairly well advanced, about six inches long and tightly wrapped. Still, far enough progressed for me to be able to determine the sex. Would you . . . Do you want to know what it was?"

Winifred rolled her head on the pillow, indicating No.

"Very wise, I think. Still, some women . . ."

"No!" she said aloud. And then in a whisper: "It doesn't make any difference, does it? Does it?" Turning to her sister, she asked: "How could it?"

Businesslike, Mercedes said: "You've been very kind, Dr. Alonzo, coming over here in the night. We do appreciate it. I suppose there's nothing for her to do now except rest up for a few days?"

"That's right. I'll stop by tomorrow and examine her a little more thoroughly, just in case."

"You're too kind. Thank you so much."

"Not at all. Good night."

"Good night."

Winifred, her head turned toward the window, looking out into the blue night, said nothing. She kept wiping her eyes with the back of her hand, and there was a faint sound of muffled, restrained sobs.

"Here's some Kleenex, sweetie."

She reached for the box and held a fistful of tissues over her eyes. Finally she said, but mumblingly, as if talking to herself: "That little girl he said he adored, his brother's child. He wanted one too. He said he did. Now I'll never know, because I didn't want to know, it was far too late, whether he had a boy coming to him . . . or the dimsal girl . . ."

"What on earth are you talking about? You've had too many pills, Win, and I'm taking them away. Go to sleep now. You're more than half asleep already. I'll get Concepçion to sleep outside your door, if you want anything. And you can always ring me at the house. Are you hearing me? Will you remember?"

Remember, Winifred repeated to herself: it seems I never do anything else but.

MERCEDES DRIVING, the low-slung convertible passed through Palm Springs and on toward Los Angeles as fast as the law allowed. Winifred had been at the Bickerton hacienda a little over three weeks and now was homeward-bound but by a different route this time. She had not been able to shake her depression after the miscarriage, and she decided, because of the rest it would give her, to return more leisurely: by boat, on the Dollar Line out of San Pedro, port of Los Angeles, through the Panama Canal, and up the east coast to New York, or at least to Jersey City, where the S.S. *President Grant* finally docked. By telephone, she had been able to get a reservation, with an outside cabin and private deck, without any difficulty. After very little discussion, she and Mercedes had decided that the slow return by boat would restore her spirits far better than the fast three-day trip by train. Funny thing was, her spirits began to pick up the moment she left the hacienda behind her, though she had truly regretted to see the last of her riding companion, Concepçion.

Just before leaving, they descended to the enormous playroom downstairs to say goodbye to Greg and his chums. Though it was a morning of brilliant sunshine, five of the boys were playing pool by electric light and two were making a hell of a racket at the Ping-Pong table. They paused long enough to chalk their cues, the Ping-Pong players to wipe their foreheads, say goodbye, come again, and then they went on with their games. Of them all, Gareth was the only one who gave Winifred a look that might have been termed personal, but it was only *politesse,* a moment of good manners, and they both knew it. There was also, though, a look of shy appeal in his eyes, as if he were saying: I hope you didn't tell anybody.

"I hate to break their hearts by leaving them like that," Winifred said lightly as she got into the front seat and Concepçion put her few pieces in the rear. "Damned mean of me to be so callous. They won't get over it for ages."

"Damned mean."

"How do you stand it, Merce?"

Her sister calculatedly took time to light a cigarette and then said: "Now listen. I like being taken care of. And I'm being very well taken care of. With bells on. It seems to me you might give a thought to the same thing yourself."

"I guess we're different people. It seems to be a waste of time, a way of getting through the days just anyhow, waiting to die."

"Do you know of a better way?"

"One ought to try being useful, somehow."

"How useful are you?"

"Forget I said anything. We're just . . . two different people."

"We are indeed. You thrive on trouble, look for it, find it, fall into it. Me, I prefer the even tenor of whatever-it-is the poet says. Don't ask me which poet, but I couldn't agree with him more. And I like, I fairly bask in, my creature comforts."

"Bask? Over a thousand pieces of jigsaw puzzle?"

"You couldn't do a thousand-piece jigsaw puzzle in a fifth-floor-walk-up cold-water flat."

"More power to you."

"You don't need to be nasty, Win."

"Far from being nasty, I admire you all over the place. I'm just not the placid type."

"Now you are being nasty. Look, there's the gas station where beautiful Bart works, in those beautiful white coveralls. Shall we stop and ask him to wipe off the windshield?"

"No thanks. You stop for me, on the way back."

Mercedes smiled. "You know, I might just do that."

At San Pedro they drove down the small incline right onto the pier. An affable porter from the steamship came running, Mercedes told him the number of the stateroom that had been reserved for her sister, he took the bags, and they got out. They went to the checking-in place, found everything was in order, and paid; Winifred still had a number of traveler's checks left and a decent amount of cash in her purse, plus her checkbook.

As they looked the other passengers over, Mercedes said: "God, what people. You can see at a glance there's nobody you'll want to know. Aren't people awful?"

"Concepçion was nice."

"Oh, I knew you liked him."

"I liked that red rag he wore around his head. And I awfully liked that beautiful silver and turquoise necklace. He wouldn't sell it to me."

"Of course he wouldn't. It represented his tribe, his people. He'd sooner die than part with it."

"Well, I wish *I* had one."

"No problem. There's a souvenir shop right over there. Come on."

"A souvenir . . . But that's not the same."

"Don't be a snob. You couldn't tell the difference."

And she couldn't. Though no two were exactly alike, they looked more or less the same: pale Mexican silver, studded here and there with unobtrusive lozenges or bits of turquoise, bright green or bright blue, with that inverted crescent moon of heavier silver below, hanging at the waist line or just above. She bought one for seventy-five dollars and considered it a bargain.

"Here, let me give it to you as a present. In memory of Concepçion," Mercedes said, "and whatever went on between you."

"We rode together. We rode like mad. You know that. But thanks loads. Gee, it's nice."

"Now," Mercedes said, as if embarrassed by her generous impulse, "the moment you get aboard, see the purser and try and get a table by yourself in the dining room. Then you won't have to talk to people."

"I'll be all right."

"And mind, you're not to brood."

"I'm all right. I'm not the brooding type anyway. At least I don't think I am."

"You've picked up beautifully. I really think you're better already."

They looked up at the ship, saw the many derricks raised skyward slantingly like inextricable jackstraws in a pile, saw thirty or forty passengers already aboard and already waving wildly to friends or relatives on the pier, a hundred feet away at most. The ship looked small compared to the gigantic floating palaces of the Cunard or White Star Lines that had taken them to Europe in the past.

"It's certainly no *Mauretania* or *Leviathan*," Mercedes said.

" 'Other times' . . ."

"Look, dear, we're just making conversation. We're as bad in our way as those frenzied people above waving artificial farewells to the people below who dasn't leave if they wanted to. All that wasted energy, those frozen smiles, it makes me positively shudder. So look. Why don't I just beat it. Get the hell out."

"Thanks for that," Winifred said, relieved. "We know how we feel about each other without all this."

At that moment a busty woman in garish clothes with canary-colored hair and white sun visor à la Helen Wills, preceded by a porter pushing a small truck laden with luggage pasted with enough travel and hotel stickers to cover almost every inch of their many surfaces, and leading on a split leash a pair of small poodles that trotted rapidly ahead as if their tiny feet hurt (one was dyed bright pink, the other Kelly green), passed importantly by. The sisters exchanged expressionless glances that said plainer than words, Now there's Southern California for you; then Mercedes turned, patted Winifred casually on the shoulder, and was gone.

The stateroom was spacious, with a made-up day bed, a wide sepia-tinted mirror covering the wall opposite the door to the corridor, a stall shower, and another door leading outside to the deck, with a section spaced off by a low wire grill indicating that it was for Winifred Grainger's private use only. She began to unpack and hang away a few things.

There was a rap on her door, and without waiting for her "Come in" (*"Entrez," "Herein," "Avanti"*), a short thickset muscular young man in an immaculate starched white uniform pushed open the door. Without once looking at her during the two or three minutes he was in the cabin, he said: "Everything all right, Madam, or Miss? My name is Matt. Remember that, it ain't hard. If you need anything, just press that button there. I'll hear you and come running. I'm the steward assigned to this corridor. Say, you didn't get your flowers!"

"What flowers?"

"The *President Grant* always sends flowers to its lady guests."

"Good old Hiram Ulysses Grant," she added, then felt foolish for having engaged him in unnecessary conversation so soon.

"Ulysses Simpson Grant, when I went to school."

"Actually it's either or both," she said without interest.

"Then how did he get to be U. S. Grant?" he said, straightening his stiff white jacket around his neat hips and regarding himself in the mirror.

(Concepçion would never have done that, she thought, then realized she had thought of Concepçion and his figure because they very much resembled each other in the purely physical department.)

"Oh, I don't know. Please! I'm trying to unpack, and you must have other things to do."

"Right. Just ring if you want me for anything. Anything." And he was gone.

She stood there holding a dress in one hand, a hanger in the other. Now why should he have said that? Even repeated it. Especially when he hadn't even looked at me at all, not once. Do I go around (ridiculous thought, but it had often occurred to her) carrying the *mark,* for God's sake?

She lunched alone on her small private deck, from a tray—it was brought to her by a comically effeminate Latin waiter from the dining room (he insisted on correcting her, grandly, by saying in pointed sibilants "dining *salon,* Ma-dame") and afterward she set the tray in the corridor outside, locked both doors, drew the Venetian blinds, and took a nap. In mid-afternoon, with the ship moving slowly down the peninsula of Lower California toward Mexico, never very far from shore so that it was like not being really at sea at all, except for the barely perceptible rolling, she lay in her deck chair with an unopened book in her lap and enjoyed the exquisite luxury (compared to the recent past) of time-out, doing nothing, thinking nothing. From inside the cabin she heard someone ring the buzzer first and then, after a pause, rap sharply on the white louvered door. She ignored it: Matt with the flowers, perhaps. Though she refused to turn her head to see, she was then aware that someone had come out onto the private deck next to hers: out of the corner of her eye she could see, whether she wanted to or not, a thick blur of white as some figure stood motionlessly there; then it went away.

She knew she was in for it now; it was only a matter of time. She hadn't the sense or the will to put him in his place; besides, she wasn't sure she wanted to. Why? Or why not? From what she had seen of him (he had seen nothing of her, apparently), he seemed a completely unprepossessing young man. But there was also something about the situation, something in the air: the private cabin, the male attendant, the lone female passenger who was herself. In the past she had given in readily, even made the first move, on far less. Even so, she wanted to be alone now; wanted to, and knew she wouldn't be, knew she would change her mind in the twinkling of an eye or one more glance at that short thick thoroughly male figure of the brash young man in the white uniform. (What was there about uniforms? Their very "uniformity" should have eliminated any attraction, because it made the creatures within a kind of stereotype, whereas the very reverse was true.) She wanted this time to think, rest, recover—*get rid of Jack Sanford*. It was a losing battle, and she knew it. She couldn't "get rid of him," she could only take on substitutes. She didn't want Jack any more, she was through with him, but she loved him still; and she remembered so many moments when he had loved her—oh, there had been no doubt of that. But if he had loved her, how had it come to nothing so easily, so quickly? He was adept at playing the social game, for gain; she was not; and that had made all the difference. But how could he have dropped it so lightly? Just how often, please (answer me that, she asked herself), does one come across love, the real thing? Whole lifetimes can pass by, and it doesn't happen. When it does happen, wouldn't you think . . . wouldn't any man think . . . wouldn't anybody want . . . ? Well, to get the most out of it, to say the very least. Love, or being in love—my God, alternatives did not arise at all! You didn't *calc*ulate these things, not when they were real. You let yourself go, with no regard to the consequences: to what other people thought, for instance, or how it affected your position in town. But—it was over. She couldn't go back to it, and she didn't want to. Even if he should give up Betty Finletter, or whoever, his importance to her (except for love, the love-making, especially the being wanted as much as she had wanted him, that most luxurious, priceless, rewarding feeling of all) had diminished. Far better to go back to Tony di Santo once in a while, or just anybody, any male, and expect nothing more than sensual pleasure in bed—no small thing in itself. Only, love was missing, that extra magic that had made her feel important, attractive, alive, fulfilled, *wanted for herself.* Raw sex could be a fulfillment too—oh, she had never belittled the value and excitement of that—but it always seemed so, was so, temporary, transient, an expedient merely.

When she was dressing in her cabin to go to dinner, there was a rap on her door again. This time she opened it. Matt the steward came in as if he had been expected, carrying a vase filled with yellow roses. Without looking at her again, without so much as glancing in her direction (she wondered again if he knew what she looked like at all, even whether he had ascertained if she was old or young), he set the vase down on her writing table, fiddled with the separate blooms for a moment, then stepped back and stood in the exact center of the room, partly turned away from her, his stubby hands on his white-duck hips, thumbs to the rear, and began to talk.

"I hope you're going down to dinner tonight. It ain't good for a lady to coop herself up like this, eating lunch from a tray and like that. You ought to get out. There might be some people you'd like to meet."

"Thank you for your concern," she said. "I'll get out. I'm getting ready to go to dinner now." She couldn't have dreamed it would be the first and last time she was to enter the dining salon during the rest of the ten-day voyage.

"Good. I'll look in on you after dinner. Before you go to bed. You go to bed early?"

Then she became aware of why he hadn't looked at her directly; he hadn't needed to. He was studying her intently in the long glass of the mirror opposite the door to the corridor; and recalling his stance and apparent aloofness before, she knew now he had been looking her over thoroughly, with studied attention, far more intimately than if he had turned toward her face to face. Unwilling to let on that she knew she had been cased in this oblique way, she looked down toward the carpet beside her chair, where rested the shoes she was about to put on for the evening.

"Thank General Grant for the roses," she said.

"That's okay. Anything you want from me, just ring."

She didn't answer. Give me Concepçion any day, she thought, and that natural, uncomplicated, unpretentious simplicity, unscheming, pretending nothing. In another second or two Matt turned from his so-useful mirror and left the room.

Dinner was not a success, though she was made a great fuss of by the head waiter. The food was good enough, and the passengers themselves ("What people," Mercedes had said; or "Such people") were really all right, including even the overdressed glittering lady who had brought the dyed poodles aboard, but she felt out of place without knowing why, wished she were back at the hacienda or, even more, home. She was lonely to the point of desolation, which was so unlike her; she who had always had resources within herself to fall back on now seemed suddenly bereft and astray. She heard the throb of the engines below and the wash of the sea, felt the ship lurch slowly to one side, then another, looked at the other passengers with as much interest and curiosity as she could muster, and did not envy the clubby chatty groups that had already been drawn together as if by some mysterious but meaningless inevitability. She thought of her Indian riding companion with the scarlet headband and the beautiful necklace; she thought of Dr. Alonzo and his cold-blooded (there was a word!) night visit. She knew she would never forget the question he had asked her and the opportunity she had had, and passed up, to "find out." But she felt she had been right not to go into that, even though she knew she would always wonder.

In middle evening Matt tapped lightly and came in.

"How you doing?"

"All right."

"Anything I can do for you?"

"No. Thanks."

"Enjoy your dinner?"

"Enough."

"Mind if I sit down a minute?"

"Aren't you on duty?"

"More or less. But I got the bells fixed in the corridor so I can hear a ring wherever it comes from. I could hear it in here just as plain as if I was at my post." He took the comfortable chair opposite her (he no longer needed to look in the mirror), leaned back and sprawled out, loosening the collar of his white jacket.

"Where is your post?"

"I got a place, couple of cabins away. Share it with three other guys. Two of them are waiters. Nice enough guys but they're not clean, you know? I mean bodily clean. Get's kind of crowded when we're all in there at night. And smelly." She must have raised her eyebrows at this, for he added: "We don't have an outside cabin like yours, with portholes, and an open door and all that fresh air. This is *nice.*"

She looked at him now, as thoroughly and perhaps as calculatingly as he had earlier studied her in the glass. He was the kind of young man who came a dime a dozen; she had seen hundreds like him, had dozens, and you couldn't beat it. Strictly working-class, with an animal vitality that filled out his white clothes, particularly in the upper thighs and shoulders so that his uniform seemed to be packed full; self-centered, most certainly selfish, out for himself and what he could get out of life (but who wasn't?); in one way, when she thought of Jack Sanford, who had loved her, he was all wrong; in another way, considering the kind of person she was herself and the position of desolation she was in, he was just what the doctor ordered. She didn't even try to resist her interest, and it must have been revealed in her expression. She resented his cockiness, his certainty that she wouldn't say no, but she expected nothing less, of either of them. It was only a matter of time; and that wasn't long in coming.

"That bed, you know, opens into a double."

"Does it?"

He made no pretense of desire, much less of love-making or even of ordinary flattery. "I'd sure like to stay here tonight."

"I knew you were going to ask that."

"I didn't ask. Never do. I don't need to."

"I'm sure of that, too."

"Then we understand each other. Okay?"

"How old are you?" she asked.

"Twenty-eight."

"I wouldn't have thought you were that much."

"I don't show wear and tear like some people. With my clothes off, you'd think I was a boy."

"You might have skipped that. Besides, I'm not much interested in boys."

"You will be in this boy. Wait, I got a couple of things to tend to. Be right back."

He was gone.

She was being used, of course, and she felt nothing about it one way or the other: no feminine pride held her back. For she was using him too, or would be, so why pretend? As she thought back on it, he seemed to have made it perfectly clear from the beginning what his intentions were, with a take-it-or-leave-it attitude. In a way she admired, and was even grateful for, his brash, conceited frankness: compared to many men she had known, it was positively refreshing.

"I never knew it to fail," he said guilelessly as he closed the door behind him and now frankly unbuttoned his jacket from top to bottom. "I've never been on one of these trips yet when I didn't find some nice babe to play house with."

How could she be abashed? He was like a child thinking out loud. "Lucky you," she said.

"I think so," he said simply.

"But did it ever occur to you that such an arrangement could be, can be, a two-way street?"

"So much the better," he said, with a broad disarming smile, "long as we both get what we want. I hate that smelly cabin with those other guys. And I hate sleeping alone. Don't you?"

"Frankly, yes."

He threw aside his stiff white jacket, untied and stepped out of his white shoes.

"You do come to the point in a hurry, don't you?"

"Why not?"

"I suppose I could call the captain or somebody and have you thrown out. For insulting a lady," she added wryly.

"But you won't."

"No, I won't. I've already decided to accept what you have to offer. Now go ahead, make something of that."

"No need to. My name's Matt, by the way."

"You already told me. Mine is Winifred, Winnie, Win, whatever you like."

"I know. I looked you up in the purser's book."

"You probably even know my financial status, and so forth."

"Not yet, but give me time."

There was a camaraderie between them—already good-humored, frank, no holds barred, almost sexless in an odd way, certainly unromantic—that made her smile, as it did him. They were going to be friends—at least that kind of friends. Outrageous though the situation might seem to others, she found it practically a relief. She wouldn't have to make any effort, play up, flatter, use words; and neither would he. If women only knew the *value* of these chance encounters, she thought, including their "therapeutic" value, maybe more of them wouldn't be so damned smug and look down their married noses at those of their sisters to whom variety-is-the-spice-of-life wasn't just a tired quotation. There are outlets for fun for everybody in this world, if you can shift gears and get onto a different plane altogether. "Fun"—what a word. Her heart was breaking, and she was alleviating the pain the best way she knew how, or the worst way; who knows?

So it began. It was just like that; as simple as that; as easy; no more to it than that. But once begun (such was his single-minded intensity, his interest in his own appetites), she found it difficult to break off. Nor did she want to, once the barriers were down. He was like an animal, with primitive concentration, broken only occasionally when he heard a bell ring in the corridor (very rarely after eleven at night). Then he was into his clothes and out of the cabin in hardly a minute; and hardly a minute later he was back, out of his clothes again, and back into bed. He slept hard, even a lot; when he was awake, his sole function in life (it was like a reflex) seemed to be to satisfy his own body, without thought of hers. She didn't think she had ever experienced in her life anything so intense, or so concentrated, or so meaningless. Talk about time-out; it was as though she had entered a world somewhere between Lethe and Nirvana, a world where satisfied appetite drugged you temporarily, for it always wore off and you wanted more; where memory and thought scarcely existed, thank heaven; where you went neither forward nor back into any kind of relationship—per-

fectly safe from disillusionment or let-down because you expected
nothing else. There seemed between them a highly active but unspoken understanding that this was all there was in the world. All?
Well, right now, what more could she have wanted? She didn't
have to think; and except for those frequent moments of almost
cataclysmic passion, she scarcely felt at all.

Their conversations, when they had them, were brief, pointless.
Such as:

"What's your name, Matt?"

"Matthew."

"No kidding! I meant your last name, of course."

"You couldn't pronounce it. Polish, it used to be, but we cut it
down to Mank."

"You don't look Polish."

"Nobody looks Polish. 'Specially in this country. Transplanted
Poles very quickly become American. More than most foreigners
is my opinion."

This seemed true enough. How many times had she seen a
bright, young, All-American face looking up at her from the sports
page more native-looking, more American than the mythical boy
next door, and then read his name below: Andy Bolshewisczitsky.

Or:

"What does your old man do?"

"Not much. Hardly anything really."

"Just like mine. He's a bum too. Only I bet your old man is no
bum."

"It doesn't matter. It's all relative."

"Say, that's a good word. I must remember it."

And again:

"Why aren't you married?"

"Oh, I don't know. I just never wanted to get married."

"Not ever?"

"I did once. For a while. But I changed my mind."

"Why?"

"I guess I enjoy my own freedom too much."

"I'll say you do."

After that first night in the dining room she took all her meals
alone in her own room or on her small private deck. This retreat

from the other passengers had little to do with What-are-they-thinking?—for such thought scarcely ever occurred to Winifred Grainger. She wanted to be alone with Matt (it was comfortable that way) and get the whole thing over as soon as possible and get home again. But what was she going back to? What would it be like? Something had gone out of her life, and she doubted whether her life would ever be filled the same way again, however briefly. Maybe she should pull up stakes and move away from Arcadia for good, start all over again somewhere else. But start what? Meaningless phrases, all of them. Like "life" itself. At least her life.

One morning, just before they passed into the Panama Canal, she woke to bright day and for a moment or two wondered (as she often had before) where she was: the cabin seemed a place, almost cell-like in its confinement, that she had never seen before. Then it came back. Matt had got up about six, dressed and gone out, and she had gone back to sleep again. Now the sun was streaming into her room, through the tied-back opened door that led to her small deck. She had lowered the Venetian blinds the evening before, from the top to the bottom, and the sun cut through the slats and patterned the floor with black-bright stripes, as if it filtered through prison bars. She looked at them in fascination and accepted the rightness of it, the peculiar justice. All the same, she told herself, I'll never do that again; either I leave the blinds up entirely, so that anybody can look in, or pull them tightly shut so they won't create this all-too-real illusion of living in a cage, of being kept caged like an animal—even a contented animal, what was the difference?—for somebody else's use. If she had communicated this idea to Matt, he would only have slapped his thick thigh heartily and laughed aloud, enjoying the allusion—as, mindlessly, he enjoyed everything.

They took forever passing through the Canal Zone; and for all that the speed of the ship had been slowed down to ten knots, and half that, and sometimes, because of the locks, much less, they made no stops at all. From her deck she watched the scarcely moving landscape of Panama, which varied from high, canyonlike gorges with slanting slides of sand and shale to low, densely thick undergrowths of vivid green jungle, almost as vivid in the darker colors as in the lighter, from which immensely tall leaning trees occasionally towered above the tangled impenetrable mass of foliage below. When they reached the Atlantic at last they moved out into a sea of a different color altogether from the gray Pacific: an ocean of rich blue, pale azure, lavender, and sometimes, toward nightfall, a tremulous mauve scattered with thousands of flakes of red gold from the setting sun.

The night before they put into port Matt said: "I got an idea."

"Yes?"

"We get into Jersey City about three P.M. It'll take me maybe an hour to report in and check out on the pier. Wait for me."

"What for?"

"Now is that nice?"

"I've got to catch the night train home."

"You could stay one more night, couldn't you?"

"But why?"

"I shouldn't have to explain. So we could have one last night together, that's why. I know a nice hotel, place I always stay at, on West 32nd Street. I'm well known there. We could stay there and say goodbye right. I probably won't ever see you again, chances are."

"Probably not."

"Well?"

"It seems kind of pointless."

"Pointless, she says! When we've got this big thing together? Come on, there!"

"Has it meant all that to you, Matt?"

"It sure has. What do you think I'm made of, anyway?"

"I never knew it till now. I'm not even sure I know it now."

"Oh, so that's the way you want to play, is it? The trouble with women . . ."

"I know what's the trouble with women. They always wind up being a pain in the ass, mostly. But I'm not 'women.' "

"So what do you say, then? One last night. A big thing."

"We can have that last night tonight."

"I mean ashore! Get out of this dump of a cabin and into a nice hotel room. See the town. Have fun. Come home together, back to

our own room. After all this time it can't make that much difference to your folks. One more day. How about it?"

"I've got to think it over. I'll let you know in the morning." And
by that, as soon as she heard herself saying the words, she knew
she was already saying "Yes" and that he understood it as such,
too. The very fact that he didn't press her any further told her he
knew he had it already sewed up. No problem.

To dock at Jersey City is hardly the ideal way to re-enter the
United States, especially when, in the past, you have been used to
the West Side piers where the big transatlantic liners from Europe
berthed, in majestic, self-important rows; but New York was just
across the river, in plain sight and all of it, so home wasn't too far
away. She had her bags taken to a diner across from the pier, one
that Matt had told her of; and there she waited. It was six o'clock
before he joined her. He had a small canvas bag with him, containing the barest overnight essentials; he had to rejoin his ship two
days later and return to California again. They took a ferry across
the Hudson and then a taxi to "his hotel" on West 32nd Street,
between Eighth and Ninth avenues, called the Vernon Arms,
where in spite of the fact that he was so well known the desk clerk
said: "What is the name, please?" He registered for them both:
Mr. and Mrs. Matthew Mank. Hell probably consists of an endless
series of disreputable hotels, she thought as they got out of the
elevator on the fifth floor and went along the shabby corridor to
their room, which faced the back, downtown. "Very convenient to
Penn Station," he said, aware of her silence. "That's just dandy,"
she said, "when I leave from Grand Central."

Their Big Night together turned out to be all of that, of course,
but the evening was something less. After eating at a cheap restaurant, he didn't feel like going to a movie or "seeing the town" in
any way, and neither did she. There was something inexplicable
about their relationship, and even their companionship, that she
found oddly comfortable, so little effort was needed. His very
amorality matched her own so exactly that she felt they belonged
together; and the fact that they had so little in common on other
levels was curiously comforting as well, like a relief from the
strains of life. They took each other completely for granted and
didn't need to mention the fact, or anything else. They were like

two strays in a confused and complex world who found in each other the complement of indifference to what went on around them that gave them the feeling of being travelers met by chance in a foreign land, hanging onto each other for no reason other than that, in a literal sense, they spoke the same language, needed each other, used each other, and so passed the time.

JUST AS daylight was breaking, a bluish light filtering in at the single window that was neither morning nor night, Winifred Grainger was awakened by the sound of a door being firmly shut. She was hardly awake, but she didn't need to turn on the light and look around to know what it meant. Still, she did just that; after lying there rather apathetically for a minute, unsurprised, she snapped on the bed light, leaned on her elbow and looked about. Matt was gone; and so were her bags and belongings. *Now* what do you do? she said, lighting a cigarette before she lay back again against the pillow, looking up at the ceiling.

Well, what you do is to wait a while, get up, go out and find a Western Union, and wire Dad for some money so you can come home.

But she didn't wait a while. She was wide awake. In a few minutes she got out of bed and looked the situation over. What had been left were a pair of shoes and stockings, her underwear, a summer suit hanging in the closet, her purse empty of everything but the canceled steamship ticket and her driver's license—the latter had been of no use to him, but neither, for that matter, had her book of traveler's checks—and her checkbook, which he could not possibly pass off as his own. Mindless Matt. Her book bag was gone too, with the other luggage, and such jewelry as she possessed: the pink jade necklace, the silver Indian necklace that Mercedes had bought for her on the pier at San Pedro, some other odds and ends—"lady trifles, immoment toys"—nothing of any great value, for she had never gone in for jewelry of quality or worth. In a pocket of the suit she found twelve dollars in cash, thank God, that he had overlooked.

She took a shower and got dressed. She was hungry; and she

had to get out and send that wire. Downstairs at the desk she asked if a message had been left for her. No; Mr. Mank had paid the bill, and the check-out time was 3:00 P.M. On the corner of Ninth Avenue and 34th Street she found a brightly lighted all-night diner. Though it was too early for working people to be up and about (she would have thought), the large place was surprisingly full. She took a stool between two other people and ordered ham and eggs and coffee.

There was no point in reporting Matt Mank, if indeed that was his name, to the Dollar Line in an effort to get her things back. She felt completely unvindictive; she had got herself into this and nobody else; besides, when she came to think of it, she wasn't surprised: it was the natural and inevitable outcome of a nothing-experience. It wouldn't have happened to another girl, because another girl would not have got herself into such a position. But what could you expect when, from the very beginning, she had almost asked for it? As for her father, Dad wouldn't protest the wire. He wouldn't care that much. And if he did care, what else could he do? Chances are, when she arrived home, he would be too embarrassed to ask for an explanation or even mention it.

She looked about at the other people and studied with casual but attentive interest those sitting at the counter opposite. They were a mixed group of men and women, oddly very much alike, though the men (Latin-looking, mostly) were rather livelier and better dressed than the women. Everyone seemed to know each other; at least they moved about a good deal, came and went among themselves, left the place on brief inexplicable errands, and came back. The women were drab without exception, and also without exception cigarettes stuck between their lips without cease, even when they were talking. If there was one thing that made a woman unattractive, she thought, it was to see a cigarette hung from her lower lip. They wore colorless clothes, dull cloth coats, unattractive dresses of no particular color with scarcely any really feminine touches at all; whereas the men, almost uniformly mustached and straw-hatted, were given to loud rings, some wearing two and even three. They were also given to amiable talk among themselves, and when a woman came over or changed her place to speak to one of them, he regarded her with a look of patient expressionless contempt. The women looked glum, lifeless, smiled not at all, and were for the most part Negro or at least mulatto. She had never seen such an unattractive bunch of females in her life. They looked inhumanly dull, almost as if in a stupor, unable to come alive, yet it was they, not the men, who came and went on brief mysterious errands. When one of them returned and hustled over to some man with a bit of news or report of some kind, he listened to her patronizingly, making no effort to please or even treat her as an equal. During her third cup of coffee, she got it.

They were whores, at the tag end of a busy night, and the men (or some of them) were their pimps, whom they were accountable to and looked up to. When she looked at the women individually, she was surprised. Utterly joyless, bereft, plainer than old maids, they seemed to be sitting out the night (or their lives) waiting—for what? They were not her idea—a romantic one, perhaps—of what whores were like. They wore no cheap finery, there was no false gaiety or flirtatiousness among them, they were not overdressed or colorful in the least: they were like stupefied, drugged-looking slaves in thrall to a more colorful species—the men in their better clothes, loud ties, jewelry, cigars, who called the shots and reaped the benefits. Not one of the women had looked at her in an inquisitive way or even an enviable way, though they must have been aware of the difference between herself and them. (Oh yes, there was a difference.) Depressed, she paid the check and left the place, to go over to Penn Station to find a Western Union office.

She wired collect, asking for a hundred dollars to be sent to her at once, explaining only that her bags had been stolen, her checkbook, traveler's checks and cash. She told the girl there was no return address; just have the money sent to this branch of Western Union and she would pick it up in the early afternoon. The girl looked at her coldly. Did she have identification? Yes, she replied, thinking of her driver's license and canceled steamship reservation. The expression on the girl's face, though professional, was thoroughly disapproving. Who the hell cares what *she* thinks she said to herself as she stepped out into the street. But she did.

She went back to the Vernon Arms to wait for a while. The room was in the back, facing the rear of 31st Street. She looked out, then took off her light suit and shoes and lay on the bed. The money would certainly not arrive much before noon.

What am I going home to? And why? I am going home to nothing simply because there is nothing else to do. She felt surprisingly free from depression; she was in a state, merely, of waiting, of standing by, as they said on the radio—that old time-out again that she seemed to live by. It was now about eight-thirty. She got up and sat at the table-desk looking out the rear window. Across the way—but not on the next street: a whole block farther beyond the next street, so that she had to look over the tenement roofs of West 31st and 30th to see—was a scaffolding several stories up, a little higher than her own eye level, on which worked two men, their backs to her, painting a wall. One stood upright, reaching, so that the whole right side of his body strained upward, his left foot just off the scaffold, as he worked meticulouly at something in a straight line. The other, though on the same level, was working a little lower down; he kept leaning over to dip his brush into the paint can (and then the upper half of his body disappeared altogether, so that all he presented of himself was his bottom and his half-bent legs), and then he stood up, the coverall adjusting itself to the new position, tighter in some places, looser in others. His head bent slightly and his body arched outward as he worked closely against the brick wall. They wore white caps, and from this distance she couldn't tell whether they were young or old. It didn't matter; they were figures of unreasonable fascination, abstract, and she could have sat there watching them all day. Why—when she knew they wouldn't be any different, look any different, an hour from now from the way they looked at this moment? All this was not one block away from her window but two: yet she saw them clearly, was with them, watched and took in their every fascinating movement as if they had been only fifty feet distant. She couldn't take her eyes away, but at last in self-distaste or frustration—for this was getting her nowhere—she stood up, turned around, got back into her suit, and went out again, to take a walk and thus help pass the time.

She went up to 36th Street, then east to Sixth Avenue and down. It was mid-morning now, a bright, clear late-September day, the time of year when New York seems at its best and most stimulating. The sunlight was white and dazzling—awful, and wonderful. She walked slowly along the crosstown street again, and again (always, was it going to be?) with time to kill. A man was approaching from Seventh Avenue—other men too, of course, but momentarily she had eyes only for this one, merely because he was the one she happened to be looking at: they could have all changed places, or almost all, and it would have been the same. This one wore neither hat nor topcoat; his suit was single-breasted, the jacket cut high and unbuttoned, his white shirt bulging loosely just above the belt; and instinctively, automatically, without even thinking to do so, her eyes dropped at once by compulsive habit to his fly. After the brief speculation that always left her a little angered with herself, she glanced up at the man's face to see what he looked like, how old he was, whether attractive or not: secondary considerations always, for these matters had come to be points of little interest, not important.

It was not that she was disappointed in what she had seen, or not seen, below; it was merely that she was insatiably curious always and had to look. Had to—just as one had to put one foot in front of the other when one walked. Sometimes she was rewarded (if that was the phrase) by the shadowy glimpse of a slight bulge or distension, extending down the left side of the pants or the right . . . and what good did it do her? But that she never thought of. Looking at the exposed fly was enough, whether she detected anything within or not. It was one of the reasons why she deplored double-breasted suits, and was glad they were gradually on their way out; if Winifred Grainger had had any say in the matter, she would have had them done away with altogether. A single-breasted suit gave you the only good look at a man, the only possibility of knowing "what he might be like" where it counted most. Thus merely walking along a street could be a kind of adventure to Winifred; but she immediately lost interest when the man approaching wore a double-breasted suit or, worse, a topcoat or overcoat. Comic though such a notion might sound to others (and she knew it, both bitterly and humorously), it was for this reason that she preferred summer to winter.

She wondered why men were always either baffled or offended by what they regarded as her intense, excessive and unnatural interest in their sexuality and physical persons. Good God they ought to be flattered; what the hell was the matter with them? Why didn't it work both ways? Why shouldn't she be interested in what they had—just as, if they were interested at all, they were interested in what she had and what she looked like between the legs? Heaven knows men were attracted to, and claimed as their personal property, those very parts of women's bodies that were different from their own. Well? Should such an interest be the prerogative of men only?

Winifred Grainger thought she had a fair idea of what the difference was between her and other women. It wasn't that she couldn't find love or even sex or just plain men—the latter had always been easy—but that she couldn't get enough different kinds of men. The male body was everything to her and it almost didn't matter to whom it belonged. Except for Jack Sanford and at most a very few others, one did not satisfy her, nor did she want the same one again, usually: she wanted, needed, had to have, more and more, and almost always a different one, a new one, one she hadn't had before and from whom she wouldn't know exactly what to expect. Those two painters splattered with white on the scaffolding this morning, one straining upward to paint the surface of the wall above his head and thus pulling tight the loose cloth and revealing the athletic lines of his body, his male body; the other bent over to dip his brush in the pail at his feet and thus creating the same effect: they stayed with her still, stamped on her vision graphically like sexual heroes—and my God they had been two blocks away! It had nothing to do with love, hardly even with sex as such, for sex in this case, or the possibility of its realization, was out— Christ they hadn't even known she had been watching them! It was an insatiable curiosity about men and men's physiques and equipment and it never left her alone. Wouldn't you think after ten days of intense sexuality with single-minded Matt in her cabin . . . ? But no; she wouldn't think any such thing, and didn't, for it was never-ending. And because of this obsession she felt a slight contempt for, and at the same time an envy of, other women. Other women's interest in men was conditioned almost always by the man's responses to *them,* whether they cared for him or not; they were far more absorbed in trying to find out, through wile and guile, how a man felt about them than they were in the man himself. This was the difference that made all the difference; that made her, in their eyes, a case. For her sole preoccupation in matters of love or sex was the *person of the man,* no matter who he was, and whether or not he liked her at all. She didn't need to know a man to be interested in him or to want him; almost she didn't even need to know what he looked like.

At the corner of 34th and Seventh, before she went into Penn Station to see if the money had come, she bought a copy of the *Daily News.* She walked along Seventh and decided to sit in the sun for a while, on those low granite steps, with those impressive, massive Greek columns towering overhead and the swirling mass of pigeons fluttering around thicker than flung confetti, their wings making a sound like ripping silk. She lighted a cigarette and picked up the paper.

On the cover was a full-page photograph of a low-browed, darkly handsome but childlike "sex fiend" whose trial for murder had been holding the country in thrall for weeks, in somewhat lesser details even as far away as California. Now the trial was over; the jury had found him guilty and the judge had sentenced him to the electric chair at Sing Sing for raping and killing two young women on a day of rampage one beautiful morning last spring. As so often before, he was shown in his mechanic's uniform, but this time the photograph was full-length and occupied the entire page. Even before looking at the impervious semi-smiling face, automatically her eyes followed the metal buttons all the way down. In shadow or wrinkle or contour nothing was showing below the abdomen, where the legs began, but bitterly, and sadly, she was only too conscious of what was there; conscious too, and sad, because she didn't really know either because she had never seen it or had it, and of course never would now and neither would anybody else. She speculated on what the young man had been through. It seemed to her such a pity that his need, if that's what it was, had been so desperate, and had led him to such grief and to such a pass. It could so easily have been satisfied, if only he had known. Known whom? And as she studied the picture, her gaze finally moving upward to where other people would normally begin, to rest on the childlike, curiously innocent-looking face, she was moved to pity. A young man she had never known and never would know, now, was on the way to the electric chair (GETS CHAIR, said the thick black headline in letters two inches tall). Soon he would be removed from the community entirely, erased from the world as if he had never been, beyond the reach of anybody; and with him gone, gone too would be that which hung concealed behind the folds of the mechanic's jumper, and there would be one less in the world—one less of the hundreds of thousands that were everywhere to be had, if only once; but one less all the same.

SHE GOT the money without any trouble—the driver's license proved identification enough—and stuffed it into her purse, under the steady gaze of the woman at the counter in the telegraph office, whose expression (the corner of one lip curled up, a hand touching the back of her head) achieved a marvelous balance between outright scorn and indifference; but Winifred was past caring, almost. There were hours to kill before her train left Grand Central in the late evening, hours even before it was check-out time at the Vernon Arms. Actually she had very little to check out, beyond two books she had left on the dresser and her toilet articles in the bathroom. Why under the sun had Matt taken some of the things he had taken? Cash was one thing; but her checkbook and traveler's checks that he couldn't possibly use . . . She started back toward the hotel.

Passing along West 32nd Street beyond Eighth, she came upon a Roman Catholic church of considerable grandeur; in any other city it would have been a small cathedral. She stood on the sidewalk looking up at the immense doors, noticed a handful of persons going in as she watched, and after a minute or two, on an impulse, she too went up the steps and inside. She had never been in a Catholic church before, but she had nothing else to do.

The immensity of the nave and the whole interior, plus the awesome stillness, impressed her. Jeweled light—flaming scarlet, royal purple, blazing gold and emerald green—shone down through the round stained-glass window at the far end; a gigantic plain wooden cross, not a crucifix, hung suspended high above the communion rail with its red cushions; there were absurd cheap representations, in marble or polychrome plaster, of the Virgin, Joseph, young Jesus with a cute lamb slung across his shoulder, in various niches—they couldn't have been more banal, even vulgar; and at one side, where the communion rail ended, was a bank of trembling lights: small candles flickering in short squat receptacles of red glass, like a burning flower bed. In the whole silent church there were not more than twenty scattered worshippers or penitents or whatever they were. Some sat with their heads bowed in silent prayer; some leaned forward, hands folded on the back of the pew in front of them, and gazed upward toward the brightly lighted marble altar and the Host (if that's what it was), as if it were the most natural, pleasant, and relaxed thing in the world to be doing, while a few sat back, resting, perhaps meditating. She herself felt awfully self-conscious, even fraudulent, but in spite of her sense of alienation she experienced a contentment here—by no means a sound interior peace, though—that was a welcome relief. After twenty minutes of this, she got up and left. She noticed that others, when they rose from the pews to leave, genuflected and crossed themselves when they reached the aisle, before turning their backs on the altar to walk down the carpeted path toward the exit at the back; but moved as she was, she couldn't have done this if her life depended on it.

Outside, next to the church, was a parish house. She saw a skirted priest, white-haired, middle-aged, going in. He bowed to her pleasantly before he mounted the stone stairs with a light step and disappeared inside. Winifred Grainger hesitated. She had heard that you, anyone, Catholic or not, believer or not, could at any time go in and, if you felt like it, Talk Things Over with a priest. She didn't believe in it; but she did know that she wanted to unload, particularly to someone sympathetic who was also a stranger. With a step far less light than his, she went up to the entrance and through the door.

A young Irish girl sat at the reception desk; she couldn't have been more than fifteen. She must have been doing this for free, of course, and would eventually get, for the time she had put in, a pat on the head or perhaps a mumbled blessing from a patronizing priest, of course. She looked up brightly. "Can I help you, Miss?"

Winifred Grainger turned aside in embarrassment. "I was just wondering," she began haltingly, "I mean it came to me—I seem to remember—that one can go into a parish house and talk to a priest at any time. Is that true? I'm not a Catholic, you see."

"Of course it's true. You're most welcome. Father Mulcahy will be down in a minute. He's just finishing his dinner. Do please step into the waiting room and make yourself comfortable. Would you like some literature to read?" she asked, holding up a fan of pamphlets.

"No thanks."

Literature—what a word. And dinner. But of course. With most people in this world, working-class people especially, dinner was at noon. She nodded to the girl and went into the stuffy, ill-furnished parlor.

Underneath a large, framed, and particularly bloody chromo of the Sacred Heart a man—well, why not say it? a bum—was rocking in a straight chair, swaying from side to side, groaning or moaning a little. She got the clear impression that his whole performance was theatrical and nothing more: what he needed was a drink. She hoped he would get it.

Within a few minutes there was a rustle of skirts and a priest came into the room. He was certainly under forty, perhaps only a bit over thirty, and he had red hair. He looked the picture of health; further, he looked as if he might have been a policeman's son, not long out of Notre Dame or Villanova, where he had won honors in football and soccer. But there was something so antiseptic about him, so non-human in a way, that in spite of his masculine good looks, his vigor, his calm self-assurance, she felt ill at ease with him. He started to speak to her, but she nodded her head toward the seedy gent dramatically moaning and rocking in the straight wicker chair, indicating that he had come first.

She tried not to listen, then, as they went through their little dialogue ("Back again so soon, Pat?" "Yes, Father, it got me, it got me"), clearly a familiar, even a tired exchange to them both. The upshot of it was that Father Mulcahy reached into a pocket of his black skirt and drew forth a coin; it may have been a dime or a half dollar, but it had the effect of accelerating the poor bum's histrionics till the tears came freely. Eventually he kissed the good father's hands, backed out of the room murmuring God-bless-yous and I'll-remember-you-in-my-prayers, Father; and Father Mulcahy turned to Winifred Grainger.

"Of course he'll only go right out again and immediately spend it on rot-gut, they always do," he said good-naturedly. Then, un-smiling, businesslike: "Well, why not? If I had as little in my life as they have, I'd do the same thing maybe. If it gives him even a few minutes' respite, I consider the money well spent." He sat down behind the desk, his elbows on its surface and his very clean white hands folded in the air an inch or two below his handsome firm chin, and indicated that she should take the seat opposite, facing him.

There was a long silence. He looked at her with elbows slightly raised, his expression showing no personal interest whatever—purely academic, as it were—and waited. It had been a long time, if ever, since she had seen a man his age so self-possessed, so handsome in a doll-like way (as if he had been carved out of wood, and then tinted), so willing to be sympathetic, yet so imper-sonal and disinterested that he hardly counted as a human figure. But he was cute, and she wished she could penetrate that enameled exterior to the man underneath, if there was one. But . . . that was not what she was here for.

"I'm not a Catholic, sir," she said at last.

"That doesn't matter. But you may call me Father, all the same."

" 'Father.' Why, you can't be fifteen years older than me, at the very most."

"Still, I am your spiritual father. It might do you good to say it, to think it, if you are in trouble. It has nothing to do with me, or you."

"But I'm not in trouble, as you probably mean it."

"Most people are."

"I just thought it might be helpful if I talked something over with someone . . . with a man who . . . whom I didn't know, because you'll probably never see me again, nor I you. I'm only in town for a few hours."

"That's what we Brothers are here for, Miss. Do not fear. Hold nothing back. God understands everything, and the great thing about the Church is that no sin is too great to be forgiven."

She had the feeling that he had said this a thousand times, to one person or another, and would probably say it a thousand times more, to others. The Catholics had an answer for everything; you couldn't beat it. She looked at those immaculate hands. The smooth shiny backs of them actually reflected the light from the lamp overhead as if they had been made of mother-of-pearl, or polished shell; but the knuckles and the wrists were sprinkled as if with shreds of gold or copper-wire filings. Very attractive, and cold as ice; too attractive, leading to thoughts she didn't want to go into now. She must try not to look at him too much.

"It seems, Father," she said, feeling so awkward in using the word, "that I've got impulses or drives that I have no control over. Whatever I'm doing, wherever I am, it comes over me sometimes when I least expect it—my God, when I don't even *want* it."

"Tell me."

"I'm obsessed by men. Physical man. His body. All of them, almost. I'm sure that sounds to you like sickness, or an exaggeration."

"Do you sleep with these men?" he asked casually but pleasantly.

"When I can. Which is very often."

"Do you think I haven't heard things like this before? I understand completely."

"But how can you, when you live a celibate life? I assume you are a virgin, aren't you?" The idea was strangely appealing to her.

"You shouldn't ask questions like that. It's beside the point. But since you have asked, I'm going to tell you frankly. I am a virgin, as you call it, yes. It's quite possible, you see. And by no means unusual."

"But if that's the case, how can you . . . I mean I don't see how you can . . ."

"Understand what I haven't experienced myself? Isn't that what you're trying to say? Well, experience as such has nothing to do with it. Sometimes too much experience even clouds the issue. The great saints have often been great sinners, granted. But that doesn't mean one has to 'experience' in order to *know*." He nodded as though she had questioned a theorem in mathematics and he had got it and been able to explain it without the slightest difficulty.

She felt completely frustrated, and decided to try to illustrate what she was driving at by citing personal examples: the personal was all in all to her—nothing else mattered. "This morning," she said, "I happened to be looking out the back window of my hotel room, when I saw, on a scaffolding—two whole blocks away, mind you—"

"What did you see?"

"No, I can't go on with it. It sounds too silly."

"But it wasn't silly to you. It was serious, and troubling. Otherwise you wouldn't be here. Wasn't it?"

"Yes. But this isn't something that's just *come on*. It's been bothering me for years. It never lets me alone. Why, this morning, walking along the street, I saw a man coming toward me . . . And I'm always catching sight of someone, out of the corner of my eye, unwillingly, truly unwillingly, who attracts me whether I like it or not, and then I'm thrown off completely, for hours. *I* didn't ask for it, or ask to be this way. I even happened to buy a paper . . ." For some reason she decided to suppress that part. The lost criminal, sympathy for the crime—weren't these just what the Church understood so well? Wasn't the hardened sinner right up the Church's alley? She tucked the *Daily News* under her skirt, as if to put it out of sight and mind, and looked at him. She was keenly aware of his clean uprightness, the unclouded blue eyes, the brick-red hair, that almost infuriating but so attractive noncommittal look on his untroubled, unthinking face, and the beautiful hands with their red-gold fuzz on knuckles and wrists.

"I suppose I should tell you," she said, "that I've just had a baby. Or a miscarriage, rather."

"Are you married?"

"No."

"Was the father someone you saw just once out of the corner of your eye, like that man in the street this morning?"

"No. I knew him, and loved him."

"Well, there you are."

"Oh yes I see. Damn it all I do see. But where *am* I?"

"We are all in God's hand."

She sighed. This was getting nowhere. "Let me tell you something," she said insistently, in an effort to make him understand that this was not just an abstract discussion. "And this kind of thing happens all the time. I live in a small town upstate. I'm driving home from downtown, say, minding my own business, thinking my own thoughts, maybe outlining in my mind a letter I mean to write as soon as I reach my desk, when all of a sudden, without my asking for it at all, *or wanting it*—that's the chief point, and I can't repeat it or emphasize it often enough—I pass a beautiful person, someone I have known all my life, walking along East Avenue on his way to the tennis courts over on Grant Street, carrying a couple of rackets under his arm, dressed in nothing but sneaks, white wool socks, white duck shorts, and a short towel slung carelessly around his shoulders—" like that Jesus with the lamb curled around His neck that she had seen in the niche inside the church, she suddenly thought; then went on: "—exposing a chest that, though I've known him for years, I had never known was so beautiful, shaped like a shield, a cuirass, hard, gleaming. He waves and hollers 'Hi, Winnie,' I holler back 'Hi, Justin,' and for hours after, though I sound like a slob to admit it, I'm practically sick. Well, not sick, but saddened through and through, and most certainly thrown off from all my plans for the day."

He nodded, like a tinted, attractive automaton.

"Or driving down Main Street," she went on futilely, with the feeling that she was talking into a void, "I see a sailor in a trim blue uniform—not a young man either, a man nearer forty than thirty, one of these professional sailors who make a life of it, with brindle crewcut, a square build, a white duffel bag resting on the sidewalk at his feet in their beautifully polished black shoes, sitting there on the bench at the trolley station, waiting patiently, self-contained, for the trolley to come through from Syracuse and take him to Rochester. He has no awareness whatever of the impression he makes, or how overwhelming the sight of him. It would be so easy to stop the car, call out, 'Let me give you a lift to wherever you're going'—my God, Timbuktu wouldn't be too far—but I can't; I can't. I go on about my business, to all outward appearances completely undisturbed, but it's a masquerade. I try to wipe the sight of him out of my mind, as I drive serenely on, but again I am saddened—there is no other word for it—because of his beauty, his *unaware* beauty, and because I'll never know him, or have him: saddened through my whole heart and soul by the transiency of life, and the foolishness of love." Without asking permission, she lighted a cigarette, and went on. "But love has nothing to do with it! You don't need to tell me that! A few months ago I was on the upstairs porch at the rear of our house, getting ready to—well, I was studying French, don't ask me why. I heard the whirr of a lawnmower going back and forth beyond the picket fence, next door; back and forth, back and forth. I stood up to see who it was; and it was—you'd laugh if you knew him—Mr. van Heusen mowing the back lawn, stripped to khaki shorts and a pair of low shoes, as he never would have done if he'd been mowing the lawn in front. And I feel like a fool to admit it, a love-sick moron, but my day was spoiled, the French lesson forgotten or impossible to concentrate on. *I* don't care for Mr. van Heusen, I have never even liked the man, but when I looked at those shoulders and that back, and when he turned around at the end of a row he had just mown and I could see the slight mass of hair shaped like a thin elm tree on his chest, and just below another line of hair, thicker, darker, disappearing under the belt of his shorts, my day was ruined. My whole day. I want to . . . I wanted to . . . Oh, *I* don't know what I wanted, but I most certainly didn't want that intrusion on my day, just then, and on my peace of mind—so-called."

Unemotional Father Mulcahy unclasped and reclasped those immaculate hands, and, looking at her dispassionately with about as much feeling as if she had been airing her troubles with the Internal Revenue Department, he said: "Don't you realize that God exists in all His creatures, that they are manifestations of His beauty, that there may even be a spiritual pleasure in responding to and appreciating, as you do, His great handiwork as exemplified by their strictly physical aspects, even—no matter what they might be like as men, as sinners?"

"Words, words, words, Father Mulcahy!"

"So? 'In the beginning was the Word, and the Word was God,' St. John tells us in the very opening line of the Fourth Gospel."

"I see we're not on the same level, the human level. This doesn't do me a bit of good. I want some practical help! If there *is* such a thing . . . What am I to do when such situations arise, unasked? *I* can't go through life so damned susceptible that I'm distracted every time I catch a glimpse of a man's body, or part of it. Think how many men there are around: you just can't avoid 'em. Oh I know this must sound to you like one long whine, 'like woman wailing for her demon lover,' but I'm getting sore! And there seems to be no answer."

He leaned forward across the desk now, his hands clenched directly in front of her. She could see he was doing his damnedest, in his placid way, to think of something that would help her.

"Just a minute before you speak," she said. "What is your first name, Father Mulcahy?"

" 'Father' is good enough."

"I'm not a Catholic. Tell me."

"Well, Philip, if you must know." He glanced down, licked his lips, then looked up at her in the most straightforward way, impersonal, strictly business—and, God damn it, appealing enough in his non-human fashion. He seemed to adjust or knit those clenched hands tighter together, and then he spoke:

"I respect everything you tell me. I know you're honest and seriously want help. Well, perhaps this will help. It's helped me and many another before me." He cleared his throat, but he did not take his untroubled eyes from her face, nor remove his white clean hands from the surface of the desk. "We have a little something—a device, if you like—called Custody of the Eyes."

"Custody of the Eyes?"

"Yes. And it works like this. It *works,* you see, or I would not presume to offer it to you as a sop. I'm serious, and believe in it myself, and use it frequently."

"I'm sure you do. And I'm all ears. Eyes too, but honestly trying to be mostly ears."

"For example," he went on, gaining confidence—though he seemed already to be the most self-confident, unperturbed creature she had ever known. "Suppose at this minute," he said pleasantly, even chattily, while she tried to ignore the irritatingly calm tenor of his voice, the relaxed yet businesslike clasp of the beautiful hands, and the eyes unawakened and unaroused out of all proportion to the sensuality of the scene he was painting—"suppose through that window there" (and he nodded casually toward a wide window that looked directly into a bedroom of a boarding house next door), "suppose for the sake of example we should happen to see, under a bright light, a naked man and woman fornicating on that wide bed. Stark naked, he is doing things to her that we are not accustomed to seeing in everyday life; she, equally naked beneath him, has her legs wrapped around his hips and they are going at it with all the zest that such moments of passion require. Or let's go further . . ."

"Oh no, let's not—let's not!" she suddenly cried, for she found, to her surprise—she who had always accepted what she called the facts of life—that she was offended to her heart's core.

"Let's suppose they are lying on their sides and have reversed positions, French-style," he went on calmly, matter-of-fact, by no means prurient, in fact healthily in a way she could only call salacious, though he certainly did not mean it, did not know enough to mean it, that way; *"soixante-neuf,* I believe it is called, and all this is graphically exposed to us as we look through the window, while sitting here at this desk. Well, what would I do if such a spectacle presented itself?" he asked, with all the calm in the world, his fingers interlocking before her eyes, the backs of the palms reflecting the light from above, pinkish-white, abominably clean. "After the first glance, accidental it is true, would I continue to watch and needlessly excite myself? Arouse myself to no avail? No. I would exercise Custody of the Eyes."

"And what's that?" she asked, fascinated, yet deeply shocked that he could speak of such things without a flicker of emotion.

"Why, I simply would not look again, or watch. What good would it do me? Why should I? I would only excite myself if I sat here taking it all in. So, I avert my gaze; put on spiritual blinders, if you like, and ignore it. I don't pretend it isn't going on; I just refuse to tease myself, for nothing, by ignoring it. In any case it's their sin, and their pleasure, not mine. So to protect myself and not get needlessly aroused when it's going to do me no good, I simply, as I say, resort to that useful Catholic 'out' that has been thought up by wiser heads than mine: I exercise the right of what I have already called—what we call—Custody of the Eyes. I refuse to indulge myself by looking. Why arouse myself unnecessarily?"

She looked at him steadily across the desk, with the kind of bewilderment he wouldn't have understood.

"Does that answer your question, Miss? Is it useful to you?" he asked, leaning slightly forward again and folding those pink-white hands even tighter, as if in emphasis.

Helplessly (though she wished she had been able to control herself, for she respected him and what he was trying to do for her), her face broke up into a small series of smiles in spite of the seriousness of the moment, smiles of mockery at herself that she couldn't control.

The hands remained where they were, but he leaned slightly back in his chair and asked impassively: "What's so funny?"

She pressed out her cigarette; the session was over.

"Philip," she said, and now her smile was forthright, but directed more at herself than at him. "Great. I appreciate your effort. Please don't think I don't. But what the hell good is it going to do me, *me,* when even while you're talking so earnestly about the Custody of the Eyes, and even while I'm trying to do my damnedest and pay attention and get something out of this, all I can see are those attractive white hands right there in front of me with the short red hairs leading my mind on to—to secret speculation about what that body of yours is like underneath that black cassock. Custody of the Eyes indeed! What am I supposed to do—go through life with my eyes shut? Forgive me."

As she got up his face blanched white first, he rapidly withdrew his clasped hands from the surface of the desk, and now, blushing scarlet, he tucked them somewhere below the edge of the desk, in the lap of his skirt, out of sight. In another minute she was gone. And then, later, having engaged a lower berth on the sleeping car at Grand Central, she went home, went home to more of the same.

MORE OF THE SAME; only worse. Sometimes her very life was in danger, to say nothing of her reputation: her reputation she herself had shot down long ago.

Of course she heard almost at once, after her return from California, what had happened with Jack Sanford; how could you not hear in a town the size of Arcadia? And there were always kind friends who saw to it that she was kept abreast of the news, particularly as it concerned her. Jack Sanford had moved from the Royale Hotel to the Finletters' big house, where he became star boarder and roomer; and then the happy ménage, the club, the taken-for-granted gathering place of a select coterie, began mysteriously to change—nothing lasts forever. The gang so long accustomed to stopping in every evening to enjoy the Finletters' hospitality, their delightful and perpetual open house, began gradually to fall away, almost without anyone realizing it at first, till there were only five or six regulars left, then three or four, then a couple, then none at all. The last to leave (saddest of all, for he had become a defeated and broken man) was Herb Finletter. As unostentatiously as possible, with the greatest tact, he moved out finally and returned to his mother's house. In mid-winter, Betty Finletter went off to Nevada, leaving Jack behind to rattle around alone in the big house (nobody called when he was there alone), and without protest Herb allowed his wife to get a divorce. When she returned in the spring, she and Jack Sanford were quietly married—even Winifred Grainger could not but agree that it was a good match. Of course he was finished at the factory, and finished socially in Arcadia. Betty sold the big house, and the two of them moved to Watkins Glen at the foot of Seneca Lake. Nobody knew why or what drew Jack Sanford there by way of a job, but in any case they moved to that pleasant town thirty miles below Geneva; and they were never seen in Arcadia again. We must assume (certainly Winifred Grainger assumed) that they were happy there.

Though none of "these news" was a matter of indifference to Winifred, she had long since, like the good sport she was, and in spite of her hurt, given him up. People thought she should have felt publicly humiliated by the whole thing, a modern example of Hester Prynne wearing a loud scarlet "A"; but she did not. She never mentioned it or talked it over with anyone but her eternal confidant Harry Harrison, during those occasional weekends or holidays when he came home from Yale; but of more pressing importance to her than the defection of Jack Sanford and his eventual leaving town (and thereby permanently leaving her) was what had happened to her in California. She told Harry in detail

(she had to tell someone) all that had occurred to her out there—
of her affair with potent Matt the steward on the Dollar Line and
how he had left her stranded in New York (a fact which she could
not bring herself to reproach him for); of her taking up with Cal
Cunningham again, meeting him in his office nights, out of nothing
but sheer boredom, plus the need for sex, no small thing in anybody's life and looming very large in hers; of her renewed affair
with the darkly handsome, smoldering Tony di Santo, who was
anything but a bore, given to few words though he was; of the
abortive affair with Henry Wales, whom she could have taught a
great deal if he hadn't been so damned smug, timid, and afraid; of
Newton Griffith, who was good enough, and George Stanton, who
was better; of the beautiful but surly gas-station attendant like a
beautiful Spartan warrior with the sheaf of unruly yellow hair
which he combed continuously (what the hell was his name?)
who, in bed, almost put them all to shame; and of her brief return,
faute de mieux for the time being, to enterprising Wally Wilcox of
the spectacular penis who had first put it into her (it couldn't be
called anything more romantic or meaningful than that) when she
was sixteen, in the basement of his Bon Ton Shoppe while ostensi-
bly pretending to show her some new material that had just arrived
but had not yet been put on display.

Meanwhile, though she did not give up her prowls by night,
Winifred Grainger, whose father had suddenly died of a stroke,
began to devote considerable time to her widowed mother, whose
eyesight was critically failing; and then, thank God (but did she
thank God? Could she, even? Was it relief? Was it anything to be
happy about? Far from it!), she experienced a danger that made
her renounce, or at least try to renounce, the insoluble obsession
that had for so long held her in thrall. She was past forty when this
happened, and for the first time in her life she experienced a sense
of the dire peril (it is not an exaggeration) that she was so often
in—like walking a tight rope continuously above a pit of snarling
tigers. Partly for the sake of her mother she did this; mostly,
though, she made the superhuman effort of control for herself. She
had often had premonitions of being caught in broad daylight in
somebody's office, say, or "taken in adultery" in the public park
with an intense libidinous stranger (no more intense or libidinous

than herself however); and though such a scandal had miraculously never happened yet, there was no guarantee that it would not happen, for she knew she had grown definitely out of control and *anything* could happen. She was not afraid; she could handle herself under any conditions and cared not a whit what other people thought—and she knew they thought plenty; but now she thought of someone besides herself—she did not want to hurt her mother.

One night, in her early forties, an experience occurred which, while it lasted, was perhaps the most exciting she had ever known; but after it was miraculously and safely past and no blood had been shed (for violent death, or its possibility, had been present throughout, and it had not held her back for a single second), she was forced to accept the reluctant conclusion that no matter how much she was drawn to these wayward, these exciting but dangerous excursions into the depths, she had no right—no right!—to play with sexual danger in this way. It was an episode that should have made her shudder with fear for her own safety, but it did not: too well she had enjoyed not only the thing itself but the dark, alluring mystery as to whether she would return alive. She didn't pretend to understand it. It just happened, that's all. It was completely beyond her control, but more beyond her expectation, she hadn't anticipated it in the slightest degree; and yet when it happened or got going, she was wide open to it and actually embraced it:

One warm June night, around nine-thirty in the evening, ten at the latest, she was wandering around the house, restless, wondering what to do: go to bed, or stay up and read a while, or maybe watch television. She was keenly aware—in fact more than usually so—of the atmosphere of the night outside the big quiet house, rich, full, glowing, sensuous, promising the perfect summer night before things begin to dry up. She started to go into the library to get a book, then instead went into the front hall and wandered outside into the mystical moist night air. Her hand on one of the small, dew-damp columns of the little portico that was the front porch, she stood there looking down at the silent dark street—almost dark, though of course there were a few street lamps. Then something impelled her—she felt it distinctly, if mysteriously—to go down there, though she had no reason for doing so. She walked slowly down the front walk and through the big gate at the sidewalk and stood there for a few minutes listening to the sound or sounds of the night (there was none, really, except a kind of beating of wings, a hum or throb of night, heard only in the inner ear). She became certain, then, that something was about to happen and she had foreseen or foreheard it all, though no such intimation entered her conscious mind as to what it was all about, why she was there, until some minutes after it had actually got going. She stood there alone, listening, waiting; but she wasn't waiting for anyone, of course; there wasn't anyone to be waiting for, no one would be coming along. Minutes later she became aware that a man was coming up East Avenue on the other side of the street, walking along quietly in the shadows of the maple trees—strolling aimlessly, it seemed. He was paying no attention to Winifred—seemed indeed unaware of her presence there in the half-dark—and she was certainly not watching or waiting for him: she was sure that he didn't even know she was standing there, most of all sure that he couldn't possibly have expected to *find* her there till he actually happened along. She couldn't see who it was or really tell anything about him at all. He passed slowly on, and in another minute or two he was farther up the sidewalk, on the other side of the street, in the mottled shadows, in the dark. Then she experienced a peculiar, almost a mystical sensation. She was drawn to him as clearly and inevitably as if he had known all along that she would be there when he came by. It was the bird and the snake; she could not have held back, once she felt this lure. Nor was it just curiosity. She didn't know what it was; she didn't think. It could have been equally an amorous attraction to someone unknown or a will to danger as a caprice of love, but she was licked before she started and she didn't hold back. Still, she seemed to be waiting for something, and sure enough, in a minute or two more, it came. She heard a small, very faint whistle, just a little birdlike trill as if a man were merely trying out a whistle, not really whistling, not meant to be heard, and maybe the whistle will work and maybe it won't. He wasn't too obvious about it. He was very subtle. She couldn't even be sure if he was whistling for her sake; but it was enough—it was more than enough, it was overpoweringly compelling, drawing, alluring. She left the gate and started slowly up the east side of East Avenue, perhaps twenty or thirty paces behind him, but on the opposite side of the street, both of them headed—seemingly casually, seemingly without any realization whatever of each other's presence in the street—along East Avenue toward Maple Avenue.

From here on, now, they acted out a ritual as if it had all been already planned, and their parts assigned, and they knew how to play them. It was the bird and the snake—but more, much more. He reached Maple Avenue a short while before Winifred did, crossed the street, and started down Maple on the far side, to the east, away from town; and when she reached her corner of Maple Avenue, opposite his, she did exactly the same thing. He walked slowly out across the street from her, showing no impatience whatever, taking his time, not looking back, apparently perfectly sure that she would follow; and every few minutes there was this strange little innocent but provocative whistling noise, almost halfhearted, almost not heard at all.

The night was dark, lovely, warm, moist, athrob with mystery and the imminence of something pending, important, terrible, beautiful, she did not know what. She followed on, by no means in a trancelike state—fully conscious of what she was doing, and wanting to know the outcome, and take part in it, whatever it would be. The accumulation of suspense as they walked along was by now considerable, and yet she believed she could have gone walking on and on throughout that whole night without showing or feeling the slightest tremor or quickening of pulse. She didn't know what their destination was to be, or what would happen when they arrived there, but that it *had* to be, for good or bad, she was sure of, and accepted. Maybe she would know the man, maybe she wouldn't; it didn't seem to matter either way. Whatever there was between them was bigger than herself, and she was held by the fatal charm, as the bird is held by the snake.

At Colton Avenue they headed straight on, down the dirt road toward Asylum Hill, leaving the familiar, safe neighborhood farther and farther behind. She should have been terrified, but she was not. The thought occurred to her at one point—and kept on recurring as she followed him farther: This is one of those times when you get your throat cut, when you don't return alive—but you go right on anyway, nothing can hold you back, and maybe it is fated, maybe it is all supposed to be, what of it?

By now they were walking single file, ten or twelve feet apart, and up to now they had not exchanged a word or even really looked at each other. What she could see of him in the shadowy cloudy night was a rather stocky figure, not tall, somewhat squarish, who might have been anywhere between the ages of twenty-five and forty-five. She had not seen his face yet, but that seemed of little consideration. She wondered, all but indifferently, if he had a knife, or a woman's stocking in his pocket, or a length of thin tough rope wound around his waist under his coat, or a roll of heavy tape.

When they started up Asylum Hill and reached the crossing of the long-since abandoned Northern Central Railroad, as it used to be called, he turned right, here, and began walking along the tracks, unused so long that grass like hay grew up between the rails and ties. She followed. Twenty feet or so beyond the road he climbed up the bank, slipping and sliding momentarily among the cinders, and now he stood there in the tall grass between the old cinder path and the solid weatherbeaten warped wooden fence beyond—waiting. As Winifred came along and attempted the ascent, he reached down and took her hand to help her up the bank. He said nothing by way of greeting; she didn't even say thank you. As she stood there facing him very close (okay, was the idea, let's find out what this is about: survival, love, or death), he took out a cigarette and lighted it. She got the impression that he was doing this solely for the purpose of seeing what she looked like, and yet instinctively she knew, she knew it as surely as she knew anything, that all along he knew and had known who she was, beginning way back there when he must have seen her standing in the dim shadows by the gate in front of her father's house. Having lighted the match, which oddly gave her no chance to see what he looked like at all, he just said, very quietly, "Hi, Winnie," tossed the cigarette away, and took her two hands in his. Then the hands went up her arms, tight. They left off at the elbow and he reached for her throat. His hands folded around her neck, so that the fingertips met in the back, just above her spine; then they relaxed, moved to her throat again, caressed her there, slid farther down, flat against her chest, till they moved into and under her blouse; they ripped the blouse open and pulled it down; and the thing began.

Without a word of exchange between them, in a kind of passion of silence, they sank to the ground as one, lay down in the cindery turfy grass, and took plenty of time to do what they wanted to do and had to do. In spite of the elements of uncertainty and also of what should have been apprehension at least if not outright terror, it was a night of concentrated, complete, mutual love-making. He was very good at it, and took his time. They knew nobody would be coming along here at all, and they took off most of their clothes without thought of caution. Moreover, when it was eventually finished, they stayed on for a time, almost fondly, holding each other, enjoying that exquisite relaxation of such a moment and even a belated spasm or two, as if they were ready to begin again. But they did not. He was pleasanter and more considerate than she had had any right to expect, and she was grateful. The thought came to her (when she was able to think again) that in the ideal society, if there should ever be such a thing, this was the sort of experience that could and should happen all the time, whenever you felt like it, no questions asked, no accounting to anybody: you see somebody you know or want, and why shouldn't you have him or have each other? Lying in his arms, after it was over, she actually loved him as if she had known him for years.

Some while later they dressed and started the long walk back, without the slightest constraint or embarrassment on either part. She felt good, and she really meant "good"; she thought he did, too. They didn't talk about it, though, or talk at all. When they finally reached her house and said good night by the gate under the street lamp there, he turned so that the harsh light shone full on his face, looked at her with a smile, and said, "Well, Winnie, now you know." "Yes, now I know," for she did know, partly; she recognized him, though she had never met him or spoken to him before. He was just a man who worked part time in McGauley's Cigar Store—Pierce somebody or somebody Pierce; he had been around town only six or seven years at the most; he appeared to be under forty, she guessed; he hung around the poolroom much of the time, and one always saw him on the street with a toothpick stuck between his teeth. But besides *Yes, now I know,* she also said, "Still, now that we do know, and even though I enjoyed it very much and enjoyed you—really very much—it doesn't necessarily mean, well, mean anything, if you know what I mean. Does it?" He said, "I get you. You mean it doesn't necessarily mean we'll ever repeat it." "Something like that." "It might, or it might not, depending. Right?" "Something like that." "Okay. Good night, Winnie." "Good night," and she turned and went back into the house, while he went on up the street.

She didn't think much about it that night; in fact she scarcely gave it a thought. But when the whole uncertain experience came to her the next day, the roof fell in. She said to herself, in a kind of fright for the first time: If I am going to go on doing things like that, taking such risks . . . Well, there was simply no possibility of it, actually; it made no sense. It was out, from now on. Out! She had reached a point on the downward descent beyond which she could not go, where she had to give it up. Renounce it. Had to. There was no choice in the matter, any more. Only thing was, and this she knew would never be any different to her dying day: she had given *it* up, but it hadn't given her up, and never would, ever.

They unpack the picnic stuff from the back of the car and start for Lake Bluff, Jack leading the way. Then he stops and turns around, facing her. He raises his index finger and points it upward, giving an imitation of a diabolical smile to show that he is kidding; but they both know he is in dead earnest, and she is too. "Ahh!" he says, a charming, satirical Mephistopheles. "We forgot the blanket. The oh-so-indispensable blanket!" And he goes back to the car.

Indispensable indeed, the thought echoes in her mind, though she can count on the fingers of one hand how many times they have used it thus far. Not many: Winifred has known Jack Sanford less than two weeks.

She feels acutely self-conscious as she stands there in the narrow path, alone, waiting for him to return from the car. She looks down at the ground, and she knows that she is smiling foolishly. It is a dreadful moment; it is always a dreadful moment; and she wants it to be over—wants it to be over so that she can get back to him and be with him and they are one together again, as they have been before. The blanket—it is as "indispensable" to her as it is to him, perhaps even more so, and if he had forgotten it, she would even have reminded him of it; yet, curiously, she hates his speaking of it, dislikes waiting for him while he goes back to get it. It puts far too much emphasis on what is, paradoxically, so important, so necessary to her and to her whole life.

Jack hands her the blanket to carry, gives her a comradely pat on the bottom as he steps around her in the narrow path and goes on toward the edge of the bluff. She follows.

This is a new place he has discovered. Before they make the descent to the deserted beach below, they stand for a moment, she just behind him, looking out over the oceanlike expanse of far, wide Ontario. Nothing stirs on the horizon, not even a faint veil of smoke from some distant lake steamer or barge; there is utter silence; it is as though they have the whole world to themselves.

Jack steps over the turfy edge to the beginning of the sandy steep slope and reaches to help her down. Then they proceed, he always a little ahead of her, through shifting giving sand that is like walking in snow drifts. The sand keeps giving way under their feet, so that each step takes them always a little farther below than it would have on solider ground.

Winifred watches him moving ahead of her, lower and lower, his shoulders and arms constantly moving for balance as he descends the uncertain path that is no path at all. In one hand he carries the picnic basket, in the other the Thermos of cold drinks. She looks at the back of his neck, she looks at his moving shifting shoulders, she looks at the backs of his rugged thighs showing through the dirty white ducks that he wears, and at the whole physical aspect of him that she already knows so well. She loves him; she cannot wait for that inevitable moment below on the beach, ten minutes from now, an hour from now, any time now; and suddenly she hears herself say to herself, exactly as though it were someone else whispering the words in her ear: I will never really know this man; never; never. I will always be a stranger to him, never really be able to be myself with him, never be enough myself so that I can forget him, and myself, forget we are two separate people, and be totally unself-conscious with him, belong to him. Why, I don't know . . . Is that the way everybody is with everybody else—really only a stranger inside? Always a stranger even with someone you love?

He reaches the flat beach below at last, a full minute before she does, and sets the things down in the sand, then turns to watch her making the last amusingly awkward movements of the difficult, chancey descent. When she comes up to him, he holds out his arms wide, as wide as he can, and gives her a smile of tenderness,

227

affection, and charm—a smile so amorous, such a real smile of love, that her heart is struck by something like a shock of sadness. She presses herself against his chest, her face in the warmth of his neck, and he enfolds her slowly and warmly in those wide arms. She says to herself silently, ruefully, as his wonderful embrace tightens around her more and more: In a few weeks—my God, in a few days, maybe—it's all going to be over and he won't love me any more.

III

A CRY OF THE HEART

THE Geneva of our story is not, alas, that coldly romantic, austere, somewhat chilling city, handsome and pale, breathing the antiseptic dry air of the French part of Switzerland, nourished by the ancient Rhône and spreading itself with decorous grace along the curving shore of that coldly beautiful lake which is its namesake (or is it the other way 'round?); no, not that Geneva, focal point of the Reformation and seat of the International Red Cross —city of world-shaking fruitless disarmament parleys, genteel *pensions* dear to the hearts of a vast tribe of American widows and spinsters whose sole purpose in life, now, seems to be a waiting for death, and city of a curfew hour, the *Politzei stunde,* as early as eleven o'clock in the evening, but (and here we are embarrassed) a small pleasant community, in upper-central New York State. We meet it now only in passing, have no time to get to know it, for it is but a moment's halt in our protagonists' precarious journey from Here to There, as they fulfill according to plan the life or lives laid down for them. This momentary stopping place, or "four corners," this bit of parochial civilization which serves as a place to stop for gas or a Coke or a hamburger, regard the commonplace local inhabitants and passersby with a sense of recognition because they are so much like ourselves, cruise the supermarket, enroll in college, patronize the whorehouse down by the tracks or take in the movies at the Strand on Main Street, and always admire the stolid nineteenth-century houses still very much in use everywhere—this Geneva, our Geneva, is worth a few lines of her own, in fact a separate paragraph, and necessarily a long one—not in the cut-and-dried spirit of the statistical gazeteer, but rather with fondness or

231

at least respect, for Winifred Grainger's sake and, to a somewhat lesser degree, Harry Harrison's.

With a population of something less than twenty thousand—a figure that remains more or less constant over the years, hardly varying by a handful from decade to decade and generation to generation—Geneva lies at the upper or northern end of Seneca Lake (perpendicular, it looks, on the map) and about twenty miles south of the horizontal Lake Ontario, easternmost of the five Great Lakes, which, unlike the charming Fingers Lakes (of which, though the largest, Seneca is only one of eleven—and let's name them for the sake of their mostly Indian names: Conesus, Hemlock, Canadice, Honeoye, Canandaigua, Keuka, Seneca, Cayuga, Owasco, Skaneateles, and Otisco)—the five Great Lakes are mighty and oceanlike, not because of their frequent turbulence and perpetually rolling breakers with their tumbling surf and shifting running sands, but because you cannot see across them; their horizon is the sea's edge itself. Not so Seneca Lake, which lies tamed and docile, pure and calm and unruffled, at the very doorsills of downtown, reflecting in its placid mirror Geneva's hotel, city hall, Masonic temple, candy store, bank, fire station, municipal garage, all upside down. Here is a well-built old city with splendid anachronistic residences and shaded streets arched with century-old trees, some of whose maples match the more ancient elms in girth of bole, height, and lacy spread of airy, densely leaved top branches. And everywhere in the city, if you are susceptible to that kind of thing, one is conscious (Winifred was very conscious of it, as always, and so too was Harry, in his lesser way, on this day of Jack Sanford's burial)—one is conscious of the lovely, sensuous, romantic landscape ("scenery" is the righter word) which surrounds the community, permeates its every street, and prodigally spreads abroad—not lavish but subtle, unmistakable to the poetic sensibility, like airs imagined or melodies unheard—that special, unique, upstate quality of beauty for which the Finger Lakes region is famed wide and far. Large nurseries are located in and around Geneva, and the word itself is a natural to upstaters: it does not connote nurses and baby-sitters, playpens and potty-chairs, nor those overdecorated cells, frightening with bright stencils of large cute beasts; rather it brings to mind familiar, nostalgic, and pleasant memories of the almost overpowering scent and always marvelous sight of acres and acres of roses, of delicate orchids, of vulnerable short-lived peonies, hairy poppies, hardier but quick-to-fade gladioli, exotic or domestic plants of every description, and the nose-tingling smell of rich black loam in the steamy hothouses with their narrow aisles of hard earth, occasional missing or broken panes overhead, and the ever-present, faintly hissing sound of inadequate or perhaps never properly turned-off faucets and sprays. The terrain and climate are ideally suited to nurseries, not really cold in the winter because of the lake, never too hot in the summer—Ontario County is that kind of country—but besides this the city is host to the Colleges of the Senecas (lovely name!), embracing Hobart College for Episcopalian men, with its handsome parklike campus, and the nonsectarian William Smith College for Women. Fifteen miles to the south, on the lovely sloping west bank of Seneca Lake, is the charming small colony called Glenora, whose few elegant, spacious cottages (for it is a small resort for the local rich) overlook non-American-looking vineyards and a gracefully descending slope to the immaculate well-behaved lake below; and directly opposite, on the eastern shore, Samson Air Force Base is located, a sprawling vast complex of semi-inhabited barracks, clinics, PX depots, hangars, drill grounds, machine shops and air strips, occupying in area a considerable number of square miles: ironical and depressing reminder of the recent great war that decided everything and ended everything once and for all a bare five years ago; and another fifteen miles beyond that, at the foot or southern end of Seneca Lake, lies the small town of Watkins Glen, celebrated in the Travel and Resort sections of Sunday newspapers for its adjoining state park (two-mile gorge, mineral springs, waterfalls, Do Not Feed the Bobcat). It is in Watkins Glen, as we already know, that Jack Sanford, made-up and combed and stiffly dressed, lies supine in an open satin-lined casket, waiting—academically, in the nature of things —for a few acquaintances to turn up and go through the motions of Paying Their Last Respects. Two of these have not seen him for twenty-five years; Winifred Grainger and Harry Harrison were both twenty during the few months when they knew him, and Jack Sanford was well over thirty. At sixty he is dead, victim of a heart

attack. Our two friends now on the way to Watkins Glen in response to the death notice sent out by Betty Finletter Sanford are
forty-five. But ages—his age as well as theirs—seem hardly conse-
quential in the face of that death or of death anyway. It is like us,
though, and only human, to hang on tenaciously all the same, and
wriggle and thrust and prod to make firmer and surer our small
precarious toehold on life, and, while we can, wrap the rope tighter
around our waists as we refuse to look down at the precipice
below.

As if Harry Harrison's unaccountably increasing depression
were not already bad enough, as they journeyed southward toward
the funeral, his appreciation of the attractive city they were driving
through was clouded by the memory of something that had happened here, years ago, when he was seventeen and still in high
school: a visit to Mother Mabel's down by the tracks that was
supposed to have given him a rich foretaste of the future but
turned out instead to be a disastrous failure, an experience that he
could only look back on with loathing—loathing of self—so intense that he knew he could never shake it. Till his last breath he
would not forget the sight and smell of the three harpies who
parted the beaded curtains and sidled into the parlor with sleazy
evening gowns slung on their skinny bodies and ghoulish grins on
their painted faces; and much later he suspected that the lascivious
smirks were occasioned less by the salaciousness of the rendezvous
than by the startling sight, to them, of the three very young men
(of which he was one) scarcely dry behind the ears who awaited
their, my God, pleasure. And it was also later that he came to
realize that his acute embarrassment and shame were caused not at
all by the fact that here he was, in a whorehouse at last, like any
proper man, but that he alone of the three boys had failed to rise
to the occasion and go upstairs like a man as he was expected to
do. Ernie Bassett and Bud Budweiser followed two of the ladies
through the beaded curtain with almost exaggerated swagger; he
stayed behind. He stayed behind, making ridiculous painful small-
talk with the third lady till she began to yawn, said she was going
to do a crossword puzzle, and left him. Miserable, he sat frozen on
the leatherette divan and waited for his friends to come down again.
How had he ever got into this? He did not know, for it was

something he had never dreamed of doing—something he didn't believe possible for anybody in the first place. Like every boy and youth and man in Arcadia, as well as in all the towns around, he had always heard of Mother Mabel's in Geneva: its notoriety was certainly more than county-wide. But in his heart and brain he had never really believed it existed; why, common sense told him otherwise. Men were just bragging, and not only could they not go through with it if it existed, but Mother Mabel never employed —was *unable* to employ—females of that kind to serve the purposes of respectable men. No lady would do such a thing as sell her body for hire (he had looked up the word "prostitute" in the dictionary): it was almost a physical impossibility, a going against nature itself. As for the "pleasure" that was often boasted of on their return by triumphant visitors to Mother Mabel's, he did not believe in that either. He simply could not conceive of it; thought it was the result of fantastic imagination merely, and not a very nice one at that, and ever after wondered why they felt they had to make up such stories—or, if the place and what happened there could be, by any stretch of the facts, true, he was baffled to understand what they could have got out of it. The lure of such a place, and its delights—these were something that had been left out of his nature. Maybe men did seek such women; maybe men did perform such acts with paid women; but it wasn't for him, if true. Several years later, in college English, while reading *Measure for Measure,* he came upon a thought that described the thing for him perfectly, as far as he was concerned, and he understood it: "Ever till now When men were fond, I smiled and wondered how." This idea expressed the thing exactly, but for that equivocal *till now* . . . Would there ever be, for him, a *now?* No, never—of that he was very sure.

As THE CAR reached the Seneca Hotel on Main Street, in the middle of the downtown section, Winifred Grainger turned the wheel to the right and they drove up the hill toward the courthouse, then left along the beautiful street leading south where the spacious parklike campus of Hobart College lay spread out on one side and fraternity houses on the other, between which, as they drove along, they caught tantalizing glimpses of the lake sparkling and shimmering in the bright October sun below. Soon they were in the country again, passing the Country Club and the grandiose Antibes, an expensive roadhouse which meant the last word in sophistication and worldliness, good food and drinks, to the many prosperous spenders who could afford it and perhaps even more to those who could not. (If New York State could borrow ancient or foreign place names so cavalierly for its settlements, like Troy, Ithaca, Utica, Rome, Syracuse, Macedon, Palmyra, Carthage and so on, what was to prevent an enterprising night-club operator from appropriating what he thought of as a *chic* name like Antibes? For the first couple of years of its existence, many clients spoke of it as "the Anta-bees"; but no matter.)

"I love this whole countryside, every mile of it," Winifred Grainger said. "There's hardly a bit of it, or a place, that doesn't evoke for me some association of the past. When you've lived in these parts for as long as we have, not only our own county but the neighboring counties mean something to us."

He said nothing.

"Geneva brings to mind one episode after another. Some little thing that was memorable in one way or another, pleasurable or otherwise. Doesn't it for you too, Harry?"

"No."

"No? Well, then, you're just not remembering things. Dances at Hobart, the Seneca Hotel, drives along the lake—that beautiful lake there . . . why, I remember one cook-out we all had, near Glenora . . ."

"A blank—Geneva's almost a blank to me."

"That sounds as though you don't want to remember, willfully."

"I wouldn't say that."

"Maybe I shouldn't remember, either—so much," she said, "but I do. So much, and too much. I can't drive by the Seneca Hotel without remembering one intense whole night there with a man I hadn't known twenty-four hours. Sometimes that's the best kind, if you'll permit the levity. Levity?" she added. "Hardly. This night was no joke, believe me. I can still see the way he crouched over me, see him turning on his side, see the taut, thick, beautiful

muscle of his thighs altering and readjusting, each time more beautifully, as he made the least move. It was one of those nights of
perfect sexuality, with scarcely any needless interruptions for conversation on the part of either one of us, because that's what we
were there for and nothing else—the kind of night and partner, for
that's all he was, that you never forget. Except—well, sometimes
they get blurred by the intervening ones, they kind of all run
together, and blur, and you wonder whether he was the one who
liked the freakish exciting tricks, or was it that guy—my God,
which guy?—in Rochester? In any case I think he had red hair, but
I'm not sure. I don't remember red hair on his body: redheads are
usually pretty hairless and white as the underbelly of a fish."

Somehow he couldn't take this, didn't want to hear it. He said
(so unlike him, to her): "Oh cut it out, will you, Winifred, for
Christ's sake?"

"You're right," she said. "There's nothing worse than repeating
oneself. I'm sure I've told you about this before, sometime or
other. I've always told you everything. Always."

Thoroughly depressed, he frowned. Yes, she had always told
him everything about herself and her lovers; and whereas he had
once taken this confidence as a great compliment, lately he had
begun to wonder—and today, somehow, there seemed to be no
doubt of his distaste, his unwillingness to be partner to such an
exchange. "One thing you haven't told me," he said, to say something, "is whether Jack Sanford ever communicated with you after
he left. If you did, I've forgotten."

"No. Never. When Jack left, he left. He cut it clean. Oh, he sent
me a Christmas card for a few years, and I think he wrote me a
small note when Dad died, but I didn't acknowledge it. There was
no need to, or wish to."

"Bitter?"

"Never. You know better, Harry. I've never been bitter about
Jack and what happened, or about Betty Finletter either. What
happened happened; that's all."

"But you loved him."

"Sure I loved him. I'll never forget him. But if he no longer
loved me . . ."

"You could let it go, just like that?"

"Drop it, Harry. We've been through all this. You know it as well as I do."

"But I know your love for him was real. That I do know."

"Well, it never changed. It's the same old sob story."

He had often admired the way she seemed to make light of what she must have felt so deeply; and he had always admired her guts, her good-sportsmanship, her earthiness, her gallantry and lack of self-pity, sometimes even the very way she expressed herself, in colloquialisms and even rough language intended (he felt sure) to mask her deeper, more sensitive and vulnerable feelings. For Winifred Grainger was vulnerable, far more so than most people he knew; but if there were anybody who was the soul of courage—and, yes, of honor; true honor—it was Winifred.

"Oh, look!" she suddenly cried out. "There, that dirt lane turning off to the right there . . . Oh-oh, now we've passed it."

"What about it?"

"Something happened to me one night there, just at that spot—and this I've never told to a living soul before. It was so unusual and yet so unforgettable I've thought of it a thousand times since—and so bizarre in its way that nobody would ever understand. I wouldn't even tell my closest girl friend this, if I had one; but listen."

A sudden small anger flared up in him, but it was immediately checked from old habit. He wanted to say, If it's all that intimate and personal, then why tell me? Who am I that you should tell things you can't tell any other person? Am I nothing at all?

"One night I was coming home from Penn Yan—it was about nine-thirty, I was alone, and just at that spot there, which we've just passed, something happened to the car: it went dead for some reason. I was about thirty at the time. As I sat there, stalled, wondering what to do—hike into Geneva for help, or wait for someone to come along—a car quietly drew up beside mine. It was a state trooper's car. Out of it stepped, casual as you please, slow, taking his time, this cute cop. He had a stunning, very sexy figure, with just that extra touch of weight which makes a man seem far more sensual than the thin ones, though all this may have been the fascination of the uniform. Slowly he sauntered across to my car and said, 'What seems to be the trouble?' I explained that the motor had gone dead, and after looking me over he said, 'Come on, Winifred, hop into my car and we'll drive into town for help.' I stepped to the ground, got into the right seat of the trooper's car, and we took off. In the light from the dashboard I saw the polished shoes, the black leather puttees shining like ebony, and the broad bright-yellow stripe running down the side of his flaring dark-blue breeches: a stunning picture. I admit I wasn't too surprised when he said, 'You're in no hurry to get home, are you, Winifred?' So he knew me, or knew my car. 'Not especially,' I said. 'But I don't want to leave my Cadillac there on the highway to be vandalized.' He said, 'We'll take care of that, don't worry,' and at once he drove off onto that side road there, little used, where there would be no traffic. When he then drew off the road onto the grass, he turned off his headlights but left on the dash lights inside the car. He pressed something below the wheel, and then pushed the steering wheel straight up and out of the way, which gave him plenty of room for movement. He unbuttoned his jacket and said, as if it were the most natural thing in the world—and it was: 'You get me ready, I've got to keep my eye on the road.' He relaxed and sprawled low in the seat then, almost lying down, and there was no question as to what he had meant."

"Just a minute!" Harry Harrison found his patience at an end; and yet some other emotion besides anger seemed to be mixed up in it.

"What's the matter?" Winifred asked.

"I don't know—only for God's sake do we have to go into this? Do you have to tell me? I don't really want to know, you know."

"Why, Harry! That's the first time you've ever said such a thing. What's wrong with it?"

"I don't know," he repeated. "I'm just not—*in*terested."

"You always have been before. At least I thought so."

"But there's a time and a place . . ."

"I'll try to remember that. Time. Place."

"Go ahead, make fun of me."

"I'm doing nothing of the kind. It's your funeral—no joke intended—if you want to do yourself out of hearing an absolutely unique and rather thrilling experience, with botanical overtones. At least I always thought of the experience in practically botanical terms, as I kept on remembering it—and I remembered it, all right—over the years. He sprawled, legs spread to give me the chance to do what he wanted me to do; almost I needed no directions at all. It was as though the thing had been clearly understood between us beforehand. I loosened the broad black leather belt, I unbuttoned his fly and unhooked the two catches that held his breeches together at the waistline. I spread back the two flaps of his pants, wide, as one would separate the leaves of a large flower or plant. The breeches, separated now, were a deep French-blue whipcord, and the petal-like opening revealed shirt tails of a lighter blue, which I also parted and carefully laid aside. It was like a rite. These shirt tails in turn exposed undershorts of a still paler blue, which I also unbuttoned and separated in their turn, and the last barrier to his naked sexuality was removed—oddly less exciting than the whole process of unbuttoning and unzipping and peeling back, from the stiff whipcord breeches, through the folds of the shirt tails, to the thin broadcloth undershorts, which now exposed him fully to my sight. It—the thing lay in folds of varying shades and textures of blue, the wrappings attractively rumpled on either side, as a precious jewel or necklace lies partly concealed in swaths of yellow or scarlet satin when it arrives in its tooled-leather box from Cartiers or Tiffanys. In the light from the dashboard I clearly saw, with a sinking of the heart that was in reality an almost unbearable thrill (though I didn't know the man from Adam), surrounded by dark and pale-blue petal-like folds of cloth, his secret, our secret, the thing without which he would not have detained me for a second—and but for which I would long since have gone on home some way or other, barren and alone: the bare flesh of a tawny lower belly, a bush of tawnier hair, and rising straight up from it, throbbing slightly, the tawny penis smooth and firm as a small column of marble that had been warmed by the sun —a beautiful sight, wrapped and enfolded yet also revealed by its petals of vari-colored blue that had been opened out so provocatively, like the petals of some large exotic tropical flower opening gradually out and coming into bloom in slow motion—a sight that I could have contemplated for hours, so that I almost regretted it when, ready at last, he turned over on me and lifted my skirt. Don't stop me, Harry. These were perfectly amazing facts of life that I haven't been able to forget for more than ten years. At thirty or thereabouts I was old enough to know better—admitted—but also I was old enough to appreciate it through and through, as a young girl never would."

"Are you finished?" he said, exasperated, depressed.

"I have no intention of going on with it, if it bothers you. Anyway, that's about all there was to it, and I think you get the picture. But finished? I'll never be truly finished with it: it's a memory that will haunt me with its beauty till the end of time. As I said before, oh, I can give all *that* up, but will it ever give *me* up?"

"I could say it was revolting. But mostly it was folly—folly completely. I don't know how you can take such things—I mean take yourself, afterward."

"No, not revolting. Folly it may have been. But it was never for a moment revolting, nor have I ever been ashamed of it. It was an excitement beyond pleasure, and I'd be a fool to regret it. My God, how many of those moments do we have?"

"Winifred, if anybody ever led a charmed life . . ."

"You mean the way I always skirted danger? Maybe the very imminence—and immanence—of danger was part of the thrill, necessary to the whole thing. I can't say; I don't pretend to know things like that. But I do know that in spite of what seems to you sheer bravado, Harry, it wasn't always so casual and thoughtless. I paid in shame and remorse, sometimes—not often but sometimes. One such instance came to mind as we passed the Antibes some minutes ago: it was one of the very few experiences that I wish had never happened—but it did. One night when I was around twenty-five or six, several years after Jack had left town, I'd been out with Cal Cunningham—I had taken up with him again; why not?—and in the early evening we'd gone to the Mohawk Hotel in Seneca Falls for a few hours. I remember we left that miserable room there about ten o'clock and drove back toward Geneva. Cal said, 'Let's drive down to the Antibes and have a couple of good drinks before we go home.' It sounded like a good idea at the time, as the fella says, but it couldn't have been a worse idea, as it turned out. We came into the place and headed for the bar, when suddenly I saw, sitting at a corner table only a few feet away, watching us with a kind of hypnotic or paralyzed expression on his face, Ralph Cunningham, Cal's younger son, who was only about twenty at the time. He was sitting there with a date, Marge Emerson—you know, they got married later—and I thought I would fall through the floor. They had both seen us and of course knew us. I said to Cal under my breath, 'Look, we've got to get out of here somehow, and as gracefully as possible—look who's over there.' I felt awful. Oh, I didn't feel ashamed for myself; I never have, really, over anything I've done, so long as it didn't hurt somebody else, that is. But I felt ashamed for poor Ralph's sake, for the crucial embarrassment and maybe even pain I was causing him, by being seen out with his father. I knew the awkwardness it would cause him with his girl as well as privately with himself— awkwardness, oh, my God!—and for his sake I'd have given anything in the world if it hadn't happened. It's cruel to be so thoughtless of others, especially when there are families involved. I was much more ashamed of that than I've ever been over my experience with the state trooper, or any other thing like it. That was nothing to what I felt when I saw how my being seen with his father had hurt, and would always hurt, poor Ralph. How could he ever explain it to Marge?"

Harry Harrison said nothing.

A full minute later Winifred Grainger said: "You see how I need you, Harry."

"No, I don't see."

"Well . . ."

AFTER DRIVING around the quiet residential streets of Watkins Glen for a few minutes, they found the Catkin Funeral Parlor on Bryant Street, left the car parked at the curb a house or two away, and walked along the shaded sidewalk toward the tall brick house with the mansard roof that had been their destination (though they hadn't known this till a few days ago) for twenty-five years. Harry Harrison suddenly froze on the steps and found it almost physically impossible to go up the steps and inside; by a supreme effort of will, he managed to follow Winifred doggedly, all but blindly, who went forward with apparent confidence, even indifference—in any case, self-contained.

To their mutual surprise, the widow, whom they had known as Betty Finletter, stood just inside the door, as if receiving. They recognized her at once, even after so many years, and she knew them. Without strain of any kind, looking handsome and smart in spite of her age (not really much changed in fact, for, it occurred to Winifred, she had been happy with Jack), she came up to Winifred Grainger, bent forward to kiss her on the cheek, and pressed both her hands in hers. She said: "Oh dear . . . I'm so glad you've come! I was rather afraid you wouldn't."

"Really? I wanted to come, Betty. I couldn't have stayed away."

"I mean of course because of . . . of . . ."

"I know. But we both loved him, you see."

"Yes. Yes. Bless you." She reached for Harry Harrison's hand and said, "Thank you for coming, Harry. Just sit down anywhere, won't you? There's plenty of room. So few people seem to be here. And actually we don't know many; we've kept so much to ourselves. Would you care to step forward to the coffin and view the body? Lord isn't that a dreadful expression? But that's what the undertaker says. What a macabre language they have, you've no idea."

"If you don't mind, I'd rather not," Winifred Grainger said. "We'll just go sit down. Please, dear Betty, don't have us on your mind. We're all right. I only hope you are."

"Oh yes. I'm all right."

They found two seats in the second row on the left, and there they sat quietly, waiting for the (as it turned out) very brief service to begin. The close room was almost stifling with the oppressive smell of floral pieces. Why did funeral blooms, Winifred wondered, all but suffocate you instead of entrance you with their powerful scent? Somewhere music played—was it a record possibly, piped in?—an organ rendition of "Beautiful Isle of Somewhere." It seemed incredibly old-fashioned, pointless, obediently ritualistic, and oddly very moving; it was difficult to hold back tears. Looking discreetly around, Winifred saw there was nobody else present that she knew. Betty soon came down front with a much older woman, probably her mother from Boston, and sat down on the right side of the aisle in the front row, her hands in her lap, dry-eyed, looking straight ahead; and when Winifred followed her gaze she saw that Betty was looking directly at the exposed face of Jack Sanford as he lay in the open casket. She herself, however, was acutely conscious—almost to the point of alarm or at least anxiety—of Harry Harrison.

He was sitting beside her, his hands clenched so tightly in his lap that the knuckles were drained of blood; but the thing that alarmed her most was the realization that he was trembling as if suffering a chill. His knees shook; and below them she could see that the lower pant legs and cuffs shook in the still air as if agitated by a nonexistent breeze. She put one of her hands on Harry's trembling knees and looked at the coffin; but she did not regard the body lying therein with more intense and concentrated grief—morbid!—than did Harry Harrison himself—to her utter mystification, of course. Did Harry find funerals too much—was he one of those people who couldn't take them? If so, it was a fact about him that she had never known. But she had a strange intuition that the reason for his agitation lay elsewhere.

The face of Jack Sanford, the head slightly tilted back, was recognizable and that was about all. It seemed smaller than life-size and of a waxen, non-human color. The body and the head were so rigid in repose that it could not be called repose at all. One did not need or want to look at him; he was far beyond the reach of anyone who had ever cared for him, and for all that it mattered to the now nonexistent Jack Sanford they might just as well not have been there. But attending such affairs was one of those things you did, and it occurred to Winifred Grainger for the first time that you "did it" far less because of the departed than for the sake of the bereaved; and for yourself. For here—here and not here was the man she had loved; had loved passionately, and partly been loved by him in return; and no subsequent rejection or coldness or even total indifference could have affected that positive, that valid and important, that rich experience in her life. Here too was the father of the child she had deliberately not had; and, who knows, the father of how many other children who might have been theirs had "things," unpredictable and unregulatable things, gone differently. The tears began, though not for anything would she have had any of it different now. Life was what it was; you took things as they came, you rolled with the punches, you accepted your lot; and when your love affair was over it was over. She felt that it would be sheer arrogance, a kind of flying in the face of fate—certainly not her right—if she should have the self-absorbed ego to complain *Why should this have happened to me? Why couldn't it have been different, why couldn't I have had what other women expect, and have, and take for granted as a matter of course?* Well, why shouldn't it have happened to her? Who the hell was she that such a thing should not have happened to? Was she a specially privileged person who should have gone sheltered through life? Look what happened to other people! And the tears came and came, so that they dropped in her lap, onto her dress; but they were not tears of pity for herself, or for Jack Sanford, or even for the child they had had and not had. They were a kind of melancholy homage to the conditions of human life, to the *way things go,* to one's helplessness in the face of adversity, so general to mankind, and to the fortitude or gallantry or just plain guts which saw you through.

A minister entered; after looking over the paltry gathering in the oppressively fragrant room, he began in the most routine manner to read a burial service of sorts, and it was clear that he had said these sentences many times and had long since lost all track of their meaning.

". . . Whatever you are doing, whether you speak or act, do everything in the name of the Lord . . ."

Without trying at all to check her tears (for to do so would have called attention to the fact of them, and, she felt, would have seemed histrionic as well), Winifred Grainger, looking straight before her, head up, let the tears flow. Across the aisle, in the front row, Betty Finletter Sanford wept also: quietly, privately, needfully.

And as the quiet service went on, Harry Harrison developed in spite of himself an inner sense of tension, almost of collapse, that was all but unbearable. He had the near-hysterical fear that at any moment, for no reason at all, he would go to pieces. Certainly he had the feeling that he might very well not, in the next few moments, be responsible for his actions. Shaken through and through in that stifling room and in the presence of that glacial body, inexplicably on the ragged edge of panic, Harry Harrison saw what he did not think it possible to see, at least on this occasion: he saw that the two women wept as one. Inwardly he was thunderstruck. He could not understand how Winifred his dear friend, who had been treated so shabbily by that opportunistic unfeeling man so many years ago, should now, *could* now, after all this time, shed tears over him, tears of love. Shaken through and through by what he saw—two women, rivals at that, mourning the death of the man they had loved—his throat worked, he found it almost impossible to breath, he thought he was going to faint. But his very panic told him that his distress, if that was what it was, was caused by more than just the spectacle of Winifred weeping over a dead lover of years ago who had never been any good anyway. Emotion such as he had never felt in his whole life—why, it almost seemed it was the first time he had ever *felt* any emotion—engulfed him, and he knew that helplessly, he who hated to be conspicuous in public, cause a scene, make a spectacle of himself, was perilously close to outright collapse. And then it dawned on him, with the force and shock of a physical blow, that nobody—nobody—would ever weep over him like that, mourn his death, or remember him, in spite of everything, with love. For he had never loved anyone in his life, had never been able to give love and thus to receive it, and the ghastly emptiness of all his past years, his arid present, and his even more desolate future, swept over him like a flood. He reached for Winifred's hand and by an effort of almost superhuman will somehow managed not to give way.

But suddenly in the quiet of that closed-in stifling room, while the automaton of a clergyman droned on without meaning the words or even pretending to mean them—suddenly, to the stunned embarrassment of some, the scandal of others, there was heard in the stillness the startling sound of a small, half-choked yelp, not loud but highly audible, a half-suppressed yelp of grief or emotion or pain, like the sound of a strangling dog—a single spasm or syllable of yelp only, but it was enough. It scandalized the small gathering as if he had suddenly stood up and given vent to a shout. And Betty Finletter a few seats away did not need to look around to know, nor of course did Winifred Grainger sitting beside him, that the spontaneous paroxysm, quickly cut off, choked back, came from the agonized throat of Harry Harrison.

Small towns like Arcadia are nothing if not "democratic." Espe-
cially among the very young, who are growing up and going
through the same school together; one house is as good as another,
one family no better than any other, any living room no matter
whose a perfect place for a party, so long as the grownups stay out
of the way.

Jeanette Sparkle, whose father works under Carol's at the R. S.
& E. carbarns and whose dizzy mother is out God knows where
for the evening (and when her mother is mysteriously out like this,
Jeanette plays hostess with a vengeance, no questions asked nor
explanations given, for everyone understands), Jeanette Sparkle
makes good use of the tiny living room of the two-family house as
the place to entertain her girl friends and boy friends with the
lights out, till the cows come home and the last dog is hung; for
everybody is keenly aware as if by some sixth or tenth sense that
any minute now the mother may come lurching up the sidewalk
and then you'd better beat it quick, in time to get out of her way or
for her not to see, if she is seeing, what has been going on in "her
home": nothing, really, just the usual game that goes on every-
where, of "Post Office," "Spin the Bottle," "Dynamite," or
"Photography" ("just step into the dark room and see what devel-
ops"). Not that anyone cares for variations or experimentation, or
even cares much for the game; it is a thing you do, and go through;
clearly the girls are in charge, it is their domain exclusively and the
boys just lumpishly follow along, putting on a fair enough show
of what is expected of them, though inwardly torn with desire

247

and embarrassment and each envying the one who acts the most nonchalant and at ease.

Hard-eyed joyless gum-chewing Jeanette and Doris and Inez and Martha and even an entirely different Carol from the one Harry Harrison is so used to and thinks he knows so well appear suddenly in the tiny clearing before the single sofa and pair of Morris chairs and announce impersonally but peremptorily that Bud Budweiser or Burt Scofield or Ernie Basset or Frank DeWitt (none of them younger than twelve, none older than fourteen) has been selected as the next candidate to come forward, step into the next room with the announcer and receive the next letter, spin the next bottle, receive the next charge or sit for the next picture.

The game goes on it seems for hours; there is hardly any conversation as such, only a few whacks on the back or punches on the shoulder among the boys, punctuated by an occasional witless guffaw as the mysterious ritual is enacted and re-enacted over and over again. Harry Harrison, almost without his knowing it, certainly without his wanting it, has been by unspoken common consent of the girls and boys alike elevated to a unique position in the tense group. Intimate confidant of the girls, sudden close friend of the boys who ordinarily do not speak with him much but now admire and envy his social aplomb and ease with the opposite sex, he has become a kind of equalizer, a necessary factor in the success of the evening, a tacitly named go-between without whom the two all but warring factions would not get together at all; and he wonders why, if he is all that necessary to the evening, all that popular with both the boys and the girls alike, even to receiving questions of advice or suggestions as to how to act from both sides—he can't help wondering why he, of all people, is so seldom summoned inside to receive a letter, a charge, or to have his "picture taken." Now and again some girl remembers to include him in the game, but he is keenly aware that it is an after-thought merely, and does not know whether to be flattered or otherwise.

248

IV

GROWING PAINS
IN ARCADIA

ONE day at about the age of forty it suddenly occurred to Harry Harrison for the first time, with the force of a blow, that the only wayward thing he had ever done, the absolutely only rash, defiant, unsocial or aberrant act he had ever committed in all his life, was to pee on the rug. He peed on the rug.

Vividly he recalled the preposterous scene, which shocked him far more, later, than it ever shocked or upset at the time those whom it was intended to impress. He was twelve. It was a rainy afternoon. Three or four of the neighborhood boys, boys he went to school with but with whom he was never, for some reason, on what might be called intimate terms, were playing cards with him on the floor of the living room in his parents' house. His mother was absent for a few hours, otherwise his friends would not have been there. She did not like the neighborhood children coming to the house, dirtying or disarranging things, nor did they enjoy being there when she was present: such was the formidable atmosphere of the house and the strangely alien character of his father and mother, who were much older than young boys' parents usually were, so that they seemed more like grandparents—certainly older than his friends' parents, and consequently they always felt uncomfortable or strained in Harry's house, never raised their voices as they did in their own homes, were careful of handling things, and generally behaved in the somewhat reserved and even hushed manner that one associated with scenes and places where growing boys were tolerated or put up with, like Sunday school and church.

They were sitting in a semicircle on the big Oriental rug in Mrs. Harrison's living room, and passing back and forth a much-thumbed deck of cards as they played a game of rummy. There

251

was little talk; they were waiting for the rain to stop so they could go outdoors and play. Harry Harrison was very conscious of the fact that they were there, in his house—in fact, somewhat keyed-up. He was grateful and even proud of their company, *his* company, and he wanted to say something or do something that would amaze or startle them, make them notice him, make them realize, for once, that he wasn't just the poor sort of fish that he knew they thought of him as being. He wanted them to remember their being here today, and remember him for it—wanted them to *discover* him.

Suddenly, completely without thought or premeditation, almost as if somebody else was acting for him and through him, he stood up—where the idea or impulse ever came from, he never knew, never could discover during the troubling weeks and months of puzzlement when he thought it over afterward. He stood there for a second looking down at them; they looked up, inquiringly. He opened the fly of his crash-linen knickers, took out his little penis, and there and then, in front of them all, he peed on the rug—on the fine Oriental rug of which his mother was so proud and which was so unlike the rugs or carpets, if any, in the houses of his friends.

There was utter silence in the little group; except for a barely perceptible embarrassment, there was really no reaction to his bold deed at all. It was entirely wasted on them—indeed they almost appeared not to have noticed it—and several minutes later, after much awkward shuffling among the uncomfortable group, they were gone as one: rain or no rain, they left the house, and left him, and went away to find some other place to play.

BARRING PSYCHOPATHIC BRUTALITIES, alas not rare enough, most people have never had the Unhappy Childhood they think they've had and even boast of. Harry Harrison's father was certainly a pill, a pompous ass, totally unreal, a stranger to his family, to others, and not least to himself. His mother was a timid, harassed little woman who seemed to have been born scared: everything she did was tentative, with an implied question mark of uncertainty. She went around murmuring "I don't think so, dear" and "Yes, dear" and "No, dear" without conviction; but one has to say something. Her husband was lord and master in the old-fashioned sense, and his word was law. He was never reluctant to give that word, with a finality and authority that left no question in anybody's mind that he knew whereof he spoke—except in young Harry's, who began vaguely to sense, along about the age of thirteen or fourteen, that his father was doing nothing more meaningful than sounding off, like a moose. Though only surmise, it was a great discovery and, after a fashion, released him from a tyranny that had never been tyrannical but constrictive, rather.

At home, indoors or out (unique among the neighbors), his father was always buttoned up to the chin (celluloid wing collar, wide black thickly knotted tie, high vest buttoned all the way down, or up, longish coat three-buttoned over that, and so on); he strode about, particularly and very conspicuously on his well-groomed lawn, with his hands behind his back, his histrionic head tilted upward as if to catch any deep thoughts that might be in the air, and his brow interestingly furrowed as if assailed with the world's problems which were no match for him. He bird-watched, he said How-do-you-do to the people who were his neighbors (he had never been heard to say Hello), and he had also never been known to address his fellow residents of the same street by their first names or permitted such a familiarity on their part; as for borrowing an oil can, say, to lubricate his lawnmower, or suggest lending his hedge clippers to a neighbor struggling with his wife's scissors . . . And he had a specialty which he was at great pains not to conceal: he loved music, particularly the works of Victor Herbert, Von Suppe, and John Philip Sousa, and frequently entertained the neighborhood on hot summer nights by putting a roller into the slot and then pumping away, humming loudly meanwhile, head tossed back, and conducting with an imaginary baton in his right hand: all this without so much as unbuttoning a button. Then too, because a well-rounded man has to have some other interests besides a pianola and a pair of binoculars, he had discovered— staked it out and made it his own domain and property—the Civil War. On his well-stocked library shelves he had a blue-bound set of *The Photographic History of the Civil War* in twelve volumes, filled with many graphic pictures by Brady all looking like handsome Winslow Homers, which would have been dog-eared had he ever handled it with anything but the most gingerly tender care, not to mention forbidding its use to anybody else. So much for the father; and actually he was not really the comic or ludicrous figure here depicted, for he was in reality a man so bound up in himself, unable to love or relax ("I'm thinking, don't bother me") that he was, if the truth were known, more pathetic, even pitiful, than otherwise. When this truth finally dawned on his son, it was by then far too late for Harry to try to break through the austere reserve. In moments of wild daydream thereafter, Harry sometimes wondered what would *ever* have happened if one day, during a moment of rash impulse, he had summoned up the unprecedented boldness to say affectionately, "Hi, Dad," or to kiss him.

As for his mother (Beulah Tillinghast that-was), she attended to her husband's wants with the distracted air of an absent-minded, indeed a distraught, nurse, who was almost certain to lose her job next week, and frequently she was heard to give in to the querulous complaint: "Oh dear, men are such . . . such . . ." When he said "Don't bother me, I'm thinking," she knew that he was absorbed in one of his big plans (being comfortably well-off and independent, he had no career and had never had one), plans which might involve anything from taking over the leadership of the Rochester Symphony and putting it on a popular paying basis, to embarking on a coast-to-coast tour for some lecture bureau, giving lectures on such varied subjects as "American History of the Lincoln Period," "Birds of Northeast America," or something more abstract and philosophical beginning with the word "Whither . . ." Fortunately for Mrs. Harrison, she was a member of the Coterie Club, the Tuesday Club, the Travelers' Club, and the Shakespeare Club, at whose afternoon sessions once a month ladies like herself discussed such things as other ladies who did not belong, the rising career of Governor Charles Evans Hughes (so handsome with that immaculate white beard and all), and the evils of nicotine, particularly as it affected women. Mrs. Harrison could hardly be said to be a very positive personality, but her moral strictures were so pronounced, unshakable, and frequently voiced, that young Harry, in his more impressionable years before he learned to think for himself, could not but be affected by them. The emotional atmosphere surrounding her was so all-engulfing that she dominated his own every emotion and thought; he reflected her completely, till his early teens, and his childhood, in that sense, was "miserable"—not really a childhood at all. But he did begin finally to have his own opinions (an uphill struggle though it was) and came to the surprising conclusion that what was true or real for one person was not necessarily true or real for another. Sometimes, so ingrained was the habit of reflecting her opinions, this seemed outright treason to the mother who meant only good for him, as all mothers did; but the process went on of itself, with his growing years, and freed him at last. An early instance of his having ideas of his own quite different from his mother's occurred one year at the annual county fair, which was held every September just before school started, in a vast dusty field on the edge of Arcadia.

All through his life (so powerfully did it affect his growing up), he would always see, in his mind's eye, the thronged grandstand, the pagoda-like tower of the official (Mr. Myers, of course; everybody knew him) who supervised or timed the trotting races, the barnlike, stiflingly hot hall where the ladies of the county exhibited their fancy work and the children of the primary grades showed their crayon drawings and water colors, and the broad, trampled, open alley, highly suspect, that was the midway with its exotic sideshows. The canvas posters billowed overhead in the hot September wind, depicting in gaudy colors such wonders of the natural world as pitch-black pygmies from Darkest Africa, boa constrictors, Siamese twins, ghastly white albinos with pink eyes, fat ladies and bearded ladies, sword-swallowers and fire-eaters—creatures as fantastic as anything the wildest storybooks could have described. On a raised platform next to the barker's stand (a man in a striped silk shirt, with sleeve garters, and a straw hat on the back of his head), four or five tired-looking ladies in grass skirts and brassieres made of tin foil, their snakey arms outstretched and undulating, swayed back and forth to the sound of a tom-tom within, while the barker urged the cynical, shy, disbelieving, or reluctant crowd, in tones that resembled the gravelly sound of a concrete mixer rather than a human voice, to step right up one and all and lay down their dimes and come in and see for themselves with their own eyes these spectacular marvels brought here to Wayne County from foreign lands and far places. Harry Harrison wanted to see them all, but his mother said they might go into just one of the sideshows, just to say they had been at the midway, provided she made the choice herself. She settled on the Cigarette Fiend as perhaps being the one exhibit least likely to corrupt; also the one most uplifting.

Holding her boy firmly by the hand, Mrs. Harrison led him into what turned out to be a very quiet little tent; he was ten at the time, and he and his mother happened at that moment to be the only spectators. Before them was a pitiful sight—to his mother, a shattering one. A lady so skinny and chalk-white that she looked like a skeleton, with sad lost eyes and emaciated lips painted a putrescent scarlet, lay exhausted, as if barely alive, and quite literally barely breathing, in a hammock that was all made out of those tiny silk-fringed carpets that used to come with packs of Turkish cigarettes, sewn together. Her awful fingers were bright orange with horrid tobacco stains, and she was smoking—powerfully smoking, drawing deeply on the lighted cigarette as if her life depended on it, and scarcely stopping even to exhale. Beneath the hammock were hundreds and hundreds of cigarette butts strewn about in the dirt, testimony to the dreadful, incessant habit. Now and again the corpselike lady coughed painfully, her bony chest in its sleazy evening dress wracked with spasm after spasm as if she would not recover again; but gallantly she pressed the bony fingers of her bony left hand against her bony chest and with the other she managed to take another fatal drag. It was a shocking example of a world of degradation remote from Arcadia, where customs and morals were simpler, where very few men smoked what were then called coffin nails (cigars and pipes were different, and manly besides) and women did not smoke at all. Of course Harry Harrison knew of such things—he had heard there were wicked ladies in Paris and some even in New York City who smoked cigarettes, but of course he had never seen such a creature. Holding fast to his mother's hand while the gaunt wasted lady gazed at them through tragic, enormous, sorrowing eyes, the eyes of the lost, and feeling his mother's emotion and reflecting it himself faithfully, he looked with pity at the human skeleton lying in the hammock all made of those tiny silk-fringed carpets, souvenirs of some brand of Turkish cigarette. Finally his mother spoke to the lady, and in the silence of the reeking tent her words stirred him deeply: "I suppose you just can't help it, can you?" The skeleton-lady's great eyes rolled upward, despairing, tragic. "No, Madam, I can't," she croaked. "Ever since I . . ." But here she was wracked by choking spasms of the chest that surely, this time, seemed fatal, and with a haggard arm whose wrist was so brittle that it would surely snap if it bumped into something, like the Turkish taboret well stocked with unopened packs of cigarettes conveniently handy, she waved them away from the hammock that was her world and the tent that was her prison. But just before they ducked under the flap to emerge into the bright sunlight of the midway again, Harry Harrison glanced back at those hundreds of butts strewn about in the dirt beneath the hammock, and the thought occurred to him, radically, that nobody, not even a Cigarette Fiend, could smoke or even begin to consume that many cigarettes in a single day: the touts who traveled with the sideshows probably saved up their butts and dumped each day's accumulation on the ground below the hammock. But if he had voiced such a cynical thought, his mother would have given him a scolding on the grounds that the moral lesson was lost on him.

Another time, when he was even younger, one quiet dull Sunday afternoon in the summertime—the unforgettable date was August 20, 1911—the news spread like wildfire through town and county that Harry N. Atwood, the daring aviator, would pass over Arcadia on his record-breaking long-distance flight, the longest that had ever yet been attempted, from St. Louis to New York, which he eventually completed in twelve days, with only twenty stops in between. About three-thirty that Sunday afternoon, Harry Harrison was sitting alone on the back porch, looking up into the sky, waiting for the airplane, for he had heard the news along with everybody else. Nobody was sure that Mr. Atwood would actually fly over Arcadia—it might be several miles north or several south —but it was thought that he would almost certainly follow the route of the canal, so helpful to him because it was clearly visible from the air, and thus Arcadia would be in on it. Before long there was a funny kind of buzzing in the air, like an angry enormous wasp. Harry sprang up and ran to the open back yard, and sure enough there it was, moving low along the sky just as ordinary as anything, passing right by the Asylum standpipe like a large slow bird and finally disappearing from view within a few minutes. In the evening word went around that the aviator had come down before sunset in Mr. Williams' pasture, between Arcadia and Lyons, and would spend the night there with the Williamses, for after all he couldn't fly on in the dark. But he would be taking off the next day before noon, to go on with his flight toward New York—and what could be more natural for the inhabitants of Arcadia, and practically every person in the county, than to go down to the Williams farm and see him take off?

It was like a holiday; all work was called off everywhere. Harry Harrison and his mother piled into the Fosters' Mora car (Mr. Harrison would have none of it) and, following the autos of the neighbors, drove down the canal road to Mr. Williams' farm. There were so many autos there—from Arcadia, Lyons, Marion, Rose, Clyde, Wolcott, Sodus, Savannah, heaven knows where else —that the Fosters had to park in another field quite a good ways from the Williams place. Men, women and children, from the hobbling old to the very young who had to be carried in arms, swarmed across the fields of beaten-down wheat and barley, climbed fences or simply broke them down, pushed one another aside to be first, and so on up to the dusty thronged pasture where the odd-looking contraption rested flat on the ground like some bizarre transparent bird with blunt double wings and a concentrated mass of outlandish gears and throttles for its insides. It was a Burgess-Wright biplane, the paper had said, and the handsome aviator stood beside it now, with a leather helmet on his head, leather-bound goggles momentarily hanging loose at his chin, leather jacket, gauntlets, and leggings impressively laced with leather thongs all the way up to his knees. He smiled obligingly for those who wanted to snap his picture with their Brownies; and Mr. L. H. Wheat, who had a real photographic studio in Arcadia, set up his fine big camera that was like a pleated accordion, adjusted the points of the tripod with knowing precision—an inch more this way, an inch or two that way—ducked under his black cloth several times to see how things looked, then finally squeezed the bulb, his wife, meanwhile, passing out cards to let people know where the finished photographs were to be had. Everybody crowded around the open airplane (for some reason Harry Harrison couldn't bring himself to do this, nor did his mother) to write their names on the weblike varnished wings, sticky-looking in the hot sun; silly, perhaps, but it was like a reaching out to the remote world beyond Wayne County, a kind of aspiring to universal contacts—for who knew to what far places that flying machine might not carry their names, in their very own handwriting? Then Mr. Atwood climbed into the exposed seat amid all those gears and pedals, waved people away with his leather arms, and there was a sudden terrible noise. People stampeded right and left to get out of the way, and in back of the wings, where the two propellers were, there was a rush and roar of violent wind; and Harry N. Atwood was off. All in a minute it was over; that strange thing that had come flying out of the future at the rate of forty-two miles an hour, *The New York Times* said, was gone, already a thing of the past. When the airplane disappeared beyond the low horizon, the whole county, tired out and covered with dust, trooped dispiritedly back to their autos, leaving poor Mr. Williams, all alone now, to survey his farm so wondrously changed and reckon up the damage.

Driving home, Mrs. Harrison held forth in her habitual querulous way but also, curiously, with an unaccustomed air of finality, somehow—and her young son Harry found to his surprise that he was not agreeing with anything she said. "Of course it's a nine-day wonder and nothing more. Nothing will ever come of it. It's freakish—a stunt. In fact I'm rather sorry I went to see it, do you know what I mean? All that dust and everything—and about what? I'm sorry you saw it too, Harry. There's no two ways about it, of course; nothing can possibly come of it—you know? God never intended for us to fly in the face of nature, to deny the elements like that, and take to the air. If He had, He'd have given us *wings* like the *birds*. It's sacrilegious, that's what it is. No, God never intended us to fly: it's going against all His rules."

Young Harry, even at that tender age, realized what a growing gulf there was between his mother's ideas and his own, and he was secretly glad of it, though slightly ashamed, too. But he knew that in the long run it meant freedom of a kind—freedom to think his own thoughts and maybe, in time, lead his own life. For he had been transported by the possibilities of the future as exemplified by that flimsy contraption of canvas and gears and levers, and by the leather man in goggles; and dimly he sensed that life was not always going to be what it had been up to now in his parents' house: utterly predictable, colorless, unexciting, and routine—above all changeless, so that one day succeeded the other with a monotony that was—well, not stultifying but unpromising to say the least.

As HAS BEEN SAID, childhood and the influences thereon are not the deciding factors that determine all future behavior (or are they?) and Harry Harrison, in spite of the grim pressures from above (that is, from his parents, and his home), gradually grew individual enough or independent enough to begin to draw away from his father and mother in his early teens—those correct infallible parents who had always known him so well and never really known him at all and perhaps never would. Like the most limited or benighted of us, he discovered resources of his own, almost as if these had been given him by someone else, for certainly they had little to do with his parents' ideas or opinions; so that he began to seem to himself (with a sense of uncomfortable disloyalty) not the child of those two semi-strangers at all. He fancied himself adopted and they had never told him, or a prince from a foreign country, and these notions became glamourous to him, something to dwell on in imagination for hours and hours—till one day he read in a book that this was a common delusion of children, and he felt himself a fraud at once, by no means unusual: he was a type—and that's the last thing he wanted to be. But alas, being a Type was to be Harry Harrison's destiny, and he eventually filled it with a fidelity that should have shattered his pride and ego but, by that time, had become so routine, so expected of him, that he was even able to derive some small satisfaction for playing out the role so thoroughly, for not kicking against the pricks, for becoming completely just what he was supposed to become, apparently, and no more—nor (and this could be said to his credit) no less.

But in first-year high school he began to bury himself in books, and not *The Photographic History of the Civil War* either. Romantic books, such as *Ivanhoe, Thaddeus of Warsaw,* the Henty books, *The Deerslayer, The Dare Boys of '76* and *The Dare Boys at Brandywine* and *The Dare Boys at Valley Forge, A Tale of Two Cities, The Mysterious Island, David Balfour, Roger Harcourt at Hillcrest School,* and the iconoclastic but enthralling *Mysterious Stranger* by Mark Twain. He read a great deal of poetry, chiefly *Evangeline, Hiawatha, The Skeleton in Armor,* and, most cherished of all, *Idylls of the King* in a version adapted for young people. He cultivated one or two special teachers at school who would Understand and thus give him what he had never had at home: encouragement, even stimulation, in the realm of ideas. He wrote, to his surprise, little poems; painted pictures; picked out tunes on the piano, as if he might someday become (which he knew in his heart of hearts he never would: he knew he just didn't have it) an artist of sorts. He lived in a world of daydream, retired into his imagination where all things were possible and he could become anything, anybody. Characters in books became more real to him than people in everyday life (chiefly his parents, but himself too), and it was nothing to believe himself rich and accomplished and gifted or heroic like some of the heroes he read about: Sidney Carton, Lancelot one day and Galahad the next, Hector (ah, Hector of the glancing plume!), and Patroclus, for whom he had, though he didn't know why, a special love—did not know, that is, why he preferred him to Achilles, unless it was because of Patroclus' beautiful death.

He loved to go downtown by himself and stand on the canal bridge looking down into the still but still flowing water. He would lean over the black iron rail of the bridge which was at the point where South Main Street became North Main Street and watch a line of barges crawling down the yellow-glassy canal toward town. Bound fast as he was in the net of a too-familiar Arcadia, it was exciting to him to think that only a couple of hours ago these same boats and the romantic unknown families who lived on them (so different from the filthy people who lived in the few shacks along the canal banks: people you just couldn't and wouldn't want ever to *know,* though they lived in Arcadia just as he did) had passed through Palmyra six miles away to the west and Macedon an hour before that, and last night they had been in Rochester—a city! The low flat barges, tethered closely together, were drawn along the sluggish waterway by a team of mules with twitching furry ears, ambling down the towpath like creatures in a dream, futilely prodded or urged on by a sweating cursing teamster walking behind; and from a drawbar suspended just below their rumps (dirty as the rumps of sheep) a thick, fantastically long rope, coated with a dripping green scum, reached all the way back to the bow of the front barge. Rarely was the rope taut; usually it swayed and swung over the water, slapping the surface now and then with loud smacks. Leaning over the rail of the bridge, only a few feet away from the rear of Winifred's father's bank, Harry Harrison would tentatively wave to the captain of the barge as the boats drew near, and he would wave back; and then, when the first barge began slowly to pass directly beneath his feet and disappear under the bridge, he turned and ran, in needless haste, across the bridge, to watch it come out again on the other side. A full minute later, it seemed, the boat re-emerged below, its blunt bow all festooned with old, worn, sopping-wet ropes that served as buffers, causing scarcely a ripple on the muddy yellow surface of the canal. A few seconds more and there would be the captain again, removing his corncob from his teeth to mop his face with a blue bandanna, but looking upward for Harry as he was looking down for him, and again they would wave a salute and sometimes smile and even laugh to each other for no reason. After the captain and the leading barge had gone far enough on, Harry would lean over the rail and let fall a big gob of spit that he had been working up, watching to see where it would land on the cargo of lumber or coal or manure. And if the string of barges took a good while to pass and if he kept looking down long enough, the most amazing thing happened, like a kind of magic hypnotic effect: it was the barges that stood still and he and the bridge that floated away.

At night, alone in bed in the dark, in the silent town, he heard the trains go through on the New York Central, letting go with their whistles at full steam as they took the curve down by the paper mill and the Country Club—*whaaa, whaaa,* whaa-*whaaa*—and he knew that the great world and the future was for him, and was waiting for him.

And then when he was twelve or thirteen, an event occurred and a relationship began that deeply and for some years delightfully affected his whole life: he was never to forget it. The event and relationship—the affectionate friendship, rather, so new to him—had repercussions that lasted for many years. For a long time it gave him a great deal of pleasure, but eventually the predictable day came when it shook him deeply, through and through, and made him, with damned good reason, fearful of that future he had begun to look forward to, like any boy.

HARRY HARRISON discovered Carol Wilson (and *discovered* is the word) the first day the Wilsons arrived in Arcadia, having moved there from Worcester, Massachusetts; Mr. Wilson had been engaged as the new superintendent of the R. S. & E. trolley company that ran between Rochester and Syracuse, with its business office and carbarns located in Arcadia. Besides a witchlike mother-in-law and a wife who became one of the mainstays of the Methodist Episcopal Church, he had four growing children, by far the most outstanding of whom was Carol, aged about thirteen and trying very hard to look (and mostly succeeding) sixteen.

Whenever a new family came to town, the children of the neighborhood gathered at the curb to watch them move in, frankly staring in pity, dismay, or admiration, as the case might be, as the family's household effects were pitilessly exposed as they were being removed from the movers' trucks for all the world to see. Tables, bureaus, sideboards, and beds, often the worse for wear, stood homeless on the front lawn, and chairs were piled up along the sidewalk, some of them upside down and resting momentarily atop the upright ones, like chairs in city restaurants after hours, while cleaning or mopping was being done. The gigantic-looking moving men with upper arms as thick as thighs moved more furniture from the big van, yanked off the padded or quilted wrappings (some of the cotton stuffing coming out as they did so, like airy amorphous gobs of fluff from ripe or decaying milkweed pods), and found room for the furniture among the other pieces that looked already so self-conscious on the grass or carried it into the house and disposed it willy-nilly about the empty creaking rooms. The books, the pictures, the private possessions, sometimes even the clothes, were all spread out for the curious to see and judge. Such an event was always terribly interesting to Harry Harrison, like going behind the scenes of life and getting intimate glimpses into the ways of a family not otherwise obtainable; he got a personal inspection of the family's goods and thus some idea of what they would be like that could not have been more accurate if he had lived with them for a week. Standing on the sidewalk, he took in the gilt-framed oval portraits under convex glass of a pair of grim grandparents or great-parents who looked very much alike in their stern, forbidding, joyless aspects; he took in the large steel engravings of *A Reading from Homer, Dignity and Impudence,* and *The Stag at Bay,* the yellow set of *World's Greatest Orations* and the red set of *Masterpieces of Wit and Humor,* the chipped china, the tin wash boiler filled with dolls, kitchenware, cleaning rags and shoes, the white iron beds, the Victor Victrola with its purple horn like a gigantic morning-glory, the carpeted hassocks like his mother's, the sewing machine with the iron treadle and the flannel-covered ironing board; and he recognized with a sense of gratification that the new family was probably not much different from his own, except that they had more children and not so much money. And when the Wilsons themselves pulled into the driveway in their old Reo, the idea was confirmed. Except for the strange license plate, they might have been born and brought up in Arcadia.

The new girl was tall for her age, and awkward, rather inclined to stoop, when she stood, to diminish her height, and to plod, head somewhat downward, when she walked; there were other children, of course, but since she was the one who seemed to be about his own age, she was the only member of the family Harry Harrison was interested in, for the time being. Too bad she carried her shoulders hunched and her head thrust slightly forward and low, in her effort (habit by now) to make herself look shorter; but she was prettier than any other girl he had ever seen (a fact that seemed lost on her impatient parents), with a beautiful, a perfect complexion, and fine, gray-blue, intelligent eyes. Her coloring was bright pink and white, the skin flawless, without blemish, and the glossy black hair was thick and apparently naturally curly; it hung in casual, charmingly disarrayed ringlets to her sloping rounded shoulders. She detached herself from her family almost at once, as if they were far too ordinary for her to associate with, and approached the little group of staring spectators her own age with the greatest aplomb.

"Our name is Wilson," she announced. "Isn't that *awful?* Can you imagine anything more ple-*plebeian?* Has anyone got a cigarette?" she asked. When no one had, she said: "Of course my real name is Nathalie, but my family call me by my middle name, Carol, don't ask me why. You know parents!" Harry Harrison and the handful of others watched and listened in silence; she knew they were forming their first impressions, and she did not fail them. "Goodness, what do you ever *do* in a place like this?" she asked. "I suppose you ride?" No, nobody rode except for Winifred Grainger, the rich girl who lived far on the other side of town. "Well, all *I* can say is," she went on, "I'm going to miss it something awfully. Back home in Worcester, ghastly hole that it is, we had our own stables and everything. I don't know what I'll ever do without my morning canter."

Then a cruel thing happened. At this very moment, Winifred Grainger happened to turn the corner and came trotting down the street on Dandelion. "Hello, guys," she said as she drew up.

"Hey, Winifred," someone called out, "let the new girl have a ride. She says she rides too!"

"Why, sure," Winifred said, and she swung her leg over the saddle and dropped lightly to the horse block.

Carol Wilson's beautiful complexion went purple from her throat to her ears. "Why, I wouldn't *dream* of taking your horse," she said. "Not for worlds! Besides, I couldn't without my—my proper riding habit and all."

A smile of silent scorn went around the little group, but Harry Harrison felt only a sudden surge of interest, a recognition, a kinship. It was exactly like the time, years ago, when he had wanted to be an Indian so badly—anything but a Harrison—that he had told one of the neighbors he had an Indian uncle, never dreaming for the moment that it meant anything more than that simple fact or had anything to do with blood relationship, and the persistent woman had called up his bewildered mother to ask on which side of the family there was Indian blood. Inwardly he thanked the gods that he had not been dropped into a strange town as Carol had (heaven only knew what tales he might not have told the wondering gullible natives), and outwardly he recognized a kindred spirit.

THE RECOGNITION WAS MUTUAL. Within a few days Harry Harrison and Carol Wilson had become fast friends. All that summer they were constant companions, and he was in and out of the Wilsons' house as frequently and freely as his own. They were on the telephone the first thing in the morning, to share a new thought that one of them had had the night before, and as soon as breakfast was over they were off on a hike into the country or lying on their stomachs under the clotheslines in the back yard reading *The Hound of Heaven* because they liked the words and the head-long rhythms, or the war poems and South Sea poems of Rupert Brooke (maybe because they liked the photograph in the front of the book: the wide, white, open collar à la Byron, the generous intellectual, sensual nose, the carefully fluffed-up profusion of blond hair). They discovered *The Rubaiyat* together and became fatalists overnight, though Carol preferred the word "predestinationists"; opposite certain favorite stanzas Harry Harrison was moved to write, in the margin, the comment "How true!" underscored, or "My religion." When school began again and they were razzed by their classmates because of the "romance," they smiled to themselves, tolerantly, indulgent of the un-understanding herd. Romance was not for them. They were Platonists; soul-mates.

Children still, sometimes they played at war with a group of others, taking over a vacant lot as a battlefield, because the roles, childish though they knew them to be, appealed to their imaginations. Carol was a Red Cross nurse, with a white cloth on her head, on the front of which two bits of red ribbon had been sewn in the form of a cross; Harry was a doughboy, and of the whole group, he was always the first over the top and the first to get wounded. He always fell early, fatally shot down, and died a lingering, sensual, most enjoyable death. He twitched and threshed on the cruel battlefield, moaning, groaning, and Carol rushed to his side, bent down, bathed his moribund brow with cool water from an imaginary canteen, and put her head down flat on his chest and listened to his expiring heart. He prolonged these deaths far beyond the bounds of realism, because he loved it—it was a kind of ecstasy, being tended by her during his painful dying moments; but often she dimly sensed, though she could not have said why, that he had long since forgotten, in his death throes, who she was. When sometimes they looked up and saw a neighbor standing on the sidewalk watching with a smile the crucial scene of his expiring moments, they quickly looked away and ignored the spectator: such people did not understand.

Their favorite day of the week was Sunday. On Saturdays they had their chores at home to do; Harry mowed the lawn or emptied the ashes and Carol helped her mother clean house. But Sunday they had the entire day to themselves. While Mr. and Mrs. Wilson were in church, Harry and Carol sat in the kitchen and she smoked cigarettes: he would take it up one of these days, for it was a habit absolutely necessary to their romantic future; that and absinthe. All afternoon they lay on the bed in Carol's room upstairs (with the door closed, and nobody thought a thing of it, least of all themselves) and read aloud to each other. This regular weekly ritual continued all through high school, long after Harry had begun to wear long pants and shaved; and still they read on and on. Nights after the Wilsons had gone to bed, they were still to-gether, but downstairs now, in the kitchen again. They made toasted cheese sandwiches and had coffee again, and smoked and talked of the nonexistent, almost mythical future. These "cheese-dreams," as they called them, became as regular and necessary a part of their lives as the Sunday afternoons of reading on Carol's bed.

Over and over again they read *The Vats* by Walter de la Mare, attracted as much by the author's name as by the elegant language of the tale. "De la Mare"—it was almost as magical as "spendthrifts of the unborrowable," "dream-ridden by mirage," "laminae," and "children of Lazarus, ageing, footsore, dusty and athirst . . ." They took turns with their favorite poets; each had his specialty, which only he was allowed to read—and of course it never mattered, it improved things rather (for you could not kill it), how many many times the poem was read nor how very familiar it became, so that neither really needed to read at all: each knew it by heart and could have recited it. One of Carol's best was *Mariana*. All his life Harry Harrison knew he would not forget the sound of her voice as, slowly, very low, with careful articulation of every consonant and an affinity for the rhythm amounting to a gift, she began:

> *"With blackest moss, the flower-pots*
> *Were thickly crusted, one and all;"*

and when she came to the mournful refrain,

> *"She only said, 'My life is dreary,*
> *He cometh not,' she said;*
> *She said, 'I am aweary, aweary,*
> *I would that I were dead'"*

shivers of thrill ran down his spine and the black hairs on Carol's arms stood up. Sometimes the door would burst open and Mrs. Wilson suddenly stood there with her hands on her hips, a figure of futile, pointless wrath, for the simple reason that to the readers, deep in their world of poetry, she just plain didn't exist. "My stars, why don't you go out into God's sunshine and get some fresh *air!*" Amused, they glanced at each other, then burst out laughing. "That's right, laugh!" the woman cried. "That's all I'm good for, I suppose! Something to laugh at!" She slammed the door and was gone.

But that wasn't why they laughed. They laughed because, along with their self-preoccupation, they also shared a strong sense of the ridiculous. They were spectators as well as participants in the comedy of themselves; Carol particularly was never able to get rid of this dual feeling (which, curiously, both enhanced and lessened their enjoyment of whatever they did together); they saw themselves as "characters" even when they were most carried away, and appreciated the spectacle as keenly and even as objectively as if it were happening to someone else. They knew they were comic to others, who of course could not possibly "understand." They were also comic to themselves, though never to each other.

They valued their humor, even when it most interfered, because they knew (or believed, or hoped) it was the saving grace that would carry them through anything. As long as they were able to laugh at themselves, they felt, they would be all right. It could be a terrible nuisance, though, which often made them feel, and alas behave, like ten-year-olds. Almost always, at the Public Library, where absolute silence was the rigid rule (so that it almost seemed the one reason people came to the library at all was to be utterly mute), they would be taken with fits of laughter for no other reason than that they were supposed to be quiet; unable to control themselves, they would be forced to separate at once or flee the place entirely. At other times, in geometry class for instance, or Latin (two studies, certainly, that made absolutely no sense whatever), the absurdity of it all would strike them simultaneously, though they sat several seats apart. Miss Longwell would expound a theorem involving "B-square" and "pi" that seemed clear as daylight to everybody else and very sensible besides; or Miss Calkins (called "Wop" because her subject was Latin) would patiently intone with a straight face: "Accent the penult if the vowel is long; if not, accent the antepenult." While other heads obediently bent over notebooks and took down this valuable information, Harry and Carol did not dare exchange the fatal glance that drew them together, magnetlike, with a power almost stronger than themselves; but the private knowledge of each other's intense inner struggle to repress their insane irrational laughter sustained them through the stultifying dullness of the hour.

IN THEIR JUNIOR AND SENIOR YEARS, Harry Harrison and Carol Wilson double-dated with another couple, mostly because a ride in someone else's car was a way to get to be by themselves, at least out of parental reach, during those evenings when Mr. and Mrs. Wilson sat at home. Bud Budweiser had a Scripps-Booth of his own and dated Dottie Kramer; Ernie Basset owned an H. C. S. which was the envy of the entire high school, and his date was sometimes Isabel Barton, sometimes Mae Richmond, and on very rare occasions (provided he could pick her up late enough and arrive back home late enough so that he wouldn't have to go to the Kandy Kitchen for a soda and thus be seen) Winifred Grainger. Very often Bud or Ernie and their dates would pick up Harry and Carol—why the foursome was necessary, nobody knew; it seemed to occur to none of them to go out alone with his girl and neck— and if they had money enough they would go to the movies first, and then drive up Asylum Hill, turn left, and park there along the little-used road lined with tall, never-silent whispering pines. Sometimes other cars were there ahead of them, but nobody paid attention to anybody else; after all everyone was there for the same reason. In the black shadows, with the magical soughing of the ever-restless pines overhead, Bud Budweiser (or Ernie Bassett) switched off the motor and the headlights and gave his silent agitated attention to an equally silent and businesslike Dottie Kramer (or Isabel Barton or Mae Richmond). In the back seat, for what seemed hours, Harry Harrison conscientiously petted with Carol Wilson, too. It seemed to be the thing to do, everybody else did it, but Harry was really more interested in Carol's company than in her physical person. After a while they would begin whispering together, exchanging confidences, opinions, and ideas in undertones, quiet but audible. And then an exasperated Ernie (or Bud) would disengage himself momentarily from his absorbed and absorbing deadlock, turn his head toward the rear and snap: "Say! Why can't you two be *quiet* back there, for Pete's sake?"

One evening when Bud Budweiser couldn't get away, Harry Harrison asked Dottie to go to the movies with him and Carol. Afterwards they stopped at the Kandy Kitchen for sodas, and then they left, the evening over. Harry escorted Carol home first to the Wilsons' house, said good night to Carol, and then started up the street to take Dottie home. Carol had no sooner disappeared inside when Dottie stopped dead on the sidewalk, put her hands on her hips, and said: "Honestly! I must say you're a sketch, Harry! A positive sketch! Why in thunder didn't you take me home first?"

"I don't get it," Harry said, in all innocence; "what's wrong?"

"Well, Carol's your girl, after all, isn't she? That what's wrong!"

"But you," he said, "you live nearer my house than Carol does, isn't that so?"

"That's a fine answer, I must say! Don't you know, you poor simp, that Carol Wilson is madly in love with you?"

"In *love* with me? Why, you're crazy," he said, genuinely surprised, not so much by the information (or misinformation) as by the fact that Dottie should have believed anything so preposterous.

"*Madly* in love," she repeated, "and honestly, you ought to be shot!"

"Now wait a minute, you just don't understand," he said. "Haven't you ever heard of such a thing as Platonic love?"

"Platonic love my foot! I know a girl in love when I see one, and Carol's simply eating her heart out for you. Pining away! And you don't deserve it when it's right under your nose and you can't see it."

The next morning, in school, the first of the day's long series of endless notes that were forever being passed back and forth between them began: "How did you get along with Dottie last night, when you took her home?"

"Well, the darnedest thing," he wrote back, "she actually said that you were in love with me. Now I ask you, isn't that too fantastic for words?"

"What did you say?"

"I told her it was time she grew up, or something like that. But it's really too silly to talk about, n'est-ce pas?"

A couple of years ago these notes would begin with a more or less abstract question calculated to start an endless discussion that they could add to and keep up all day long, such as (from Carol): "Do you think girls are older than boys?" or "Do you believe in God? But of course I shouldn't insult your intelligence by asking such a puerile question." He would look up the word *puerile* and then answer that he certainly did not believe any such thing and sincerely hoped that she certainly didn't either. But now, in their third year in high school, their exchanges became more literary. Carol would take a full sheet of paper and begin: "Do you believe that life is a measure to be filled or a glass to be drained?" or: "I've just this second decided that my favorite character in all literature is Lord Harry Wotton in *The Picture of Dorian Gray*. Who is yours?" "The wicked but fascinating Lord Harry is mine too," he would reply, "and I certainly think that his philosophy 'Cure the senses by means of the soul and the soul by means of the senses' is the most marvelous dictum in the annals of philosophy." Once one of these notes was intercepted by Miss Parker, their English teacher. She kept it all morning while they died a thousand deaths. When it was returned to them in the afternoon, words and phrases had been encircled by Miss Parker's blue pencil and the margin filled with admonitions of "unity," "redundant," "unclear," "rhet." and "punct." and "sp." Their next note began: "I honestly think Miss Parker is absolutely the world's best sport and it's a positive crime she doesn't get married." "Isn't it though?" the answer came back. "Think of all that marvelous character and personality and brains going absolutely to waste!"

It was Miss Parker who introduced them to the art of dramatics —in a very real sense, to the marvelous world of the theater. She taught elocution as well as English. One night in their junior year she gave a recital of her readings at the Presbyterian church. Harry Harrison and Carol Wilson sat in the balcony, skeptical, prepared to be bored by *The Charge of the Light Brigade* and *The Chambered Nautilus* and *The Sandpiper* ("Across the lonely beach we flit,/ One little sandpiper and I . . ."), which they had often heard her recite in school. But to their astonishment and delight, Miss Parker's program on this memorable night included nothing of the kind: nothing, in fact, that they could even have dreamed of. She did *A Message to Garcia, The Old Folks' Christmas Eve,* and *Lasca.* The climax of the evening was a thrilling rendition of something called *The Fall of Pemberton Mill.* It was grand, there was no other word for it; she opened up to them both a whole new world. Solely by the magic of voice, gesture, and expressions of the face—theatrical art, in short—Miss Parker graphically, unforgettably, gave everybody present the full and awful effect of the collapse of the rotten mill: the warning shuddering splitting crack, the crunch of the heavy timbers, the rain of plaster and wood, the whirling looms plunging through to the basement, the panic of the hysterical, trapped workers. Harry Harrison was enthralled. Momentarily he had a sudden desire to be an actor, too. That night, late, he stood in front of the bathroom mirror at home and Pemberton Mill crashed all around him, several times.

ONE SUNDAY NIGHT while they were eating their toasted cheese sandwiches and drinking coffee in the Wilson kitchen, under the unshaded single light bulb that burned above them, Carol said, as if thinking aloud, almost as if speaking to herself: "I suppose every man has some girl in his life that he didn't marry."

"How do you mean?" he asked.

"Oh, just the girl back home that he grew up with and always meant to marry but somehow never did. Maybe that's what I am. Maybe I'm that girl, for you. Isn't that a vile and hectic thought?"

It certainly was, he protested righteously, deeply offended; and rubbish besides. True, they had never talked of marriage in so many words because, after all, marriage was just one of those things. Actually they didn't need to talk about it, did they? They of *all* people! It sort of took care of itself, if you loved each other; it probably just happened without your needing to do anything about it beforehand; but certainly the idea of marriage was as much a part of his future as the fact that he would have a million dollars and also win distinguished honors in whatever field he eventually chose to go into. He thought of marriage as one of the rewards of life that came to you almost of itself. You certainly didn't do anything about it beforehand or by way of preparation any more than you deliberately set out to win the Nobel Prize. Besides, if you grew up with a girl and always meant to marry her someday, what could possibly prevent it? Why wouldn't she, of all people, be the very one?

"Maybe because," Carol said, "they know each other too well."

"But listen! I should think," he argued, "the very fact that they knew each other so well would be just the thing that made their marriage! Certainly they wouldn't want to marry anybody else!"

"How can we tell?" she said, absently stirring her coffee. "Maybe there's not so much incentive to marry, when you know all about each other. Maybe people are more attracted to each other, maybe it's realer, when there's some mystery involved."

"Oh, don't be so juvenile!"

"Listen, you!" she suddenly said sharply. "Don't be so juvenile yourself as to say 'Don't be so juvenile'!" The unintentional humor of her spontaneous retort took them both by surprise, and they burst out laughing—together again.

THE TELEPHONE rang. Harry Harrison heard his father answer it. The conversation was brief. A moment later he came into the den where Harry sat reading *Tithonus,* hearing in his mind's ear how marvelously Carol would get off the haunting opening lines:

> *"The woods decay, the woods decay and fall,*
> *The vapors weep their burthen to the ground,*
> *Man comes and tills the field and lies beneath,*
> *And after many a summer dies the swan . . ."*

"Burthen," he said, half aloud; what a marvelous word. Then he saw his father enter, pace back and forth, his hands behind his back, and buttoned up to the chin as always. Respectfully he put the book down.

His father cleared his throat; it was almost like an elephant trumpeting. Then he said: "Young Bud Budweiser just called you. He asked if you were home. I said yes and would give you the message. Well, it turned out that he wanted you to go to Geneva with him and Ernest Bassett tonight. Now why should he want you to go to Geneva with him, tell me that?"

With an honest show of innocence, and at the same time with an unexpected boldness, he said: "Why, *I* don't know, Dad. Why did he say he wanted me? You answered the phone."

"The two of them were going over to Geneva to spend the evening. Why should one have to go all the way to Geneva to do that? You can spend the evening at home just as well, where you belong."

"Now, Winfield," his mother said querulously, hovering in the doorway. "A boy's got to have *some* fun."

"Not that kind of fun!" his father said emphatically.

"What do you mean by that?" young Harry asked, bridling as much as he dared to. "What kind of fun?"

"I don't approve of young men . . . Let's say I don't approve of *my son* driving around the countryside at all hours with other boys in fancy cars with wire wheels and mufflers off and cutouts wide open, to astound the public. It's ostentatious, extravagant, and . . . and . . . poor taste. Not the behavior of gentlemen."

"But at least Bud has a car of his own, and if it happens to have wire wheels, well, that's not my fault, is it? *We* don't have a car at all, and I think we have just as much money as—and perhaps even more than—the Budweiser family."

"That cuts no ice with me, Harry. I don't spoil you, and I don't intend to! Is that clear? So long as I live we won't *have* a car in this family; we have no need of one. Walking—or good old shanks' ponies, as your grandfather used to say—is plenty good enough for able-bodied people. Spartan living, my boy, Spartan living; that's what I approve of."

"Yes, Dad."

"Now, Hubby . . . Now, Winfield . . ."

"Go and call your friend Budweiser. I told him I'd give you the message. If the pair of you, or the three of you, must go chasing around the country at all hours of the night . . ."

"Thank you, Winfield. You have a good heart."

"Beulah, pray leave the room. I want to talk to your son. Privately, man to man."

Wordlessly, his mother threw a distressed, pathetic glance first at her husband, then at Harry, and obeyed as she always did. When they were alone together again, Mr. Harrison clasped his hands more firmly behind his back, tilted his head higher, and strode about, speaking to the ceiling. "I suppose you're old enough to have heard of a notorious place in Geneva—a house of ill-repute where vile men go and pay to do vile things?"

"No, I haven't," Harry said.

"You haven't? I thought everybody knew of it."

"Dad, what I said isn't quite true. I *have* heard about it, but the truth is, the real truth, that I never believed it. I never believed there was such a place, true and honest I didn't, and don't, though the guys in school often joke about it."

"Joke!"

"Yes, but I think they're making it up. Decent men wouldn't go to a place like that, and women wouldn't—well, do such things. I've always thought it was just talk, and still think so."

"Do your friends young Budweiser and Bassett patronize this place?"

"Gosh no! Because I don't think it even exists. Do you? I mean it couldn't . . ."

After a few more strides his father said: "Very well. I agree with you. Now go and call up your friend; I told him I would tell you he called."

Vastly relieved but feeling guilty as hell (did he *really* not believe in the place? And if so, how could this be possible, when he had heard of it too often to doubt its existence, much as it went against his morals), Harry Harrison went to the telephone that rested on its little box halfway up the front stairs, on the landing, and, picking up the receiver, he asked Central—or Madge, whom he knew as he knew everybody in town and with whom he had often had little chats before he gave her the number—to please get him the Budweiser house.

"Bud? Harry Harrison. Dad said you called me."

"I sure did. Boy, have I got a great idea—but I couldn't tell *him*. He'd have had a hemorrhage. It's got to be just between you and I and Ernie Bassett, and, well, maybe Madge, if she's listening. Hey, Madge, get off the line, can't you? Well, for a change she wasn't listening, I guess she must be busy—I was just trying her out. Well look. What do you say to the three of us driving over to Mother Mabel's tonight and giving the old girl a call? And having a workout for ourselves at the same time. Wouldn't that be swell? Boy, do I need it! As for cash, about three bucks apiece at the most would take care of the whole thing, if that's what's worrying you. What do you say, kid?"

Kid! Bud Budweiser was seventeen, the same age that he was; and so was Ernie Bassett. "Nothing's worrying me," said Harry, putting up the kind of front the occasion required.

"Okay then, Ernie and I will pick you up at your place in about twenty minutes at the most. I swiped a pint or two of the old man's bathtub gin to see us through. Not that we need it, only sometimes it's more fun that way. Boy, are you in luck tonight! You're going to get a piece of tail that . . . Oh-oh, I hear Madge clicking. So what do you say? Okay?"

He couldn't say no, he didn't want to go; he couldn't even say okay. He said, his heart sinking, his stomach cold with chill; "Meet you out in front. Thanks, Bud, for thinking of me."

A few minutes later he was sitting on the concrete horse block at the curb in front of his house, waiting for the Scripps-Booth to drive up. Why had he said, Thanks for thinking of me? And why in the first place had Bud Budweiser—or Ernie Bassett—thought of him at all?

When the car drove up and he climbed into the front seat beside his two friends, he had the uncomfortable feeling that he was being used (they weren't all *that* good friends, or even intimates), but they were so cordial and friendly, so gaily ribald and dirty-minded and hearty and wise-cracking, that he rose to the occasion himself (under the social pressure of the evening, as it were) and by a tremendous effort matched them crack for crack—successfully, too, or at least it seemed so. They had swigs all around from Bud's father's pint of bathtub gin (awful-tasting stuff, but they slapped their chests with gusto and relish, with loud affirmations of "Boy, is that great *stuff!*") and started out of town for Geneva.

The atmosphere in the crowded front seat was heavy with a boisterous sexuality; the air reeked of four-letter words, every one of which made Harry Harrison uncomfortable—he had never, for some reason, been able to use the word *shit,* for example, much less worse words like *poontang.* But poontang was what they were after, or so at least they said; and, boy, were they going to get it! Plenty! Bud Budweiser thought he might later drop a manly hint or two, casual-like, to Dottie Kramer about where they had been and what they had done, and he knew that far from being shocked she would only admire him the more. Ernie Basset had no need, it seemed, of any such confidences, casual or otherwise; he himself was oh far too used to that sort of thing to need to air the experience or think much of it one way or the other: when you came right down to it, poontang was the same the world over, one was like any other, put a pillow over their heads and you wouldn't know the difference, and he yawned ostentatiously to make his point.

But when they drove up in front of Mother Mabel's, a shabby clapboard house badly in need of paint down by the railroad tracks, changes of a sort seemed to come over the little group: Bud Budweiser became very deferential and polite ("No, after you; really, you go first"), Ernie seemed preoccupied to the point of worry, but Harry Harrison remained the same as before: timid, unsure, and frankly distasteful of the whole thing, though he managed to summon up a brave crack or two that astonished himself as much as it did the others, who oddly enough seemed to regard it now as somewhat out of place.

Mother Mabel, conventionally blowsy, uncorseted, hair falling down, met them with indifference at the door, allowed them to come in, then called peremptorily, shrilly, as if summoning three recalcitrant daughters who were no good and never would be: "Dorene? Milly? Hortense? Shake a leg and come down at once! There's some kids here."

Ernie Bassett attempted sociability, for propriety's sake. "I guess you don't remember me, Mother Mabel. I been here often. 'Member the time . . ."

"No, I don't. But maybe I know your father. Bassett, didn't you say? From Arcadia? Got a red mustache and thin hair and could use a few pounds of weight, that right? We don't much care for the skinny ones. Besides, they're poor spenders, seems like."

Harry Harrison and Bud Budweiser exchanged an expressionless glance which yet managed to convey surprise: the description was so apt, even to the "poor spender," that they were sorry for Ernie that he had spoken at all.

Three of the Girls came in. Two of them grinned pointlessly from ear to ear; the third—it was Hortense—looked so bored, preoccupied, and even sorrow-struck that she seemed on the point of bursting into tears because of the tedium of it all. The boys stood up politely. Harry took Milly by the hand and uttered some halfhearted pleasantry that died even before he had reached its final syllable; but Budweiser bravely put his arms around Dorene's waist and shook her so familiarly that she squirmed out of his grasp and stepped back. "Don't *do* that," she said. "That's not what you're paying for." Mother Mabel, after rearranging her loose shiftlike garment and tucking in a stray hank of hair, said, "Well, have fun, kids," and left them at once. Milly said, with a ghastly smile: "Well, boys, what are we waiting for?" "*I'll* show you what we're waiting for," Ernie said heartily, and within another few seconds he and Bud had disappeared upstairs with their arms around their girls in comradely fashion, as if they had known them for years. Hortense sat down at the other end of the leatherette settee where Harry Harrison sat in stony silence, yawned voraciously, then turned to regard her prospect.

Thus they sat for ten minutes or more, while Harry, not even wondering what was going on upstairs and what the boys were doing, tried to withdraw from the tête-à-tête as if he did not exist. After Hortense had done her nails she arose with another yawn and said: "I got a crossword puzzle I'm working on, if you'll be so kind to excuse me. So long"—and he was left as he wanted to be left: alone.

When Ernie and Bud descended four or five minutes later, wreathed in smiles of triumph and all but rubbing their hands together in relish of happy, very recent memories, they took their leave. Suffering an agony of embarrassment (yet, curiously, not touched or inwardly upset at all), Harry explained that he had discovered he had forgotten to bring some money and thus couldn't take Hortense upstairs. "Aw, you poor guy," Bud said, "why didn't you tell me? I could have lent you a few bucks. Boy, you don't know what you missed! That right, Ernie?" During the drive home, Harry Harrison's one thought—without reason, he knew, for he had not put it to the test—was: Gosh, if *that's* all sex amounts to, you can have it.

TURNING UP at Carol Wilson's house an evening or so later, to take her for a walk (they loved walking around the dark village park, then sitting for hours in the deserted bandstand to talk), he found that Carol was not ready yet. He joined Mr. Wilson on the nearly dark front porch, heavily screened with vines, and sat down to wait. Very much on his mind was the fiasco of his evening with Ernie and Bud at Mother Mabel's in Geneva; but equally pressing, for some reason, was the memory of the conversation he had had with Carol a few evenings earlier, in the kitchen, while they ate their cheese-dreams and unexpectedly got into that baffling conversation about the possibility of not-marrying-the-girl-you-grew-up-with, and all that stuff.

He sat on the porch with Carol's father, waiting. They sat in complete silence. Harry Harrison occupied the porch swing, and swung casually back and forth in the dark; Mr. Wilson meditatively puffed his pipe in a rocking chair, pausing now and again to knock it out on the railing before refilling again.

Abruptly, without any warning, Harry Harrison found himself wondering what Mr. Wilson was thinking about; and then, almost as abruptly, he seemed to know, by intuition. For the first time in their relationship he became acutely, uncomfortably, conscious of the fact that Mr. Wilson was Carol's father, a crucial circumstance that suddenly seemed charged with new and profound meaning: father of the girl he had been spending so much time with, for so long, and so intimately.

The silence grew longer, heavier, and more oppressive as the two of them sat there. The only sounds to be heard in the utter stillness of the summer night were the occasional bang of a June bug against the screen, the intermittent spit of the carbon arc lamp that was the street light in front of the house, and the iron screech of wheels half the town away as the R. S. & E. trolley made the turn on upper Main Street and headed out into the country toward Rochester, thirty-some miles away to the west. Momentarily he expected Mr. Wilson to take the pipe from his mouth, expectorate over the railing into the nasturtium bed below, lean meaningfully toward him, and say: "Well, young man?"

He listened anxiously for footsteps inside but Carol was taking forever. He felt he couldn't sit there another minute longer; with an effort he resisted an impulse to get to his feet, blurt out some apology, and make for home. And then, as suddenly again, to his inexpressible relief, it came over him all at once what his role was to be, what was expected of him and even being waited for: the inevitable, the only possible role, so right and natural and normal that it could not but give complete satisfaction to all parties concerned: Mr. Wilson; Mrs. Wilson; Carol, too; and not least of all, even himself. He cleared his throat and began to speak; and as he heard his own words, he felt a new power in himself, the power of being able to please, to say what was expected of him—a power that led him on and on, improvising at will.

"Carol's a wonderful scout, do you know that?" he began. "Probably, as her father, you don't know it, don't see it as I do, but she is. I don't think any fellow in this world ever had a finer girl or a more interesting and stimulating girl. She's got a wonderful mind, too. And I just want you to know, Mr. Wilson, that I appreciate it. I appreciate your trust in me, too, you and Mrs. Wilson, and I just want you to know, in case you've ever wondered, that I wouldn't, well, violate that trust for anything in the world."

He paused as if to note the effect, but there wasn't any. Mr. Wilson just knocked out his pipe on the porch rail, restuffed it, and he went on again.

"I know you don't worry about me and Carol, even though you don't really know why you have no need to worry. The reason is I've put a great deal of thought on the subject, and I have ideals about it. Very strong ideals."

Mr. Wilson prodded inside his restuffed pipe with a kitchen match and said nothing.

"I mean when I get married someday, I want to be able to know that my wife has never loved anybody else first, or—or been made love to by anybody else. And how would I have the right to expect any such thing, myself, if I myself had played around on my own beforehand and been unfaithful?"

Aware of the silent attention and of course maturity of his audience, he felt older with every syllable he uttered. He was speaking man to man, and it was a fine feeling. It gave both weight and wings to his words.

"I want to keep myself just as clean and straight before marriage as I expect my wife to keep *her*self. I think love is a very important thing, maybe even one of the most important things in life, and we haven't any right to trifle with it or—or besmirch it. And when I said a minute ago about being unfaithful, I meant with her too. Because if you and the girl you intend to marry—if the two of you, well, tasted things together beforehand, you would be just as unfaithful to her as if it was somebody else and not you. And unfaithful to your*self* too, and to the institution of marriage. But I guess there was maybe no reason for my saying any of this, really. It's the way any decent man would feel, and I'm sure," he wound up, "it was just the way you yourself felt about Mrs. Wilson."

Silence descended again. He looked up confidently to note Mr. Wilson's reaction. There was none. He couldn't have said what he expected the man to do or say, but he certainly didn't expect Mr. Wilson to go on sitting there in silence like a bump on a log. His feet up on the rail, the man sat puffing silently at his pipe as if Harry hadn't even so much as opened his mouth. What on earth was he thinking? Still more, what was he thinking of *him?* Didn't he ap*prec*iate it at all? Luckily Carol came out on the porch at this moment, Harry got up from the hammock and joined her, and the two of them went down the steps and off up the street. But he told Carol nothing about his "conversation" with her father. It was one of the few things in his life that somehow he did not feel the need of communicating to her. He didn't know why, but something told him he had better keep it to himself.

A DAY in the city, an afternoon in the bookstore, a movie, an evening at the theater, a red-letter day!—they had made their plans down to the minutest detail, budgeting every single minute; and one Saturday morning they were off. It was a day the memory of which would color all the rest of the dull winter months ahead; nor did the excitement of this have anything to do, in particular, with the fact that the movie was *Camille,* at the Piccadilly, starring Nazimova and Rudolph Valentino, and the evening was to be spent at the Lyceum Theater where Nance O'Neill and her touring company were appearing in a Spanish play called *The Passion Flower*. No matter how full the hours or how rigidly planned, there was always the possibility of the unpredictable adventure—the adventure, yet to be encountered, that might well mean a turning point in their lives. For who ever knew about these things in advance, or even at the time? Only long after, in retrospect perhaps, would the fact reveal itself that there had been any adventure or turning point at all.

To Harry Harrison, Rochester meant the place where, in company with his mother and literally led by the hand, they bought their shoes, and his suits, and her hats. Once she had taken him to see *Chu-Chin Chow,* and last year (oh, memorable matinée!)

Robert Mantell and Genevieve Hamper in *Macbeth*. Because of these two experiences, the city meant to him the glamour of the theater. It had given him a foretaste of what the great world had to offer when he and Carol were finally grown up and on their own and had escaped Arcadia at last.

At nine-fifteen on the morning of the great day they were on their way, on the trolley. It was fun when Mr. Jenkins spotted them and raised his eyebrows kiddingly as he punched their tickets; he was from Arcadia, and they had known him since they were children. The trolley sped on through the countryside, whistling shrilly at the crossings; they watched the farms and fields slipping rapidly by, disappearing, as it were, into the past. At Palmyra, Macedon, and Egypt other passengers got on, bound for a day of Saturday shopping in the city. All of these towns were known to them as places seen from the trolley window, to pass through and leave behind—a promise of the big city waiting for them beyond.

They arrived shortly after ten and at once made for Scrantom's bookstore. With her nose for "finds," Carol discovered and bought a copy of *The Undertaker's Garland*. Harry was lost in the rare-books room, reveling in limited and illustrated editions. From time to time he emerged and called Carol away from the current-books counter.

"Doesn't it make you sick? Look at this set of *Casanova*. The bindings! And these illustrations—look at them! Aren't they wonderful? Let's ask the man how much."

"Don't be silly, Harry," Carol said in one of her feet-on-the-ground moments that often deflated him. "It's probably nearly fifty dollars. After all, ten volumes . . ."

"I can ask, can't I?" He summoned the salesman, a middle-aged man who looked like an usher in church. "How much is this *Casanova*, please?"

"That set, I'm sorry to say, is already subscribed for, young man, but I'll be glad to order another if you'll leave your address."

"What does it cost?"

"One hundred and sixty dollars. Would you care to take along a descriptive folder?"

"Thanks," he said, "we were just looking."

Carol's mother had given her money to buy a new dress for school. Before noon they had been in and out of three different dress shops along East Avenue. Harry liked helping Carol decide on a dress; he sat on a little chair and looked her critically up and down each time she came out in a new one. Indeed he was so critical that Carol could not decide, and she would not choose a dress he did not like. She remembered a hat that had been spoiled for her by that very thing; she had become angry and said: "From now on, Harry Harrison, if you're any friend of a girl, don't you ever dare tell her that you don't like something she's wearing! It so happens this is the only hat I can afford for some time, and now every time I put it on I'll only remember that you don't like it— and I'll hate it!" So Carol did not buy a dress that day because she could find none they both agreed on. It is possible that he saw several he liked, but he was enjoying his role as critic and quite forgot that she was honestly looking for a dress to buy.

Over their chicken croquettes at the Pine Tree Tearoom, Carol suddenly announced: "Do you know? I've decided I'm not really an atheist after all. I guess I'm an agnostic."

It was wonderful; he was very impressed. But also he was somewhat taken aback. He couldn't help wondering why, if the word and its meaning were known to Carol, he had never heard it before.

They decided against the Valentino movie after lunch. Just being in the city was enough; it was more fun walking along the busy streets among so many strangers and speculating on their private lives than wasting a couple of hours seeing a movie that would eventually turn up in Arcadia anyway. Once, half a block ahead, they recognized old Mrs. Scofield and her great-niece Elda, who lived on Dalton Street. They ran forward and took hold of her arm just as she was turning into Eastwood's Shoestore. "Hello!" they both shouted at once. "Why, hello, children!" she shouted back, joyful as they were at the sight of someone from home. When they had passed on, they looked at each other and began to laugh. "Why on earth should we make such a fuss?" Carol said, "over seeing somebody we know and don't particularly care about anyway? If we ran into each other downtown, at home, we'd hardly trouble to speak."

On Spring Street they came upon a curious shop below the sidewalk, so that its sign—HUMPHREY'S, Old Books—was on a level with their knees. They descended the steps and went in. The place was dark and musty and crammed with books, on shelves, tables, mantels, the floor. An old man with a goatee, wearing a smock and pince-nez with a black ribbon, peered at them from the back of the shop. "He looks as though he's gotten up for some part," Harry whispered. "Yes, and rather overdoing it. Somebody probably once told him he was picturesque and he never got over it. But isn't he sweet?" she added. Harry picked up a small bronze bust that frowned among a litter of prints and examined it admiringly.

"Do you know who that is?" the old man called from the shadows.

"Why, yes, sir. It's Dante."

The old man came forward, squinting at them with interest. "Young man, you're the first customer I've ever had who recognized it."

"Really? It doesn't seem possible," Harry said. "I don't see how anyone could help but see—"

"Well, they never have! And do you know who this is?" He held up a copper medallion with a very familiar profile.

"This one's easy. It's Beethoven."

"Would you like it?"

"How much is it?"

"I said would you like it!" he repeated sharply, the "character" that he was. "If not, I'll give it to the young lady."

Harry Harrison was embarrassed. "Why, it's awfully nice of you, but—"

"Don't hem and haw." He dropped the medallion into Harry's coat pocket. "Now if the young lady is as discerning as you are, we'll find something for her." He turned and sloped into the back part of the shop. Harry and Carol could only look at each other. Then: "Girl!" the old voice called out. "Come here!" Obediently, like two children, they moved back to where he stood with an open portfolio spread out upon a littered table.

"Now, young lady, who painted this?" He held up a small but very good tinted print of *Primavera,* mounted on thin board.

Carol bent over it in the dim light. After a cautionary glance at Harry, she said, "Is it . . . El Greco?"

The old man threw Harry a look of disgust and gave vent to an audible snort.

"Why, Carol! You know it as well as I do," Harry said. "It's Botticelli. How could you have missed?"

"Oh yes. Of course." She bit her lip and frowned at Harry.

"Well, young lady, take it just the same. It's one of the great things of the world. Look at it every day. Botticelli—it's a name to remember, girl!" He dropped the mounted print into a manila envelope and gave it to her.

They were almost too surprised to thank him. Only when they were out of the shop, an hour later, could they talk freely— excitedly—about the experience and that dear eccentric old man. And Carol said: "I could really kill you, Harry Harrison, honestly! I knew it was Botticelli all the time, and you knew that I knew!"

"Then why didn't you say so?"

"Oh, just my own pecuiar kind of tact, I suppose. I simply couldn't find it in my heart to take advantage of the old darling. If we'd gone on identifying everything in the place, he'd have ended up giving us the whole shop. I bet he doesn't make a penny as it is, do you?"

When they entered the dining room of the Seneca Hotel at six o'clock—to them a very grand place—a knot of waiters broke up at the far end of the room and dispersed to their various stations. No other diners were in the place. A distinguished-looking man in a tuxedo approached.

"Tea, sir? Or dinner?"

"Isn't it open yet?" Harry asked. "I mean there seems to be nobody here."

"Presently, presently. Two?"

"Yes, please." They followed him to a small table at one side of the room, he held a chair for Carol, turned on the small pink-shaded lamp on the table, and handed them menus.

"Anyway," Harry said when the man had gone, "we can watch the people arrive."

"And, look, let's get to the theater early, too," Carol said. "That's always half the fun, don't you think? All those new faces, people we've never seen before and will never see again."

But later, seated in the balcony of the Lyceum, they lost track of everything else, including the other theatergoers about them, in their study of the program. It promised an exotic excitement. "THE PASSION FLOWER, A Translation of the Spanish Play *La Malquerida* by Jacinto Benavente y Martinez." Wondrous title! And in the cast of characters there was a man called Faustino. Thrilling names! Already Harry was planning the note he would send across several aisles to Carol when school began again on Monday morning, but whether he would sign it "Faustino" or "Jacinto" he hadn't yet decided.

For two hours, after the curtain rose, they were lifted out of themselves, carried away into another world, a world of smoldering Latin passions; but when, too soon, it was over and the lights came on again and their neighbors in the surrounding seats began getting into their wraps and glancing at their watches as casually as if nothing had taken place on stage at all, they felt a curious letdown. It had all been exciting and wonderful, but they had looked forward to it for so long; and now ahead of them lay only the dull routine thought of home. Was all the promise of the future nothing but anticipation?

They moved along Clinton Street with the crowd. They found a small night restaurant called the Black Cat. They had more than an hour before the last trolley left for Arcadia, so they went in. They seated themselves in the strangely quiet place and ordered cheese-dreams. But the waiter lingered a moment before going for the order; he seemed to be looking them over speculatively, for some reason. Then he asked in low tones if they would like anything to drink. Harry brightened and looked at Carol.

"Imagine! A speakeasy."

She nodded. He glanced about the room to see what the few others were having, but all he could see on the various tables were coffee cups. "What have you got?" he asked the waiter.

"Port, sherry, and whiskey," the waiter said.

"I'll have port-sherry," said Carol.

The waiter cleared his throat. "It's two different drinks, Miss. Port's one and sherry's another."

"Of course—how stupid of me," she said, ignoring as best she could Harry's smile of delight. "Sherry, please."

"And I'll have whiskey," Harry said.

The waiter turned and left.

"You needn't laugh," Carol said, laughing herself, now. "You'd have made the same mistake if you hadn't ordered such an easy one."

The waiter returned with the cheese-dreams and the drinks in coffee cups with saucers. Harry drank his whiskey with his cup in one hand and a glass of water in the other; he couldn't have got it down otherwise. Carol slowly sipped her sherry.

"Hasn't it been a heavenly day?" she said. "Don't you just hate having it end?"

"I hate it. I don't feel any more like going home," he said, "than I feel like going to the moon."

"*I* feel like going to the moon!"

"In another hour it will all be over. We'll be on our way home—we'll even almost *be* home, by then. And then tomorrow night we'll be doing the same old thing we did the night before that and the night before that, the same thing we'll be doing next week and next month and next year and so on till Kingdom Come."

"Oh no we won't, Harry Harrison!" she said with a passion that surprised him. "Now you listen to me! The day will come, Harry— and I'm holding out for that, otherwise I couldn't breathe another day—the day will come when we'll be on our own—free!—in New York or maybe Europe; and our next minute will be as much of an uncertainty as our next year!"

"Or our next meal, maybe!"

"Why not? *I'd* just as soon wonder where my next meal was coming from, for a change. You'd appreciate the food more!"

"No kidding," Harry said, leaning forward—caught up, as always, by Carol's enthusiasm—"isn't life interesting, really? Isn't it full, and exciting, and stimulating!"

"It could be—it's going to be! I can't understand these people who go around complaining about the emptiness of existence. It's either a pose, or else life is just too much for them!"

"That's it! They aren't up to it, aren't big enough for it. They're blind! They haven't got imagination enough to see its—its multi-colored hues."

"And its million possibilities!" she cried, responding to him just as he always did to her. "Think of all the things there are to do in this world—just *think* of them, Harry! Why, life isn't half long enough! I know I'll never be able to read all the books I want to read and see all the places there are to see. And the people! If I lived to be five hundred I still wouldn't get to know half the people I'd like to know. Life just isn't *long* enough!"

"I hate to bring this up," Harry said, "but it's time for the last trolley home. Now isn't that just life for you?"

"No!" she cried spiritedly. "Certainly not! *That* isn't life, and I'm never going to believe it is for a single minute, never! Oh sure," she said, her voice dropping lower as she began gathering her things together, "I'll go home and all that, and go right on doing all the things that are expected of me, for a while. But if people think I'm conforming, if they think I'm giving up like everybody else—why, they just don't *know,* that's all! Nobody we know even suspects for a single second who I really am, and who you are—who *we* are! Do they?"

LATE ONE NIGHT, a few weeks before Commencement, Harry Harrison sat at the desk in his bedroom writing a poem. Hot though it was, he closed the windows and pulled down the shades so that tomorrow the neighbors wouldn't be able to report to his mother at what hour he had turned out the light. It was one of those wonderfully mystical midnights when everything came right: conception, form, the very phrases themselves, even the difficult rhymes, seemed to fall into place on their own, almost as if he had nothing to do with it. He felt that he was but the instrument or vessel of some mysterious agency above and bigger than himself. From somewhere outside in the large hushed night a roving creative spirit descended and operated through him, chose him as the voice for the thing to be said. He felt the awful responsibility of the moment and the gift, and held his breath in terrifying, delightful suspense as the unpremeditated words came and came. At two o'clock in the morning he read the completed poem with tears in his eyes, tears of humility, gratitude, and a peculiar, very special, certainly un-understandable (he believed) emotion to anybody else; then carefully he copied it all over again fresh and clean, and printed above it, in block letters, the perfect, the inevitable, the only possible title: CHEESE-DREAMS.

He didn't sleep the rest of the night; he must have read over his handiwork twenty times before morning, with increasing admiration and satisfaction each time; and after a very early breakfast he was already on his way, cross-lots, through back yards, to Carol's house.

Carol brought her cereal out on to the back porch to sit with him on the top step and finish it while he read the new poem; her mother meanwhile glanced through the kitchen window at the pair of them and shook her head in exasperation over she knew not what. Harry Harrison, with Carol looking over his shoulder as he liked her to do, read slowly, self-consciously, but with a thrill of pride:

> *"Ambrosia and nectar, wine and viands of the gods!*
> *What were these compared to ours—sandwiches of cheese and*
> *toast?*
> *How we'd sit on Sunday evenings by your cosy kitchen stove*
> *Lingeringly eating; and it was our favorite boast*
> *That our cheese-dreams, as we called them, rivaled any sumptuous*
> *feast:*
> *A more luscious dish could not have been prepared—for us, at*
> *least.*

> *And we'd plan the thrilling future. Did we really mean it all?*
> *(How could you ever think, child, that we'd never, never fight?)*
> *And if it didn't make me smile I know that I should weep*
> *When I think of what a scale of dreams we'd range each Sunday*
> *night . . .*
> *Oh, Life is vastly funny, for how short ago it seems*
> *That we sat beside your kitchen stove, and made—and dreamed—*
> *cheese-dreams."*

When he had finished reading, he sat there beside her on the top step of the back porch in breathless anticipation, and silence, unwilling to break the spell of her complete enthrallment by any question or comment. He knew that Carol's first spontaneous praise would be better than anything he could solicit. But it seemed that *she* didn't want to break the spell, either. She put aside the bowl of uneaten cornflakes, took the poem from his hand, and read it over to herself. By this time he could contain himself no longer.

"Well, for Pete's sake!" he said. "I mean gosh almighty. After all! Come *on!*"

"I simply don't know what to say," she finally said, quietly. "You . . . You've said it all."

"But I haven't said a word!"

Her voice was barely audible. "I mean in the poem."

"Oh, really? Do you really think so?" His spirits rose. "That's what a poem is supposed to do, speak for itself. And it really does, doesn't it! I mean it says so much."

"Volumes."

"Oh, I knew you'd like it!"

"Only thing is, it sort of reminds me of another poem you wrote—all for me, you said—with the title 'Bright Star, Would I Were Steadfast As Thou Art.' "

"Oh, that! Why, that was nothing. It was only a kind of imitation of Keats."

"I know."

"But this one is so different!" he said. "I mean it's so modern and all."

"There's one thing though," she said tentatively.

"What's that?" he asked eagerly, welcoming any criticism. "The part about 'luscious dish'? I don't think it's right myself. It's so kind of, well, jejune. Wait, is that the word I mean?"

"I don't know whether it's jejune or what," she said, ignoring his question. "I was only thinking. You won't like this, Harry, but I can't help wondering if you'll ever grow up to your poetry."

"Now look, you don't need to be insulting!"

"I'm being no such thing," she said. "You're not a real poet, Harry—at least not yet. But at the same time the *idea* of your poem is so mature, so prophetic, that it leaves me with—with practically nothing to say."

"Well! That's better!"

ON A HOT SUMMER AFTERNOON in late August, a few weeks before they were to go their separate ways—she to Holyoke, he to Yale—they went on a long hike into the country, to their favorite spot and "discovery"—quite like the old days. As usual they took along a canvas bag full of books—*Jurgen, This Side of Paradise, The Moon-Calf,* the poems of Francis Thompson—for of course they would spend the afternoon taking turns reading to each other much-loved and well-marked passages from some of their favorite works. As it turned out, they didn't crack a book, as Carol's father would have said.

Just beyond the East Arcadia Cemetery they left the main road and cut across through the fields to their private haven, their own domain, a couple of miles farther south. Their walk passed through fields where far from costive cows grazed, and paralleled a wide, meandering but at this time of year very shallow brook: their brook. Now and again frogs plopped out from under their very feet as they walked along the bank of the brook, and, now bright green, swam off into deeper waters very gracefully in spite of the awkward-looking, thrusting motion of their back legs. Purple, white and sometimes yellow flags—iris, they were more properly called—grew in abundance along the banks. In August the fields were denuded of their bright colors: gone were the buttercups, the blue flowers they didn't know the name of, the white daisies and the black-eyed susans, and the vivid, small, almost coppery red devil's-paint brush; but the fields were alive—indeed the whole atmosphere was alive—with "molting" milkweed which had burst their dried pods and taken to the air: hundreds of thousands of tiny fluffy stars that floated across the fields and off into the blue like miniature delicate balloons. Goldfinches had taken over the whole landscape, it seemed, as if it were still spring, as if they had just come back: they swayed on stalks of thistle and burdock, or flew about the field in that peculiar zooming and falling flight that is like hedge-hopping. A distant dog was heard barking, about nothing, you could tell from the intonations of his bark: just talking to himself. A train whistled somewhere. Undisturbed cows mooed when they thought of it. And Carol Wilson and Harry Harrison, though familiar with every inch of the way, watched their step from old habit, because of the lavish deposits of ordure left behind by cow, horse, smaller animals, and sometimes by man himself, or boys, who had passed this way before them, often not many hours ago, along the brook path. Hand in hand, silent for a change—not talking at all, so that they were both self-conscious about it—Harry and Carol walked on and on.

The next field was ablaze with goldenrod, tall stalks, topped by the brilliant orange-yellow of their lacey blooms. Before climbing the fence they could only stand and stare at the beauty of all this, all but overpowering in its vivid, lavish rash of color.

He asked, "Have you ever had hay fever—do these things make you sneeze?"

"I don't think so," she said, "but it wouldn't matter if it did—not today it wouldn't. Today's a very *special day,* you do know that, don't you, Harry? I don't know whether to be sad or glad—do you? Look at that field, Harry: another Harry's Field of the Cloth of Gold—just *look* at it! And whatever happens, I mean if we begin to sneeze or anything, wouldn't it be worth it? Who could possibly care about a sneeze or a sniffle in the face of—of all this? It's glorious!"

They found the wide place in the stream they knew so well, under a weeping-willow tree with quivering thin leaves and very thin limbs that could hardly be called branches at all because they drooped straight down weakly as if in perpetual sorrow, the place along the brook that always reminded them of Ophelia's watery grave. They paused here and looked down into the transparent running shallows of the stream. *There is a willow grows aslant a brook, That shows his hoar leaves in the glassy stream; There with fantastic garlands did she make Of crowflowers, nettles, daisies, and long purples That liberal shepherds give a grosser name, But our cold maids do dead men's fingers call them* . . . However much they might pity Ophelia, they lingered here dry-eyed, of course—after all, one does not weep at *Hamlet*—and then passed on.

Still silent, still not having said a word between them, they went through the darkish little wood beyond, the damp ground shifty with skunk cabbage and ancient rotting leaves, and emerged into the brilliant sunlight of the open field just below the three little hills that were their private secret place, their home. The hills were little more than big mounds, they were short-turfed as if regularly gone over by lawnmowers (but it was sheep who kept the grass so closely cropped), and winding through the small lower plain was the broad brook, doubling back upon itself at times, so that from above it resembled a kind of maze, its sedges well barbered, its waters clear and flowing slowly, at no point narrow enough to jump across. *Brooks too broad for leaping* . . . They climbed one of the hills to lie down at the top and look out over the enchanting countryside, underneath a densely planted row of chestnut trees as formal-seeming as the aspens or cedars that defined the limits of long *allées* on old-world country estates in foreign lands, Belgium or Lombardy.

Carol opened the canvas bag, took out the books, and, with the copy of *Jurgen* in her lap, unopened—with no intention now, somehow, of opening it at all today and maybe not ever again, she said: "Miss Parker told me something the other day. It must have been an unguarded moment, for what she had to impart to me was very personal. She said: 'If ever any two people were made for each other, abso*lute*ly made for each other . . .' " She hesitated, and then added: "But maybe I shouldn't be telling you this. In fact I know I shouldn't."

"Why not," Harry said, "gossip? Tell me, I want to know who they are, of course. Everybody loves news like that, and I'm no exception."

"Well, if you must know, she was talking about us, of all people. You and me. Me and you. Us."

"What a nice compliment! But we must remember that Miss Parker, being an old maid, is, well, an incurable romantic."

Coarsely Carol suddenly said: "Aw, go way back and sit down."

"Why, Carol!"

"I knew I shouldn't have told you."

"Why not?"

"Just for instance," she said, glancing upward at the chestnut trees and lighting a cigarette.

Though he wanted to be with her more than anybody in the world, Harry Harrison sensed that this was going to be a difficult afternoon, and automatically his guards went up. He put his el-

bows on his knees and studied a curious rock formation at the foot
of the neighboring hill, maybe a hundred feet below. On this side
of the twisting brook, which reflected the afternoon sun as far
yellower than it appeared in the sky, rose a low pile of pale-gray
rock, almost white in the sun, reaching no higher above the field
and scarcely higher than the water in the wide multicurving brook,
than the heavy flanks of a reclining elephant would reach: nothing
spectacular, nothing challenging or dramatic, but it could be seen
even from this height that the spread of rock was veined with
quartz and its contours worn by time to a smoothness and even a
seemingly palpable softness most unrocklike. The broad undulating mass (at any moment it seemed it might billow and swell, as if
something stirred underneath) was a piece of timelessness, of a
time going further back into the past than a man's memory goes—
of no time, so to speak, or untime.

"Nothing's ever been said between us about our loving each
other," Carol was saying, "do you realize that, Harry? Oh dear, I
know I'm saying all the wrong things."

"Nothing needs to be said, does it? We just do. Isn't that
enough? Isn't that better than words?"

"Do we?"

"Don't we?" he bridled.

"I wonder . . ."

"We most certainly do! At least *I've* always thought so."

"That I never knew."

"The trouble with women," he said, "is that they've always got
to be reassured forever and ever—got to be *told*. Good grief, why
don't they just *know?* Men get kind of tired of having to say it all
the time."

A full moment later Carol said lightly, mockingly: " 'In sooth I
know not why I am so sad. It wearies me; you say it wearies you.' "

"That's marvelous. I'd forgotten how good it is. How does it go
on?"

With a sigh like exasperation but more like deep fatigue, Carol
said: "Something like 'But how I caught it, found it, or came by it,
What stuff 'tis made of, whereof it is born, Something-something'
—oh, I don't know, does it *matter?*"

"It matters because it's one of the best passages ever written, that's all."

"Yeah, that's all. Well, maybe it's enough."

He refused to be taken up by this, or let on that he "knew." When Carol got into the double-meaning department, which happened only every few months, he bowed out, played dumb, because it only spelled trouble. He looked down the hill. Beyond the torturously serpentine brook, which was too wide for the grazing sheep to jump across, tall grasses swayed in the warm breeze. The afternoon sun beat down with increasing warmth, and beneath the soles of his feet the earth seemed to beat, too, as if with the hum of the turning world or of life itself. He watched the marauding bands of goldfinches skimming the field below in sharply scalloped hops, falling and rising like skipping stones. He smelled, even from this distance, the smell of the thick carpet of pine needles in the larger woods beyond the gray, elephantlike mass of rock; and a smile of welcome mirth came over his face. Maybe this would help things. "I've just thought," he said, "of a wonderful line. 'Nature I loved, and after nature, me.' "

Carol said: "Philosophers say, or somebody says, that when two people love each other or are in love, one is happier than the other. The question is, which is the happier one: the one who is loved or the one who loves? If it's the latter, then I think it's pretty damned cold comfort. But I see I might as well be talking to myself. In fact I *am* talking to myself."

"Carol Wilson, this isn't a bit like you. What on earth's got into you today?"

"Oh, shut up, can't you?"

"Well, of course if that's what you want."

"Oh, it isn't, Harry. It isn't for a minute. Dottie Kramer was right. I love you, I'm in love with you, and—and I could kick myself around these three hills for—for admitting it. I'm a *fool*. It's one of those things a girl just doesn't do!" Almost at once she added, whether for his relief or not he didn't know: "Listen: here come the sheep. You can not only hear them, with their silly bleating; you can smell them."

A drove of filthy, dirty-tailed sheep filtered down the hill from between the rows of the chestnut trees. They gave Harry and Carol a wide berth, but not till after standing in their tracks for some moments, staring at them as if they had never seen human beings before; then with many a falsetto or deep-toned *baaa,* they trotted farther down the hill to drink at the wide brook and to nibble at the sedge there, whose grass grew a little more lushly than the close-cropped growth that sprouted on the crests of the three, formal, little hills.

"Well, I'm going to lay off," Carol said. "I apologize; I really hate to be that kind of woman; something got me, and I got going. It wasn't a bit fair to you, or to me either."

Harry Harrison felt a complete stranger; he was uncomfortable with Carol for the first time in his life, and he had a dreadful premonition that it would not be the last time. What had become of their wonderful friendship? He knew it was he who was in the wrong (if wrong there was) and only he; but he had no inkling why. Silent, refusing to yield an inch, he lay on his back staring up into the cloudless sky. Why couldn't they read one of those books, for heaven's sake, as they used to? That's what they had brought them along for, wasn't it? But he felt helpless to suggest the idea, for some reason, and gauche besides: gauche, of all things, with his dearest friend in all the world. He lay watching an all but motionless hawk with wide-spread stationary wings wheeling slow against the white-blue of the sky, turning and turning in listless circles: soaring freely and slowly against the heavens like a flung scimitar.

"I'm not going to say another word, I promise," Carol said, already saying far more than that, to their mutual discomfort. "But don't you feel badly about, well, leaving home?"

"Not in the least."

"I guess that's not what I really meant."

"What did you mean?"

"Oh, *I* don't know." She took a deep breath and then said, with all the heart in the world, and some effort: "Look, Harry. I honestly think—I true and honestly believe—that someday you're going to amount to something rather wonderful in this world. Even though," she added ruefully, her voice dropping very low, "I'm not so sure of my own place in the picture."

"Gee, Carol, thanks," he said; for all that had reached him was the extravagant compliment.

RETURNING TO TOWN hours later, still troubled, still silent about the nature of that trouble (whatever it was, because neither could have named it), they emerged from the loved brook path onto the dirt road that led back home, past the East Arcadia Cemetery. Slowly they walked along the high iron fence, looking through the widely spaced spindles at the familiar beauty and restfulness of the old place. The bridal wreath and mock orange bushes were only partly in bloom, or in ragged, colorless bloom this late in the season, but they were still attractive as they nodded drowsily in the pleasant heat of the late afternoon, above the small heaped mounds and their ancient thin headstones, all so much alike, some of them dating farther back than the Civil War, the war that had never taken place except in history books.

Now they passed one of the special fascinations of the place: the tomblike vault (in fact it *was* a tomb) partly above ground, partly below, where the dead were kept in the winter months till the frost had left the ground in the spring and they could be properly buried in the softer, thawed earth. The massive doors of the tomb had tapering hasps of wrought iron, shaped like spearheads, and in the center were four holes cut into the doors for ventilation, in a quatrefoil design, like something in church, on the altar, say, or at the end of the pews. For years it had been fun, somehow, to stand on tiptoe here, your hands flat against the rough splintery surface of the thick wood, and press your mouth up close to one of these designs and shout something (anything) through the holes. From inside, an echoing roar came back to you, ringing again and again louder and deeper than your shout; and in the sensitive tips of your fingers flat against the door you could feel the tingling vibration of the stirred-up tumult of sound within. Harry Harrison was tempted to step up to the door and go through this performance again, as it were for one last time. But for once he felt self-conscious about it; something held him back. Even he knew it was time to put away childish things.

THEY WROTE each other often—or, that is, she wrote and he answered. Gone were the old abstract discussions they had loved so well; gone too, almost entirely, the personal. Mostly the letters, sometimes to the point of artificiality, seemed a kind of demonstration of an unwillingness to give up, to concede that it had all come to nothing, to accept the fact and admit, right out loud, so to speak, that they'd better try to forget each other and begin all over again with someone else. But how could either one forget the person who had been his dearest friend?—such a friend and otherself as each knew he would never find again, regardless of what might have been missing in their familiar, comfortable relationship of so many years. So many years? At eighteen and nineteen and twenty, six or seven years of the past is a very long time.

Of course they saw each other, for dates, when they met at home again during the holidays: Thanksgiving, Christmas, spring vacation, and so on. But they did not really get together in anything like the old way, with plenty of time, till the following summer came 'round and they were home from college. The high point and crucial point of that summer—the turning point, and each of them knew it at once, the moment it had passed—occurred one weekend when Winifred Grainger invited them out to her place at Parson's Point for the Fourth of July holiday. They looked forward to it keenly. Each knew that it could be, and should be, a memorable weekend. And it was; it was.

Neither Harry Harrison nor Carol Wilson had been much taken with Jack Sanford when they first met him, but they were glad for Winifred that she had a new beau and one, moreover, who seemed genuinely in love with her. She was proud of him, and they were proud of him for her, because, unique among the many men who had gone around with her (except for those few occasions when Harry himself took her out), he thought nothing of being seen with her in public places; and the more formal or gala or even crowded the occasion, the more he seemed to enjoy himself with her. He was a man of distinct charm and personality, and because of his debonair, outgoing, irresistible quality, one could easily overlook those lesser faults (social climbing; making the most of the occasion; winning people over; scoring big, if possible) that somewhat detracted from his genuineness. But he was good-looking, and witty, with personality to burn: just right, it seemed, for Winifred Grainger.

It was fun dashing across the black chill bay, with the speedboat *slap-slapping* the dark waves and all but taking to the air as it hit *slap-slap-slap* the top waves only, with Harry Harrison and Carol Wilson huddled behind the second windshield, toward the rear, in the exact center, so that their clothes would not be sprayed, even soaked, by the waves thrown into the air by the bow. Before them, between the two windshields, Winifred, expert as always, kept her mind on what she was doing with characteristic concentration, holding the wheel and watching for moored sloops or buoys; while Jack Sanford, enjoying himself like a kid, turned again and again to raise his eyebrows in thrill at the pair in the rear, for conversation at this speed was impossible.

As they pulled in beside the Yacht Club, Chet Hastings, who was waiting for his girl to turn up from Auburn Island in her own Kris-Kraft, caught their painter—was that the word? wondered Harry, who knew little of these matters—with which to make fast the speedboat; getting ready to get out, he looked forward to the evening as to the most festive occasion, because it was theirs, in a way: they were together. Jack Sanford handed them up to Chester Hastings, and with light, joyous jumps they made the pier. Inside, the orchestra was playing "The Sheik of Araby," and Harry and Carol looked at each other with a smile that was like self-congratulation: it couldn't have been better.

The tune changed, and Harry and Carol moved inside the dance hall. It was wonderful being there again; they knew almost everybody in the place; but surely the most striking couple there, or at least the most handsome woman, was Betty Finletter, who was dancing with Stan Hewitt. She wore a simple sleeveless dress of palest pink shantung or raw silk with an apple-green leather belt; her blue-black hair was bound—a marvelous, imaginative touch—with two narrow grosgrain ribbons of pale green and pink; but it was her figure, her alertness, her complete and flattering attention to the man she was dancing with that was her distinction. This was not lost on Jack Sanford, who stood at the side, when Winifred was occupied elsewhere momentarily, his face showing open, frank, unguarded admiration—as who could blame him.

As Harry took Carol in his arms and Winifred and Jack moved off cheek to cheek on the dance floor, the trap-man whisked the snare drum with his flyswatter and the singing pianist gave a winning, even a flirtatious smile—for it was that kind of evening—to everyone who danced by. "I never knew . . . I could . . . love anybody . . . honey like I'm . . . lovin' you." It was too much; it was perfect; it was what a dance should be, among old friends, amid settings long familiar, long loved.

After dark—the real dark that descends late in early July—everybody got into their coats or wraps against the cool night, and moved as one, outdoors, for the fireworks, to the wide pier of the Yacht Club overlooking the bay. And judging by the "Ooohs" and "Ahhhs" that went up, the spontaneous cries of "Oh, look at that one!" and "Oh, look at *that* one!" it was an enormous success. Not surprisingly; for was ever a pyrotechnical display, when people are happy and in the mood of gaiety, *not* a success?

Then the evening changed, mysteriously, unpredictably—it couldn't have been helped; no one could have forseen it—when after the return across the bay to the sand bar, Winifred with her usual skill brought the speedboat into the wide slip at the boathouse, cut the motor, and they were home. Almost at once Harry Harrison, who didn't have the faintest reason why, was overcome with a feeling of oppression that amounted almost to a smothering sensation.

The four of them went up the steps into the neat, compact cottage at the Graingers', painted off-white inside, with a few nautical or marine touches here and there—nothing ostentatious or "cute"—and Winifred lighted the lamps. On a broad table under a hanging brass-bound lamp of thick ribbed glass there was an array of bottles and an ice bucket in case they wanted night caps, and sandwiches wrapped in wax paper.

"Food, kids, in case you're hungry." Winifred indulged herself in a loud, whining, almost animal-like yawn. "Me, I'm dying."

There was an embarrassed silence, while Jack Sanford, bright as ever, looked from one to the other with a grin.

"You know where your rooms are," Winifred said. "Or room is; but that's up to you."

"We know," Carol said, noncommittally.

"I didn't tell you before because I thought it might shock you," Winifred said.

"Shock us?" Carol said. "We're not shocked."

"Certainly not," Harry added. "Not by anything!"

"Well, in any case," Winifred said, "Jack and I are sleeping in Jones's bed in the boathouse. So, night-night. Pleasant dreams." And they were gone.

After a moment Harry said: "Well, I think it's nice, myself."

"Why?"

"Well, I mean, that they don't have to be strained by our presence, or do otherwise than what they'd want to do. You know?"

"Oh sure," Carol said, starting up the stairs.

"You mean al*ready?*"

"Why not? It's late. For your information—just so we don't collide, I mean—I'm taking Mercedes' old room, on the lake side."

"Okay," he said. "There's a spare room on the bay side, for me. Sleep well!"

"Thanks," Carol was heard to say as she disappeared along the upstairs hall.

Harry Harrison sat down on the small cretonne-covered sofa. He looked around the room for a long minute. Then he got up and inspected the books in a small bookstand under the stairs. My God, there wasn't a book in the entire collection, of maybe fifty in all, that he would be caught dead reading—except possibly an "adaptation" of *The Arabian Nights*. He smoked a cigarette. He looked out of the windows at the lake side: nothing to be seen whatever. He looked out the bay side; and he saw the light burning in the single upstairs room above the boat slips; it was a raw, bare bulb on the end of a wire, weak, and unshaded at that, but tonight it seemed to burn with a beat, an intensity and self-renewing throb, that was like the continuous sweep and hot searching blaze of the revolving beacon of the lighthouse just beyond Charles Point.

He didn't wonder what was going on between the two of them up there in Jonesey's cot and room; he just didn't want to think about it. He did wonder if Carol had fallen asleep in her room on the lake side. He hoped she had and that he was farthest from her thoughts and consciousness. Perhaps after a little while longer he could decently go to bed himself, if he was very quiet about it.

About ten minutes later he put out the downstairs light, remembering to leave on the blue night light at the top of the stairs as he had been told to do, and went up.

He was surprised to find his bag open and his clothes spread out on the bed in the room he would have chosen himself: Agnes apparently had chosen it for him. No sound came from the room at the other end of the hall where Carol slept; no streak of light showed under the door. He undressed quickly without turning on a light, using the dim blue glow that came from the hall, and got into bed in his BVDs, shivering pleasantly in the chill of the sheets and the damp night air that blew along the sand bar. Then he lay on his back with his hands under his head, listening.

The only sound that could be heard in the night was the occasional *putt-putt-putt* of an outboard-motor boat far off across the bay somewhere and the constant sound of surf from the lake shore, followed by the wash and backward-sliding of the pebbles that always strove to return to the sea again but never succeeded, for they were each time thrown back up upon the sand by the next rush and spread of surf. It was nice being here. The day had turned out very well after all, like an unforeseen adventure. For all that they had said in the past about the sameness of their lives and the dullness of always knowing what was going to happen to them every minute, here they were, for the first time in their experience, spending the night under the same roof, a thing they had never done before. Sleeping in the same house gave them the advantage and novelty of knowing that first thing tomorrow morning they could take up right where they had let off, just like living together, when you came to think of it. Finally he turned on his side, in his favorite position, pulled the blankets snugly around his shoulder, and settled himself for sleep. He was just dropping off when he thought he heard Carol call out his name.

He lifted his head from the pillow and listened. He was right; her voice came again.

"Harry . . ."

"Yes?" he answered back.

There was a pause. Then: "Come here a minute."

Was something wrong? He got out of bed and padded in his bare feet to the hall door. "Funny thing is I was going to come and see you anyway, but I'm not quite undressed yet," he said loudly. He waited a minute more, apprehensive, then went down the hallway toward her door. "What is it?" he said from the doorway.

From the darkness of her room the voice said, "Come here a minute," and it was not a voice he had ever heard before. It sounded a tentative note, timid, unsure, so unlike the positive Carol he knew so well: more like a child afraid but imploring to be reassured. He stepped into the room.

She was barely visible in the dim night, but as his eyes became accustomed to the shadows he saw that she was lying rigidly straight in bed, almost starkly. Then her arms went up stiffly, held out to him. He sensed the tremendous effort behind the move and his heart sank. He moved forward, sat on the edge of the bed, and lay down beside her. At once her head was on his shoulder, but turned downward, almost away from him, and he heard her deep intake of breath that was like a kind of shudder.

He was never to know, later or ever, how long they lay together like that, she under the blankets, he outside, yet clasped together. But it was a stranger he held, and he was a stranger lying there, no one known to her at all. He was two people, one thinking, listening, waiting, wary, the other obeying wishes that were not his. To pull back the covers and get into bed with her was impossible, somehow; it was a move he could not make if his life depended on it. To get up and leave was more impossible still. And meanwhile to go on lying there, and lying there, created in him a suspense that became more unbearable by the minute.

He sat up. His feelings were a whirl of confusion. He had never been so puzzled by himself, never in his life. He did not know what he wanted and did not want, and there seemed no way of finding out. He wished there was someone he could turn to for help, some dear friend, but for once Carol was not that person; the responsibility was his alone. Sitting on the edge of the bed, he looked down at the silent figure waiting. And she who had always been so familiar to him, so comfortable to be with, like another self—she had become a puzzle, too. As he looked at her in the half-dark she seemed to change and again change before his very eyes. When she was his dear Carol, the idea of passion was farthest from his thoughts. When she was woman, the lover, love, he felt lonely and longed for Carol. Oh, what did others do—how was it with them? Were they so uncertain, too? Did they need more time?

Needing time, then, he heard himself say—but it was as if someone else were speaking through him or for him—"Wait a minute while I get a cigarette." He got up from the bed and went back to his cold room. He fumbled in his pants pockets for the cigarettes, lighted one, then shook out another one for Carol so they could smoke together, and went out into the hall again.

Her door was closed. He put his hand on the knob and turned it. It turned, but that was all. With a shock of panic he realized that he was locked out.

He stood there for a long silent moment to let the sudden pounding of his heart subside, then tapped lightly on the door. "Carol," he called in a low voice, "let me in." And again: "Carol," and still again, and yet once more. There was no answer or sound from the other side of the door. He was shut out.

He returned to his room and climbed back into the cold sheets, shivering, to spend a night of desolation that he thought, as the hours stood still in dreadful accusing silence, would never end.

The silence and rejection still held in the morning. Carol said not a word to him at breakfast, before Winifred and Jack came in. After she had finished her cereal and coffee she said, "I'm going to walk along the sand bar to Lake Bluff," and she got ready to go. It was a good three-mile walk, there and back.

When Winifred and Jack came in from the boathouse at nine-thirty, Carol was just about to start and Harry was cleaning up the breakfast dishes. Harry looked up brightly, and brightly he called out: "Good morning, Winnie, morning, Jack. Isn't this simply a spiffy day!"

Winifred didn't need to look from one to the other to know something was wrong. Something had gone seriously amiss, or there had been a misunderstanding, or even a quarrel.

Harry Harrison's bright expression and cordiality belied this—

belied it, and at the same time gave it away. "We've already been out," he said heartily. "Think of it, I walked to Charles Point, and Carol's taking off for Lake Bluff."

"You must be crazy."

"Oh, we're crazy all right," he said gaily.

Carol said nothing; Harry Harrison felt foolish because of his own bright talk, which he didn't seem to be able to control, and he respected her the more for her silence.

"I've always wanted to walk to the Bluff since I first saw the placc," Jack Sanford said. "Will you take me, Carol?"

"Not on your life," Winifred said. "At least not now. Breakfast first."

After she had gone, and then Jack Sanford too, Winifred Grainger said: "Well, tell me."

"Tell you what?"

"Whatever happened? Something happened."

"You're imagining things. It's that operative imagination of yours, that insatiable curiosity, that sees things that aren't there."

"You know? I believe you're telling the truth in spite of yourself. 'Nothing happened'!"

"I don't know what you're talking about."

"But if anything happened to me," she said, "as obviously happened to you and poor Carol, I'd be the first to tell you."

"Why do you say 'poor Carol'?"

"Because she's unhappy."

"She'll be okay."

"Then I *was* right. Something did happen."

"Winifred, will you lay off, please? It's of no importance. Carol's all right. And so am I. We've had a *very* good *time*. We slept like logs, thanks to those very good beds, among other things."

"We didn't, and I think we're the better for it. Little sleepy, maybe, but . . . try it sometime."

IN MID-MORNING, while reading and not reading a copy of *The New Yorker,* he glanced out and saw that Carol was skipping stones, idly, by herself, along the lake surface. After a minute he went out. He sat down on the low wooden steps and said: "Hi! Did you enjoy your walk to the Bluff?"

She didn't answer.

"Where's Jack?" She'd have to answer that one.

"I don't know, I thought he was back. Isn't he? Anyhow he left me part way and returned. I guess I'm not very good company today. Can't blame him much."

He knew they were miserable together and that she was suffering as much in her silence as he was in his.

After a while she sat down beside him and halfheartedly put forth one more stone into the oncoming surf. When she finally spoke, the voice was different. It was calmer than before, older, listless and indifferent to the words, and yet a note of the barest suggestion of humor was in it.

"I wish you were my son, Harry. I'd love to bring you up."

Not daring to, yet daring it all the same, out of the corner of his eye he glanced at her, to see if it was all right to smile. It was.

The relief and gratitude that flooded over him then was like joy, like being reborn. Inwardly, with his entire heart, he thanked Carol. Oh, more than ever, she was his best, his dearest friend; but the friend whom—from now on, for both their sakes—he must be most careful of.

BUT DURING HIS MOST PRIVATE, most alone moments—and he had many of these moments of aloneness—he could not deny to himself that the episode ("episode!") had thoroughly frightened him, and scared him through and through in fact, had made him doubtful of his future and of himself. He thought: If I could hurt somebody like that, somebody who was my dearest friend in the whole world, what could I not do (what might I not yet do) to someone I cared for less; and who had there ever been that he cared for so much as for Carol? He did not necessarily or deliberately avoid Carol after that evening that had been so shattering to them both, for in reality there was no need to; it was early summer, school was just over, and he had been promised a trip abroad with a group of nice boys from Rochester. Preparations for the tour, thank heaven, were taking most of their time. Eight boys were going, and they were being shepherded around Europe by a history teacher from East High in the city, one Al Newmarck, or Dr. Newmarck, as he preferred to be called. Dutifully Harry Harrison wrote notes to the parents of the other boys who were going— rather pointlessly, it turned out, since none of them wrote to him and perhaps even wondered why he had written them in the first place. There was a front-page article in the Arcadia *Blade* about the coming trip abroad, and Harry's photograph was printed beside it—which caused quite a stir, or he thought it did. The week they left to board the *Mauretania* in New York, he called up Carol to say goodbye. They exchanged a few studiedly jovial pleasantries about travel and one's first trip abroad, including a bold reference to the necessary dirty postcards (as necessary as one's passport, for heaven's sake), and that was that. He met Dr. Newmarck and his new friends at the Ansonia Hotel on upper Broadway (how impressed he was by the view from their balcony, looking down Broadway toward the bright lights of Times Square, and by the fact that there was actually a lively playing fountain, illuminated from behind by colored lights, in the dining room) and after what they considered a wild night on the town (speakeasy, cafeteria, insanely fast ride on the subway), they took off the next day.

For Harry Harrison, the turning point of the tour came about by accident, so to speak. In Zürich they took a walking tour into the ancient woods behind the Grand Hotel Dolder and were suddenly caught in an almost savage thunderstorm and downpour including hail. The summer air turned icily chill almost in a minute, and they took shelter, during the torrential rain, in one of the shining, peeled, varnished-looking *gasthauses* to be found every few minutes among the cedars. There were no windows, only oblong openings without panes of glass, and an always open door. Result: Harry Harrison caught a bad cold, and by late afternoon he was running a fever of a little over a hundred degrees.

That evening there was a round-table discussion in the dining room of the Baur-au-Lac, gloomy on the part of Harry Harrison, concerned on the part of Dr. Newmarck, while the rest of the little group were indifferent. The tour was to go on to Vienna, then down through Albania and on to Greece. But Harry Harrison didn't feel up to the trip, much as he had looked forward to seeing Athens and the Parthenon. It was finally decided that they should go on without him—there was no telling what his cold would lead to, for he had never been robust—and Harry would go home. It was his own choice. He had felt strange in Europe, and with his new friends. He had no sense of belonging there, or with them. So it was arranged: he would take the night train to Paris, while they went on to Vienna and Greece; and from Paris, the first boat home. Unaccountably, he even felt relieved.

THE *Bahnhof* at Zürich was clangorous with activity, jarring on Harry Harrison's nerves. Travelers hurried through the gates as if the world were coming to an end. Porters in faded smocks and caps ran here and there shouting curses at one another. Bells rang; there was an iron rumble as baggage was trundled along the stone floor; on all sides could be heard excited talk in half a dozen languages. Momentarily the crowd gave way before a company of young men carrying two or three vaulting poles each, moving through the station like a marching thicket: like Birnam Wood, Harry thought. At one of the gates a man and woman stood wrapped together in oblivious passion as if they were never to part. In the glass-covered train shed slanting blocks of pale sunshine trembled in the air above the steaming locomotives that were panting as they prepared to leave for Paris, Munich, the Engadine, the South. Harry Harrison's luggage was already aboard the Paris express; and now with several minutes to go, he walked back along the stone platform to look over the magazines in the waiting room. He came upon the couple still wrapped in silent embrace at the gate, oblivious to all else, and, turning his glance discreetly away, he passed through to the newsstand. He chose a *London Illustrated News* and the *Züricher Blatter,* and a soft voice spoke in English at his shoulder.

"Gentleman, will you go with me?"

Abruptly he pulled back and found himself intimately face to face with a young woman of about his own age, which was barely twenty. She looked up at him with inquiring lifted eyebrows and parted lips. Then she nodded reassuringly and spoke again.

"Yes? You will like me, gentleman. I am nice."

Unable for a moment to speak, he looked back at her. There was something appealing about her, or pathetic; but of course it was out of the question. It was out of the question anyhow, train or no train, and he tried to control his rising exasperation because, he told himself, he did not want to hurt her feelings.

She placed her hand on his sleeve and he felt the gentle pressure of her fingers through the tweed jacket. Her mouth curled in a faint smile, she tilted her head, and her eyebrows rose again, pleadingly.

He found his voice, and the sound of it startled him. "No, no! You don't understand!" His helpless anger increased because he didn't know what he meant by this, didn't know what it was that she didn't understand. "Excuse me, please!" He pulled his arm free, remembered to lift his hat, and hurried off to his train.

He hoped he hadn't offended her. At the gate he paused and cautiously looked back. He saw she was still there, idly leafing through a magazine as he himself had done, yet at the same time already watchful for the approach of another: even as she turned the pages, her casing glance moved this way and that. Relieved, he went through to the train shed. Of course what she didn't understand, he told himself, what she couldn't have known, is that I am ill.

WHEN HE arrived home, all he knew of his European experience was that he had got nothing out of it, or very little. He looked forward to college again. All that was certain in his life (and how certain was that?) was that he would return to Yale in the fall and take up a major: architect of country houses. Why this? He had discovered a knack for draftsmanship and could easily put down pretty, by no means original, houses of a certain style and cost that would fit into American communities, especially around Rochester. To help himself in this, in his relations with his few colleagues and the growing numbers of acquaintances as the years passed and his profession got under way, he had mastered a technique that seemed to cover all emergencies. He wondered what had ever become of the promising boy he had once been, the outgoing, interested boy, where had that boy gone, what had become of him? Knowing no answer to this, he cultivated a technique of personality, and it worked. To all outward appearances it worked; and what else was needed beyond outward appearances? It helped him immensely after he left college, and it never diminished the number of friends he couldn't help acquiring along the way, in his profession; but he knew—only he knew—that he was a prisoner, for all that he was in demand socially; his life, successful though it was, showed no promise of ever being anything but utterly empty. He knew this, and accepted it, and kept it to himself. He was cut off, somehow, lonely with the loneliness of being alive.

Some people feel comfort in crowds, a sense of belonging, security. Harry Harrison is one of these; all his life (and it's nothing to what is coming up) he has needed the protection of being with others, even when he knows "inly" that he is most unlike them— an alien. It makes him feel a member of the human race, to which, in secret moments, he almost feels he has no right of membership at all; a state or sense of isolation that will get worse as time goes on. But there are also times when crowds—well, it's something like this:

The night of the Yacht Club dance, when everybody quits the dance floor and piles out onto the crowded pier in the dark overlooking the bay, to see the fireworks, Harry Harrison is in the forefront of the mob, arm in arm with Carol, his date. They have the best possible position for seeing the barge half a mile offshore from which the fireworks will go up and the elaborate display begin. He is (it must be repeated) arm in arm with Carol, but for all the electric physical intimacy that runs between them he could just as well be with someone else—a stranger. For some reason it just does not occur to him to give her an added break by taking her in his arms and lifting her up onto the great oil-smelling square-shaped beam that marks the last edge of the pier so that she can get and even better view. It is Jack Sanford who unaccountably and instinctively does this for him, and for Carol. Harry Harrison is relieved, glad that Carol has been lifted up to a better view.

Now he moves back a step or two, giving way to others. In the dark around him he hears one woman say to another, kidding yet *deadly serious: "Time like now reminds me of the night I discovered, well, how the hell can you have a fight with your lover, or sustain a fight rather, while you're standing shoulder to shoulder perforce singing the National Anthem, for God's sake? You wouldn't remember him but there was this Bill Whoozis—big thing for a while. And one night we were at this nightclub-speakeasy together, in Albany, fighting like mad all evening long about God knows what, who remembers now? And just as I reached the absolute point of walking out on him, and I mean for good, the band suddenly plays, don't ask me why, 'The Star-Spangled Banner' of all things! And do you know what happened? Did I feel a horse's ass! We stood up along with everybody else, by God we stood there shoulder to shoulder seething like mad inside but going through the motions of being awfully cozy or patriotic or something on the outside—all this 'solidarity' stuff that makes you sick to think of but somehow or other, don't ask me why, works after all. And you know what happened? By the time we reached the lines self-conscious as all hell 'The land of the free and the home of the brave,' I'd forgotten what we'd been quarreling about and so had Bill. You know what I mean? Oh look! Look!"* Slightly wobbly at first, the first rockets are beginning to go up from the float.

Harry Harrison knows exactly what she means. You cannot maintain a quarrel while sharing, however halfheartedly, something from the outside with somebody else. And though he is not at Carol's side, or linked with her arm in arm as before, he is sharing the gorgeous pyrotechnical display with her along with everybody else in that close-packed crowd. For reasons that he is unsure of himself (but they are real! real!), he wishes the beautiful fireworks would never end. Here, on the pier—miles distant and an hour away from the cottage room or rooms he will shortly have to decide upon after they have returned to Winifred's place across the bay—here there are no problems: all is comfortable and pleasant as high school was all last year. Here is only celebration of stunning beauty in the sky. No time now—no need—to think of serious test or trial, of responsibility pending, waiting, unavoidably.

Let the Ohs and Ahs soar up mindlessly! Let the night sky be split or rent with dazzling evanescent color! Let the sky come down with color and flaming light! Let it not cease! Let the summer heavens explode in joyous flame and noise, while they all celebrate, as one, the glorious Fourth! For when it stops, and the night is dark again, and people start on their way homeward contentedly, contentment alas for Harry—contentment as he has always known it with his dearest friend Carol—will alter, become something else, suffer a profound sea change, for better or worse. Oh, look at that one! God, just look at that one!

V

CLOSING IN

THE car was a good five minutes out of Watkins Glen, speeding up the slope along Seneca Lake toward Arcadia and home, before either one of them said a word. Then:

"Did anything happen back there?"

"Nothing happened."

"Did I say anything?"

"Nothing."

"I mean, anything I shouldn't have said?"

"You said nothing, Harry dear. Forget it."

"But there was something . . ."

"Yes, there was something. But it's nothing to blame yourself for. It was only human. You just sort of broke down for a minute. Could have happened to anybody."

"I feel awful. I can't tell you how I feel. I've never felt like this in my life. I learned I'd been in hell. Been living in hell. And never knew it till today. I can't explain it."

"You're explaining it, all right. But you 'explained it' fully as much back there in that awful funeral parlor when you gave way to that funny little yelp."

"Heaven knows what people thought."

"Who cares?"

"Awful. A grown man . . ."

"You are now. But there've been many times I thought you weren't."

"Did Betty Finletter hear?"

"It couldn't matter less, I told you."

"Dear Winifred. An hour or so ago, on the way down to Watkins Glen, when you told me that story about Cal Cunningham's son—and I didn't want to hear about the state trooper—you said, 'You see how I need you, Harry,' and I didn't see. I do now. We need each other."

"Well, as long as we both know, we don't need to talk about it. Feeling is the thing, Harry."

Then, abruptly, there was that sound endemic to the American landscape anywhere—slam of brakes, screech of rubber—and Winifred Grainger swung the wheel sharply-suddenly to the right, recovered just in time the straight progress of the onrushing car, proceeded half a mile farther in silence, but slower, then pulled to the side of the road, drove onto the grass, and shut off the motor.

"Do you mind if we wait a moment or two? Nice view anyway."

"Certainly not. We've got all afternoon. And it is a nice view."

"That wasn't like me, Harry. Losing control for a second, there, and crossing the white line."

"Just what I was thinking: not a bit like you. You're the best driver I've ever known."

"I must have been daydreaming, thinking of something else. In fact I know I was." She shook a cigarette from an open pack of Pall Malls on the seat between them and lighted it. After smoking in silence for a moment she said, with a suggestion of a laugh in her voice—that self-mocking laugh that he knew so well—she said with a ribald sigh: "Oh, I tell you, Harry. Looking at a man's ass will be the death of me yet."

"I didn't notice . . ."

"You didn't? That man back there, that young farmer—or for all I know that middle-aged farmer because I didn't look at his face—standing at the side of the road in beautiful washed-out denim pants, bending over a bale of hay or whatever, his back to us and showing that beautiful, narrow, male ass encased tightly in the faded blue cloth—so attractive . . . It's going to be the death of me someday, you wait." Now she did laugh. "It's the story of my life; you can put it on my tombstone, as my epitaph: 'A Man's Ass Was the Death of Her.' "

He said nothing. After a moment she added: "Though I don't

know why I say ass. The ass is no use to me. It's what's up front that counts."

"Winnie, for God's sake. Cut it out."

She turned toward him on the front seat, and without rancor of any kind, rather with an exuberance or almost hearty affirmation, she said: "Listen, you. If I can laugh at these things, laugh at myself, why the hell can't you? I know I'm ludicrous. Come on, let's get out of the car and walk down the slope a little and sit in the sun. Such a beautiful view—Valois Castle over there on the far bank, and the lake like silver . . ."

They sat down in the long grass a hundred feet or so below the car. The magnificent countryside beyond the lake, part vineyards but mostly a patchwork of neat farm lands, was resplendently clear and near in the mid-afternoon sunshine of that late-October day. It looked like parts of France, nor was this only because the white castle of Valois made it so.

The hour was a time-out for private thought and shared thought. Winifred Grainger, for all her ribaldry, had been deeply moved by what she had felt at Jack Sanford's funeral; and the unexpectedly keen sense of loss she had experienced at the sight of the body of the man who had been the father of the child she had not had had stirred her to a sense of grief she had thought she had outgrown these many years. As for Harry Harrison, he felt utterly shattered. Something or someone had suddenly pulled the rug out. His life, such as it was and what was left of it, appeared to him unmistakably for the first time in its true, cruel guise: meaningless, useless, a blank. He had been shocked to hear himself give way to that sudden audible intake of breath in the stillness of the funeral parlor, but it was nothing to the bleak tragic glimpse that overwhelmed him of the emptiness, the pointlessness, the lifelessness of his own life. Neither of them was in the mood for conversation, yet unconsciously they felt an unwillingness to let each other go. They were stuck with each other and they knew it.

At one point Harry Harrison suddenly said: "Winifred, why don't we get married?" And then, embarrassed, he felt constrained to add, with that masquerading facetiousness so characteristic of him when he was most serious. "Oh, I know I'm no bargain. At best I can only offer you," he said lightly, "a second-hand life."

Winifred smoked her cigarette in silence, without answering. And then after a while, as old friends will, they began to talk, as much to themselves as to each other. And what they said, then, did not go anything at all like this:

WINIFRED: I know a man whose hair—a man neither more nor less attractive than many another, but a man—whose hair lies straight back from either side of his temples, flat to his ears and beyond, with a sheen like the finest bird's wing, glossy, smooth, clean, beyond words attractive, so that you want to touch it with your fingers, stroke it, lay your palm flat against its beautiful un-ruffled surface. And why? Because the hair itself is so beautiful, or the man is? No. Neither is in any way extraordinary. It's only because one is obsessively conscious, *I* am conscious, that some-where in the picture there is the human penis. I have a friend, I have had him often, but never enough, who, like many men, though women don't usually know this, like to be made love to fully as much as they like to make love: fifty-fifty, the perfect balance. Sometimes, in a state of pleasant exhaustion or relaxa-tion, he lies stretched out full-length on the bed, on his back, one leg slightly bent. His skin is perfect, ivory-white, and hairless; the body is beautifully shaped, the long legs glorious to look at. He lies perfectly still, eyes shut, one arm under his head. But at the least touch the whole wonderful creature comes slowly alive. I have only to put my finger, say, just under the underside of his knee, that most beautiful spot, and then the leg moves as if with a life of its own, apart from the rest of the body, or moves and stirs as if it had been pulled or moved forcibly: as if it knew in itself my desire and admiration and accommodates itself to me accordingly and at once. These, I tell you, are the great moments in life—moments you cannot forget. I saw a photograph in a magazine over which I pored for hours, a publicity picture put out by some museum, showing how a certain marble statue, a male nude by Canova (I'm sure from the athletic realism of the figure it was nobody better than Canova), was being moved from a platform in the rear of the gallery onto a truck. The camera showed a husky,

towering giant of a truck driver in one of those nondescript coveralls reaching up to lift off, and set into place on the open platform
of the truck, that cold exquisite beauty, his arms around the perfect marble figure, and his shoulders and back and legs straining
under the burden as he guided the Canova into position; and I
don't need to ask you—or rather you certainly don't need to ask
me—which was the more beautiful of the two, the beautiful nude
that was an imitation of life, or the crude, living—alive!—man
himself. I was walking along East Avenue in Rochester one afternoon and saw a little group of women bent over in front of an
antiquarian's shop, examining with the keenest attention a small
row of exquisite miniatures in gold frames on the tiny parquet floor
of the shop window, and missing the—the only thing that counted.
For just beyond and in back of the miniatures was something they
did not see at all and were in fact almost ostentatiously unconscious of: a workman, in workman's clothes—oh, most "unes-
thetic"—standing on the floor and facing the street. He was wash-
ing the window, swabbing the upper half with a wet sponge,
reaching as high as he could reach, then wiping the water away in
straight lines downward, with one of those rubber-edged wipers.
And each time he reached upward with the sponge, straining
higher each time, while all those busy women focused on the gold-
framed miniatures at his feet, his gray work shirt separated from
the belt at his waistline, and the pants dropped down a little lower
by an inch or two each time, and you saw—*I* saw—part of that
beautiful, bare, flat abdomen, with a slender line of fine silky hair
running downward from his navel. I could go on for hours, hours,
for I've lived a long time and I've always been too highly aware.
As a kind of therapy, let's say, or distraction, I've taken up languages, studied music and painting, flown my own plane, read
books and reread them; but you can't get away from it. Much have
I traveled in the realms of art, and much good it has done me! I've
been to the Sistine Chapel in the Vatican twice. I wanted to see the
frescoes on the ceiling, and what did I see? Oh, the glory was there,
all right, the glory—but, for me, once I saw that magnificent figure, all concentrated in the legs of Jonah, the thighs of Jonah, the
partly twisted, backward-leaning torso of Jonah, the full bare
thighs and legs of Jonah, I was done for. Such beauty of man, and

done by a man, conceived, executed and celebrated by a man! If Michelangelo could glory in it, why can't I? Oh, I do, and still do, and will always so; but that's all I saw—the glory of the masculine flesh and figure, the calves and thighs and legs and the very feet of Jonah. Such beauty, such legs and thighs, such beauty of man, one man, *a* man—man. And Jonah was only one of hundreds up there; how many hundreds? Yet all I saw was Jonah, I separated him from the others, isolated the personal. Don't tell me that the nude in art is abstract! I sat on a bench, the mirror spread flat on my knees; I held it tightly looking into it, looking upward at the legs and thighs and torso of Jonah, the legs and thighs, those beautiful thighs, and I was a prisoner then, held there, trapped, transfixed for a tortured hour or more, torn between rapturous admiration and anguished, anguished desire: getting everything out of the beauty of Jonah—getting everything, and nothing. I'm sure that Michelangelo never in all these many years had such an idolator of his art as I was then, never such a single-minded admirer, as I shook my head again and again in appreciation and awe, and in gratitude too for his vision, his vision and mine, yet seeing only Jonah and those thighs and legs. I was stopped there, stuck, needing to look no farther than those thighs and legs, for that is all there was and is anyway, except the penis that is always somewhere there in the picture. And in spite of these lofty experiences, this reaching out to art or literature or something better, something bigger than myself, what has my life been, anyway—since eighteen, my God—but a headlong plunge, or wallowing if you like, into varieties of lust, constantly changing, constantly different and "new." Shakespeare said it for me, in one of the later sonnets: written for me, nobody else. In an almost angry torrent of deliberately harsh-sounding, strong, and wonderful words, he says that *"lust is Purjur'd, murd'rous, bloody, full of blame, Savage, extreme, rude, cruel, not to trust; Enjoy'd no sooner but despised straight; Past reason hunted, and no sooner had, Past reason hated . . . Mad in pursuit, and in possession so . . ."* All this he calls *"Th' expense of spirit in a waste of shame"*—and don't I know! But shame? Shameful? I wonder. For without such episodes in my past, my life would have been unbearable.

HARRY: People who think I'm so clever wouldn't believe what a clown I am, what a clown I've always been, and ignorant. Not even you, Winifred. Oh, it's laughable now, but do you know this, would you believe it? I was a grown man, supposedly a mature one, before it dawned on me one day that when men sang of their baby, as they do in popular songs, *I* actually thought that they *meant* a baby, like an infant in a crib. Many, many years ago, dancing with Carol at the high-school dances on Friday nights after the basketball game in the gym, when the orchestra played "When My Baby Smiles at Me," I used to think, like a goddamn fool, now wasn't it nice that someone should write a popular song on the subject of a man's love for his *baby*—offspring, of course—after all the slushy junk they used to write about moonlight and roses and "you in my arms." Farther back, there was that sickeningly monotonous song with the jerky rhythm, "Everybody Loves a Baby, That's Why I'm in Love with You," and so help me, I used to picture—oh sap that I was and am and always have been—a tender loving young father bending over a crib or bassinet in the nursery and crooning to his adored little girl. And later, when Mary Martin sang and danced so enchantingly that song called "My Heart Belongs to Daddy," I thought—oh God, I feel sheepish about it now—that she was singing about her father and how good he was to her, even though all during the song she was parading back and forth across the stage doing a strip-tease at the time—which *maybe* I thought a little odd, but I don't remember that I did. Now why is it that somewhere along the way when someone sang about his "baby" smiling at him or when Mary Martin sang about her "daddy"—why was it that someone, somewhere, somehow, didn't tell me what it meant? The whole point is: nobody told others what it meant, they just knew instinctively; and if ever I needed to be reminded that something had been left out of me that was only too alive in others, that something was missing in me—and *I* was missing everything—I have only to think of those idiotic songs that meant so much to all the boys and nothing to me.

WINIFRED: If I've learned anything in my life of any value, I've learned that I can blame nobody else for whatever has happened to me. No one: not my mother and father, my beautiful sisters, any traumatic shocks, as they say nowadays, that might have happened in childhood: I blame no one but myself, and I don't blame myself much at that. I've had to learn, for there is no other way out, to accept the things I cannot change, accept the way things are, and myself. There is a French expression: *nostalgie de la boue*—homesickness or nostalgia for the gutter. That's me, Harry; I was born that way; it's as simple as that. I have a hunch—I can't call it a theory because I don't know enough about these things—but I have a hunch that people are born the way they are and nothing would have made any difference. It would be pretty crummy of me, for instance, if I went all the way back to age eleven and blamed Cal Cunningham for seducing me on the lake porch of his cottage that night. He didn't seduce me; I was ready for it as he was; I seemed to know all about it and take to it without previously really knowing a thing. And I can give you an instance to show that it was native to me, perhaps even inevitable, just waiting to be brought out, an instance that went farther back than my first encounter with Cal. Many years ago, on a visit to New York when I was certainly no more than eight or nine, if that, Mother took me to the Metropolitan Museum while Dad attended some bankers' convention. We came inside the vast main entrance. We turned to the left and started down what was then called the Hall of Emperors. Every ten feet or so was a larger-than-life bronze or marble statue of a Roman male in the nude, each with a calm but stern expression and the well-barbered head of a businessman, very like my own father. Brother! Did Belle have an ordeal coming up—and more power to her for the way she rose to the unexpected occasion. She paused self-consciously but conscientiously before each naked figure, bent forward dutifully to read the name of the emperor on the metal plate, then straightened up and glanced upward with a cultured studious expression and dilated nostrils at the head and shoulders above the bronze or marble naked torso; and immediately, though I think I had never before even faintly known that there was the slightest difference between the physical body of a man and a woman, I was aware that Belle felt very keenly the responsibility of the occasion and would do her damnedest to bring it off without revealing the trace of a wince. Her very strain, of course, told me everything. Holding my hand tightly in hers, she allowed her eyes to travel slowly, unflinching, from the neck to the chest, to the belly, and all the way down the body to the feet.

Even at that tender age I knew that come hell or high water, Belle was determined not to avoid looking at That Thing; and of course I got it. Before we passed on to the next figure where we were to stop and go through the whole grim performance again, Mother heaved a deep admiring sigh, and with enough volume almost to conceal the nervous tremor in the voice, she said: "My! Certainly is a fine figure of a man." Chin up, Belle turned away from the overpowering nakedness of that torso, to the next one, and I felt a hot little excitement stir within me, an unaccustomed and strangely physical tension. And then I saw that about thirty feet away a uniformed guard was watching us; watching me. Silently, hypnotically, he commanded my gaze; a current as of an electric attraction sprang up between us in the vast space of the hall, intimate and secret, creating its own atmosphere, excluding my mother, the nearby strollers, and the whole world—*in*cluding only myself, and the naked Roman, and the guard, beneath whose uniform (I knew it now for the first time) there reposed, in the flesh, a copy of the figure on the pedestal. Reposed? Hell no! For as I watched him helplessly, drawn to him, unable *not* to look, I saw that he had put his left hand in his pants pocket, and saw how the hand moved there, stirred, under the cloth, and how, unsmiling, almost frowning, his eyes drew me to look there, and to look again. Repeatedly he compelled my glance; and now, each time I looked at him, he began slowly to move away a little, backing away, walking backwards, his restless hand stirring in his pocket as if with a life of its own as he moved slowly backward, facing me all the time so I could see the hand astir in the pocket, so that I would not miss seeing it, toward the door to the next room, and then I saw him go down the iron stairway to whatever was below, but looking back at me all the while, away from my mother and the others; and plainly as if he had spoken aloud in commanding words, I sensed his futile secret invitation—and my own frustrated desire—to follow him.

HARRY: I'm sorry, Winnie, the marriage thing makes me sick, and I know it is far more of a commentary on me than on the human race to say so. But—but when I see, as I did last night, driving home through the traffic, just after work, a car stop in the middle of the street and hold me up and hold everybody *else* up—oh, for only a few seconds, granted, but so thoughtless of others, all the same—while a woman, not old but not young either, trots out from the curb and opens the right-hand door of the car in the middle of the street and steps in, and leans over toward her husband while he leans toward her, for a kiss—a kiss!—an automatic utterly meaningless kiss at that time of day and under those conditions—meaningless because she can be seen a second later diving into her purse for something while he glances out the window on the left at something else, till he starts the car again—all momentary, understand, and taking no time at all really, but at the same time holding me up and all those other cars behind me for a full inconsiderate minute, all merely to indulge in the pointless ritual of a husbandly-wifely kiss as if by rote or even reflex— when, as I say, I see something like this, I find myself going instantly into an almost irrational rage because they're such idiots —such idiots! And even while I'm thinking this, my blood pressure rising higher by the second, I'm at the same time fully aware—oh, I am, I'm all too keenly aware of it!—that idiots though they be, they have something in their life that I've never had, even though that Something may have shaken down into something else as routine, meaningless, inane as this. And oh my God, when you hear, as you seem to be hearing more often these days in our towns, the idiotic, infuriating, incessant sounding of horns as a wild caravan of motor cars decorated with pink and white streamers goes tearing through the streets after a wedding, with the bride and groom wrapped together in the back seat of the first car kissing like mad, insanely, for all the world to see—all this, mind you, immediately after a solemn ceremony in a church—and all those other idiots, wildly blowing their horns, trailing the married couple in rudely noisy cars, *ad*vertising the fact that a private and holy rite has just been observed; and not only that, but advertising equally—why, the thought is inescapable!—publicly advertising what is to follow, in bed, between the nuptial pair only a few hours hence—if they can *wait* that long, the fools!—then I shudder for them, in shame for the married state and for the very race itself: such idiots, bound to propagate, such pathetic, asinine, helplessly hopeful idiots, not only blind but doomed. Heaven knows the misery they're headed for; yet heaven knows too, and I know, it will be the kind of misery that I will never have—and one might

even say a better misery than mine. Oh the pity of it, Winifred—
the irony!—that we actually rejoice when a young and promising
couple steps up to the altar, and weep tears of joy, joy, because
we are so touched—yet all the while we know bitterly that only
hell will come of it, that they will gradually, subtly, insidiously
murder each other over the years with all the weapons of devotion
—all in the name of a sacrament sanctioned by custom and the
church, in the name of fidelity, ideal partnership, loyalty, love,
ticking off the anniversaries one by one, one by one, way up into
the tens and twenties and thirties, all the more trapped the longer it
lasts and is applauded and approved and celebrated by others. I
tell you, Winifred—oh, I tell you!—there ought to be a *civil law*
against marriage because of the awful things that marriage does to
perfectly good, well-meaning, and innocent people. Take a marriage we know of, take a marriage among the married people we
know, our friends—take any marriage. Well, *you* take it—because
I want no part of it—but I warn you: don't look too closely at it,
let it keep its distance, stay aloof, unexamined. How many times
have I met and come to know and to like and even to envy in my
poor way a certain married couple, and I have thought: This, at
last, is the ideal marriage; here, finally, is a truly happily married
couple. And what happened? The nearer I got to the heart of
it—the closer I came to knowing them as a married couple—the
more clearly it became apparent that the marriage was by no
means the ideal thing I had thought it to be: the couple—and both
of them so nice, too, so deserving of something better, if there is
such a thing—weren't happily married at all—were in fact miserable together—and I would withdraw, I had to withdraw, for I had
found out what I should not have known about them. Those ads
we see in the glossy magazines, usually for gorgeous wall-to-wall
carpeting or color TV, showing overdressed forlorn pretty women,
angularly posed in green taffeta evening gowns, my God, alone in
the *luxe* interior, responding soulfully to the beauty of their luxurious possessions. Not for nothing is there no man in sight. Whom are
they all dressed up for anyway, walking around in gold sandals on
all that thick pile? And if they doffed their satins and lay down,
what would they do for the guy, the always absent guy, or he for
them? Love in marriage is a thing that doesn't exist. I know a

man—unique, he must be—who loved a girl too much to want to marry her, and destroy her, or be destroyed. All-important is the pile, the nap, the décor, the exotic frigid solitary respectability, and the lonely luxury, while the guy's out chasing somewhere, looking for love. Of *course* there's no man around; who needs him when you've got high fidelity, plants trailing from the ceiling from vulgar braziers, and a multicolored cockatoo swaying on a gold ring before a lattice of fake *chinoiserie* for background? No, Winifred, do not look too closely into *any* marriage. Count yourself lucky, Winifred, just as *I* am lucky. And yet, only you and I know, too, how luckless. Only we know.

WINIFRED: You can't win in this life, Harry. But one shouldn't generalize. Of course I'm speaking of myself—for myself: *I* can't win. All those escapades, those affairs long or short, those one-night stands—they got me nothing. They add up to nothing. They promised nothing to begin with but momentary transient thrill— mostly all forgotten now, or merely specific undetailed isolated memories attached to some vague gent I no longer remember, the details and the men almost indistinguishable one from another. But those that are not forgotten, those that hang on and linger, and nag at you more than the affairs carried through to a climax of sorts, so that you never, never— Well, it's like this—and here's a paradox that in my case is downright immoral, *much* more immoral than the affairs carried out: downright subversive even to think about. And I've never stopped thinking about this particular one. How could I, when it never came off? For the affair you never get over is the one you didn't have. What that can mean is: Go ahead, do anything, the light is green, don't hold back or you'll have regrets, unforgettable unerasable regrets, that will devil you till the end of time. For instance: A number of years ago, too many, really, for me to remember the details so clearly—but I do, I do, and that's the hell of it!—something happened, or didn't happen, that should have meant nothing to me for the very reason that it didn't happen. For this is the point: Because it didn't happen, I remember almost excruciatingly the whole thing, I've thought of it six thousand times, gone over it again and again in my memory that remembers what didn't happen and wishes that it had—and now I'm stuck with it for good and all, forever, it will

haunt me to my dying day, because—and *here's* A-Thought-for-
This-Week—because, well, for a change, for once, I behaved just
like any other girl, just as any sensible, armored, "good" young
woman would behave—not like me at all, untrue to myself, in fact.
I don't care how many men I have had since, or may yet have, if I
go back to the old life again, I know I will never be able to erase
from my haunted memory the one that didn't "happen": the one
that got away, one can say, or, rather, the one that I was fool
enough or conventional enough, for God's sake, not to take up and
enjoy, fulfill myself with him if only momentarily, and thus get him
and it out of my system. It doesn't pay to "behave"—not for me
it doesn't. Don't ask me why I ignored it and looked the other way,
in a manner of speaking. I can't possibly explain it, I've felt a
damned fool about it ever since, it's a complete mystery to me why
I reacted as I did, or didn't react at all. A moment of virtue?
Never! For me, that moment of virtue was sheer aberration. I was
twenty-five, and not bad-looking; at any rate still young enough
and attractive enough to attract a man without my having to do
anything about it on my own. It was mid-summer. Belle and Dad
were staying at the Point at the time, and Irma was with them. I
was alone in town, alone in the house: I believe I had some
appointments with the dentist that week and was staying in town
alone till he finished the job, all alone in that big house of ours
where *no*body would know what happened: the perfect set-up, and
I threw it away. But threw away, I was to learn later, bitterly,
something that couldn't be thrown away, because, though I didn't
so much as lift a finger in acquiescence, I have carried it with me
ever since, so that it gnaws at my vitals still; and believe me, that's
no empty phrase. I had asked Dad if I could have a telephone
installed in my room upstairs, on my desk, and he had given the
okay and even ordered it for me. It so happened that the telephone man arrived with his black metal kit on one of those hot
days when I was staying in town alone: don't tell me that such
things are accidental. There's a divinity that shapes our ends, and
so forth. I let him in, when he rang, and took him upstairs to show
him where I wanted the phone installed. It was a very hot afternoon. He set the black tool kit on the floor near the bed and
opened it. I sat in a chair watching him for a while as he squatted

there on the floor, in very thick dark-blue pants, boring a hole in the wainscot to connect the wire or whatever. His back to me, he squatted there on his heels in perfect, easy balance, in that classic sexy position of the catcher at home plate. I kept looking at him; and if you know me, I was "thinking things." The heat was stifling. *I* was in a light summer dress, but he had on a heavy work shirt and those thick dark-blue pants, which looked like heavy old-fashioned wool or cheviot at the very least—none of this chino or denim stuff you see nowadays. Just as I heard myself on the verge of saying, "Why don't you take those heavy pants off and be cool, *I* won't mind," I got panicky—so unlike me even then—restrained myself by some superhuman effort, got up and got out of there fast. But I didn't go far: I went out to the upstairs porch adjoining my bedroom, and then kept passing compulsively by the open doorway, looking in. He paid no more attention to me than if I didn't exist: so far as I know he was totally unaware of the atmosphere by now so highly charged, but of course I thought that atmosphere existed only within myself. It didn't, as a matter of fact, as I was to discover later; when one feels a thing as strong as I was feeling this, the other can't help but sense it, I don't care how dull he is. A word about the man himself. He was about five feet ten, maybe thirty-five years old, slender, blondish, cute: the typical American male and husband. He lived outside of town in Marbletown and had a wife and three children. He was pleasant-looking to an extraordinary degree, and as the time passed he began to seem the most pleasant-looking, the most attractive man I had ever seen: the ideal playmate, the kind one dreams about. But of course —oh, I know it now—that was because he was the only one around, and we were alone together. His name was Andy, wouldn't you know. Andy: it suited him perfectly. Once in a while, because I kept coming in and out of the room—at one point I offered him a drink, which he declined—we had a word or two together, but there was no hint in our conversation of anything brewing, at least on my part. Finally he finished the job, shortly before five, and started to brush away the sawdust and clean up the mess generally. He phoned the office, asked them to ring back and see if it was working right, it was, and then he stood up with a smile and said, "Well, there we are, Winnie, the job is done." God, it seems everybody in the county called me Winnie—I must have been awfully well known, even then; but I didn't mind. He put his tools away in that black heavy metal kit they carry, snapped the catches, and then he said, polite as all hell—why are telephone men always so agreeable? Is it part of their training? Anyway they have a personality and a charm all their own—he said: "Look. Would you mind awfully if I left this heavy tool kit overnight?" He smiled quizzically, with utter charm, the head tilted slightly to one side, the brow attractively, even artfully, furrowed, and the expression on his cute face said plainer than day, *You wouldn't turn me down, would you?* The idea was that it would save him going back to the main office, and he could get home to the wife and kids in time for supper. "Just let me leave it here on the floor, next to your bed table, and I'll stop by and pick it up first thing tomorrow morning, a little before eight, that all right?" I said, "Why, certainly, Andy, just leave it there and get it tomorrow"—never dreaming what I was letting myself in for. "Thanks a lot, Winnie, you're a big help. Don't bother to show me out, I know the way. Gee, thanks a lot. You're a damned good scout"—he gave me a last smile and was gone, down the front stairs and out. But he was *not* gone: that black kit was there on the floor next to my bed table, I knew he'd be back in the morning, and my ordeal—my struggle with him, you can call it—began. It was a dreadful night, a night of ridiculous suspense, I've never been through anything like it. I promise you, I'll never put myself through such a thing again, or, more accurately, never *not* put myself through such a thing again. Believe me, it don't pay! Knowing that he was coming back in the morning, early, and not only coming back but coming up to my bedroom—because *I* couldn't lift the damned thing to carry it downstairs, and he hadn't—I was torn this way and that, indecisive as an idiot, wondering, even planning, how to "receive him." Would I be dressed or not dressed? Would I run downstairs in my shift and let him in, then run back and get into bed? Or would I descend, sedate and fully clothed, wait in the lower hall while he went up and got his kit, and then let him out, aloof and reserved, like a lady? You know the latter plan didn't win. But I wore myself out that evening considering every possibility, and of course I spent a terrible night, sleepless, imagining all that could happen. Result: I stayed in bed till I heard the front doorbell ring, by then completely unstrung and at a loss. It rang just before eight. I threw on the lightest of wrappers, ran down the stairs barefoot, and opened the door to him. Then I ran back up. I could hear him behind me, coming slowly up the stairs as if he was pursuing the most ordinary normal routine. When he came into my room, I was already back in bed. The black kit rested on the floor beside the night table; I could have reached down and touched it. All night long it had been burning a hole in the floor, so to speak; or, you might say, it glowed in the dark of my sleepless night after I had turned my light off. I can't tell you how potent an image it had become. A mere tool kit, imagine!—and no play on words is intended. Andy sauntered across the room as casual as you please, a small smile on his cute face—nothing fresh or insolent, just an amiable little smile that seemed to indicate he was ready for anything. Beyond my wildest expectations, he sat down on the edge of my bed, then, and looked at me, still smiling pleasantly, as if privately amused; and not only sat down, but leaned across me and placed his hand flat on the bed on the other side of me. And there, under that angle of that stretched-out arm and his body, feeling the heat of both, I lay like a green girl. I thought of—but I had thought of them all during the night, planned them—a dozen things to say, a dozen openings. "Would you like to lie down for a few minutes and take a rest?" "Is there anything I can do for you?" "You're such a nice-looking guy, since last night I've thought of nothing else but your return this morning." Even: "Come on, take those clothes off and hop into bed." But none of these things did I say. I was mute. Mute, and at a complete loss, don't ask me why. I knew by the amused expression on his face that he was not only ready and willing but even expected a little play, maybe even wanting it as much as I did, but for once in my life, to my astonishment, I held back, ignored the very atmosphere of amorous tension that enfolded us both—why, I was almost stern! I can't explain it. He sat there talking agreeably about nothing for several minutes, smiling intimately—not too much, but not too little either—and I—God help me—acted as if I didn't know what it was all about. After about ten minutes he stood up, smiled down at me pleasantly and amused as if he knew my every thought, which he did; then picked up that goddamn kit and left. You can't imagine what this did to me. I had let him go, when it was right there in my hands. And—and I have suffered for it ever since, or at least never been able to forget it, only too conscious of what I had missed. Whereas, if I had turned back the covers, or if I had put my hand on his thigh which rested alongside my body, against my body . . . But I didn't, and I've been paying for it ever since. For once in my life I restrained myself, I was "a good girl," and for weeks after I was tormented by the memory of it. Me being me, the normal and natural thing would have been for me to take him. But I didn't, and I paid dearly for my so-called control. So: what do you make of *that,* Watson? The moral is, Let yourself go, get it over with, so that you can forget it. And who would call that a moral, or being moral? By my standards, considering my obsessive memory, ever since, of what didn't happen that morning, *immoral* is the word.

HARRY: People think I have an ideal life. I suppose everybody thinks that everybody else has an ideal life. What they don't know! Affluent enough, I have an apartment at the Sagamore. I have that nice place at Parson's Point, across the bay from yours. I'm independent—whatever that means. I'm good at my profession; I know I am, or I wouldn't be so much in demand as an architect of country houses, even though those country houses all look as if they came a dime a dozen. But it's what people want, and all I can do. The best I can do, I mean. I have no complaints, except the eternal loneliness—loneliness even while I am surrounded by so many companionable friends around Home Acres. I play the game of popularity like mad; it doesn't hurt me any, but why do I do it, what do I get out of it? I'm the best man at so-and-so's wedding one year, and the next year at so-and-so's, even though neither one of them really knows me at all. They only think I'm a great guy, and that's the criterion of happiness. I'm the godfather of other people's children, I'm the fourth at bridge, the extra man at dinner —good old Harry who can always be counted on to fill in—I suppose because I really have no life of my own. Men envy me or think they do because I have "freedom." And because I have freedom they want to get me married, like themselves; underneath they can't really stand it; they're always saying what I need is a good wife, and after a few drinks they nudge me in the ribs and say "We know! You old fox you, you probably get more than you can handle, but we know you're just waiting for the right girl to come along." The women are just as bad. *Just* as bad? They're murderous. They want to marry me off. They know a certain divorcée, with money, of course, who was just made for me. I'm willing to meet these—these eligibles, I play the game, I play up, but I never have the slightest intention of going through with it. I can't! I'm relieved when the prospect, as it sometimes turns out, is a Catholic and therefore can't remarry; then I put on an act of charm, but not quite pursuit, that would shame Casanova, all the while hating myself the more for my deception, then going home to lonelier quarters, a stiller, emptier life. I don't pretend to justify it; actually I haven't a leg to stand on, except my inborn—yes, distaste. These women are perfectly nice for the most part, and who am I that I have to be such a snob? Why can't I give a little, as they do? When I think of them as intimates, as someone who might be a part of my life, someone whom I could and should make love to, go to bed with, at least embrace, I shudder. Did you ever see one of these women, not even middle-aged sometimes, usually tightly brassiered and poured into their girdles—did you ever see them with their clothes off, a few minutes after undressing? Well, to be honest, I've got to admit I haven't, myself, but I know damned well that after all that heavy corseting and zippering and binding, their soft overblown bodies must be a mass of welts and reddish marks and oh, God. As for dancing with them *with* their clothes on, and putting your arms around their waists in their densely brocaded dinner suits, they might as well be encased in armor plate. And the voices! Where is that woman of whom it can be said today, "Her voice was ever soft, gentle, and low; an excellent thing in woman . . ." They bray! As for the hair and the hairdos—the dyed flax, the orange mops, the pink or lavender or platinum: how can they possibly think this makes them desirable? They become standardized, turned out by the hundreds, and by the machines; and yet—thousands of other men seem to find them attractive enough to play with and make love to and even to marry, so what's the matter with me? What's missing? I don't ask this in pity of self. I'm honestly wishing to know—too late. But

I'm afraid I do know too well what the reason is, if there is a reason. It isn't that I hate women, it isn't that I dislike other men. Androgynous—that growing American type! My God, one could say that the miserable tragedy of me is that I didn't even have enough drive to be a homosexual! No, it's just that I—I loathe myself, can't stand myself, can't, and could never, get outside of myself. How I need you, dear Winifred whom I no longer have the right to ask.

WINIFRED: "I think I could turn and live with the animals. They do not sweat and whine about their condition, they do not lie awake in the dark and weep for their sins, not one is dissatisfied, not one kneels to another, not one is respectable or unhappy over the whole earth." What an irony if I have been both, if Whitman in speaking of the animals is including me, even though I try not to sweat and whine about my condition. Have I lived like an animal, sensually? Am I an animal, only? Perhaps. But I think there's more to it. Much more. I believe my excessive, my long and obsessed search has been spiritual. Smile at the word if you like, but I think, for all that the search is a dead end, for all its preoccupation with the flesh and its self-defeating climaxes—I think the hunger has been a spiritual one. I think it has been a spiritual hunger all along, a kind of adoration of the male, a worship of man in the body, a seeking of God in man. Too lofty? I don't pretend to know. I only know I have adored, as Catholics adore the Virgin, physical man. Over and over and over, I have paid his body homage and worship—over and over again, times without count, forever trying to satisfy a hunger, a rapture, a need, a passion of sublime *respect* that has been spiritual all along. Yes, I have been ridden by spiritual hunger, possessed by it, and have never been satisfied physically because perhaps it is spiritual and nothing less; perhaps I have failed because always I sought to satisfy my consuming spiritual hunger in the persons of men, not in man, in man who is God.

HARRY: I don't think of Carol much, or often, I don't allow myself to, not because it's all water over the dam and long ago, but because I'm not proud of having hurt her so deeply, and myself missed so much. She loved me, and I gave nothing back. She loved me, but truly I only realized how deeply when, a good ten years after she had married Stewart Clyde, she asked me down from the city to have dinner with them one night, at their home. I knew what an effort it cost her, not only because Stewie thought I was an odd bird to say the least, if only for having turned her down, but because of herself; yet I went just the same, putting on a front as debonair as Benedick or Mercutio. A moment after I had arrived at the house, Carol and I got going, like old times, happy to be together. We talked our heads off; we had so many things to say to each other that I stayed in the kitchen with her the whole time she was preparing dinner, while Stew read his newspaper in the living room. Finally the table was all ready and the food put on, Carol called Stewart in from the living room and in a semblance of mature silence and good manners we waited while Stew carved the roast. Then there was a pause—an awful pause, it seems to me now, and I couldn't understand the reason for it. Stewie looked from one to the other of us, impassive, and then he said, matter-of-factly: "Carol, what are we going to eat on? There are no plates on the table."

WINIFRED: Harry, dear old friend. This noon while we were having lunch at my place, before we started out for the funeral, I said to you, "No, Harry, life is too short" when I heard you proposing what I think you think you were proposing. "Life is short," the philosophers tell us; "life is short." But no! no! no! no! no! they've got it all wrong! We might as well get used to it now, be fair to ourselves and accept ourselves while we can, for life is long! Life is long! long! and for better or worse we're stuck with what we are, it will not change or lessen, it will ride us to the end, to our very last moments. In our forties now, we may think it will be easier in our fifties or at least in our sixties; but listen to me, for I know this in my bowels: Our daemon whatever it is, yours so different from mine but just as inescapable—our daemon will not ever leave us, right up to the end he will ride us like fate, and there is only one answer, bleak enough but an answer. Take it! Take it! Accept, and don't expect anything back. And if we are able to do that, will we be the happier for it? That I do not know. I only know there is nothing else we can do, and maybe we'll be the better if not the happier for being honest. Oh, Harry, I've often wanted to say to you, and I want to say it still: Get *in* there,

Harry. Get *into* life in some way. Sweat some. Get your hands dirty, your feet wet. Take your pants down. Get laid. Get loved. Get hurt. But do something! Let yourself *go!* But maybe you can't. Maybe it's all far too late, and maybe you never could anyway. We are what we are, we can't be different people from what was handed to us at the beginning. We're born one way, or another, or another. Most of us can do nothing about it; I am as badly off as you, maybe worse. But I, at least—I could renounce! You can't even do that, for there is nothing for you to renounce. And that, my poor friend, seems to me the saddest thing that can be said about you—the saddest. I think you really thought you were proposing marriage to me this noon, but what was it worth? It sprang out of fear of the future, only—the barren years coming up. And in spite of what you thought was your seriousness you tried to make light of it by adding in your poor facetious way: "At best I can only offer you a second-hand life." Uh-uh. All wrong, Harry. All wrong, my dear friend. Mine is the second-hand life—used, shopworn, tarnished—maybe even, according to some people's lights, rotten. But yours—yours is a life lived at second-hand—life seen through a plate-glass window: safe, untouched, bloodless, bloodless. Oh, Harry . . .

THUS THE TWO FRIENDS TALKED, through the dark afternoon of the soul, and nothing of what they said between them, to each other, went anything at all like what has been set down above. What they really said were the same things that other people say, what everybody else says, like:

"The days are getting shorter, notice how the sun's already cooler, the shadows longer, Belle will be watching the clock . . ." and: "I guess fall is the best time of the year after all, isn't it, though I like spring well enough too . . ." and: "Remind me to get some gas when we get going, the tank's pretty low . . ." and like that . . .